THE DRAGON AND MRS MUIR

DRAGON WITCH SERIES, BOOK ONE

CONNIE SUTTLE

To Walter, Joe, Larry, Dianne, Sarah, Mark, Denise and Brett.
Thank you.

ACKNOWLEDGMENTS

As always, this book is the result of collaboration. If it weren't for the support of my editor, my cover artist and my beta readers, it would be less than it is. All mistakes, as usual, are mine and no other's.

About the Author:
Connie Suttle lives in Oklahoma with her husband and a conglomerate of cats. They have finally banded together to make their demands, which has proven disconcerting to all humans involved.

You may find Connie in the following ways:
Facebook: Connie Suttle Author
Twitter: @subtledemon
Website and Blog: subtledemon.com

ALSO BY CONNIE SUTTLE

Blood Destiny Series:

Blood Wager

Blood Passage

Blood Sense

Blood Domination

Blood Royal

Blood Queen

Blood Rebellion

Blood War

Blood Redemption

Blood Reunion

Blood Recall

Blood Alliance

Legend of the Ir'Indicti Series:

Bumble

Shadowed

Target

Vendetta

Destroyer

High Demon Series:

Demon Lost

Demon Revealed

Demon's King

Demon's Quest

Demon's Revenge

Demon's Dream

God Wars Series:

Blood Double

Blood Trouble

Blood Revolution

Blood Love

Blood Finale

Saa Thalarr Series:

Hope and Vengeance

Wyvern and Company

Observe and Protect*

First Ordinance Series:

Finder

Keeper

BlackWing

SpellBreaker

WhiteWing

R-D Series:

Cloud Dust

Cloud Invasion

Cloud Rebel

Latter Day Demons Series:

Hot Demon in the City

A Demon's Work is Never Done

A Demon's Due

Seattle Elementals Series:

Your Money's Worth

Worth Your While

BlackWing Pirates Series

MindSighted

MindMage

MindRogue

MindMaster

Black Rose Sorceress Series

The Rose Mark

Rose and Thorn

Black Rose Queen

Queen of Thorns and Roses

Future Wars Series

Buffer Zone

Black Zone*

Lion and Raven Series

Raven, Red

Exile, Ancient*

Dragon Witch Series

The Dragon and Mrs. Muir

The Dragon Queen of Seoul*

Other Titles from SubtleDemon Publishing:

Malefactor

Transgressor

Underhanded*

by Joe Scholes

*Forthcoming

A NOTE FROM THE AUTHOR

This book is an homage and a huge thank you to the people of South Korea. During 2020, when the pandemic hit and everything shut down, there was only so much on the cable channels in the US that I could stand after a while.

That's when I discovered a few K-dramas on the main pay-for-streaming channel, and then, because I fell in love with what I'd seen there, I went looking for more.

I found the motherlode in an Asian streaming channel.

Thank you, South Korea. What little sanity I retain, you helped me preserve. With your help, I was led into a new world of television and movies that I might never have seen otherwise. Not only did you help me get through a terrible time, you made me laugh (*Clean with Passion for Now* comes to mind) and cry (*Crash Landing on You*—I used up at least two boxes of tissues).

Those are only two of the many, many movies and series that I watched, just to keep myself sane in a world turned upside down. I now have a new list of favorite actors (I watched Park Seo Joon in *What's Wrong with Secretary Kim*, and then watched him in *Itaewon Class*—yeah, I was leaning forward in my seat and asking "Is that the same man?" Hint—it is, and he's just that awesome).

I also came away with a few new words, even after reading subtitles in English.

That's sort of how *The Dragon and Mrs. Muir* came about—it's a love story for a country that helped me without even knowing that it helped me.

And, as always, any mistakes regarding terms, the people or the culture are mine and mine only, so I ask for forgiveness and patience from those who know better.

Finger hearts to the fiftieth power,
Connie Suttle

CHAPTER 1

$\mathcal{I}$t was on every news station in the country—and on many foreign news outlets as well. *Attack at Wedding Leaves at Least Fourteen Dead, Many More Injured*, the headlines proclaimed.

The wedding was an outdoor affair, on a beach with the Gulf of Mexico in the background. In all, seventy-two were injured, and the body count rose to seventeen. Local hospitals were filled with bleeding attendees, and, at one point, the bride, her bloodied white wedding dress cut away and spilling onto the emergency room floor, went into cardiac arrest.

Her groom died at the scene.

In the room next door, an elderly wedding guest also suffered cardiac arrest—not from a bullet wound but from shock, combined with advanced age and a weak heart. Both souls walked out of their respective rooms.

One wanted to live.

One did not.

THREE YEARS LATER, TWENTY-SIX-YEAR-OLD PHILOMENA MUIR STOOD in line at her neighborhood Bean Brewery, staring into space while a couple ahead of her ordered hazelnut cappuccinos.

"That's her," someone sitting near the window hissed at her companion. "The widowed bride."

A slight jerk was Phil's only reaction to the comment; she'd gotten used to it by now—the pointing, the whispers, the avoidance of those who became uncomfortable once they heard about her wedding.

Phil closed her mind to the rest of the conversation, determined to get her vanilla latte and leave, rather than sitting next to a window to enjoy the sun and her coffee at the same time.

As she'd originally planned.

Why do they always hold up a hand to hide their mouths while they're spreading lies and gossip? Phil asked herself for the umpteenth time as she briefly glanced back at the ongoing conversation.

"Same?" The barista at the register smiled brightly at Phil.

"Same," Phil agreed, forcing a smile in return.

A few minutes later, Phil carried her latte and a napkin in her left hand while pushing the glass door open with her right.

That's when she saw him the first time.

He was Asian.

He was also beautiful, from his straight nose and sensuous mouth to his expensive charcoal trench coat and cream-colored turtleneck.

The last and perhaps most tragic thing about him, however, was the spelled dagger protruding from his chest, dangerously close to his left armpit. Tailored cuts had been made in his clothing to accommodate the deadly object.

Phil blinked twice at him before looking away. She knew, even if nobody else did. People and creatures who didn't want to be seen shouldn't be stared at.

She'd known that kind of thing since her waking after the wedding massacre. The groom had just been given permission to kiss his bride as the ceremony drew to a close.

Then, the bullets flew like angry hornets and nothing had been the same since.

Still, the moment this man passed less than three feet away, her heart squeezed in her chest. There was no blood on his clothing, so it wasn't a fresh wound.

Unsettling vibrations emanated from the dagger itself, and she couldn't help noticing that the hilt was decorated with green jewels.

Emeralds, she told herself.

He must be in pain.

His footsteps were heavy and aimless as he wandered farther away.

Don't get involved, a tiny voice whispered. *Nobody else can see or hear him.*

"Shut up," she mumbled to the warning voice and began walking after the man.

KWAN THOUGHT ABOUT STOPPING AT THE COFFEE SHOP, BUT SOMEONE was coming out the door, causing him to automatically step aside to avoid them. The woman couldn't see him after all, and he had no desire to get hit by the door or bump into the woman, especially if either event might jostle the dagger.

The pain from jostling the dagger would leave him weak and suffering for days, and he needed to eat soon.

A few steps past the coffee shop he stopped, suddenly wondering where, exactly, he was and how he'd gotten there.

Vashon Island Real Estate was displayed on a sign above a business across the street.

Pacific Northwest, United States, floated into his brain.

"Hold this." A paper coffee cup was shoved into his right hand. He scented vanilla syrup blended with the heady aroma of coffee and steamed milk. Reflexively, he gripped the cup as instructed, while blinking at the face that had somehow appeared before him.

"No!" he shouted as both her hands cupped the dagger's hilt.

Pull it out and you'll die. Those malicious words still sounded in his mind—clear, filled with acid humor and as fresh as they'd been when he'd first heard them—more than two hundred years before.

"No!" he shouted louder.

The woman paid him no mind whatsoever, and his vision failed. He felt himself falling before darkness came.

CHAPTER 2

Kwan woke with an indrawn gasp, finding himself sitting on a rough concrete sidewalk and leaning against the brick wall of the real estate agency he'd noticed earlier.

Was it earlier?

Was he truly alive?

Hands automatically searched his coat, making sure he was in one piece and that he still had his belongings.

Everything was where it should be.

Except.

Frantically, he lifted the left side of his trench, and then pinched the fabric of the turtleneck where the dagger should be.

Dizziness and nausea almost defeated him before he could think clearly again. *Where was the fucking dagger?*

Hastily, he pulled the slit in the turtleneck wide, gazing at the skin underneath. A dark, reddening scar and a few smears of blood could be seen.

Kwan cursed in Korean, his first and native language. "Where is she?" he fumed. *Had she taken the dagger?*

How had she taken the dagger?

He was the only one who could touch it—the spell on it was very specific.

Mist came rolling in off the waters surrounding the island as he worked to control rapidly rising heartbeats and shallow, worried breaths. With a shaking hand, he reached up to rub his eyes.

You have to get up, he scolded himself. *Eat something, too*, he added. *Then, you need to find out what happened to her.*

His shoes scraping on concrete and the fabric of his trench catching on rough brick, he pushed himself up the wall, swaying only a little when he was fully upright.

Eat, then find a hotel, he commanded.

Was there a hotel with a restaurant?

Pulling out his cell phone while staggering down the sidewalk, he intended to find out.

THREE DAYS OF RARE STEAKS IN THE RESTAURANT, WITH PLENTY OF rest and a few slow walks in-between, Kwan gradually built up his strength.

You should find the woman, flitted through his mind continuously.

There'd been no news of a tragically poisoned female, no body, no missing person reported—nothing. The dagger would have killed even the hardiest human in only a few hours, with most dying shortly after touching the damned thing.

At this point, he hoped he'd find the body first, so he could thank her. Whatever she'd done had relieved centuries of terrible pain. Hell, he'd even washed the scarred area in the shower and barely felt a twinge.

Had Dal lied?

No. Dal was deadly serious, Kwan scolded himself. *Did he know the dagger was no longer where he'd stabbed me all those years ago?* The betrayal and pain flooded Kwan's mind. Did his attacker have a link to the dagger, which would alert him if it were removed?

Dal should have arrived by now if that were the case. His hate was too strong for him to allow Kwan to regain his strength. His enemy would strike again and quickly, knowing that if he ever did heal completely—well, Dal would prevent that if he could.

And at all costs.

Find the woman, Kwan's conscience nagged.

"Fine," he snapped, grabbing his new merino coat off its hanger and slamming out of the hotel room. *Coffee first,* he promised himself.

Bean Brewery was three blocks away. Maybe he could walk off his anger between here and there.

PHIL FRETTED FOR THREE DAYS AND REFUSED TO GO BACK TO TOWN, although visions of a rotting corpse that nobody could see outside the real estate office terrified her.

"What else could I do?" she muttered for perhaps the fiftieth time. Who knew what or who he was? Had she made a mistake? Was he now terrorizing small towns or digging up cemeteries because she'd helped him?

"I need Bean Brewery." Shaking herself to remove nightmarish thoughts, Phil studied herself in the bathroom mirror, decided that her jeans and sweater were clean enough to be seen in public, brushed her hair and fled the bathroom before she could change her mind.

"I MUST BE CRAZY." PHIL FLUNG THE DOOR OF HER COMPACT SUV open three blocks from Bean Brewery. She hadn't taken into account that it was Saturday and everybody plus their pooches would be there shopping, gawking or eating before or after hitting the public beaches, parks or the lighthouse.

"I could have walked from home in the same amount of time it took to get a parking place." Tightening her favorite gray sweater around herself to fend off the cold, Phil marched toward the coffee shop like a soldier to battle.

As expected, the line was out the door and down the sidewalk when she arrived. Tourists and Seattle area locals loved Vashon Island and flocked there whenever they had time to wait for the ferry.

Taking her place at the end of the line, Phil stubbornly crossed her arms and inched her way forward, while other newcomers lined up behind her.

"Triple vanilla latte," Kwan ordered in perfect English the moment he arrived at the Bean Brewery counter. "Extra hot. Name is Kwan—K-W-A-N."

He watched as the employee scribbled his information on the cup and slapped it down next to the espresso machine. After paying and dropping a dollar and change in the tip jar, Kwan moved away to wait for his drink.

With drink in hand after waiting ten minutes, he squeezed through the door, holding his cup high so as not to spill a drop. Walking past the waiting line to get back to the hotel, he nearly stumbled when he saw her.

Oblivious to his presence, her arms wrapped tightly about her waist, she stood in the morning cold, waiting to get through the door.

Alive.

She. Was. Alive.

Impossible.

There was only one thing for him to do at that point—flee across the street, become invisible to everyone else, and wait for her to leave so he could follow.

Anyone who could remove one of Dal's spelled daggers and survive was a wonder and a miracle. He wanted to find the source of each of those things.

If she knew how to protect against that—*well*.

Revenge might be had after all.

HALF AN HOUR LATER, PHIL EMERGED FROM BEAN BREWERY WITH HER cup in one hand and a bag containing a heated croissant in the other. She felt as if she'd been in line for two days, while the crowd sucked away all her energy.

Should have known better than to jump in the middle of all that. She shook her head as she began the three-block walk to her vehicle.

Across the street and careful to stay out of Phil's line of sight, Kwan peeled away from the brick façade of the real estate agency and moved to follow. Blinking in surprise, he found her climbing into a black, compact SUV parked almost in front of his hotel.

Now what?

Luggage rack, moron, he chided himself.

Would he fit? Would she realize?

Kwan hadn't changed in more than two centuries. The dagger prevented it—it was one of Dal's most malicious insults.

Careful, careful, he sighed as he lifted himself upward with effort to clutch the metal rails atop the car with his front claws. Back claws searched for purchase at the rear of the vehicle, causing it to rock momentarily.

Inside the car, she froze. Kwan could scent brief fear and confusion. Finally, mumbling to herself, she sipped coffee before pinching off a part of her pastry and stuffing it in her mouth.

Letting a breath out slowly, Kwan settled himself on the luggage rack, twisting and turning to fit his bulk on such a small space.

Please don't drive too fast, he mentally begged as the car was started and put in reverse. His left claws were far from full strength— he'd have to build that up slowly, following years of disuse.

The car never went above forty miles per hour, and once it turned off the main road, Kwan was able to enjoy the forested area they traveled through.

What surprised him was their destination.

The house was enormous, with an amazing water view and curved, glass walls fronting the structure.

She doesn't dress like she owns the place. Maybe she's a servant, Kwan mused as the car was parked in a courtyard surrounded by the U-shaped mansion. Surely, the owner would be driving something far more luxurious than what he'd climbed onto.

Once she was out of the car and heading for the entrance, Kwan leapt off the SUV, causing it to rock slightly and its springs to squeak.

Now that I know where she is, I can come back at a better time. Kwan flipped out his wings, hoped they'd get him back to the hotel and took flight.

"HE COULD STILL BE TERRORIZING THE COUNTRYSIDE," PHIL SIGHED AS she flopped onto her favorite sofa in the great room. Outside, the mist had blown off the water and she could almost see Rainier in the distance.

"At least I didn't see him or his decomposing body." Lifting her latte, she drank, realizing she'd almost finished the extra-large cup on the drive home. The croissant had been eaten, pinch by pinch, before she'd gotten halfway home. She should have gotten two instead of one.

"You don't need to eat two of those things," Phil reminded herself. "Go do some work."

She received a text from Xinnie after walking into her upstairs office.

Got any lettuce?

You stock the kitchen. If it's there, it's yours.

Xinnia and her husband, Ray, were the estate's only full-time employees, and were the only family, adopted or otherwise, that Phil had in Washington State. Xinnie and Ray supervised the part-time cleaning staff and the landscaping company hired to do the heavy work. They lived in separate quarters over the back set of garages, which had its own kitchen, living area, bathroom and two bedrooms.

Phil's remaining family was in New Mexico or Texas, and she didn't talk to many of them more than once or twice a year.

There's plenty of romaine. I'll take half, Xinnie sent a smiley face with her reply.

Okay.

Do you have something healthy to eat for dinner?

I can do my own thing. Enjoy your weekend and stop worrying about me.

Does your own thing involve pizza, Chinese takeout or burgers?

Maybe one of the above. Maybe all three. Who wants to know?

Ray wants to know.

He does not, so stop that right now.

Ray is laughing.

As well he should.

He does want to know if we can borrow some movies.

Why do you even ask? You know I don't care. Even if I'm watching what you want to see, you can sit with me and we can watch together. Besides, I'm in the middle of a K-drama on the streaming app. I'm set for the weekend.

Did you go out for coffee this morning?

I did. It was a mistake. I could have had three cups at home while waiting in line for one at the B-B.

You forgot it was Saturday again, didn't you?

Are bears Catholic?

That's what I'm talking about, right there.

Hey, mind your own beeswax on your days off. I can be absent-minded and eccentric if I want.

You're twenty-six. How absent-minded and eccentric should you be? You could always let us fix you up. We know some decent guys.

I've never fired anyone before. Should I start with you two?

You can't live without us and you know it.

Yeah. I do know that. But the absolute last thing I need is to be fixed up with somebody. Okay?

Philomena, you can't let that rule your life. Let go of it.

I need more time.

Fine. If you want something decent to eat, let me know.

I will. I need to work, now. Have fun.

"She's gonna write herself into an early grave if she doesn't find somebody to help carry that load of guilt around," Ray shook his head after reading the last of Phil's texts.

"I know. It was hard enough letting go of her grandmother. I was worried Phil would just sell this place and move to New Mexico."

"But she didn't," Ray pointed out. "She's here, and she hasn't changed much of anything her grandma set up. She just sits in front of that computer day and night, unless she decides to go to that coffee shop in town. I tried to talk her into getting a dog or cat, but she just hides inside that thick shell and won't come out."

"Ray, hon, I might be exactly the same if I saw you gunned down in front of me," Xinnie frowned up at her husband. "And on her wedding day? How traumatic was that?"

"I know." Ray's arms wrapped around Xinnie and held her tight. "She used to smile all the time, didn't she? Before all that mess happened."

"They still haven't caught the bastards who did it, either," Xinnie mumbled against Ray's chest. "I swear I'd shoot them myself if I found out where they were."

"A bullet might mean they die too fast," Ray sighed. "They need to suffer for what they did."

"We can't fix the world," Xinnie said, pulling away. "We can only fix what little we're able."

"I know that's right."

"Serial commas much?" Phil leaned forward, frowning at the plethora of commas she'd used on a single page of her latest manuscript. "I should not write while I'm tired and out of sorts. What time is it, anyway?"

Glancing down at the right corner of her screen, Phil almost shrieked. It was nearly ten and she hadn't had lunch or dinner. "Maybe I should have bought that second croissant."

Pushing her chair back and rising to stretch her arms high

overhead, she stood like that for several seconds, hoping to clear the kinks in her back and shoulders.

A few minutes later, she lounged in front of the open refrigerator door, contemplating whether to eat cottage cheese or have a turkey sandwich.

"Turkey sandwich it is," she said, pulling out the sliced turkey, mayo and a fresh tomato. At least the toast would be warm, even if the rest of the sandwich wasn't.

KWAN WRESTLED WITH HIS THOUGHTS WHILE PILING CLOTHING IN A suitcase. If he just showed up at the woman's door—no, that would certainly be the wrong thing to do. What had his kind done in the past to show appreciation to humans who'd done them favors or made sacrifices?

Money?

He had plenty of that, but after seeing the house, she could also be wealthy.

He could offer to ruin enemies, but he wouldn't be at full strength and capability for weeks if not months. He might not be able to fulfill a promise right away, and timing was most important in matters such as this.

Begging?

No. He was terrible at debasing himself.

Wait.

Perhaps there was something that wouldn't—couldn't fail. There was precedent in Dragon Law itself, plus another action to counter the penalty of said Dragon Law. In fact, that particular action had been a highly-prized status in the past.

Yes.

That should work. He would go to her, inform her of her mistake, and then describe her new status in detail.

What if she threw him out before hearing everything he had to say?

There was a way around that.

He knew where she was, and it was next to impossible to remove a dragon, once he had chosen a location for his lair entrance. Prying up an entire mountain with a toothpick could be an easier task. He'd make arrangements and tell her after the fact.

Yes. He would go tonight, make himself at home in an empty room, and then he would inform her of her liability and subsequent station. She would be grateful; he could tell her what he wanted from her and build up his strength at the same time.

Then, when all was ready, he would strike back at Dal.

CHAPTER 3

Phil lifted her face from the desk's surface, blinking in the morning sunlight pouring through her office window.

A paperclip which had stuck to her face during the night, dropped with a muted tick onto a pile of paper while she attempted to clear her head.

Why had she gone back to work after eating the night before?

Why?

"Coffee," she mumbled, slapping hands on the desk and pushing herself upward. "Ow," Phil complained as she took a muscle-stiffened step toward the door. "Ow. Ow, ow, ow."

"Not gonna take the stairs. Elevator," she urged her body to move along the catwalk that separated the high-ceilinged gallery between upstairs bedrooms.

"Why can't I go to bed at a decent hour and sleep like normal people?" she moaned, sliding through the open elevator doors and tapping the first-floor button.

Closing her eyes, she almost fell asleep standing upright in the elevator on the way down. "Coffee," she breathed, shuffling out of the elevator and heading in the kitchen's general direction.

"Coffee. Shower. More coffee." Sweeping a hand through long,

15

tangled, honey-blonde hair, she narrowed her eyes at the too-bright sunlight streaming through tall windows facing the front of the house. "Why are you shining today?" she whined. "Put some clouds on, for Pete's sake."

"Are you acquainted with weather spells, too?"

Phil turned, blinked at the man she'd seen only once before and shrieked before fainting.

KWAN BARELY HAD TIME TO MOVE THE UNCONSCIOUS FEMALE TO A nearby chair before another female shuffled into the kitchen. This one was perhaps twenty years older than the one who'd fainted.

She couldn't see him and failed to notice the other woman for a few moments.

"Huh?"

The unconscious one was coming around. Quickly, Kwan scooted behind the chair, so she wouldn't see him immediately and perhaps faint again.

"Phil?" Concern was in the other woman's voice as she hurried toward the chair.

"Xinnie?" The one called Phil blinked at the other woman.

"What happened? Are you all right?" Xinnie leaned down to touch Phil's forehead.

Her name is Phil? Isn't that a male name? Kwan frowned at the two women.

"I uh," Phil searched for words.

Would she tell the other woman that she'd seen a man? What would she tell the other woman? Kwan waited anxiously to hear the answer.

"It's nothing," Phil waved away the question. "I fell asleep at my desk and drooled all over a pile of edits. I probably have low blood sugar or something." She patted the arm of the chair twice. "Then, I found myself here. No idea how or why."

"Let me get you some orange juice. Sit there until I get back." Xinnie hurried toward the kitchen.

"Coffee," Phil called out to Xinnie's retreating back.

"Juice first," Xinnie's words were flung over a shoulder.

Once Xinnie was out of sight, Phil turned in the chair and glared at Kwan. "You still here?" she snarled. "Get out of my house."

"I cannot," he replied, his words haughty. "I spent most of the night moving the entrance to my lair. It cannot be moved again for several months."

"Your lair." Slapping her hands on the chair's armrests, Phil struggled to stand. "Only a few supernatural creatures build lairs. Which kind are you?"

"Which kind do you think?" He crossed arms over his chest and returned her glare. "How do you know this? Very few humans have ever been informed or retain that information."

"Sit down," Xinnie was back with a tall glass of orange juice. "Drink all of this, missy." She held the glass out at arm's length.

"Drink all of it, missy," Kwan mocked, obviously enjoying himself. "She can't see or hear me, and you probably know that. Go ahead, reply and make her think you're insane."

Her bottom lip pushed out in an exaggerated pout, Phil took the glass, sat as instructed and began chugging orange juice.

"There—all gone," Phil stood and stepped around Xinnie.

"Where do you think you're going?" Xinnie demanded.

"To get coffee. Then, I'm going to take a shower. Don't follow me." Phil stomped away.

"You think I'd follow you when you're in that mood?"

"I wasn't talking to you."

"Is she seeing ghosts again?" Xinnie's muttered words made Kwan blink in surprise. He wanted to ask questions of Xinnie, now, but couldn't reveal himself.

Should he follow Phil?

Stupid question, Kwan chided himself. Of course he should follow her. She was now his familiar and no longer had a say in the matter.

KWAN WAITED IN PHIL'S SITTING ROOM, ADJACENT TO HER BEDROOM and opposite her bathroom, from which he could hear water running in the shower. While he waited, he studied himself in the mirror mounted over the fireplace; this was the perfect room for reading and having tea, he decided.

Comfortable chairs and a sofa before the fireplace made him want to build a fire while he waited, but he worried that Phil might faint again and there were questions to ask.

The mirror above the fireplace revealed a face he knew well—he was considered quite handsome in his homeland. He'd carefully brushed thick, black hair away from his forehead; he worried that leaving it not parted and natural would make him appear less severe and commanding.

His best feature, according to the females he'd met in the past, was his mouth. *Lips full and sensuous*—more than one had described it that way. With a new familiar, the guidebook always said to take a firm hand and therefore, he certainly had to look the part. Schooling his mouth into a grimmer line, he nodded.

This look should do nicely.

He'd also dressed in a charcoal pinstripe suit with a black turtleneck sweater, adding to his commanding demeanor. He wouldn't tolerate backtalk from a familiar—the guide said to keep things professional at the beginning, so the familiar-in-training would know what to expect in the future. He'd allowed it earlier, since he'd caused the female to faint.

No more of that, Kwan promised himself, straightening the lapels of his suit. If she didn't like her new circumstances, she had no one to blame but herself, having removed the dagger from his chest and touching him in the process.

The water cut off in the bath; she'd emerge soon. He hoped she'd have some covering on; he didn't want to chastise her too much in the beginning.

Kwan was tapping a slippered foot with impatience when she walked out fifteen minutes later, but at least she wore clothing.

Slouchy clothing.

A loose, long-sleeved gray shirt and black lounge pants, if his recollection of less-than-acceptable clothing was correct.

Were those—white socks on her feet? White socks and black pants? The nerve!

With a towel, she continued to rub damp, long hair. It was untidy, yes, but not completely unacceptable. He wouldn't complain about that just yet.

"I thought I told you not to follow me," she snapped, noticing his presence.

"I'm glad you brought that up," Kwan began in his best lecturing tone.

"Get out. Of my. Bedroom."

"You do not have permission to speak to me in such a way," he retorted.

"Okay."

"Okay?" He only had time to blink once before he was flung out of the house and dumped in the koi pond. Kwan sputtered, his hair and face dripping, while a lily pad hung precariously off a shoulder.

"She ruined my suit," he snarled, pushing himself up and onto his feet. He couldn't go back in looking like this; he'd be forced to reenter his lair, clean himself and change, then return to confront the woman with a man's name.

"I should have employed protection spells; I knew she had magic," he mumbled, taking in the sorry state of his garb.

What kind of witch was she? No other human could toss an ancient dragon like that. Did she have Sun magic, perhaps? Air? Earth? Water?

If she were a black witch, she'd never have helped him to start with. That was the only possibility he could omit.

"Soul magic?" he whispered reverently.

No, he answered his own question. A Soul Witch would never do such a petty thing as dumping him in a lily pond. Besides, his kind hadn't seen or felt a Soul Witch for more than two centuries. If she were a Soul Witch, his radar for such power would surely be pinging.

Kwan, report.

The message slid into his mind from Prince Jiah.

Kwan hesitated.

Has the dagger truly been removed? And you still live?

Yes, my Prince. Unconsciously, Kwan bowed, as if he were in the presence of Jiah himself.

How? Explain this miracle.

A witch, my Prince. I am preparing to question her. She holds the secret.

Have you confined her? Have you truly made her your familiar? You have never done such before. Please explain your actions.

No, yes, yes, and you already know everything I do, Kwan was pained to answer with such honestly. *Your secretary should have the scroll already.*

I'll retrieve it. Where are you?

Outside the witch's house in the Pacific Northwest of the United States, Kwan replied.

A western witch?

Yes.

Hmmmm. This may not sit well with the Council. I wish to meet her at your earliest convenience. I must determine whether she is worthy of you.

Kwan wanted to say that at the moment, it didn't sit well with him, either and he wasn't sure whether *he* was worthy enough in this particular case. He held back the urge. *I must go; the witch should be informed of her new status,* Kwan stated instead.

Very well. Send regular updates directly to me. Don't bother going through Secretary Kim. I await your next visit with great anticipation; I haven't been able to embrace you for two centuries due to Dal's malicious prank.

You call it a prank. I believe it to be attempted murder.

We have no evidence to the contrary, and we have argued this point into the ground in the past. Come soon; I wish to see you and your familiar with my own eyes.

Yes, my Prince.

S

"Ghost tossed out?" Xinnie chopped onions and sliced mushrooms in the kitchen.

"Hard," Phil nodded. She'd come to the kitchen for a coffee refill after editing a chapter in the latest book.

"Good. I get the shivers every time," Xinnie confessed.

"Most are harmless," Phil poured half-and-half into her fresh cup of dark roast.

"This one?"

"Has a smart mouth," Phil thumped the carton of half-and-half on the counter. "Probably been around for a while and thinks women are still property."

"Too bad he couldn't stick around for a history lesson, then." Xinnie dumped the mushrooms and chopped onions into the sauté pan and added four tablespoons of butter. "Beef stroganoff for dinner," she added.

"With rice?"

"If you'd rather have rice than noodles."

"Yeah—rice." Phil gave Kwan a nasty look as he stood across the island from her, frowning deeply.

"We must talk," Kwan sniffed.

"Yeah." Lifting her coffee mug, Phil, wearing a murderous look, skirted the island and stalked past Kwan.

"I am nobody's familiar," Phil hissed at Kwan. "I didn't give my permission. I only pulled that dagger out of your armpit because I felt sorry for you. Now, you think a life of servitude to your majesty is a fitting reward? Damn. I knew I should have left well enough alone."

Phil paced inside her office while Kwan watched, distaste revealed in every tense muscle of his body. Did the woman have no sense of order? Books and papers were stacked on every flat surface inside the spacious room, while others were piled on the floor.

"How can anyone walk safely through this mess?" Kwan complained, hoping reason would arrive in the woman's brain sooner rather than later. Being chosen as a dragon's familiar was a position of highest honor.

"I'm a stacker. I come from a family of stackers. I know where everything is, this is my office and I prefer it this way, thank you."

"Clean it up. I cannot think properly amid this chaos."

"You want another bath in the koi pond?"

"I have surrounded myself with protection spells. You will not catch me off guard again."

A moment later, Kwan pulled a lily pad off his face with a disgusted grunt. "Aish," he muttered in frustration.

"BEFORE YOU SEND ME TO THE KOI POND AGAIN," KWAN HELD UP A hand while Phil shot him an angry look, "I'm hungry, and why did they name you Phil?"

"It's short for Philomena, and dinner will be ready in fifteen," Phil rose from her desk while her face softened. "All you need to do is act civilized," she added.

"I am civilized."

"Not from what I've seen so far. You appear to be intent on my being servile to you. Ain't gonna happen, dude."

"Dude?"

"Koi pond?" Phil's left eyebrow lifted in speculation. Kwan winced and braced himself.

"Please, no—you've ruined two suits already," Kwan released a pent-up sigh when he remained standing at the door to Phil's office.

"I'll replace both—if you remain civilized."

"Perhaps we should write an agreement? I cannot undo my choice of familiar; the Prince has already sanctioned it."

"Well, then, Mr. Dragon, what's your real name?"

"How did you know?"

"Only the dragons have a Prince. The others have a King or Queen."

"Sadly, this is true. Our King was killed."

"I know. Is it a personal loss to you?"

"Somewhat."

"My condolences."

"Thank you." Kwan bowed reflexively.

"By the way, I figured out which bedroom is now the doorway to your lair. I told Xinnie not to clean it or the one next to it. It's to keep her safe," Phil added.

"Wise," Kwan acknowledged. "Should I change for dinner?"

"You look fine."

"Should you dress for dinner?"

"There is nothing wrong with what I'm wearing. Have you never met anyone who wrote before?"

"Not in recent times."

"I don't need to be dressed uncomfortably while I'm trying to figure out who done what and where," Phil said. "I don't need a fight with my clothes instead of a fight with the bad guys. Therefore, no tweed jackets with leather elbow patches, or whale-boned corsets and blouses buttoned up to my chin."

"You are too thin as it is. I would take those corsets and burn them."

"You'd have to stand in line for that, dude."

"Surname?"

"Muir. Widowed. Anything else?"

"You cannot be past your twenties, and already a widow?"

"It's a lengthy, uncomfortable story. How long do you plan on being here?"

"It will take approximately seven months for approval to move the entrance to my lair again after I've already moved it—these requests travel slowly throughout the hierarchy." Kwan didn't add that he had no desire to move the entrance, but if he did, he'd be forced to take his familiar with him.

"Are you planning to remain unseen the whole time? It could get awkward after a while."

"Ah. I suppose a remedy might be found."

"Original language? There aren't any native dragons in the US."

"Korean."

"Awesome. You can become the Korean translator for my books—in name only, of course."

"Hmmmm," Kwan considered the suggestion before nodding once. "Yes. Perhaps you can inform your employees that I will arrive in two days. I and a suitcase will be at your front door at an appointed time."

"Just remember—Xinnie and Ray are family. Mistreat them and you're gone."

"As if," Kwan sniffed. "After dinner, I shall prepare a document for your perusal tomorrow. I hope we can reach an amicable agreement."

"Awesome."

"Do you say awesome overly much? I find it irritating."

"Koi pond?"

"I will learn to live with this."

"Ray and Xinnie like to eat and watch the news," Phil explained later as she filled a plate for herself after serving Kwan a generous portion of beef stroganoff. "I can't stand to watch the news, nowadays. It aggravates me in ways you cannot possibly imagine. During the week, Xinnie usually cooks in this kitchen and takes dinner to their quarters afterward. They're off on weekends, so I fend for myself."

"What about cleaning? This house is too large for one or two people to maintain on a part-time basis."

"We have a cleaning crew that comes once a week—on Thursdays. Usually ten to fifteen people, depending on what needs to be done. Xinnie supervises and lets them know what to clean and when. They're never allowed inside my office."

"Ah. The wreck," Kwan agreed softly. "Do you have chopsticks?" He tapped the fork he was given.

"Hang on." Phil rose and opened a drawer of the built-in buffet. "Will these do for now?" She handed him paper-wrapped wooden chopsticks from a nearby Chinese restaurant.

"This will do. Tomorrow, I will bring my own."

"Awesome."

Kwan stiffened for a moment, then broke the chopsticks apart with a disgruntled snap and began to eat.

"Noo," Phil moaned as she woke at her desk the following morning. She meant to go to bed. She'd fallen asleep in her chair—again.

Peering out the door of her office, she didn't see Kwan anywhere. Walking as silently as possible, she strode toward the stairs and trotted down them.

That's when the ruckus started outside.

"Kwan," a bass voice sounded, shaking the front windows.

"What the hell?" Phil didn't bother opening the door—she ran through it, employing Tree magic.

The dragon was a green-scaled monster, who couldn't get closer to the house than twenty feet into the waters of Puget Sound. Phil had set her spelled boundary that far for safety reasons.

"Ah. The weakling familiar," the dragon spoke with difficulty around a forked tongue. "Is your master too afraid to come himself?"

"Fuck you," Phil shouted at him, while casting Sun, Air and Water magic. The boom and fireworks of the dragon's unwilling exit disturbed the waters, causing a backwash that covered half of Phil's front lawn with saltwater.

"Dammit," she muttered. "We just planted those flowers."

"Where did Dal go?" Kwan appeared with a slight pop at her side.

"Well, he's somewhere in the vicinity of the French Southern Territories," Phil shrugged her shoulders. "Dang, that was tiring." Turning, she walked back through the door while Kwan watched.

"Tree magic?" He scented the air until the flavor dissipated. He'd come too late to sniff the spell she'd cast to remove Dal.

My Prince, the familiar has removed Dal from my presence, Kwan sent.

How?

I was not present when the spell was cast. I will learn more soon.

I suspect it is a good thing she touched you first; elsewise you may not have gotten past her barrier.

I concur.

When was the last time there was a witch familiar?

Perhaps four centuries?

Yes—I recall that as well. An Earth witch, if my memory serves. That one could never do something like this. Is Dal close by? It will take much strength to send him far.

Dal is not within my sensing range, Kwan replied.

More than fifty miles, then? I am rethinking my position on your choice of familiar, my dearest friend. It appears you need extra protection while you recover from the wound left by the dagger. Your witch is proving herself useful.

That remains to be seen, Kwan mused. The Tree magic he'd sensed wasn't enough to send Dal anywhere. Philomena had used some other magic to remove Dal from the area. More than anything, he wanted to know what it was.

I will report as things progress, my Prince, Kwan ended the conversation.

I look forward to your reports.

"You're getting a what?" Xinnie sounded incredulous when she and Ray received the news that a houseguest was arriving the following day.

"I don't have any books translated into Korean," Phil sighed. "He'll stay here and work for around six months. His English is excellent; this way we can discuss whether we've hit the mark with the translations."

"Do I have to serve noodles or rice all the time?"

"I don't think you'll have to change your routine. Besides, there are Korean restaurants all over Seattle."

"You're giving him keys to a car?" Ray frowned.

"If he has a license."

"Can we trust him?"

"Don't worry. If he gets out of hand, I'll send him to a hotel."

"Is that why you blocked off those two bedrooms upstairs?"

"That's why. He can clean up after himself. There's no need for anybody to go in there and pick up after him. I understand he's a neat-freak anyway."

"How do you know that? You haven't met him," Xinnie sounded unconvinced.

"He saw my office—we had a face-to-face on the computer," Phil bent the truth to suit her narrative. "I thought he was going into cardiac arrest over it, too."

"It wasn't cardiac arrest. It was pure revulsion," Kwan wandered into the kitchen where Phil, Ray and Xinnie were talking.

"Phil, your hair is fluffing out," Xinnie remarked. "Is it the humidity?"

"Humidity—like the level in the koi pond," Phil grumped.

"Just passing through," Kwan hurried his steps.

"WHAT IS THIS?" PHIL HELD UP THE NEATLY-LABELED BLUE FOLDER with a thumb and forefinger. The tab read *Agreement between Master and Familiar*.

"I cannot wait to read this," she hissed as Kwan appeared in her office doorway. "A revision is already needed," she tore the tab off the folder and tossed it in the wastebasket.

"Which part?" Kwan folded arms over his chest.

"How about we start with *Agreement between Kwan and Phil*, until Kwan can move his ass out of her house?"

"Did you really send Dal to the French Southern Territories?"

"Yes."

"Then we can rename the folder."

"Awesome." Phil flopped the folder open in her hands and began to read.

Item 1: Derogatory name calling of one party by the other is not allowed.

Item 2: There will be no forced relocation to the koi pond.

Item 3: Each party is charged with the protection of the other.

Item 4: Entry into Kwan's lair is prohibited unless invitation is extended.

Item 5: Expenses incurred to serve both parties will be shared by both parties.

Item 6: Lying between parties is expressly forbidden. The penalty for such will be decided by the Dragon Prince.

Item 7: If a party refuses to answer a question, the other party is not allowed to press the issue. (also refers to Item 6).

Item 8: Gifts may be given by either party and must be received graciously by the opposite party.

Item 9: Neither party is allowed to belittle the other.

Item 10: Philomena must consent to visit Dragon Prince Jiah with Kwan within fourteen days of the signing of this document. This is required by Dragon Law and cannot be avoided.

Item 11: Should either party be wounded, the other must render aid to the best of their ability.

Item 12: Each party must be mindful of the comfort of the other party.

Item 13: Neither party is allowed to invade the other's personal space without permission. This includes bedrooms, bathrooms and offices.

Item 14: If either party harms the other, intentional or otherwise, aid, comfort and an apology must be rendered. If harm is severe, the Dragon Prince will level punishment.

Item 15: Sustenance may be provided by either party, but no party should be forced to provide all sustenance. Each party must practice patience with the other's preferred tastes.

Note: Other Items may be added, as agreed upon by both parties. Existing Items may be revised as the need arises.

Beneath the list of items were signature and date lines for Kwan and Phil.

"Wow. This is almost civilized," Phil blinked at Kwan in surprise.

"I wrote three documents. I substituted this one in the folder after you ripped off the original tab."

"Let me guess—the other two had lots of master and familiar listed in it?"

"Ah, something like that. Yes."

"I still don't want to sign it." Phil floated the folder to Kwan. "Nobody asked me if I wanted this. I get that you can't move out of the house for a while, but for me, consent is everything."

"You removed the dagger without my consent. In fact, I told you no —twice."

"Oh, sweet Jesus," Phil covered her face with a hand.

"You also put your hands upon *my* body without *my* permission," Kwan reminded her. "For humans, that alone can draw a death sentence. Are you prepared, Mrs. Muir? Making you my familiar will satisfy the Dragon Court, should they learn of such a violation."

"You were in pain," Phil hissed, dropping her hand and staring at Kwan. "I couldn't," she sighed and lowered her eyes. "I knew it would kill you if you tried to pull it out yourself. It wasn't a fresh wound, so you'd been carrying it for a while. No doubt the asshole that showed up this morning figured you'd get tired of hurting after a while and pull it out just to end it all."

"You knew he was the one?"

"The malevolence in him matched the dagger, dude." Phil lifted her eyes to blink at Kwan.

"What happened to the dagger? Do you have it? I still don't understand how you were able to remove it without harming me."

"I didn't remove it."

"What did you say?"

"I didn't remove it."

"Then where is it?"

"I didn't remove it. I disintegrated it. I may or may not have cauterized the leaking blood vessels surrounding it afterward, depending on how the Dragon Court views *that* kind of thing."

"Nobody disintegrates a spelled dagger."

"Well, you don't have to believe me if you don't want to. I'm going downstairs for a snack. Feel free to stand in my doorway as long as you want."

Phil brushed past Kwan on her way out the door, but he didn't follow.

My Prince, the familiar has a rather unique ability, I think.

Tell me when you come to visit and make it soon.

⁂

"RAY IS GRILLING STEAKS," PHIL SIGHED WHEN KWAN JOINED HER IN the kitchen, asking what was for dinner. "We'll put a salad together, and roast corn on the cob. Is there anything you want to add or subtract?"

"That sounds quite good," Kwan replied. "I still need your signature," the folder appeared in his hand. "The Prince already knows you willfully touched me without permission and is prepared to file a case with the Dragon Council on my behalf, whether I wish him to do so or not."

"Then take out the koi pond thing."

"No."

"Then how am I going to tell you when you've crossed the line?"

"You could use words."

"Right. Like you were so willing to listen."

"I was forced to reeducate myself in modern practices where business agreements and relationships are concerned. I will even pay rent and my part of the utilities."

"Or you could really translate one of my books."

"I confess I don't read modern literature."

"Figures."

"I worry that Dal will return," Kwan mused.

"I extended my barrier," Phil countered. "The entire island is now covered."

"What kind of witch are you?"

"I don't want to tell you."

"Very well, but I warn you, I can be quite observant, patient and persuasive. If I guess correctly, will you tell me so?"

"Sure," Phil closed her eyes and drew in a breath. "That was sarcasm, by the way. Can we add a sarcasm clause to the agreement?"

"When we agree upon the parameters. Sign, please," he opened the folder and tapped her signature line.

"You, first."

"Very well." An old-style fountain pen appeared in his hand. Kwan signed with a flourish and added the date. "Your turn."

"I really, really, resent you for this," Phil said, taking the pen from his fingers. "See if I help anybody out in the future."

"You're left-handed."

"I can see your observational skills are already at work," Phil leaned down to sign her name and date the agreement.

"Tch," Kwan snorted in reply.

"WHAT'S HIS NAME AND WHEN WILL HE BE HERE TOMORROW?" XINNIE asked as she and Phil chopped tomatoes and red onions for the salad.

"His name is Kwan, and he'll be here before noon," Phil replied. "Oh, can I get an extra steak cooked—in case I'm hungry later?"

"Well, look at you," Xinnie laughed. "We'll have a couple extras—you can have one and we'll take the other."

"Sounds great. Make it rare, please, so I can heat it up without making it chewy."

"Will do."

"Good choice—thank you," Kwan leaned on the end of the island, watching the two women work.

"How do you feel about not having the house to yourself on weekends?" Xinnie asked.

"It'll be fine. Who knows, maybe he'll want to go out and amuse himself," Phil waved a hand. "There are plenty of good restaurants in Seattle."

"Are you really going to let him drive one of the cars?"

"If he has a license. He can drive the compact SUV—it's still dinged up from my last trip into town. He probably can't do much worse than that, don't you think?"

"Aish." Kwan pushed himself away from the island and stalked away.

"Does that mean you'll actually drive the Mercedes?"

Kwan stopped in his tracks. "I'll drive it," he said, turning around.

"I'm not letting him drive it," Phil tore lettuce and dropped it in the salad bowl.

"What if he's nice looking? Will you let him drive it then?" Xinnie teased.

"Xinnie, don't try to fix me up, and I mean it."

"You have a problem with Asian men?" Kwan was back at the island, demanding an answer.

"I was just thinking—after you've spent so much time watching K-dramas and Asian movies," Xinnie pinched Phil's cheek affectionately.

"I have absolutely no problem with Asian men," Phil said, refusing to look at Kwan. "I love K-dramas, Taiwanese dramas, Chinese dramas, et cetera and so forth. That doesn't mean I ought to jump the first Asian guy who comes along."

"Phil, it's been three years," Xinnie's voice softened.

"Nobody needs to tell me how long it's been."

"I didn't mean to upset you." Xinnie rubbed Phil's back. "It hurts to watch you kill yourself with work and never go out, except to the coffee shop. Your grandmother would be worried sick if she were still here."

"Gran can't help either of us, Xinnie. You know that. I'm going for a walk." Phil jerked away the apron she wore and almost ran for the door.

"I guess that's what happens when you lose sixteen members of your family and your husband, all on the same damn day," Xinnie muttered when the door slammed behind Phil.

Kwan blinked at Xinnie for a moment before following in Phil's footsteps.

"WHAT DO YOU WANT?" PHIL REFUSED TO LOOK AT KWAN, WHO PACED her through the forest surrounding her home. She scrubbed a stray tear off her cheek and trotted ahead of him.

"I need to buy a computer and ah, one of those tablet things, I suppose. To make me look professional when I officially arrive tomorrow."

"We can go find that after dinner."

"I think the steaks are ready; I can smell them from here."

"Xinnie will leave mine covered on the island—you can have it."

"Yours will be medium rare. I prefer rare."

Phil stopped walking. "Fine. It doesn't do any good to try and run —it always comes back to haunt me anyway. Let's go feed your face; you're probably starved."

Kwan hesitated for several seconds as Phil turned and retraced her steps to the house. *How did sixteen relatives and her husband all die on the same day?* Kwan decided he would solve that mystery.

Soon.

CHAPTER 4

"You can get settled in tomorrow. Thursday is cleaning day, so I'll be out until late in the afternoon," Phil told Kwan as they ate at the kitchen island later.

"Do I also have to be out?"

"Only if you want to be. I can't handle the noise of the vacuum or the gossip that goes on the whole time the cleaning crew is here."

"Where do you go? The library?"

"Cleaning days are my rollerblading days. Sometimes I hit Pike Place Market afterward, especially if Xinnie wants fresh fish."

"Rollerblading?"

"Inline skating? There's an indoor skatepark in Seattle that's relatively quiet on weekdays."

"Where are we going tonight—for my computer?"

"There's an electronics store in Tukwila."

"Will we take the Mercedes?"

"If you promise not to scratch it."

"The ah, scratches on the other vehicle were unintended." Kwan shifted uncomfortably on his chair.

"Then you can pay to get it fixed."

"I suppose I will. Thank you for not being angry."

"It's just a car."

"It's not your Mercedes."

"Exactly. Gran bought the Mercedes for me as a wedding gift. I drove it here from Texas—afterward."

"Afterward?"

"After I got out of the hospital. If you hang around here long enough, you'll find out anyway. The information is all over the Internet. Please go to a reputable website for details. Keywords are *Texas bride* and *wedding massacre*. Don't do it while I'm anywhere nearby." Phil held up a hand when Kwan reached for his phone.

"Very well. When will we be going out?"

"In half an hour."

"I will wait." Kwan shoved the phone in a pocket and went back to his food.

"This one," Kwan pointed to the top-of-the-line laptop. "With a leather case. I also want a tablet with accessories," he informed the electronics team member at the Tukwila shop.

"You into gaming?" The team member asked. "This is the best gaming laptop we carry."

"Yes. This is what I want. No more questions, please."

Phil stood nearby, keeping her mouth tightly shut. Kwan was determined to sink more than six thousand dollars into a laptop, a separate keyboard and accessories, plus an iPad. The store was closing in less than fifteen, and Kwan appeared to be in a hurry to get out the door before then.

"Do you want anything?" Kwan turned to Phil.

Pressing her lips together, which forced one of her dimples to appear, Phil shook her head.

"Tch." Kwan turned back to the team member, but not before he revealed a half smile.

"I promise not to dent or scratch the car," Kwan wheedled after placing his purchases in the trunk. "Let me drive."

"No."

"Very well." Kwan lifted his head disdainfully and walked around to the passenger side. "I've never driven an S-Class Coupe. Go ahead—keep it all for yourself."

"Reverse psychology will get you nowhere if my Mercedes is involved." Phil pulled the door open and climbed onto the leather seat.

Kwan reluctantly slid onto the passenger seat and shut the door. "I will go with you Thursday and scrutinize your skating skills."

"Perfect."

"Ah. We should attend to the sarcasm item soon, should we not?"

"Absolutely. Seatbelt."

"THE WI-FI PASSWORD IS THIS?" KWAN FROWNED AT THE SLIP OF PAPER Phil handed to him.

"What's wrong with it?"

"AngryOrphanHag96?"

"I'm going to bed, now. Good-night." Phil left Kwan standing in the kitchen while she bounced toward the stairs, ponytail swinging.

"You'll be writing in half an hour," Kwan called after her.

"None of your business," she shot back and raced up the steps.

Kwan busied himself for the next two hours getting his new laptop and tablet set up, then dithered about giving Phil his email address.

Would she give him hers in return?

What about her phone number?

If she refused, he could find those things on his own, he decided, before stepping through the portal to his lair. Tonight, he would sleep there. He would knock on the door at the appropriate time the following day and slide into his role as translator. He looked forward to asking Xinnie and Ray questions.

He also wondered whether it was impolite to ask the mixed-race couple about their lives and how they came to work for Philomena. Had her grandmother hired them? They fit perfectly with Philomena, who obviously cared deeply about both.

Resolving to find the information one way or another, Kwan stepped through the portal at the back of his chosen bedroom, became his scaled-and-clawed self, stretched, unfurled his wings and flew toward his sleeping chamber.

"ARE YOU SURE HE HASN'T BEEN IN SOME OF THOSE SHOWS YOU'VE watched?" Xinnie whispered as she and Phil watched Kwan disappear into his bedroom just before noon the following day. "He's pretty enough to eat."

"Xinnie, you're a married woman," Phil reminded her dryly.

"Doesn't mean I can't look. Ray gets all the benefits anyhow. I'll make sure the exercise room is clean and aired. That man definitely works out."

"Remove that gleam in your eye," Phil sighed. "Feel free to show him the exercise room after lunch."

"I'll go finish that up now. You think he likes chicken salad on a croissant?"

"I suspect that he can find his own food if he doesn't. I'll give him the keys for the SUV when he comes downstairs for lunch."

"He really has a license?"

"It's a New York driver's license, and it hasn't expired. He emailed a photocopy last night." Phil didn't add that she still had no idea how he'd found her email; she hadn't given it to him.

"YOU'LL HAVE TO TELL US WHAT YOU LIKE TO EAT," XINNIE SMILED AT Kwan as she set his sandwich in front of him half an hour later.

"There are plenty of restaurants in the area, too," Phil frowned at Xinnie.

"You'll have to take me to your favorites." Kwan enjoyed the slashing look Phil gave him.

"The keys to the compact SUV," Phil pulled keys from her sweater pocket and pushed them across the kitchen island toward Kwan.

"I may lease something for myself to drive while I'm here. I'll give these back if that happens."

"Digging much?" Phil hissed at Kwan when Xinnie walked away for a few moments.

"Merely stating my intentions. I found I had many plans to make while setting up my equipment last night."

Phil held back her retort; Xinnie returned with a fresh cup of tea for Kwan.

"Don't forget; you must travel to Korea with me in the next two weeks to sign the contract with the Korean publisher," Kwan gave Phil a malicious smile.

"What?" Xinnie and Phil chorused.

"I see I shall be forced to be your memory while I'm here," Kwan chuckled.

"I don't think," Phil began before Xinnie clamped a hand on her wrist.

"Then remind her to eat and sleep," Xinnie smiled sweetly at Kwan. "I can't be here every minute to ride herd."

"Ride herd?"

"Oh, sweet Jesus," Phil rubbed her forehead.

"Boss her around. She doesn't take care of herself, and any editor or publisher should be concerned about that."

"Xinnie, stop talking," Phil muttered. Kwan was enjoying the exchange—he leaned back in his chair and crossed arms with apparent interest.

"I still have to clean the floor in the exercise room—feel free to use it whenever you want," Xinnie told Kwan. "I'll go do that right now."

"Thank you," Kwan dipped his head to Xinnie.

Phil waited until Xinnie was out of the kitchen before rounding on Kwan. "Do not get comfortable," she hissed at him.

"But I am," he raised his hands and linked fingers behind his head. "This is quite enjoyable, I think. I'll make the arrangements for the visit to Korea."

"Please tell me we're going to the southern part," Phil sighed.

"And if we weren't? I assure you, protection would be provided, should we visit the north. We dragons do not recognize the boundaries humans place upon our country."

"I don't want to visit the north."

"Why? You'd be in no danger."

"It's not me who'd be in danger."

"What are you saying, Philomena?"

"When you stop being a pain in my neck, maybe I'll tell you."

"No name calling," Kwan pointed out their agreement.

"Statement of fact. My neck is so kinked from stress I can barely type."

"Then stop typing. Give yourself a rest. You can drive me to an auto dealership. I have a lease to sign."

"What do you intend to lease?"

"I have an address for the dealership. Finish your lunch and we'll go."

"THIS IS OUR NEWEST F-TYPE R COUPE. JUST ARRIVED YESTERDAY," the salesman led Kwan and Phil to a white Jaguar parked on the showroom floor. "Fully loaded. Speed, style, you'll turn heads for sure with this one."

"I see I've been left out of this conversation. If you need me, I'll be sitting over there," Phil pointed to a bench surrounded by tall, potted plants.

"Ah, I didn't mean," the salesman coughed.

"She will be fine. I find this vehicle adequate. Prepare the lease, please."

"The Mercedes you arrived in—you wouldn't consider selling it, would you? That's a limited edition in mint condition. It'll bring top dollar from a collector."

"How much do you like koi ponds?" Kwan asked as the salesman led him toward his office.

"Koi ponds?"

"It means that vehicle will never be for sale."

"Ah."

"I ALREADY TOLD XINNIE THAT WE WOULDN'T BE BACK FOR DINNER, SO she didn't have to cook," Phil grumped at Kwan when the new Jaguar was driven around to park beside her Mercedes.

The entire process had taken more than three hours, because Kwan wanted to drive the Jaguar back to the house.

"Then where do you want to eat?" Kwan frowned as the salesman got out of the Jag and handed the keys over.

"Depends. Do you want seafood, Korean, Chinese, Japanese, Mexican, American, French, Thai or fast food?"

"Seafood will be fine."

"Why? I thought you'd go Korean for sure."

"Seafood is the first on your list. I think it is your first choice, whether it be conscious or subconscious."

"There's a good place near Pike Place Market. I'll text you the address." Phil pulled out her phone and sent a text.

"How did you get my number?" Kwan demanded, causing the salesman to turn back quickly.

"Turnabout is fair play, don't you think?"

"Aish," Kwan frowned and turned his head.

"I'll call ahead and try to get us a table," Phil slid onto the seat in the Mercedes and shut the door. "Feel free to fume and fuss while you're driving," she added, starting the car and putting it in gear.

"New relationship," Kwan nodded to the salesman. "Thank you for your assistance." He buckled his seatbelt and pulled away to follow Phil.

"The owner liked Gran's books. When I finished the last one for her, he started reading my stuff, too." Phil opened her menu, blocking Kwan's face from view. The restaurant she'd chosen was so popular it was nearly impossible to get a same-day reservation.

Kwan, his curiosity piqued, had asked her about it.

"Has her publisher asked you to continue her series?"

"They've asked."

"And?"

"I'm thinking about it. Gran had a few notes written on future books, and the one I finished did really well. I don't want to ride her coattails, though. I have my own ideas, and they're lucrative enough."

"I've arranged for a two-week visit to Seoul and the surrounding areas," Kwan said. "We leave in four days."

Phil's menu dropped, allowing her to glare at Kwan over its top. "Prince Jiah has commanded our presence. I had nothing to do with the timing."

"Right. How the hell did I get involved in all this?" Phil sighed, lifting her menu again.

"You willfully touched me, remember? That is forbidden in my culture."

"Maybe your culture sucks when it comes to rendering aid."

"That is the only reason you still live," Kwan replied, his words haughty and unrelenting.

"Hmmph. Try to kill me. *Try*."

"I am practicing patience."

"Right. You're full of patience. I get it, now."

"You have no idea," Kwan muttered.

"May I take your drink order?" A waiter arrived at their table.

"Bring a bottle of the Rombauer Chardonnay and two glasses, please," Kwan said.

"I want a Perrier with lime," Phil said before the waiter could turn away.

"The wine is very good," Kwan began.

"I don't drink much."

"One glass?"

"We'll see. We're driving, remember?"

Moments later, the wine and Perrier were served and another waiter appeared to take their order. "King crab legs with sautéed vegetables, and a Caesar salad out first," Phil handed her menu to the waiter.

"King crab legs with potatoes au gratin," Kwan handed over his menu. "Also with a Caesar salad out first."

"You'll like the potatoes," Phil sighed when the waiter walked away.

"Why didn't you order them?"

"It comes in a dish big enough for two or three people. I can't eat all that. Besides, squash and zucchini are in season and really fresh right now."

"Here," Kwan poured half a normal portion of wine in a glass, then handed it to Phil.

"I shouldn't drink on an empty stomach."

"You'll have a salad soon enough."

"Fine."

"Here's to new vehicles and an upcoming trip."

"Neither of which I'm happy about," Phil clinked her glass with Kwan's.

"Bring nice clothing. You cannot appear before the Prince dressed as you do for writing. Bring a dress for a formal occasion, and a few skirts, at the very least."

"I'll decide what to bring, thank you."

"You cannot go about in jeans and track suits all the time, thank you."

"Where, exactly, will we be staying?"

"I've booked a hotel in Seoul, but we will spend the first two nights at the Prince's palace."

"Why not stay there the whole time?"

"Because Dal will arrive on the third day. There are many things to discuss, and he will stay at the palace when he arrives."

"Oh. *That* asshat."

"Murder is not allowed in our race. Even though Dal committed a great crime, he will not be killed for it. Only treason will bring a death sentence, and only if the entire Council and the Prince agree."

"So Dal has friends in high places."

"You may arrive logically at that conclusion."

"What you mean is that Dal is also on the Council."

"You are most perceptive."

"Yeah."

PHIL AWOKE TO DISTANT THUNDER, WHILE RAIN HIT HER BEDROOM windows with the lashing force of a heavy wind.

"How?" Raising her head, she took in her surroundings.

She couldn't recall getting into bed.

She couldn't recall dressing in her pajamas.

She couldn't recall the drive home.

She did recall that she'd had two and a half glasses of wine the night before.

Her phone buzzed on the nightstand; someone was texting her. "What?" she demanded, swiping the phone on to see the text.

I touched your person without permission. However, you were unconscious at the time, so I was compelled to render aid. Apologies —K.

I want to kill you. RIP—P.

I hired a busboy to drive your car home. Your insurance is already active. It was for the best—K.

I'm hiring a hitman. It's for my mental health—P.

A hitman will not last five seconds against me—K.

Kwan found himself flailing in the salty waters of Puget Sound, his phone still in his hand.

BTW, the agreement only says koi pond—P.

"Philomena!" Kwan banged on her locked office door, still dripping from his unexpected dip into cold water. "Open this door immediately."

"Your phone is waterproof; I checked," Phil shouted back.

"We will amend the agreement. *Now*."

"I like it as is."

"I will break the door if you don't open it." Kwan flung his weight against it, making it and Phil's office walls shake.

"Damn," Phil muttered, rising from her desk. "I'm coming, keep your shirt on."

"My shirt is ruined," Kwan yelled the moment Phil opened the door. "Look at this." He pinched expensive, wet silk with two fingers.

"I'll buy you another one."

"Fine. We will shop today. You owe me three suits, three shirts, two pairs of slippers and socks and underwear."

"Can I just give you money and send you out on your own? I have work to do. You can go drive that fancy car of yours."

"You will come with me. Dress to go out. I'll meet you downstairs in an hour. This is the least you can do for making me miserable and ruining my favorite suits. Also, we *will* be amending the agreement."

"Suit yourself. Pun intended," Phil snipped.

"Get dressed. Go, now."

"You're in my way."

"I can be more in your way." He took a menacing step forward. "I smell of fish, too. Would you also like that?"

"I'll go get dressed. Please move."

"Tch," Kwan hissed, turning aside to let Phil pass.

At least her jeans are black and don't have rips or tears, Kwan surveyed Phil's outfit with a critical eye. *Short-heeled boots are nice. Shirt and jacket are suitable enough. Earrings are too small*, he decided.

"Is that a purse?" Kwan stared in surprise at the tiny strap she'd flung over her shoulder.

"It's a wallet on a string. It doesn't hurt my shoulder," Phil gave Kwan a dark look.

"Your shoulder hurts?"

"My collarbone was broken in three places by one of the bullets that hit me. It aches at times. Gets worse if I hang a heavy purse or laptop over it."

Kwan took a moment to close his eyes and calm his breathing.

He'd seen the scars—couldn't help but see them while removing her clothing and dressing her in pajamas the night before.

The shooter meant to kill her and everyone else at her wedding. Kwan's hands clenched into fists.

"Very well. I will remember this in the future."

"Do you know where you want to go?"

"Yes. I have already studied the map."

"Good. You drive. I'm not feeling very steady right now."

Kwan leaned his head to the side, acknowledging her words. They walked downstairs together, heading toward the back of the house and the door into the garages.

"You look good in everything—take whatever you want," Phil told Kwan later, when he couldn't winnow his purchases past five suits. "I know those suits I ruined weren't off the rack, so I owe you a lot."

Shirts and ties were also laid out for Kwan's consideration. "If you want all of them, that's fine. Get measured, dude. It's past lunchtime," Phil said.

"I'll take all these, plus the dress shirts and four turtlenecks," Kwan told the sales assistant.

"I'm buying," Phil slid off her chair and opened her purse. "Here." She handed the man a credit card.

"Philomena Muir? You're Beatrice Lang's granddaughter, aren't you?" The clerk blinked at the name on the card. "She's still considered a local celebrity. Your books have the same feel to them. My wife reads everything you write."

"Gran was special, and there will never be anyone who could replace her," Phil said. "Thank your wife for me."

"I will. She'll be upset that she didn't meet you."

Kwan watched the exchange in silence. Philomena sounded professional and assured. Her fingers, tightly clenched together, told another story.

Kwan's measurements were taken after the sale was rung up. "Did you have breakfast?" he asked as he and Phil walked toward the shop's front doors. Kwan carried four clothing bags; Phil offered to carry half, but he'd refused. His suits would be altered and ready in two days, after Phil paid a fee to expedite the process.

"My stomach was too queasy for breakfast," Phil admitted. "Now I'm hungry."

"Food first, then shoes and other things."

"Awesome."

Kwan didn't even flinch at the word; he stuffed the bags in the trunk of his Jaguar while Phil slid onto the passenger seat and shut the door.

"Are you missing your rollerblading day?" Kwan asked, putting the car in gear and backing out of the parking space.

"No. I told you I wasn't steady today. If you hadn't wanted to shop, I'd be at the library, hiding in a corner."

"Does this happen often?"

"Now and then."

"Want Chinese?"

"They have great pork lo mein at a restaurant not far from here."

"Give me the address."

Kwan was grateful for the list of foods that Xinnie slipped him—he'd asked for Philomena's favorites and Xinnie had provided a list quickly. *Phil will never turn down pork lo mein*, Xinnie had written.

Kwan surreptitiously watched Phil enjoy her food while he ate steak and rice. The cook was happy to accommodate his special request and the food was good, just as Phil promised.

"We will definitely come here again," Kwan sighed, setting a credit card on the small tray brought by their server.

"They're good about leaving out the MSG for me," Phil sighed. "I know lots of people have a phobia about it, but I'd eat it if I could rather than making trouble."

"It does affect some people," Kwan agreed. "I have seen this for myself."

"Thank you for not lecturing me."

"Has that happened?"

"Yes. Not here, but at other restaurants. Want coffee? There's a shop two doors down."

"I'd take a latte."

"Me, too."

Kwan was pleased that Phil's color looked better after she'd eaten and promised himself never to force alcohol on her again. "Fog and mist coming," he said softly as they strolled toward the coffeeshop.

"Yeah. I can feel it," Phil nodded. "It'll be here before our coffee is ready."

She can sense the weather. Kwan placed another checkmark on his list of witch-types. The Prince was anxious to get more information on Phil; no doubt he'd heard something from Dal already about the unexpected trip he'd been forced to take.

Familiars were off-limits to other dragons and considered personal property, which, by Dragon Law, couldn't be harmed or violated. Dal was cunning enough to get around the laws without implicating himself, however.

I hope Philomena never learns that she's considered personal property. Kwan wanted to shake his wings and ruffle his scales at the thought of where he could land if she did.

Phil could remove another spelled dagger, should Dal choose to attack him again. For that to happen, he had to be agreeable rather than grumpy. He'd never intended to take a familiar; that wasn't his way of doing things. Nevertheless, Philomena had come along and things had changed.

"Two large vanilla lattes," Kwan ordered when they reached the coffeeshop counter.

"Are you buying, or should I? This is your outing," Phil blinked at him. Perhaps for the first time, he noticed that she was only as tall as his shoulder, even with short-heeled boots on.

"I'll buy the coffee."

"Awesome." An almost dimple twitched on the right side of Kwan's chin. It only appeared when he was deeply chagrined or amused. "That's nice—you have an almost dimple," Phil pointed at his chin.

He couldn't decide whether chagrin or amusement was the proper term after she'd used the forbidden word, so he let it go. "Name?" the barista asked.

"Phil," Phil replied.

"Okay, Phil," the woman smiled at Kwan before writing the name on both cups.

"Eh?"

"Let it go," Phil urged as Kwan handed cash to the barista.

After paying for their drink order, Kwan followed Phil to a table near the front windows. He clamped his mouth shut when Phil turned, grabbed his elbow with both hands and jerked him backward.

That's when the giant squid broke through the coffeeshop's windows with an ear-shattering rain of broken glass.

CHAPTER 5

"We're not hurt," Phil told the detective and a squad of police officers who'd arrived at the coffeeshop to investigate the incident.

Kwan, standing behind Phil, nodded his agreement.

If Phil hadn't pulled him back and protected them both somehow, well, he wanted to shake out his wings and roar in fury at the thought.

"Why and how would somebody launch a giant squid at a coffeeshop?" Another man joined the team of forensic investigators who hurriedly took photos and set up small, numbered markers around the scene.

"You're the marine biologist?" The detective asked.

"Yes. This is unheard of—these creatures are not only impossible to find, they don't live long in captivity."

"The barista was having a panic attack, so they're taking her to the hospital," another officer arrived to inform the detective.

"Do either of you need medical assistance?" the officer asked Phil and Kwan.

"We are fine. How much longer will this take?" Kwan asked.

"I think we're about done. If I have follow-up questions, I'll contact you."

"Come out through the back," the officer beckoned. Phil and Kwan walked behind him until they reached the back door.

"Where is your car?" the officer asked.

"Two blocks down," Kwan replied. "We came for coffee after having lunch at the Chinese restaurant."

"They serve great food," the officer agreed as they made their way to Kwan's Jaguar.

"This your car? Nice," the officer breathed when Kwan unlocked the car with his remote.

"I'm glad we walked to the coffeeshop," Phil sighed. "Kwan, can we go home? I think I've had enough excitement for today."

"Drive safely," the officer called out as Kwan settled on the driver's seat and started the car.

"I think he did this," Phil stated softly as Kwan backed out of the parking space.

"He?"

"The one I sent to the French Southern Territories."

"I was thinking the same thing." Kwan changed gears and drove the Jaguar to the parking lot entrance. "Home it is."

"Does he have some way of finding you?" Phil thought to ask later, after they'd parked the Jaguar on the ferry that would return them to Vashon Island.

"He must have," Kwan gripped the steering wheel tighter. Phil watched as his knuckles turned white.

"We need to fix that. You have nice hands," she told him.

"Eh?"

"If you ask a hundred women what the first thing is that they notice about a man, they'll say everything from his eyes to his backside," Phil looked out the window at the cars parked all around them. "I always notice the hands."

"Why? That sounds odd," Kwan frowned in her direction.

"I look at how well they're kept. The shape of the fingers, the veins on the back. I wonder what those hands have done for a living. How many gifts they've given or received. Have they been a comfort to others, or have they been used to harm anyone?"

"I will never consider hands in the same way again," Kwan whispered. "What is the second thing you notice?"

"Mouth and eyes. Whether either of those things are accustomed to smiles or laughter. Those are only the physical attributes, mind you. If I say I first study the light around someone, most people will freak."

"Yes, I suppose they would," Kwan agreed. "What will you do to fix our current problem—that of Dal finding us, somehow?"

"Prevent him from finding you," Phil turned her head to blink at Kwan. "I'll set a concealment spell. He won't know where you are unless you're standing next to him."

"That sounds useful. How long will it take, and will there be any side effects?"

"It's a spell set around you, not *on* you," Phil explained. "You'll never know it's there. I'll have to wait until tomorrow or the day after to set it—I'm too shaky and unsettled to do it right now. Don't worry, once we're back on the island, we're safe. It's already spelled against him and anything else he's had an interaction with."

"Sounds complicated."

"That depends on your definition of complicated. I've already concealed this car and I'm worn out. Something this small shouldn't drain all my energy like that. That's why yours will have to wait for a day or two."

Kwan stilled at her words. He hadn't noticed her casting any spell. How and when had she done it?

"We're here," Phil sighed with relief and closed her eyes as the ferry maneuvered into position; they'd arrived at the Vashon Island landing. "Let me know when we get home," she added.

"I'M EXHAUSTED. THE HOUSE SMELLS NICE," PHIL TOLD XINNIE WHEN she and Kwan walked into the kitchen. Xinnie's eyes widened at all the upscale shopping bags Kwan carried.

"Shopping always wears her out," Xinnie told Kwan. "Phil, go take a nap. You look like you've been at ground zero in a buffalo stampede."

"You have no idea," Phil slouched toward the stairs.

"You think she'll make it?" Kwan asked.

"If she didn't have the strength, she'd take the elevator," Xinnie murmured.

"Very well. I'll drop these off in my room. Also, Philomena asked me to inform you that our trip to Seoul has been moved up; we leave Sunday evening."

"How long?"

"Two weeks."

"I'll ask for vacation time for Ray and me. He wants to take a road trip."

"I hope you enjoy your time off." Kwan nodded to Xinnie before following in Phil's footsteps.

"I'M UP," PHIL CALLED OUT AFTER SOMEONE TAPPED SOFTLY ON HER bedroom door. She'd slept for nearly three hours before waking in a haze. She and her clothing were rumpled and out of sorts when she pulled the door open.

Kwan stood outside, his head canted to the right as he studied her appearance.

"Don't say it," Phil held up a hand to stave off comments.

"Have you started packing?"

"No. We still have two and a half days. Give it a rest, dude."

"Your dinner turned cold an hour ago."

"Yeah." Phil ran fingers through her hair, trying to tame it after she'd slept so restlessly.

"Shall I ride herd, now?"

"Let me straighten myself up."

"I'll wait."

"Not necessary."

"I. Will. Wait."

"Fine. Give me ten minutes." Phil took off toward her bathroom and the closet beyond that.

Kwan checked his *Vacheron Constantin* wristwatch; if she didn't reappear in ten minutes, he'd complain.

Maybe.

"All right. I'm here," Phil turned sideways so she wouldn't touch Kwan on her way out the door. "What's for dinner?"

"Cold lasagna."

"Oh, man," Phil stopped halfway between her bedroom and the stairs. Her shoulders drooped as she tilted her head back.

She'd twisted her hair into a bun and clipped it with a piece of jewelry. Kwan blinked; she'd changed into a long, aquamarine skirt and white tank, over which she wore a matching, long-sleeved aquamarine shirt. Her pose at that moment stilled his breath; her throat and the line of her neck were exposed. He had no idea why it fascinated him so much.

"Come on," Phil sighed. "I'll nuke it."

"Still good?" Kwan asked later as Phil took her second bite of microwaved lasagna.

"Yeah. It's just the idea of putting a piece of art in a microwave." Phil cut off another bite with her fork.

"Xinnie's lasagna is a piece of art," Kwan agreed. "I was very pleased and had two portions."

"We've had a rough day," Phil lifted her glass of sparkling water and drank. "If the guy who lobbed the giant squid at us today is in Seoul the same time we are, what's to stop him from trying this crap again?"

"Your spells?"

Phil's fork stilled. "I don't want too many knowing what I can or can't do, and I despise tests."

"Why?"

"I have my reasons. You'll have to live with that answer."

"If the Prince requires," Kwan began.

"I don't belong to your Prince, or anybody else for that matter. There's a reason for that as well."

"Prince Jiah has made the study of witches one of his favorite hobbies. It's not often that he comes across anyone so talented," Kwan tried another tack.

"For your sake and the Prince's, please quench your curiosity."

"I'll arrange a private meeting."

"Right. I still won't answer questions. I have my reasons, as stated before."

"The Prince is most curious, and it is required that you meet him."

"Then this will be awkward, yes?"

"Aish," Kwan muttered.

"Are you packed?" Phil asked.

"Almost."

"Then go finish that and let me eat in peace. Your whining is getting on my nerves."

"I am not whining."

"Fine. Complaining, then."

"Not complaining."

"Harassing?"

"Ah," Kwan lifted a finger to lecture her before reconsidering. "Very well. I will finish packing. Eat." He shoved his chair back and left the kitchen, his stride and posture as stiff as any dragon in human form might make them.

Phil's resolve collapsed the moment he was out of sight; she felt weak and drained after their exchange. *Why was he so relentless?*

A Prince who studied witches as a hobby?

What the hell was that all about?

Will his English be as good as Kwan's?

Phil felt that only trouble would come of all this, but she couldn't refuse; refusal would only draw more attention, and that was the last thing she needed.

She is balking at answering questions and refuses outright to be tested, Kwan informed Prince Jiah. *Something troubles her about this, but I cannot find the cause.*

Can you be certain that the attack earlier was Dal's doing?

I feel confident in that assessment, as does Philomena.

Why is he carrying this so far? Jiah allowed his private thoughts to extend to Kwan. *He is barely fit to serve on the Council and he knows this.*

Jealousy, of course. I still cannot find the source of the spell on the dagger.

Have you asked your familiar?

Not in so many words. What I know for certain is that Dal cannot perform this level of magic on his own.

You were the only one to touch it, Jiah reminded Kwan. *The rest of us could not without causing your death.*

I am aware. I have my doubts that today's incident can be wholly attributed to him, either.

That is also my concern. He has been watched carefully for more than two centuries, but nothing has been detected so far. We have no evidence otherwise. What time are you scheduled to arrive Monday?

In time for a noon meal, in the Seoul time zone.

Very well. I will see to the arrangements.

I ask for a small welcoming party. Philomena may be overwhelmed if there are too many.

She must meet the Council and many others eventually.

I understand.

"WE'LL HAVE OUR EVENING MEAL WITH PRINCE JIAH AND A FEW COURT regulars," Kwan told Phil on Sunday morning. Xinnie and Ray had left on their road trip the day before and wouldn't be back until Kwan and Phil returned from Seoul.

"Are they waiting on us to eat?"

"It will be their noon meal, due to the time difference," Kwan explained.

"Are we supposed to stay awake after that? Time differences always do me in."

"If you are weary, you only have to tell me. I will make arrangements for you to rest in your palace suite."

"I'd rather stay at the hotel the entire time."

"You cannot. That would be an insult to Prince Jiah. He is only allowing us to stay at a hotel at all because of Dal's arrival."

"Was Dal already planning a visit or is he coming because you are?"

"The latter, I'm sure."

"How did he find out?"

"There are few secrets among dragonkind."

"Lovely. Chalk up another massive mistake on Phil's lengthy list."

"Philomena, I am grateful for what you did for me. It took me a short while to realize it, but you did something no other could do, I think."

"You're welcome," Phil sighed, hanging her head. "I have to go pack, but I need coffee, first."

"Do you always wait for the last moment to pack?"

"This is different. I'd already be packed if it were somewhere I wanted to go."

"You don't want to see Seoul?"

"I want to see it. I just don't feel comfortable with the uh, other stuff. Too many things could go wrong. You don't see it that way, I know, but that's my problem in a nutshell."

"You will be welcomed warmly by Prince Jiah."

"I don't doubt it. But you said studying witches is his hobby. I don't want to be studied, scrutinized, dissected, examined or baited."

"Aish, I shouldn't have told you that," Kwan sighed, closing his eyes.

"Well, forewarned is forearmed, I think the saying is. Do you want coffee, too?"

"I'd prefer tea if you have any."

"I have tea. There's a great tea shop in Pike Place Market. I love the smell of it, but I only drink it if I'm reading."

"What kind do you have?" Kwan followed Phil toward the butler's pantry.

"Several—from white tea to black and a few in-between."

"I'll have the Chinese silver needle, please," Kwan breathed as he surveyed the tea shelf.

"It's good," Phil nodded, taking the cannister down and pulling out the metal brewing container from her tea maker. "This makes around two cups," she added.

"Does this machine make good tea?" Kwan leaned in to examine it.

"Yes. At least I'm happy with it. Xinnie bought it for me for my birthday last year."

"Xinnie is a gem."

"Yes, she is. As is her husband. I'm glad they took a vacation."

"How did Ray lose his leg?"

"You noticed, huh? Ray doesn't like to let anyone know he's got a below-the-knee titanium replacement."

"I didn't want to ask him or Xinnie."

"Xinnie and Ray were in the same combat unit in Afghanistan. Ray was madly in love with her, but he was black, she was white, and he outranked her. When their armored vehicle was hit by an IED, Ray's leg was badly damaged. He still managed to pull three people away from the wreckage before it blew up. Xinnie was the first one he rescued."

"Did his efforts result in the amputation?"

"Yeah. They might have saved his leg if he hadn't dragged it back and forth three times. He has a purple heart and a distinguished service cross. Personally, I think they owe him a medal of honor, too."

"How did they come to work for you?"

"Gran hired them six years ago. I inherited this house and begged them to stay. They hold me up whenever I feel like falling down."

"Xinnie told me they'd work here for nothing, but you pay them top dollar and provide food, housing and full benefits," Kwan said, taking his freshly-brewed tea from Phil.

"They're family and earn every dollar and then some," Phil squared her shoulders. "I'd be in a loony bin somewhere if not for them. Happy tea drinking. I'll take my coffee and go pack."

Kwan wanted to talk more, but he held himself back as Phil walked out of the butler's pantry. He couldn't barge into her bedroom and talk while she packed—not without her permission. The agreement specified it.

He doubted he'd get permission if he asked. *Philomena is dealing with personal demons*, Kwan sighed and shook his head. "I'll take my tea outside and enjoy the view," he mused aloud before taking a sip of the tea.

"Good flavor," Kwan said after tasting it. "Philomena was correct."

"Show the scars; don't show the scars," Phil held up a black evening dress and a white one. The black dress was a mermaid style with a scoop neck and long sleeves. The white was a strapless A-line with a sweetheart neckline and ruffled side slit.

"Scars it is," Phil hung up the black dress and carried the white one to her suitcase. "I guess I need heels and jewelry, too."

She'd already checked the average daily temperatures for Seoul in March—layering was the best option, so she'd packed accordingly.

"Philomena, we leave in an hour," Kwan knocked sharply on her door.

"I'm closing my suitcase," she called out.

"Are you taking a laptop?" Kwan lifted an eyebrow when she opened the door less than a minute later.

"I have something similar to work with. It's already packed up in my office. Why?"

"I can let you borrow mine," he dipped his head to hide his expression.

"I'm afraid to touch your laptop. It's scary. How long have you been gaming?"

"Nearly a decade—I was losing strength and mobility in my left hand—because of the dagger. Gaming helped me build it up again."

"Well, that makes sense. Good for you. I hope you enjoy it."

"I ah, do. It distracted me from many of my troubles."

"We all need something like that. For the past three years, it's been writing and K-dramas for me. Plus, I'd probably starve if Xinnie and Ray didn't take care of me."

"The Prince teases me relentlessly for engaging in youthful, human games, although I have convinced him to play now and then."

"No experience is wasted," Phil gave him a smile. "As long as it isn't hurting anybody, you do you. Let me get my bags and I'll meet you downstairs."

"No, meet me outside my bedroom. We'll be traveling through my lair."

"Huh?"

"It's the fastest way."

"You know, I'm sorry I didn't ask you before how we were getting there."

"It's only frightening to the unsuspecting."

"Right."

"I'll take these," he pulled her roller bag and the overnight bag sitting atop it out of her bedroom. "Get your laptop or whatever it is and come to my bedroom door. The journey isn't a long one, once the entrance to a lair has been properly established."

"What the hell was I thinking?" Phil fumed moments later as she flung a purse over her shoulder and lifted the handle of the bag holding her fancy tablet, plus a full-sized wireless keyboard and mouse.

"Come," Kwan opened the door when she arrived. "The back wall is the actual entrance. It will be dark," he warned.

Phil blinked; a wall of blackness lay just beyond the king-size bed in the room. "I don't want to," she began.

Kwan gripped her wrist; Phil shrieked as she was stretched and pulled through an endlessly dark and chilling tunnel.

"PHILOMENA?" SOMEONE CALLED HER NAME.

Someone was also slapping her left wrist.

"Huh?" She couldn't force her eyes open.

"The Prince is waiting. Wake now."

"We can place her in a cold shower."

Phil's eyes popped open at the sound of an unfamiliar voice. She struggled in Kwan's grip so fiercely he was forced to let her go. Phil was also on her feet swiftly and glowing with light, her hair crackling and lifting as if she were near lightning.

"Philomena!" Kwan barked.

Phil turned eyes on him that had become electric blue; he hardly recognized the woman in front of him. "Now is not the time for threats, dragon," a strange, cold voice spoke.

Phil's head turned to look upon the one who'd made the threat. He'd backed away and was now pressed against the door of the bedchamber where she'd awakened.

"Philomena," Kwan lowered his voice. "You are frightening Secretary Kim." He didn't add that he was also frightened—and more than a bit worried.

Phil's eyes darkened to their normal shade of blue as she blinked at Kwan. "My apologies," she said, sounding more like herself.

"Thank the skies," Kwan released a sigh. "Secretary Kim, inform the Prince that we will arrive in his presence shortly."

Secretary Kim couldn't speak; he could only jerk his head in a nod before rushing out the door.

"He's a *dokkaebi*—a goblin in your language," Kwan said, as if that would explain everything. "He has perfect recall and terrifying record-keeping skills. You can't pry secrets out of him with a lever, and he's served as the Prince's secretary for nearly a century."

"Uh-huh. Great. I feel like crap, now, and we still have to sit down and make nice with people I don't know."

"Philomena, we will speak of what just happened afterward. For now, we are late. Is there a need to visit the bathroom before we proceed?"

"No."

"Very well. Follow me."

SIX DRAGONS IN HUMAN FORM SAT AT A LARGE, ROUND TABLE IN WHAT Kwan described as the Prince's private dining room. Phil did and didn't want to look at each one present as she followed Kwan toward the cloth-covered table.

"My Prince," Kwan bowed deeply to the dragon dressed in an imperial robe, pulling Phil down with him. The bow lasted three seconds—Phil counted.

Two chairs waited; she let Kwan choose first before taking the other.

"I am pleased to see you, Cousin," Prince Jiah welcomed Kwan warmly. "Introduce us to your familiar, if you will."

"This is Philomena Muir, a novelist and witch, from the Pacific Northwest," Kwan's gaze swept the other guests.

"I've read several of her books," the only other female in the room announced. "I enjoyed them immensely. I was forced to beg Prince Jiah for an invitation when I learned you were coming. I am Min-ha," she introduced herself.

"I am very pleased to meet you," Phil smiled and dipped her head. She wanted to kick Kwan—it was obvious that the entire race of dragons knew who, what and where she was. She didn't like that.

At all.

The others were introduced, all Council members, Phil learned. Food and drinks were served, then, and the talk turned to Kwan and the dagger. Phil could barely force her food down, although it was very good.

"Ms. Muir, you are fortunate that Kwan chose you as his familiar; you could be facing a death sentence for touching not only him but such a valuable item from a dragon's hoard," Min-joon remarked, his words as bland as if he were discussing the weather.

"I believe Kwan may also be fortunate not to have that nasty thing stuck in his armpit still," Phil replied as sweetly as she could manage. "Crisis averted," she added.

"There may be a problem with that," another Council member,

Myeong, stated. "The dagger belongs to Dal. He may ask that it be returned."

Kwan was shocked when Phil turned to him and asked softly, "May I touch your hand?"

Hiding his surprise, Kwan nodded. Phil's hand covered his lightly.

He blinked as Phil's voice entered his mind. *I'll let you take point on this one.* She showed him exactly what was about to happen. *They'll think it's you. Now, hold up your free hand.*

Light formed around Kwan's uplifted hand, and the dagger materialized above the table with a loud pop, making everyone except Phil and Kwan jump.

"Do you wish to return the dagger to Dal?" Kwan asked Myeong.

"I ah," Myeong stuttered.

"I thought that might be the case," Kwan sighed. "I believe I shall leave it in this room for Dal to retrieve on his own."

The dagger was flung against the wall so fast the eye couldn't follow and was buried hilt-deep in the stone wall of Prince Jiah's private dining room.

"Thoughtful," Prince Jiah smiled at Kwan. "An excellent solution, cousin."

"It was nothing," Kwan waved his free hand. Phil's hand slipped away from the other, leaving Kwan feeling less than whole, somehow.

"Is the, ah, spell still in effect?" Myeong asked.

"The spell is altered," Phil answered. "The only one who can safely remove it from the wall is Kwan."

"Perfect," Min-ha clapped. "You should put this in one of your books."

"THANK GOODNESS THAT'S OVER," PHIL SLID DOWN THE WALL OF THE suite she'd arrived in. "I'm exhausted."

Kwan watched her collapse with consternation. "How?" he demanded.

"Which part?"

"You sent that—power or whatever it was, through me."

"I didn't—I merely shaped what you already have. Are you okay? Hurt anywhere?"

"No," he snapped. "I want to know how it was possible."

"I can't answer that. I do know that it's only possible with another powerful being or creature. You're both."

"Jiah wants a private meeting," Kwan grumbled.

"Of course he does."

"He says that Myeong won't go anywhere near the wall where the dagger is."

"You have telepathy."

"Yes. It's not common among my kind but frequently appears in my family."

"Would that be why the Prince calls you cousin?"

"Perhaps. What should I tell others when they ask about my feat in the dining room?"

"Tell them I'm rubbing off on you, I guess."

Kwan surprised her by laughing aloud.

CHAPTER 6

*P*hil slept for seven hours after what she considered the dining room debacle. Kwan had left the room before she went to bed; she had no idea where he'd slept until he wandered out of an alcove, dressed in a robe and toweling wet hair.

"What?" she shrieked, pulling the sheet up to her chin.

"There's another bedroom through there," he pointed behind him. "It's the one closest to my lair on this side. Your privacy hasn't been compromised, although there is only one bathroom, which we must share. Besides, I have seen," he hesitated for a moment, taking in the sight of her, "much of you already. Why are you upset now?"

"Gah," Phil flung the covers away and slid off the bed, fairly bristling in the black, silky pajamas that she wore. "I treated that like a visit to the gynecologist," she snapped at him. "Sometimes, you have to convince yourself it's a necessary evil and get on with your life."

"Tch," Kwan sniffed, although he tried to hide the smile that came after.

"Is there anything to eat in this place? I'm starved," Phil knelt beside the small fridge located beneath a decorative table.

"That will have water, soft drinks and juice," Kwan replied as Phil opened the door. "I'll send for something from the kitchens—unless you'd like to go out."

"Out?" Phil sounded hopeful.

"Get dressed. I'll take you—as a reward for the dagger's return."

"If I'm the one who dematerialized it, then I can arrange to rematerialize it," Phil sighed. "I didn't want to recreate that evil spell, though. Give me fifteen." She stood, ran to her suitcase and grabbed clothing before rushing toward the bathroom.

"IT'S SIMILAR TO CREATING A LAIR OPENING, ONLY THIS IS FOR THE USE of anyone who stays at the palace," Kwan explained as he led Phil down the steps of a building in Seoul. "We're not far from the Itaewon District, actually."

"Ooooh, I always wanted to go there," Phil clasped her hands together in excitement.

"It's quite cool out—you were wise to dress this way," Kwan took in her outfit of white turtleneck beneath a blue, thick-knit funnel-neck sweater. Black jeans and black athletic shoes finished her outfit.

"Are you visible or not today?"

"Why do you ask?"

"So I'll know if people are staring at you or me."

"Will they not stare at both?"

"Not if you're visible. Their eyes will be glued to you, dude."

"Which would you prefer?"

"I'd prefer that they stare at you."

"Hiding, Philomena?"

"Whenever possible."

You have no idea how many will see your beautiful skin and glorious, thick blonde hair and swoon, Kwan thought. "Very well," he agreed. "I shall be visible at your side."

"Awesome."

"Get whatever you'd like to try," Kwan told her later as they sat at a small table inside the restaurant he chose.

"Cool. Kimchi, then, and uh, pollack soup, maybe," she slid a finger down the menu card on the table. "That's probably all I can handle for now. Does rice come with the soup?"

"If you want it."

"Yeah."

Kwan told their server what they wanted, and soon enough, the table was filled with food.

"Nice—maybe a bit spicy, but still great," Phil lifted another bite of kimchi with her chopsticks.

"You don't eat spicy food?"

"Not often. Soup is great, though. Nice flavor."

"Try the pork," Kwan set a piece of meat atop her bowl of rice.

"Mmmm," Phil nodded as she ate it.

"This is cucumber salad, rolled omelet and radish salad," he pointed out three small bowls containing side dishes.

"All right, I'll try some." She placed a little of each on her rice bowl and tasted. "Okay, cucumber salad is awesome," she nodded. "Radish is okay—omelet is great. Thanks," she smiled at him.

"People are staring at you," Kwan said, stifling a grin.

"Huh. Not likely."

"I believe they're wondering if your hair color is real." Sure enough, a girl at a nearby table hid her face when Phil turned to look.

"Well, at least it's that and not the widowed bride thing," Phil sighed, turning back to Kwan. "There are residents on Vashon Island who love to point me out to whomever, wherever."

"That's extremely rude."

"That's what some people do. To them, I must be deaf and impervious."

Kwan paid the check later; Phil followed him out to the sidewalk. "Our hotel is in the opposite direction from where we started," he told her. "There's an Internet café across the street which also serves espresso drinks and great food if you're looking for local cuisine."

"I've heard about those," Phil said. "Is there a coffeeshop in the hotel, too?"

"Of course. You will not be deprived of good coffee."

"What's next?" Phil asked.

"Our private meeting with the Prince."

"Yay."

"We will certainly tend to the sarcasm item in the agreement."

"Yay squared."

"You may nap afterward."

"Are you reading my mind or something? This time difference is murderous."

Kwan refused to smile.

But he wanted to.

PHIL FOLLOWED KWAN'S LEAD AND BOWED BRIEFLY WHEN THEY arrived in Prince Jiah's study. "Please, sit," he invited, indicating a sofa across from his comfortable chair. "Would you prefer tea or coffee?" he asked, waving Secretary Kim over.

"Philomena and I would prefer vanilla lattes," Kwan replied.

"Similar tastes—most fortunate," the Prince smiled. "I also want a vanilla latte. Secretary Kim, will you tell the kitchen to prepare the drinks?"

"Yes, my Prince." Secretary Kim dipped his head and strode quickly toward the door.

"It's quite surprising, actually," Kwan replied, crossing his legs elegantly once he was settled on his end of the sofa. "Coffee is how we ah, found one another."

"Were you invisible at the time?" Prince Jiah's eyes narrowed in speculation.

"Of course."

"Not many witches have the ability to see past our shields," Jiah turned a curious gaze on Phil.

"I couldn't do it three years ago. I suppose four minutes of flatlining in a hospital emergency room may have had something to do with it."

"Kwan forwarded information to me. I have many questions,

although we will save most of them for another day," he backtracked once he saw the look of dismay cross Phil's face.

"It's a sensitive matter," Kwan covered when Phil's audible sigh was shaky.

"Understood. Now, tell me about your meeting," he commanded. "From both points of view."

"I was at a loss when I received word from Secretary Kim that I'd spent twenty years already in my apartment in New York. I suppose I relocated many times while I worried about where I should go," Kwan answered first.

"You can only stay in one place for twenty years?" Phil asked.

"That is so for all dragons who have arranged a lair entrance among humankind," Prince Jiah said. "We do not age, you see."

"That makes sense," Phil leaned her head back and gazed at the ceiling for a moment.

"Your coffee," Secretary Kim arrived with a tray. "Prince Jiah, Prince Kwan," he bowed as he set cups in front of Jiah and Kwan first, although the honorific brought Phil's head up and around quickly.

"Philomena," Secretary Kim lowered his head to her as he served her drink. Phil's eyes widened as he winked at her before rising.

Prince Jiah waited for Secretary Kim to retreat to a corner of the room before speaking again. "Yes, Kwan is next in line to the throne, although he wants nothing to do with it. Dal is third in line, although he is older than Kwan. It is a decision I made against Kwan's wishes, but it was one I made to protect our race. I would only trust him to rule if I were unable to do so." Jiah reached out to pat Kwan's shoulder, giving him a brilliant smile while he did it.

"Well, that explains a lot," Phil's words were desert dry as she lifted her cup to drink.

"Dal doesn't have telepathy," Kwan informed Phil. "The Prince and I are often in contact. As to my meeting Philomena," he turned toward the Prince, "I found myself in the Pacific Northwest after relocating many times. I was consumed with worry, and the dagger became painful as I tired. Before I could stop her, Philomena appeared before me, handed me her coffee and relieved me of the dagger. I fell unconscious almost immediately, but woke in a safe place a while later, wondering why I still lived."

"Is this what happened?" Prince Jiah turned toward Phil.

"Yes. I was coming out of the coffee shop when I saw him walk past. At first, I told myself not to get involved, because I knew others couldn't see him. It's generally a good idea to leave people like that alone," she said.

Prince Jiah nodded his agreement. "Continue," he said.

"I knew he was in pain, and I could certainly see the reason—the spell placed on the dagger sent out waves of spite and evil. It was a split-second decision to dematerialize the dagger. I'm still not sure whether Kwan would have allowed my help if I'd bothered to ask him."

"Honesty. So refreshing," Jiah smiled. "I can only speak for myself when I say I am grateful that you removed that filth, although it does go against Dragon Law."

"I keep hearing that," Phil leaned back against the sofa with a troubled sigh.

"Do not worry yourself, Philomena," Jiah soothed. "Kwan is well again for the first time in more than two centuries. He was unable to allow anyone to touch him during those long years, and it prevented him from flying, which may have been the worst of the torture Kwan endured. I am grateful for your interference in this case, as you have prevented untold years of suffering in his future. Now, whether he appreciates the help or not, he has done everything he can to protect you under the law."

"I know." Phil closed her eyes.

"The time difference makes her weary," Kwan said.

"Then by all means, take her back to your suite," Jiah said. "If you need anything, let Secretary Kim know. We will speak again soon."

"Your personal shield is up, so Dal can't track you," Phil sat heavily on the side of her bed.

"You knew I intended to go out?"

"I figured you would—you don't have a tired vibe right now."

"I will return in two hours. If you are awake, we will have dinner."

"All right."

"Sleep well."

Kwan walked toward his lair entrance rather than the door. Phil flopped onto the bed and dragged an extra blanket over her, huddling into its warmth.

"*DragonPrince8888* is back online," was whispered excitedly throughout the Internet café where Kwan logged in and entered a game. The whispers made him smile; they'd missed him somewhat.

Now, he only had to choose a quest and play.

Kwan felt elated when he left the Internet café nearly two hours later—he'd broken his old record on a quest already. His elation was short-lived, however, when he saw Dal walking toward the building which housed the common lair entrance.

Philomena? Kwan was forced to attempt telepathy.

Huh? She sounded sleepy. Kwan felt immediate gratitude that he could connect with her this way.

Dal is heading toward the Prince's palace, he warned.

I'll be okay. Maybe you ought to tell the Prince.

I will. I shall be there soon, he promised.

Stay behind him. Don't let him know, Phil issued a warning of her own.

I will.

My Prince? Dal is arriving early at the palace, I believe. Yes—he just entered the common lair building.

I shall make everything ready, Jiah replied. *Philomena's safety will be assured.*

She knows he's coming. Don't do anything out of the ordinary—she is prepared. I will arrive shortly.

Kwan counted seconds impatiently; he didn't want to follow in Dal's footsteps too quickly.

He found himself looking forward to the confrontation, however.

And Dragon Law be damned.

PHIL RUSHED TO CHANGE CLOTHES; SHE'D SLEPT IN WHAT SHE'D WORN earlier. Kwan wanted to tear out Dal's throat—she could sense it. Now wasn't the time to try to talk him out of it, either.

Wearing jeans, a pair of Chuck Taylor low tops and a T, she sprinted out of the suite, only to find Secretary Kim waiting outside.

"Come with me," his words were terse. He took off at a run, with Phil racing behind him. Dal was already in the Prince's receiving room when they arrived, three seconds before Kwan skidded to a stop on the marble floor.

"Kwan!" Dal shouted, the echo of his booming voice circling the oval receiving area.

Dagger, Phil shouted mentally at Kwan, who'd suddenly become an immense, red dragon.

Dal flung the dagger at Kwan's eye as the Prince shouted and became a gold dragon. Kwan's lean dragon twisted in midair to avoid the dagger, all while flying toward Dal, massive teeth bared.

Secretary Kim dropped to the floor to stay out of the fray; Phil raised her left hand. Light poured out of it; someone shrieked in pain and surprise while the chamber shone so brightly nothing could be seen by a naked eye.

Secretary Kim understood what happened, however.

Someone had been hit by a dagger. Someone had disappeared. The third had hit the opposite wall so hard the rock wall crumbled, revealing the room next door.

CHAPTER 7

"You have to ask, Philomena. Ask now," Kwan hissed as Phil reached for the dagger in Prince Jiah's throat.

"May I touch you? Please say yes," Phil shook so badly she almost couldn't get the words out.

Tell her yes, Jiah was forced to send his reply telepathically.

"He says yes. Hurry, Philomena," Kwan begged.

"She needs help to steady her hands," Secretary Kim appeared at Phil's side.

"I'll do it," Kwan reached out to take Phil's hands in his. With a nod, she acknowledged his touch before reaching out to cup the dagger's hilt with both hands. *We can't touch it*, Phil informed him. *If we do, we all die.*

"I won't let you touch it," Kwan breathed against Phil's ear. Phil swallowed with difficulty and nodded before extending her energy. Light formed around her hands as she sorted the threads of the spell on the dagger.

This one—was more complex and deadly than the one Kwan had borne. This one was meant to kill, only Phil had taken away half of its forward thrust when she removed Dal from the chamber.

Jiah was compelled to remain in dragon form; if he changed, the dagger would pierce his carotid and he'd die within moments.

"The spell is gone," Phil breathed. "Let me cauterize the wound before removing the dagger."

"Thank the skies," Secretary Kim sighed.

"Here we go; I'll try to keep the pain to a minimum," Phil soothed the Prince, whose large, golden dragon eyes were wide with shock and fear.

With Kwan's assistance, the dagger popped out of existence within Jiah's throat, only to materialize outside it. Kwan was forced to catch Jiah as his human body collapsed.

"Filth," Phil muttered, using Air and Earth power to bury the dagger in the opposite wall. "Is the Prince all right?" She knelt next to Kwan, who held fingers against the Prince's neck.

"His heart rate is elevated, but everything else appears to be fine. Secretary Kim, contact Healer Jo, please."

"I have already sent a message," Secretary Kim replied. "He should arrive soon."

"I am here," a deep voice called out. "Treason, is it?"

Phil moved out of the healer's way so he could check Jiah's vitals.

"This is a good piece of work," Healer Jo nodded after placing his hand over the rapidly healing wound. "Vessels cauterized, very little bleeding—yes. Exceptional work for such a short amount of time. Kwan, will you take him to his chamber? I'll tend to him further from there."

Phil and Secretary Kim watched as Kwan lifted Jiah in his arms and carried the Prince out of the receiving chamber, closely followed by the Healer. Once they were gone, Phil, with a shaking hand, raked fingers through her hair.

"Thank you for your swift actions," Secretary Kim turned to her. "Had you not been here," he didn't finish.

"Yeah. I get that. Something else is at work here and you know it, don't you?"

"I have known it since before I arrived to serve the Prince," Secretary Kim agreed. "I have a question, however."

"I hope I have an answer."

"Where is Dal?"

"Well, I sent him to the bottom of the Marianna Trench. I have no idea where he is now."

"I hope I never anger you," the *dokkaebi* smiled.

"I doubt you'll ever come close," Phil sighed. "I need some water."

"Then come with me. There is water and several in the kitchen anxious to meet you."

"YOU'RE HAVING COOKIES AND MILK? THE ABSOLUTE NERVE," KWAN complained when he found Phil in the kitchen an hour later.

"Prince Kwan," Secretary Kim bowed. The other kitchen staff followed his lead. Only Phil didn't move; she stared straight at him, a hurt look in her eyes.

"I am teasing," Kwan sighed. "Prince Jiah is alert and feeling better. He has questions, Philomena. Secretary Kim, your services are also required."

"That's going around," Phil said, dropping half a cookie onto the plate set before her. "Thank you all for the snack," she told the kitchen staff. "I hope to visit with you again later."

"Come, then," Kwan offered Phil his arm when she slid off her chair. Curling her fingers around the crook of Kwan's elbow, Phil followed him out of the kitchen. Secretary Kim was happy to follow.

No doubt the Prince would have new regulations to draft, and a charge of treason to level against Dal, who would no longer be considered an heir to the Dragon Throne.

"SEVERAL OF DAL'S CRONIES WILL NEVER AGREE TO THE TREASON charge; they'll wriggle their way around the truth of it," Kwan complained to Jiah while Phil listened carefully and Secretary Kim took notes. Jiah held Kwan's hand tightly in his, refusing to let go.

"Pressure can be applied," Jiah began.

"If there is a single no vote, the charge will fail," Kwan reminded the Prince. "I am not confident enough in a unanimous decision. That will allow him to keep his position on the Council. I suggest that you remove him from that position instead—you hold that power, my Prince. Banish him from the court and the palace forever."

"You wanted to kill him earlier—don't deny it," Jiah snapped.

"I don't deny it. When I learned that I was not his only target, my eyes were opened wider, I think."

"In what way?" Jiah now held Kwan's hand in both of his, as if pulling comfort from his friend and heir.

"May I speak?" Phil asked.

"Yes," Jiah replied.

"No," Kwan insisted.

"She will speak," Jiah frowned at Kwan, who closed his eyes in defeat.

"Think about this for a moment," Phil said. "I removed the spells on both daggers. This spell was far more complex than the first one. If you think for even a moment that Dal has the capability of creating those spells, I can assure you that you would be very wrong."

"He can pay for spells," Kwan's eyes now blazed in anger at Phil.

"Not this kind. Either he has sixteen talented covens working together, and that's a stretch, or he has one very powerful ally. My suspicions fall in the latter category."

"Then you side with Jiah—on bringing Dal to trial on a treason charge before the Council?"

"Nope."

"Eh?" Kwan and Jiah chorused.

"Think about it this way," Phil said. "Right now, we know who the real enemy is allied with, don't we?"

"What are you saying, Philomena?" Kwan's voice softened.

"Somebody who is powerful enough to provide those spells—I doubt he or she is in this for the money. They can get money anywhere without having to work that hard for it. No—they need a way to get to you, Prince Jiah. Failing that, they need access to dragon ears everywhere. There's a motive in all this, unless I'm very, very wrong. They want something, and I wouldn't trust that motive for every precious thing on the face of the Earth."

"I agree with Philomena," Secretary Kim said, surprising Jiah and Kwan. "Any *dokkaebi* would feel the same."

"How should we proceed, then?" Kwan's eyes narrowed as he studied Phil.

"This is a setback, temporary or otherwise, for the opposition. How long can you drag out the process of deciding Dal's fate?"

"A month, perhaps six weeks," Jiah replied.

"Then push that to the limit. I hope you have trustworthy spies; I think you'll need them. You should be concerned about where Dal goes, who he sees and what he does during that time."

"We cannot be complacent; that much is clear," Jiah agreed.

"I may be of assistance in the spy department," Secretary Kim offered.

"I'll leave that to you. Let me know the ones you choose; I'd like to speak with them first," Jiah said.

"Of course."

"I have one more question," Kwan frowned again at Phil. "How did the dagger change course? Did you do that?"

Secretary Kim snorted in disbelief.

"It changed on its own," Phil snapped. "He threw it toward you, but you weren't its target—the Prince was. Any onlookers would automatically expect it to be tossed in your direction. I think the one who created the spell was hoping you'd be blamed for deflecting the dagger toward the Prince instead, killing two birds with one stone and leaving the Dragon Throne wide open for Benedict Dal."

"Aish," Kwan fumed.

"Yeah."

"DAL IS BANISHED FROM ALL OF KOREA, AND IS NOT TO COME WITHIN one hundred miles of the Prince or of me," Kwan flopped onto a chair inside their suite and cast a troubled glance at Phil. "Will you provide a shield for the Prince like the one you did for me?"

"I will, but it will have to wait until tomorrow. Depleted energy, you understand."

"Yes." Kwan pinched the bridge of his nose with a sigh. "Today could have been—disastrous."

"Yeah."

"Should we have Myeong followed?"

"Along with two others at the table when we first got here."

"Give their names to Secretary Kim."

"I will."

"If we return to Vashon Island, Secretary Kim wishes to send a colleague with us."

"Huh? What do you mean, if?"

"You must understand that the Prince is feeling somewhat ah, vulnerable, right now."

"Okay, I get that."

"We may have to cancel our reservations at the hotel."

"Yeah." Phil's shoulders drooped. "Tomorrow, I'll spell every atom of this palace against the menace of Dal. If Myeong or the other two show up, I'll have an alarm set up to notify the four of us."

"Four?"

"You, the Prince, Secretary Kim—and me, of course."

"Excellent. Philomena, there's something else I must tell you."

"What's that?"

"The Prince wants us to move to the Royal Wing. This is my old suite—from before I was named First Heir. I insisted on keeping it. The Prince will feel safer if we are closer to him, now."

"Okay. Fine. I'll pack up."

"No need. Someone is coming to do that for both of us."

"I insist on carrying my computer bag."

"I will carry it for you."

"Fine."

❦

"PRINCE JIAH'S SUITE IS ACROSS THE HALL."

"If this is First Heir's suite, how big does his have to be? A third-world country could fit in here," Phil sighed, staring at the high ceilings in the massive space. There were three bedrooms, each with their own spacious bathrooms and closets, a sitting room with windows looking down upon the side of a mountain, a study with a fireplace and library, a dining room and a small, fully equipped kitchen.

"His is larger than the size of your home on Vashon Island. We dragons need our space."

"Yeah. I saw how much space you need," Phil hunched her shoulders.

"Does that frighten you?"

"No. Not really. I'm just coming to grips with what I've gotten myself into, that's all. Will the entrance of your lair be moved from your old suite to this one?"

"That will be accomplished tomorrow. I have to be involved in the relocation."

"Okay."

"I see you're still worried."

"What do I tell Xinnie and Ray?"

"We'll think of something. Stop fretting, Philomena."

"HOW ARE YOU FEELING?" PHIL ASKED PRINCE JIAH THE FOLLOWING morning at breakfast. He'd insisted that she and Kwan join him to eat.

"Quite well—we tend to heal quickly from ordinary wounds."

"I'm grateful for that," Phil told him.

"As am I," Kwan said, dipping chopsticks into his rice bowl.

"You don't eat rice at breakfast?" the Prince asked Phil, who'd ignored her bowl of rice completely.

"Uh, only if it has butter, sugar and ah, milk in it," she admitted, feeling embarrassed.

"We can provide those things."

"No—please. I usually don't eat much at breakfast."

"Tell the truth, Philomena. You often skip food altogether and drink coffee only."

"Is this your version of telling embarrassing stories about someone's childhood?" Phil frowned at him.

Jiah laughed. Kwan slow-blinked once at Phil before smiling.

"When will you place the spell around the palace?" Kwan asked as he continued with his breakfast.

"It's done. I just needed some sleep before I did it—it was first on my list this morning. Your personal shield is also in place," she dipped her head to the Prince.

"This will keep Dal away?" Prince Jiah asked.

"He'll be forced back if he tries," Phil told him. "You'll also get a mental vision if Myeong, Min-joon or Min-ha arrive."

"You have suspicions?" Jiah asked.

"Yes."

"We're closing off Dal's lair entrance within the palace," Kwan said.

"He has a suite here?"

"As Second Heir, he did," Jiah nodded, stabbing breakfast pork with his chopsticks. "The decree removing him from that title, as well as removing him from the Council, has been distributed."

"What if he chooses to add heat and remove moisture from certain areas—to prove he is still powerful?" Kwan asked. "We cannot remove his abilities without a majority vote by the Council."

"He can dry out areas on a whim?" Phil squeaked. "Please tell me he won't set the stage for wildfires in the Pacific Northwest."

"We can't promise that," Kwan sighed, setting down his chopsticks.

"Just when I think things can't get any worse," Phil shuddered.

"WHEN WAS THE LAST TIME HE STAYED HERE?" PHIL ASKED AS SHE, Kwan and Secretary Kim surveyed Dal's suite.

"Not in the last fifty years, at least," Secretary Kim replied. "He refused to allow anyone to clean it without his permission, which has resulted in this filth."

Phil nodded; the entire place was covered with dust and cobwebs. "You know there's a spell here, somewhere," she cautiously stepped toward Dal's closet.

"I feel it, too," Secretary Kim agreed.

"Be careful, Phil. It could be a trap," Kwan warned.

The closet was mostly empty, with only a few dusty articles of clothing hanging from the rods. High on a shelf was a wooden box. Unlike everything else, the box was clear of dust.

"Yeah—he had plans, all right," Phil muttered. "I can't feel anything from the box itself, so I'll place a shield around it and bring it down. You two should step back, just in case."

"Philomena," Kwan expressed his disapproval in the way he said her name.

"It's okay, just back up a little bit. I don't think we're going to unleash World War Three, here."

The box floated gently off the shelf, while Phil guided it with uplifted hands. "We'll move it to the bed," Phil turned when the box reached her level.

Once the box was settled carefully on Dal's bed, Phil employed Tree magic to lift the wooden lid.

Kwan, Secretary Kim and Phil blinked when they discovered three daggers and a vial inside the box, which was carefully packed with cotton.

"Well, aren't we prepared to cause chaos," Phil breathed.

"The vial holds the spell," Secretary Kim began.

"Yes. It holds enough to spell all three daggers."

"Render it harmless, please," Kwan said. "I shall inform the Prince."

"All right." Phil held her hands over the box and began sorting the spell threads to destroy the vial's contents.

"Damn, that's tiring," she said, allowing her shoulders to slump once the task was complete.

"The Prince asks that we bring the box and its contents to his suite," Kwan said. "After the spells are removed. Is everything done, Philomena?"

"It's done. The daggers are only plain daggers and the vial is empty."

"Thank the skies," Secretary Kim said. "Shall we?" He turned toward the door.

"It didn't have a speck of dust, when everything else did," Phil explained to Prince Jiah. "I believe he brought this with him when he arrived this time."

"He has a home in Busan; that's where he stays—or where he stayed before he was banished," Secretary Kim observed. "I believe we should also search that location, my Prince."

"Yes," Jiah agreed. "Kwan, I place you in charge of that task. We'll decide what to do with the property itself afterward."

"It now belongs to the Crown," Secretary Kim told Phil, who appeared confused. "It is quite large and opulent."

"We will go tomorrow," Kwan said. "I believe Philomena needs to renew her strength."

"That is acceptable," Jiah said. "Secretary Kim, please ask Undersecretary Oh to attend me tomorrow. I believe you will better serve me if you go to Busan with Kwan and Philomena."

"I will ensure that all is well," Secretary Kim bowed to the Prince.

"Is it safe to clean Dal's room, now?" Jiah asked Phil.

"Yes. It's a total pit, though."

"I'll send an entire cleaning crew," Secretary Kim said.

"Throw everything away inside the suite. I don't want to keep anything Dal has touched," Jiah ordered.

"It will be done, my Prince."

"Lunch?" Kwan knelt beside Phil's chair. She'd chosen a leather wingback chair beside a window in their suite to sit while she rested and considered recent events.

"Please say we can go out. I'm feeling—stifled," she confessed.

"Cabin fever?"

"I just can't get rid of the claustrophobic revulsion I felt after walking into Dal's suite."

"Then we need fresh air. Come; dress warmly and we'll go out."

Less than an hour later, Phil and Kwan left the Seoul common entrance. "Want to try the restaurant at the Internet café?" Kwan asked.

"Sure. I smell an ulterior motive, but I think you need the distraction, too," Phil smiled up at him, revealing a dimple.

"I am touched that you understand," Kwan teased, holding a hand over his heart.

"Uh-huh. I'm hungry. We'll eat first, then satisfy your gaming urge."

"Today, we will be seen," Kwan said, steering her in the café's direction.

"Look, everybody. Pretty man, right here," Phil elbowed him gently.

"Tch."

"I need the protein. The top of the bun is too much," Phil said as she cut another piece of her now-topless cheeseburger. "I'm glad they had this on the menu."

"With a nice hotel across the street, they're more likely to cater to various tastes," Kwan said. He'd ordered rare sesame steak bites with rice and side dishes.

"This place is bigger than I thought it would be," Phil said. "I've never been inside one before."

"This one is rather large but caters to the clientele. You can order snacks and drinks while gaming, too."

"I'm surprised they haven't named a suite after you, yet."

"I'm not here often enough," Kwan sniffed. "That's why I bought a new laptop, remember? My desktop is still in my New York apartment."

"I feel so sorry for you," Phil teased.

"You should. I was also attacked yesterday."

"Awww—and nobody fussed over you. Poor thing."

"Yes. A tragedy," Kwan nodded.

"I'll buy your lunch, then. Will that help?"

"Yes. It is customary to treat someone in this scenario."

"You make me laugh," Phil told him. "I'll pay for your gaming today, too."

"Will you pay for a neck and shoulder rub?"

"They offer that here?"

"Obviously."

"Fine. You can have that, too."

The exchange at the counter after they finished lunch took place in Korean; Phil could only understand a tiny bit of it, so she stayed quiet.

"Get everything you wanted?" she asked Kwan as he led her toward a flight of steps.

"Yes. The massage comes first, then drinks," he said. "We have a couple's suite upstairs. You can check your email or nap on the sofa if you want."

"Can I get into MS Office?"

"Yes."

"Awesome. I can get some writing done."

"We're here to relax and enjoy ourselves."

"Aish," Phil muttered.

"Your first Korean word. I'm so proud of you."

"You have such low expectations of me."

"Prove me wrong."

"Okay, that's an insult."

"I have others—would you like to hear them?"

"Huh?"

Kwan's arms crossed tightly over his chest. "You don't exercise, and you need to in order to build your stamina. You don't eat properly.

I received an email from Xinnie earlier, asking about both those things. How can I tell her you are doing well when, in fact, you are not? You didn't eat half your lunch, even with the top bun removed from it."

Phil's face paled and her eyes grew wide. Here they were in the middle of an Internet café, with at least twenty people now listening to their conversation. Bright pink spots appeared high on her cheekbones.

He'd chosen a public humiliation? Tears pricked Phil's eyes.

"I can get myself home, thanks." Phil almost ran out of the building.

Ten minutes later, she was wiping tears in her own kitchen on Vashon Island. She'd left Seoul, which was sixteen hours ahead of where she'd landed. There, it had been a few minutes after one in the afternoon. In Washington State, it was shortly after nine the night before.

"Fuck you and your equine transportation, Mr. Kwan," she sniffled. "Twice over."

"Do you need lessons in dealing with humans?" Secretary Kim glared at Kwan. "That tactic only works with some humans, not all of them. If you can't tell the difference, then don't do it."

"I received bad advice," Kwan sighed.

"From whom?"

"The human woman who leases my properties in New York."

"You asked her?" Secretary Kim was aghast. "That—that—bitch wants you for herself. What kind of advice would someone like that give you for a perceived rival?"

"What? She has always treated me with kindness and concern," Kwan argued.

"You have me listed as an emergency contact. Do you have any idea how many times she's called, digging for information?"

"Why haven't you told me?" Kwan demanded.

"I told him not to—you had enough to worry about," Prince Jiah entered Secretary Kim's office. "You have to find a way to get

Philomena back here before your trip to Busan tomorrow, or would you like to see if there are more spelled traps there for you to fall into on your own?"

"With permission to enter Kwan's lair, I will fetch Philomena," Secretary Kim slammed a folder onto his desk.

"Kwan will go. He will make things right, by the Prince's order," Jiah glared at Kwan.

"Kwan will go," Kwan sighed. "I will say the truth, as it is part of our agreement."

KWAN DIDN'T FIND PHIL INSIDE HER OFFICE, AS HE'D EXPECTED. Instead, he'd found her asleep on the sofa in the sitting room of her suite. Her breathing was irregular, and her body jerked every few seconds.

Immediately concerned, he knelt and lifted a hand.

Should I touch her? He asked himself, then added, *something is wrong.*

Phil drew in a gasping breath while Kwan fought with himself over what to do. Her eyes opened, wide and frightened. Once Phil focused on Kwan's face, she clutched his shirt and jacket in shaking fingers.

"Thank God," she pulled him forward and rested her head on his shoulder. "I'm so glad you're not dead."

CHAPTER 8

"I'm not mad at you now—I got an email from Secretary Kim." Phil, wrapped in a blanket and curled up on her sitting room sofa, explained things to Kwan.

He sat on a nearby wingback chair; he'd made cups of hot chocolate for himself and Phil. Phil, who appeared shaken, still, sat cupping the mug in her hands.

"You're saying that new friends you meet always show up in your nightmares of the wedding?" Kwan went back to Phil's previous explanation.

"Yeah. It's terrifying, watching them get shot and die in front of you, even if it is only a dream."

"Dragons don't die so easily from bullets, Philomena."

"Rational thoughts seldom intervene in nightmares, Kwan."

"Point taken. Are you feeling well enough to go back to the palace with me? The Prince still wants us to visit Dal's home in Busan tomorrow."

"I suppose. Let me rinse out this mug, first."

"Bring it with you; you've barely touched your hot chocolate. Is there anything else you want to take with you this time?"

"More sweaters and jackets," Phil sighed. "Hold on, I won't be long."

"Take your time, Philomena. I am in no hurry."

Fifteen minutes later, Phil brought out another roller bag. "I packed my inline skates," she told Kwan. "Maybe I can get more exercise doing that. Running or walking are too boring to do every day. Next time, try talking to me first," she added. "I'm good with constructive criticism."

"I am embarrassed that I did not," Kwan admitted. "My interactions with humans have been limited to business only in the past."

"Don't worry about it," Phil said. "I've made my share of mistakes and I've dealt with humans all my life."

"Come, then. We will return to the palace and allay the Prince's worries."

"THE CHICKEN IS DELICIOUS," PHIL TOLD THE KITCHEN STAFF AS SHE, Kwan, Secretary Kim and the Prince sat at a table prepared for an informal meal. "I've always loved spinach, but this is exceptional," she added, dipping into the spinach side dish served with her meal.

"We are pleased," the cook gave her a slight bow. "If we know your preferences, we will serve you better," he continued in Korean. Kwan translated for her.

"Tell him I'm sure I'll love whatever he makes," Phil told Kwan.

"Eel and octopus?" Kwan lifted an eyebrow at her.

"Well, maybe not that," Phil sighed. "Most fish and crustaceans I like, though. And, if you're nice, I'll even make you some lobster alfredo. That has plenty of fat and calories in it."

"You cook Italian?" the Prince asked.

"I can cook Italian," she said. "Chicken parmesan, anything alfredo, spaghetti Bolognese, et cetera."

"Can you make Xinnie's lasagna?" Kwan asked.

"It's Gran's recipe—she taught both of us how to make it," Phil replied. "If you want lasagna, you should let me know a day in advance—it takes lots of time and effort, plus getting all the ingredients."

"I would like that," the Prince nodded. "Also, I think I will go to Busan with you in the morning. I haven't been out of the palace in months."

"I'll notify the guards," Secretary Kim said, pulling out his cell phone.

"This common entrance will take us to Busan," Kwan told Phil the following morning after breakfast. He led their party, which included the Prince and four guards, toward a red door just outside the Royal Wing.

"Kwan owns the building where we will arrive," Secretary Kim said.

"Then I'll spell it against Dal, too," Phil said.

"After we visit Dal's home—we need you at full strength, Philomena, in case he has laid traps."

"You're right," Phil nodded. "I'll wait."

"I don't know whether I'll ever get used to traveling like that," Phil said, sounding out of breath when they reached the building in Busan.

"We have transportation arranged to Dal's house waiting outside," Secretary Kim checked his phone.

"I'm sorry to separate you like this, but it is for the best, you understand," the Prince's chief of security said when he loaded Kwan and Phil in the second vehicle after getting the Prince and Secretary Kim safely inside the first. Only one guard would ride in the second vehicle—the other three were with the Prince.

"We'll be okay," Phil told him. "I've already placed shields around both vans."

"Thank you." The chief of security closed the door and tapped the side of the van, letting the driver know it was all right to proceed. He then joined the others inside the Prince's van, which pulled out to follow Kwan and Phil.

"Pretty," Phil exclaimed as she watched scenery fly by on their way to Dal's home.

"He has an ocean view," Kwan said. "The building and property are worth billions."

"In won or dollars?" Phil asked.

"Won. Millions in US currency."

"You weren't kidding," Phil breathed as she studied the massive structure once they'd arrived. "You say the Prince owns this, now?"

"It belongs to the Crown, not specifically to the Prince."

"Okay."

"Shall we?" Kwan asked, indicating the steep steps leading to the main entrance.

"Let's go," the Prince said, once he and Secretary Kim stepped out of their van, followed by all four guards.

"Oops," Phil said, stopping halfway up the steps.

"What is it?" Kwan stopped beside her.

"Do you see them?"

"Them?"

"Honey, there are at least a hundred ghosts gathered around the entrance," Phil warned.

Kwan blinked at her in surprise.

"I see them," Secretary Kim replied grimly. "Shall we find out why they're here, Philomena?"

"Secretary Kim and I will go ahead," Phil told Kwan before nodding to Secretary Kim. "I can't imagine why this many haven't moved on."

"It is highly unusual," Secretary Kim agreed. "My Prince, stay a safe distance behind us, please."

The guards tightened their perimeter around both Prince Jiah and Kwan, much to Kwan's dismay, as Phil and Secretary Kim made their way to the top of the steps.

"Dressed in rags," Secretary Kim breathed as he and Phil cautiously approached the waiting spirits.

"Victims," Phil whispered. "Extremely poor ones."

"Release us, we beg you," a male spirit separated himself from the others and glided forward. "We are trapped here."

Phil and Secretary Kim exchanged a glance.

"Who trapped you here?" Phil asked, trying to keep her voice calm and steady.

"It calls itself *Seokga*, but that is not what it is. It has allied with the dragon to do his will because its body is not—healthy."

Secretary Kim translated the spirit's words for Phil, who released a ragged sigh. "This isn't good," she breathed.

"You think it could be *dalgyal gwishin*?" Secretary Kim asked softly.

"If it is, it's extremely powerful, although that could explain why the spirit says it isn't healthy."

"This is not good," Secretary Kim echoed Phil's assessment. "Can you release all of these? Those I know who possess that talent can only do one or two at a time."

"I have to unravel the spell holding them. Whoever or whatever this is—they're a master at spell-making."

"Why did it bind them here?"

"No idea, unless it's drawing on what little power the spirits have left."

"Perhaps that's why there are so many," Secretary Kim surmised.

"Reassure them, then. Tell them we'll try to destroy the spell that holds them to this plane."

"*A dalgyal gwishin*?" Prince Jiah blinked at Kwan.

"Philomena says it has to be an extremely powerful one, if that is the case," Kwan replied.

"I would like to escort the Prince back to the van," the chief of security informed them.

"I'll stay here," Kwan said. "For your safety, cousin," he nodded to Jiah.

"I dislike backing away," Jiah complained.

"I understand. Nevertheless," Kwan countered.

"Very well." Jiah turned to go back, surrounded by three guards. The chief of security stayed beside Kwan.

"At least we can hear clearly," Kwan sighed. "I dislike that Philomena and Secretary Kim may be in danger."

"What else can we do, Prince Kwan?"

"Nothing at the moment, Chief Ahn," Kwan replied. "I do not have Philomena's skill at dismantling spells."

"Secretary Kim is not without certain ah, talents and resources," Chief Ahn remarked.

"True."

"I have to find the source of the spell—it must be in the house somewhere," Phil sighed. "There are probably even more ghosts inside. That means I'll have to walk through them to get to the source."

"Uncomfortable at best," Secretary Kim agreed. "I will accompany you."

"No—stay here, just in case," Phil held up a hand to stop him. "You'll be the only one standing between the Prince and disaster if something happens."

"This is untenable," Secretary Kim muttered. "Dal has gotten away with far too much. This—this is a violation of natural laws, and no dragon should do such obscene acts."

"He didn't do it himself—his ally did. He just handed over a convenient place for the binding."

"This angers me greatly."

"Well, it pisses me off, too. Keep your fingers crossed, or whatever it is you do to summon good luck," Phil told him. "I'm going in."

She expected many ghosts inside the house, but she hadn't expected it to be packed with them. She couldn't move without walking into or through one. The icy feelings of despair, fear and anxiety of each victim threatened to overwhelm her.

As she moved closer to the center of the house, the spell throbbed harder against already raw nerves. Phil could almost hear her heart pounding in her chest.

Was this truly a trap? It couldn't have been laid recently—so it couldn't be specifically aimed at her—could it?

Philomena, are you safe? Kwan's worried mental voice reached her.

My body is safe enough. My emotional state is taking a few hits.

Describe this, please.

There are ghosts everywhere. I can't move without walking into one. That gives me their final feelings of fear and despair, and I still haven't located the source of the spell that holds them here.

Philomena? Secretary Kim's voice came next. *The spirits outside the house are becoming agitated.*

Same, here, she replied telepathically. *I must be getting close. Do you know any tricks to calm them while I do this?*

Not at the—wait. Yes. Let me take care of this for you.

Huh?

I shall create a vision for them to follow. You must be close to the spelled object for this to work, you understand.

Oh, no, Phil breathed into Secretary Kim's mind.

What?

Children. The ghosts of children are guarding it. Get back. Get everybody back. The spelled threads are woven through—damn. This is impossible. The enemy has tied its spell threads to their ghosts.

SECRETARY KIM RELAYED PHIL'S MESSAGE TO KWAN AND THE PRINCE, demanding that both move away from the structure.

I'm not leaving her in there to die, Kwan insisted.

Get back here, Jiah sent a mental shout.

I'm going in, Secretary Kim announced.

No! Kwan and Jiah commanded.

Get back, I'm sorting threads as fast as I can, but the spirits are attacking me, Phil informed everyone at once. *I think it must have,* she sounded out of breath, even telepathically.

Must have what? Kwan pleaded when Phil's sending was cut off.

Oh, sweet Jesus, Phil's message was filled with a mental sigh, just as a rumbling and cracking of wood and plaster began. Like a carefully planned and executed implosion, the entire, massive building collapsed in a thunderous cloud of dust, splinters and finally—fire.

"Philomena," Kwan screamed, his red dragon flowing up the high steps in swift ripples. Secretary Kim's clothing appeared scorched as he threw off a pile of rubble and scrambled for a solid place to climb out of the pit left behind.

Two guards, who'd also turned to their dragon forms, were behind Kwan; one leaned over the edge of the pit so Secretary Kim could climb up his copper-scaled, ridged back.

In the distance, a siren wailed—someone had already called local authorities.

"We have to leave," the second guard spoke as he held Kwan's dragon back from the burning pit. Secretary Kim was now on solid ground while the stench of smoke and burning thickened.

"Philomena," Kwan wailed as his guard struggled to push him away from the fire.

"Keep your shirt on," Phil appeared beside his dragon, out of breath and covered in dust and debris. "We need to leave. I don't have enough strength left to move anything." She bent over, coughing and retching.

"We are not without resources, my Philomena," Kwan now looked human as he reached down to pull her upright. "Get us out of here," he snapped at the guards.

"As you command, Prince Kwan."

EVERYTHING HAPPENED IN A BLUR; PHIL UNDERSTOOD SHE WASN'T quite herself. Her lungs had filled with dense smoke, but she couldn't draw a decent breath to cough it out. The trip to the palace had two steps but she didn't recall seeing more than a brief glimpse of the lair entrance in the Busan building, and was nearly unconscious when she arrived at the palace.

She woke in fits and starts; each time, anxious faces peered down at her before unconsciousness came again. Strange nightmares filled her dreams; nightmares of the deaths of children who shouldn't have died. Of adults who shouldn't have died.

All had a single, common denominator—they were poor. Many were homeless. All had no easy access to healthcare.

Dal's ally had combed slums and homeless camps throughout Asia, including North Korea, China, Thailand and Viet Nam. In Phil's nightmares, she walked through barren landscapes filled with the dead and dying.

She knew that the spirits of the dead hadn't crossed the veil; they'd been collected and then tied to spells. "We're all in danger," she breathed, waking herself with her own voice.

"Philomena?" Kwan's face slowly cleared as she blinked up at him. "Huh?"

"Thank the skies," Kwan stood straighter, pinching the bridge of his nose with a hand.

"Huh?" Phil repeated, before a coughing fit hit her.

"Cough it out," Healer Jo appeared on the other side of the bed. "I can only do so much for humans; my specialty is dragon medicine. The *dokkaebi* physician has been of more help than I, but he is resting, now."

"Water?" Kwan offered a glass when the coughing fit ended.

"Yeah," Phil croaked, reaching for the glass.

"Let me help," Kwan sat on the side of her bed and wrapped his hand around hers as she gripped the tumbler and lifted it to her mouth.

"Thanks," Phil sighed after nearly emptying the glass.

"When you're feeling better, Prince Jiah wishes to ask questions," Kwan said. "But that is of no concern right now."

"I get that—I'm exhausted," Phil let her head drop back to the pillow. "Is Secretary Kim okay?"

"He is fine; he exerted very little of his power and had only entered the building shortly before it collapsed," Kwan explained. "He has been fretting about that ever since, claiming he should have gone in with you at the beginning."

"No. Tell him that would have been too dangerous," Phil flopped a hand on the covers in denial. "I appreciate the thought, but we're lucky we didn't all die."

"Aish, I knew this was worse than we thought," Kwan complained.

"Yeah."

"You should eat. I asked for broth from the kitchen; it should arrive shortly," Healer Jo smiled.

"You've been down for forty hours," Kwan explained as Healer Jo left the room. "We were terrified that a human hospital would prove necessary."

"That's okay—I don't like those places either."

"Awake at last," Secretary Kim followed a kitchen helper into the room. The server set a tray on Phil's bedside table; it held a bowl of broth, a small orange juice and water.

"No coffee?" Phil complained.

"No caffeine for today," Secretary Kim replied. "Tomorrow, perhaps."

"Do you feel steady enough to sit in a chair and eat?" Kwan asked.

"I'll try it. I hate eating from a bed."

"Tell the others she's doing well enough to ask for coffee," Secretary Kim told the server, who smiled and left the room.

"Thank you, Lee Min," Phil called after him.

"You're welcome," he poked his head inside the door and grinned at her.

"He'll be walking in the clouds all day because you remembered his name," Secretary Kim said. "Prince Kwan, she must be in a chair to eat, if you recall."

"Ah, yes. Do you hurt anywhere before I lift you up?" he asked Phil.

"I think I can hobble," she countered.

"I don't want you to tire yourself unnecessarily."

"Fine. Lift away," she waved a hand.

"Thank you. I will."

"How many did you see?" Prince Jiah asked Secretary Kim later, after Phil had eaten and gone back to bed.

"Three, and clearly," Secretary Kim replied. "She is certainly a Soul Witch, my Prince."

"The mightiest on record had four souls within him," Jiah nodded thoughtfully. "This explains how she can safely remove these spells." He toyed with the gold tortoise that Kwan had found in Phil's jacket pocket after they'd arrived at the palace. "Such an immense spell to be placed in such a small object."

"She performed a miracle, releasing all those spirits and neutralizing the spell at the same time," Secretary Kim agreed. "Physician Ong and I know this as a fact."

"We are indebted to the *dokkaebi* physician," Jiah told Secretary Kim.

"He was honored to help a Soul Witch, my Prince."

"Still, should he ask for a reward," Jiah said.

"I will give him that message."

"How many other spelled objects are waiting for the hapless to stumble across?" Jiah mused.

"I am terrified at the thought of it, and word has it that Dal has disappeared altogether."

"I'm sure he knows that I wish to question him—and his cronies," Jiah growled. "Where are those who Philomena named?"

"Messages have been sent; we await replies."

"They're either with Dal or hiding in a tree, a mountain or a river somewhere."

"We agree on this much, then. Either they are embarrassed that they sided with him, or they're in too deep to climb out."

"I can walk to the bathroom by myself."

"I will carry you to the door."

Phil and Kwan glared at one another. "Fine," they chorused together. Kwan snorted a laugh.

"I will walk you to the door," Kwan amended.

"Thank you."

Phil only wobbled a little as Kwan kept a hand on her arm. "Don't lock the door," he warned as she stepped inside the spacious bathroom.

"I wasn't gonna," she snipped, closing the door in his face.

A few minutes later she opened the door. Kwan, waiting nearby, sighed in relief and moved to help her to the bed.

"Eggs and toast for dinner," Lee Min was back, carrying a tray and grinning.

"Oh, thank heavens," Phil said. "That broth didn't last long; I'm starved."

Another server walked into the room, carrying a tray for Kwan.

"Hey, yours smells better," Phil complained as he helped her sit on a chair to eat.

"You may nibble," he told her. "Eat your eggs first."

Phil ate her eggs and a piece of toast; Kwan sliced tiny bites of steak and served them with a small portion of rice. Phil consumed both with good appetite.

"That was really good, thank you," Phil leaned back in her chair and closed her eyes with a sigh.

"You look more like yourself now, and I am grateful," Kwan replied. "Perhaps tomorrow we can visit with Prince Jiah."

"Yeah. He needs to know what happened, as much as I dislike talking about it."

Secretary Kim arrived with Lee Min later. Lee Min carried the trays and dishes away; Secretary Kim asked to speak with Kwan and Phil.

"What's up?" Phil asked him after Lee Min left the suite.

"After the debacle at Dal's home in Busan, I sent out messages to others of my kind, hoping for assistance with our investigation. Some of them ah, work within government agencies, you understand. Shortly after I notified them of what we found in Busan, I have been receiving messages in return."

"What are they saying?" Kwan appeared concerned.

"The most troubling are from two who work with the NIS," Secretary Kim replied, referring to the Korean National Intelligence Service. "They have seen reports from regular agents who have closed off the buildings and had them condemned."

"They've found more places controlled by spells, haven't they?" Phil's breath caught.

"It seems that way. At first, they thought they were investigating a human trafficking ring, but that was merely a cover. Some have been arrested on those charges, but we doubt they knew of actual ah, events taking place in those buildings."

"Where are they?" Kwan asked.

"As you may have guessed, it's near the northern border."

"They're bringing them from North Korea?" Phil's hair began to crackle.

"Slavery itself is still happening there," Secretary Kim frowned. "How easy would it be to offer a bit of money for those already in captivity?"

"This is awful," Phil mumbled. "If I ever find the ones responsible," she didn't finish.

"Philomena, I would very much like for you to go to these places, if for no other reason than to tell us if they are housing spelled objects. However, Kwan and Prince Jiah must give their permission."

"Kwan?" Phil rounded on him, anger in her eyes.

"I will not refuse," Kwan held up a hand. "But first, you must be well enough to do this."

"I will present this to Prince Jiah," Secretary Kim sighed, "now that Kwan agrees."

"We really need to find out why they're doing this," Phil crossed arms over her chest with a determined gaze. "Why did that fool tie children to the last object? This makes no sense."

"He tied the souls of children to the object?" Secretary Kim gasped.

"Yeah. It was—I had to uh, untie them first, before destroying the spell threads."

"Perhaps to slow you down long enough to destroy you?" Kwan was now more concerned than ever. "What would happen to those souls had you not removed those ties?"

"They can't cross over," Secretary Kim sounded angry. "Even those who escort souls cannot remove something like that. I wonder if I might contact some of them?" His question was spoken softly, and to himself rather than to Phil or Kwan.

"Beg the Prince for his permission, then," Phil said. "After I've rested, I'm willing to go."

"Very well. There is also something else, Philomena," Secretary Kim said.

"What's that?"

"Will you call me Tae Yong? Secretary Kim is formal, but I wish to be less formal, if you are willing."

"Tae Yong? What a nice name," Phil smiled. "I'd be happy to do that."

"Very well," Secretary Kim rose from his chair. "I shall approach the Prince with the news I have, and the requests from my colleagues."

"Philomena, he never allows anyone to call him by his name except the Prince and me. You are highly favored by the *dokkaebi*," Kwan smiled at her.

"When he mentioned those who escort souls, what was he talking about?"

"The Korean term is *jeoseung saja*, but you may call them *sasin*. It's shorter and means reaper," Kwan explained with a shrug.

"Yeah. They don't use that term where I come from. They want to be called guides."

"Have you met any?"

"Once or twice," Phil shrugged. "Usually, they come through hunting a particularly troublesome spirit, who just refuses to go quietly."

"Come through?"

"My house."

"Have you spoken to them?"

"If they ask questions, sure."

"Aish."

"Stop worrying. I saw a ton of them at the hospital when I woke up
—after the ah, you know."

"Nevertheless, this troubles me."

"It shouldn't. They're very polite."

"Politeness is not the issue, Philomena."

"Don't worry; I won't go down without a fight."

"*Aigoo*." Kwan rubbed his forehead.

"Hey, another word I understand. Thanks."

"Tch."

CHAPTER 9

"Other than slowing somebody like me down, I don't have an explanation as to why he'd tie souls to a spelled object," Philomena answered Prince Jiah's question at breakfast the following morning.

"It's certain, then, that Dal has a malevolent ally," Jiah nodded. "He cannot perform these spells, and definitely has no power over human souls."

"Why would Dal align himself with such?" Kwan mused aloud.

"To get what he wants," Phil replied.

"Ah. Yes, there's that," Kwan agreed.

"We still haven't located his cronies," Secretary Kim interjected. "This is beginning to worry me greatly."

"Me, too," Phil nodded at his words.

"I have given permission for you to go with Tae Yong when you're feeling better, Philomena," Prince Jiah told her. "We must eliminate these spelled objects and buildings before they cause further troubles."

"I will go as well," Kwan said, his words stiff and unrelenting.

"That goes without saying, as you're her guardian," Jiah acknowledged. "As I am yours, if you recall. That gives me guardianship over both of you, should it prove necessary. When will you feel well enough to look into this matter, Philomena?"

"I'm feeling much better," Phil said. "How about tomorrow?"

"I'll set it up," Tae Yong smiled. "It will be rainy and cool; please dress accordingly."

"I will make sure of it," Kwan replied.

"You in charge of my life again?" Phil asked, blinking her eyes with false innocence.

"I was never not in charge, once we met."

"Uh-huh."

"Who else will stop you from drinking too much?"

"That was your fault, and you know it."

"Tch."

"When and where did this happen?" Prince Jiah hid a smile.

"Seattle, two weeks ago," Phil grumped.

"We went to a seafood restaurant, and ordered practically the same thing," Kwan explained. "It appears we both enjoy king crab."

"Was this before or after the giant squid incident?" Tae Yong asked.

"Before. It still makes me mad that he killed a giant squid—they're too rare," Phil complained.

"You mean Dal?"

"Yes."

"That is a violation of our code of honor," Jiah sighed.

"Everything he's done lately is a either a violation of our laws or our code of honor," Kwan pointed out.

"True enough. Ah, I should have done something before now, but I was too concerned for your life after the dagger incident."

"Dal was supposed to be looking for a way to remove it," Tae Yong sniffed. "That was an outright lie, as was the staging of the accident that placed it in Kwan's chest."

"He made it look like an accident, and then promised he'd find a way to get it out?" Phil was aghast at Dal's treachery.

"At first, it sounded legitimate enough. Only later did we come to suspect the entire incident, but it was too late to get the Council ruling overturned," Secretary Kim told Phil.

"This whole thing gets worse as time passes," Phil shook her head.

"At least the dagger is in a place where it can't harm anyone else on its own," Jiah said. "Everyone avoids that area, now."

"Let me know if you'd like to move it," Phil offered.

"It can stay where it is—it's a reminder that attempted murder and treason won't be tolerated in my palace."

"At least something positive came out of all that," Phil said, "although it was pure coincidence."

Secretary Kim's cell phone rang. He checked the number, then showed the screen to Kwan.

"Answer it—on speaker, please," Kwan said.

"Who?" Phil asked. Kwan held up a hand to stop the question.

"Good evening, Ms. Nielson," Secretary Kim said smoothly.

"Mr. Kim, I was just calling to find out whether my advice for Mr. Kwan worked out."

"Concerning?" Secretary Kim lifted an eyebrow at Kwan.

"His fat friend—did it work for her?"

"Fat?" Kwan's outrage was clear.

"Mr. Kwan? I had no idea you were with Mr. Kim. How did it go?"

"Oh, hi," Phil announced before Kwan could gather his wits to speak. "You're the one who almost caused a riot. I hope it wasn't intentional; if it was, karma may bite your ass—really, really hard."

"Well, I never," Ms. Nielson sputtered.

"And you will never. I'll forward your termination papers later. Gather your things, Ms. Nielson. I no longer wish to employ you as my building manager," Kwan vibrated with anger as he spoke.

"She's still fat," Ms. Nielson shouted before hanging up.

"Well, that was enlightening," Phil sighed.

"I'll take care of it," Secretary Kim said. "No need to worry."

"I hope you don't regret firing her," Phil told Kwan. "Good help is hard to find."

"She only does a good job with the hope that she can dig her nails into Kwan's bank account," Secretary Kim observed. "Pay it no mind; this has been coming for a while."

"We've already discussed dismissing her—several times," Kwan reassured Phil. "Until today, it was merely a bother we didn't find time for. Now it has proven necessary. Would you like to take a walk with me? To clear our heads?" he asked.

"Maybe. Where?"

"Wherever you like. We haven't explored much of the Itaewon district, yet."

"Okay—that sounds nice. I really do want to see it."

"I'll get everything set up for tomorrow," Secretary Kim promised. "Enjoy your walk, Philomena."

"Thank you, Tae Yong." Phil dipped her head to him. His smile brought an answering smile from her.

"COFFEE," PHIL SIPPED AND SMILED. SHE AND KWAN HAD FOUND A coffeeshop only a few minutes into their walk and decided to stop for vanilla lattes.

"Quite good," Kwan agreed as they sauntered along the sidewalk together. "Thank you for buying."

"No worries. I wanted to stop; you humored me."

"Philomena, I will humor you whenever possible."

"Really? That's nice."

"Are you warm enough?"

"I'm good. I'm used to weather like this. The Seattle area gets downright cold at times, and with the wind and moisture coming off the water," she shrugged. "I received an email from Xinnie and Ray; I told them to take an extra week off and go to Vegas on their way home, my treat."

"Did you tell them you're extending your stay here?"

"I did. There's so much to see, and I've done very little in that department, so that really wasn't a lie."

"How much do they know—about you?"

"Some. They knew Gran had hidden talents. As her granddaughter, they understand I can do the same things. I don't want to trouble them with the other stuff unless there's no other way."

"Xinnie knows you can see ghosts; I recall that much."

"She does, but then Gran could see them, too. Not a big deal unless you make it a big deal."

"Yes—understatement appears to be a talent of yours."

"Better that way," Phil agreed. "Uh, gaggle of admirers coming this way," Phil warned Kwan.

"Aish. This is why I prefer to remain invisible."

"I can keep their cameras from recording anything," Phil smiled at Kwan.

"Then do so." Kwan took Phil's free hand in his and smiled at the young women who were snapping his photo with their phones.

"All done," Phil said, once the gawkers had passed.

"Thank you. Shall we go in here?" He steered her into a jewelry shop.

"Need a new tie clip?"

"Perhaps."

Instead of looking at tie clips, however, Kwan led her toward the glass counter which displayed gemstone earrings beneath its surface.

"Gifts will not be refused," he quoted their agreement.

"Then I get to buy you a tie clip."

"You can buy whatever you want. As will I."

An assistant arrived as if summoned. Kwan asked to see several pairs of earrings in jade, emeralds, sapphires and rubies.

"I don't have any jade jewelry," Phil admired the carved jade and diamond earrings.

"The ruby and diamond drop earrings are quite nice, too," Kwan pointed out.

"Those are longer than what I normally wear."

"But they will look stunning on you," Kwan said, before speaking to the assistant in Korean.

"Did you just buy both pairs?" Phil frowned at him.

"I may have."

"Aish."

Kwan chuckled. "Tie clips next?" he teased.

"Yeah."

"I like this," Kwan said when Phil pointed out collar bar pins. "They can be worn with a shirt and sweater."

"Then we'll get one in platinum and one in gold," Phil said. "For now." She pointed out the ones she wanted to buy and handed the assistant her credit card.

"I feel like I'm not keeping my end of the bargain," Phil said as she and Kwan left the jewelry store. "I only spent around fifteen hundred, US. You spent around ten grand."

"If Jiah were here, he would insist on buying for you, too," Kwan stopped and smiled gently at Phil. "You saved his life. He is grateful. As am I."

"Gah," Phil leaned her forehead against Kwan's chest. "Please stop. It was nothing."

"Ah, welcome contact," Kwan pulled Phil closer. "I don't wish to cause embarrassment to you in any way, but these gifts are deserved. Come, it is lunchtime. We will find something good to eat."

"HE INSISTED ON COMING WITH US," AGENT YOON INFORMED Secretary Kim.

"A human observer in this situation could become problematic," Secretary Kim sipped tea at a shop Agent Yoon suggested.

"One of his closest associates disappeared while investigating in the area," Agent Yoon lifted his cup to drink. "Agent Park and I believe he is trustworthy enough to allow it. Also, he is *baksu*, a shaman, although that is not commonly known within the NIS. He has already performed a ritual outside one of the structures but was unable to see past the spells cast upon it. If the witch can contact his missing friend at all, he greatly wishes to know of it."

"Philomena will have the last word on whether he stays," Secretary Kim nodded his acceptance.

"Of course. Thank you."

"Are there other structures near the ones under investigation?" Secretary Kim asked.

"In one case, yes. The other was once a chairman's house that has fallen into disrepair. The owner was the first reported missing."

"Which, in your opinion, is worse? Philomena may not be able to handle both on the same day, you understand—the property in Busan drained much of her strength, and she was forced to inhale poisonous vapors."

"An ordinary witch would not have survived," Agent Yoon sighed. "I will be most interested in watching how she deals with this."

"As are others," Secretary Kim replied dryly. "I am fully convinced of her abilities."

"You have witnessed what we have not," Agent Yoon remarked. "This way, we will achieve two goals at once, eh?"

"Let us hope for that, then."

ONE OF PRINCE JIAH'S GUARDS DROVE PHIL, KWAN AND SECRETARY Kim to the first building the following morning. Local police removed barriers to allow the van through. Phil leaned down to peer at their surroundings as the vehicle pulled to a stop.

Outside, as Secretary Kim predicted, it was raining. Phil had dressed in a warm turtleneck and sweater, and over that she wore a navy parka. Jeans and boots covered the rest of her, but she still shivered slightly when the driver opened the door for her.

"It's this way," Secretary Kim led her and Kwan up steep, narrow steps until they arrived at a rather square building, nestled closely with two other, similar buildings.

Outside those, three people waited for them.

Phil studied them; two were waiting, their curiosity evident in eyes and posture. The third—he was desperate and fearful.

"You've lost a friend, haven't you?" She turned and walked toward him, as he stood a few steps away from the others.

Secretary Kim translated her question quickly.

"*Ne*," the man answered in the affirmative, before breaking into a spate of Korean.

"He says he senses no spirits around either building, but something isn't right," Secretary Kim told Phil.

"I feel it, too," she said. "I'll know more in a minute." Secretary Kim relayed her words; the agent dipped his head to her.

"Philomena, what are you planning?" Kwan was at her elbow quickly.

"For now, I'm going to put a hand on the building. I may be able to sense the spell without having to go inside first."

"Then be careful."

"You do the same; step back and tell the others to move at least twenty feet away. If this one implodes like the last one," she didn't finish.

"We'll move back," Secretary Kim said, before relaying her message to the agents.

Once they were far enough away, Phil stepped forward and placed her left hand on the side of the building.

Sending images now, she informed Kwan. *Agent Choi will be included.*

Gamsahabnida, Agent Choi sent his thanks.

CHOI JI-HOON CLOSED HIS EYES; HE FOUND HE COULD BETTER SEE THE images the western woman sent—until she found Ha-jun's remains, chained to a metal spike on the floor.

I'm sorry, she spoke in English. He understood some of her language, and he felt it more than his brain could process the translation.

The spell is here, she went on, as her inner vision moved from room to room until she arrived at a small area in the back. Like before, Choi Ji-hoon *felt* her intent rather than fully understanding the words.

I'll go in, now. Please keep everyone else back—if the door is opened, they'll die.

Ji-hoon's eyes popped open, only to watch as the woman walked straight through the building's wall.

Nearby, the one named Kwan cursed softly. Somehow, Ji-hoon understood that, aside from the woman, he was the only human present. Later, he'd ask Agents Yoon and Park about it.

Ha-jun, he reminded himself, forcing other thoughts away as tears threatened. Ha-jun had walked into a trap; one he could never see or sense. Like Kwan, Ji-hoon wished to curse, but kept his mouth tightly shut. There would be time for mourning—*later*.

There are no spirits here; either the trafficking victims were killed elsewhere, or their spirits managed to cross over, Phil reported, causing Ji-hoon to jump.

Is the spell set to bring down the building? Kwan asked.

I'm not sensing that here, Phil replied. *Hold on, I'm about to start working on it. Disconnecting now.*

"She'll be fine," Secretary Kim reassured Kwan, who fidgeted after Phil cut off contact with him and the agent. "She doesn't need the distraction," he added.

"I'm sorry I didn't introduce myself earlier; I was surprised to see the one you brought. I am Agent Choi Ji-hoon," he bowed to Kwan and Secretary Kim.

"Ah. You imagined we'd brought a pretender?"

"I will work on my prejudices," Ji-hoon apologized. "I am ah, at a loss—seeing my friend inside has me unsettled."

"I am sorry," Kwan dipped his head to the agent. "It is understandable in these circumstances."

Only the spell on the door is left, Phil informed Kwan, Agent Choi and Secretary Kim. *Keep everybody back; I'm about to turn it into splinters.*

The wooden door blew outward, with no sliver of it large enough to make a toothpick. Phil came striding out, a frown on her face.

"I removed the shackle and chain from the body," she told Secretary Kim, so he could pass the message to Ji-hoon. "Tell him his friend died shortly after he opened the door. He didn't suffer through torture or anything like that. They chained the body to make it look that way."

"We'll get a forensics team up here," Agent Park said. "Ji-hoon, go home and rest. We will keep you informed."

"May I contact you later?" Agent Choi asked Phil in Korean.

"He has questions," Phil laid a hand on Kwan's arm as he was about to protest. "I can do that much, I think. You can be there if you want."

"I do."

"Call this number," Secretary Kim translated Phil's answer and handed a business card to the agent.

"Get one of the officers to drive you home," Agent Yoon called out.

"We have questions, too," Agent Park sighed after Ji-hoon's departure. "We could feel the spell unraveling inside, but it happened far faster than we could ever believe."

"This was only a way station," Phil said after Secretary Kim relayed Agent Park's comment. "There are other stops, I think. I got very little information from here."

"Are you tired, or should we go to the second building?" Secretary Kim asked.

"Let's see what's going on with it," Phil said. "This wasn't a big deal—except for the poor guy who died."

Half an hour later, they parked beside a wide gate outside a large home. "Don't touch the gate," Phil said the moment she stepped out of the van. "It has a tagging spell attached."

"Tagging spell?" Agent Park asked.

"Anyone who touches it can be tracked by the one who laid the spell, and it's not for friendly purposes, I assure you. They could be marked for death and not know it."

Agent Yoon pulled his cell phone out to make a call immediately; he spoke rapidly in Korean once it was answered.

"He's asking for a list of anyone sent by the police or the NIS," Secretary Kim explained as Kwan's hands descended on Phil's shoulders from behind. "And for camera recordings from across the street, in case civilians are involved."

"Philomena, will you be able to remove those tags?" Kwan breathed next to her ear.

"Yeah, but how many could there be?" Phil drew a ragged breath. "They're easy targets, wherever they are."

"We will go to those we can find. In the interim, can you remove this spell now?"

"Yeah. Let's do this."

"May I stay in contact while you work?"

"If you want to; there shouldn't be blowback from this one."

"Then proceed." Kwan's fingers tightened on her shoulders.

Phil closed her eyes and began to search for threads of the spell. Kwan blinked before closing his eyes, too; through Phil, he could see the threads for himself; they were twisted and knotted together, like a waiting spider's web designed to trap and capture human prey.

Kwan wanted to ask questions but didn't; Phil's concentration on unraveling the trap required her full attention.

With meticulous precision, Phil began unraveling the spell from the outside edges first, working her way toward the more complicated center. As she closed in on that tangled knot, it attempted to withdraw from her power. She was forced to cast a spell of her own to hold it in place. Kwan felt the rush of her energy as she pushed it toward the center knot.

Grinding his teeth, he continued to watch as she fed more power into her spell. The knot reacted to her continued efforts to take it apart —*was it designed to protect itself?* Kwan knew little about the construction of spells—he'd never seen one unraveled like this before.

He doubted many had witnessed this for themselves—not on this level. Phil had reached the center; the knot began to struggle viciously. Phil leveled another burst of energy against it, rendering it to a quivering mass of spell threads, which she carefully picked apart.

Every thread dissipated in his mental image once Phil unknotted the last of the spell. Her shoulders sagged; Kwan shifted his hands to her arms to hold her up.

"The caster didn't want us to get past this one easily," Phil sighed.

"Is it safe to go through?" Agent Yoon asked. "Our department is working on the list of those who came in contact with this gate."

"You can go through now," Phil said. "I need to sit and rest for a minute. Whatever you do, don't go in the house until I can check it."

"I think we understand that now," Agent Park told her.

Kwan led Phil back to the van and opened the door so she could get in. "Are you all right?" he asked her softly.

"Yeah—the one who did this put some effort into it."

"I saw," Kwan nodded.

"Are you well?" Secretary Kim now stood anxiously behind Kwan.

"I'm good—just tired. We may have to wait to deal with whatever's on the house. Are there any spirits in the yard?"

"We have found none so far," Secretary Kim replied.

"We can see bodies inside the house from the back windows," Agents Park and Yoon arrived after a quick look around the yard.

"Can you smell decomposition?" Phil asked.

"No."

"Then there's a blocking spell in place, at the very least. Uh, Kwan?" Phil moved to look around him.

"Philomena?"

"You were asking about guides? One is standing at the gate, now."

Kwan turned quickly, to find Secretary Kim and the two agents watching the guide. "I thought the black hats were only a story," Phil sighed.

"Philomena? The *sasin* wishes to see you," Secretary Kim turned back to her.

"Just when you think the day can't get any weirder," Phil muttered.

"THE SPIRITS ARE LOCKED INSIDE THE HOUSE," *SASIN* MOON SAID. "WE dare not pass the threshold."

"Yeah, I can feel the spell from here," Phil agreed.

They'd moved from the front gate to the steps leading to the porch.

Phil understood that the blocking spell was the least of her worries with this place.

"You said the first building was only a way station," Agent Yoon observed. "Were the victims brought here and killed?"

"It looks that way," Phil agreed. "The first building may have been little more than a meeting place for the traffickers to dump their cargo. The buyers didn't want them to see this place, I think."

"You cannot report what you do not know," Agent Park said.

"You think there are slavers from the north bringing cargo to the border, and meeting with a secondary team from this side, which pays a fee and then delivers the slaves to these buyers for a larger profit?" Phil asked.

"That would make the most sense."

"I guess they filled up the Busan property with enough ghosts, so they're either doing the same with this one or locking spirits to bodies until they find another location," Phil said. "This is giving me a headache. I don't think we have much time, here—if we want to save those inside from a fate worse than their deaths."

"Surely we can wait a day," Kwan began.

"We don't have a day," Phil hunched her shoulders. "How willing are you to lend energy to me to get this done now?"

"I am the most logical one to lend energy," *sasin* Moon interjected. "You know a death spell is wrapped within the others placed here."

"I will not allow it," Kwan hissed.

"It will not harm anyone who is not marked for immediate death," the *sasin* argued.

"You guys hash it out; I'm going in," Phil announced and walked through the wall.

"Don't follow her," Secretary Kim held Kwan back when he took a step forward. "It could blow up in our faces if you do."

"How do you know?" *sasin* Moon demanded.

"Because it's my fault that the house in Busan imploded," Secretary Kim admitted. "I ran into the building against Philomena's instructions. While I was shielded against harm by her spell, my entrance triggered a destruction spell left by the enemy. If Philomena says to stay outside, she means it."

Does the Prince know of this? Kwan's mental words to the *dokkaebi* held anger.

He does. I told him immediately.

"What should we do?" Agent Yoon asked. "She requested help and didn't get it. Will she have enough strength left to deal with this?"

At that moment, the front door flew open, and all windows in the house were raised. "The gate spell was the worst of it," Phil said, walking out the door while attempting to brush heavy dust from her parka and jeans.

"My underlings are here," *sasin* Moon said, as reapers poured into the yard by the dozens.

"Must we stay for this?" Kwan asked tersely.

"It is no longer your problem," *sasin* Moon insisted.

"I need a drink," Agent Park said. "This day has been unnerving."

"I'll buy," *sasin* Moon offered.

"Wait. You drink?" Phil's eyes widened in surprise.

"I also have a cell phone—to order chicken and beer. May I have your number?"

"You may not," Kwan bristled.

"I will pass messages," Secretary Kim intervened.

"Very well." *Sasin* Moon handed his cell phone over. Secretary Kim entered a phone number and gave the phone back.

"What are we drinking?" Phil asked.

"Philomena, you know your limitations, I trust?" Kwan sniffed.

"When I pass out, I've had enough. Damn, this day has been total crap."

"I will drive," Agent Yoon offered.

"I call, as they say in English, shotgun," *sasin* Moon declared. "I know a good place not far from here."

"Noooo, no more soju," Phil complained when *sasin* Moon tried to pour a second shot for her. "One is plenty, thanks." She slurred her Ss; Secretary Kim hid a smile.

She sat between Kwan and Secretary Kim, while Agents Park, Yoon and *sasin* Moon sat together on the opposite side of the table.

"I'll have another," Kwan held out his shot glass. *Sasin* Moon poured graciously.

"Awww, you have such nice hands," Phil leaned her head against Kwan's upper arm and wrinkled her nose at him.

"You do notice those first," Kwan chuckled.

"Yep."

"She really is drunk on one glass of soju," Agent Park said.

"Hey, I'm right here," Phil wagged a finger at him.

"You should never ignore the witch in the room," *sasin* Moon philosophized.

"Nobody should ignore a grim reaper, no matter where they are," Phil teased.

"True enough," *sasin* Moon agreed, emptying his glass and pouring another. "Thank you for helping me sort out that problem, by the way. It caused a backlog for us."

"What about the mess in Busan?" Secretary Kim asked.

"That was a large part of our recent backlog. We didn't know until today how that problem was solved."

"You should let me know when that happens again," Phil told him. "Can I get some water?" she asked Kwan.

"I'll get it," Agent Park stood and walked toward the water cooler nearby.

"That's why I asked for your number," *sasin* Moon said.

"Work with us, too," Agent Yoon suggested. "I'll give you my number."

"I never knew I'd have grim reapers and goblins on my contacts list," Phil said. "It's like a dream."

"More like a nightmare," Kwan deadpanned.

"Water," Agent Park set a paper cup next to Phil.

"Thanks." She lifted the cup and drained the contents.

"Are you ready to go home, Philomena?" Kwan asked.

"Maybe. I need a nap."

"We'll go first," Kwan said, rising to his feet and pulling Phil up with him.

"I'll come with you," Secretary Kim agreed. "Please, stay and enjoy yourselves," he added when Agent Park began to rise. "Contact me if you have questions or something of concern crops up."

"I certainly plan to do so," *sasin* Moon agreed. "Want another round?" he asked the agents, who agreed quickly.

"Am I still dusty?" Phil asked after she and Kwan arrived in their palace suite a few minutes later.

"Minutely. Do you want a shower now or later?"

"I'll take one now. I don't want to get the bed messy while I nap."

"Go ahead, then. I'll wait until you get out."

"Okay."

Phil didn't take much time in the shower; her eyes were trying to close as she washed off the dust of the day and shampooed her hair.

"All done," she said, her voice betraying weariness as she walked out of the bathroom wearing a robe and pajamas.

"I'll wake you for dinner later," Kwan promised, taking her hand and leading her to the bed.

"Okay."

Phil took off her robe and climbed into bed; Kwan covered her up. "Sleep well, little witch," Kwan leaned down to whisper. Phil was already asleep when his lips gently touched hers.

CHAPTER 10

"What would you like to do today?" Kwan asked Phil at breakfast the following morning.

"After yesterday, I get what you mean when you say I need to build up my strength," Phil said. "I have my roller blades; I just need to find a skatepark or something where I can get some exercise."

"There are indoor and outdoor venues," Secretary Kim said. "Olympic Park is nice if the weather is suitable. I will research indoor facilities."

"I can skate outside if it doesn't rain," Phil said. "Once I get warmed up, I won't notice if it's cold."

"Should I come with you?" Kwan asked.

"You don't have to. Why don't you go kill imaginary characters at the Internet café? I'll meet you there after I'm done."

"I will go to the Internet café with you," Prince Jiah said. "I haven't done any gaming for a while. Reserve a private suite for us, Kwan."

"Wow, look at you, getting out of the house and all," Phil teased Jiah. Jiah grinned at her.

"I'll arrange for a car to take Philomena to the park," Secretary Kim said.

"You don't have to. I can get myself there and back again."

"She can," Kwan acknowledged with chagrin. "I have seen this for myself. Make sure to keep your cell phone with you at all times," he lectured her. "Call 112 to reach the police if there's an emergency that doesn't involve you. Call 1339 if it is a medical emergency that does not involve you. Let me know telepathically if the emergency involves you."

"Okaaaaay," Phil nodded. "If your character dies in a game, you can keep it to yourself."

Secretary Kim snickered.

A FEW SKATERS AND SKATEBOARDERS WERE ALREADY MAKING THEIR way along walks and paved areas when Phil arrived. Setting her bag down on a bench, she pulled out her skates. "Oh, they bike here, too," she breathed as a couple rode their bicycles past her.

Stretch first, Phil reminded herself after lacing up her skates. *Place an invisibility spell on the bag*, she added, after stuffing her belongings beneath the bench.

Rising, she sent herself rolling toward the far side of the paved walkway. Once there, she bent double, her hands on both calves to stretch muscles.

Then, she crouched low, one skate extended before her, and rolled along like that for a short while before changing over to the other leg. After rising to full height, she twisted her waist while holding elbows.

"That ought to do it—for today," she said and began to skate down the walkway, her strides even and graceful.

"I HAD TO SHOWER AFTERWARD," PHIL SAID WHEN KWAN GAVE HER A questioning look.

"It's nearly lunchtime," Kwan complained.

"I had fun and got some exercise—you suggested it, remember?"

"He's upset because his character suffered a setback," Jiah grinned at Phil. "I, on the other hand, was killed several times."

"I'll buy your lunch," Phil patted Kwan's shoulder. "Where would you like to go?"

"A meal will not assuage my anger."

"Can you eat while you're in a snit?"

"I can eat."

"Awww, you're so cute when you're grumpy," Phil patted his cheek gently.

"Do you see how I am being patronized?" Kwan turned to Jiah. "I should amend our agreement."

"You can't amend our agreement without my agreement," Phil reminded him.

"Guards," Jiah turned to summon the two dragon guards standing by the door. "Shall we go have lunch?"

"These dumplings are really good," Phil lifted another plump dumpling with her chopsticks and bit into it.

"This restaurant is one of my favorites," Prince Jiah said. "It isn't fancy or expensive, but the dumplings are extraordinary."

"And I get to drink the broth straight from the bowl. This is so awesome," Phil sighed.

"I'm pleased to see your appetite has improved after exercising," Kwan told her.

"I hope I'm not too sore tomorrow; I'd like to skate again. I saw all kinds of cool stuff today."

"Olympic Park is quite beautiful," Jiah agreed. "I suspect that there are other such locations where you can skate."

"I'll ask Tae Yong."

Phil spent the afternoon writing; she'd fall behind if she didn't plan her days better. Kwan was in a meeting with Jiah and a handful of Council members, so he hadn't complained about her spending time in the suite to write.

Her cell phone buzzed; she lifted it from the desk to see who'd texted her.

Where you are? Was translated from Korean to English in a screen shot from Agent Choi Ji-hoon's phone.

Phil pulled up the English to Korean app on her phone and took a screen shot of the translation of *home*, then sent it to Agent Choi.

Meet? Came next, followed by *Talk?*

Okay, she replied.

Here? He sent a follow-up image of a coffeeshop. At least the website had an English version available, so she could see the location.

When? She sent her next translated image.

Thirty minutes?

Sure.

Agent Choi rose from his seat when Phil walked into the coffeeshop half an hour later. *I'll get coffee and join you*, she said, sending a mental image of what she planned, along with one of him sitting down again.

He gave her a brief nod and took his seat while she went to the counter to order a latte.

Phil sat across from Agent Choi and set her cup on the table. *We can talk and understand one another, but we must be touching for the spell to work*, she told him.

Without hesitation, he extended a hand. Phil reached out and covered his hand lightly. "Now we can talk," she told him. "You'll get your language, I'll get mine."

"This is terrifying and amazing," Agent Choi blinked at her.

"It is. I don't do this with anybody I don't trust."

"I am honored."

"So, what's going on?" Phil asked.

"I was able to contact my partner after performing a cleansing ritual," Agent Choi said. "I asked for information. What I received is troubling."

"I would imagine so," Phil nodded.

"I fear that we may be dealing with a very powerful *dalgyal gwishin*."

"One of those faceless spirits?"

"Yes. I am concerned about what this one was before its death."

"Okay—that could definitely be a problem," Phil acknowledged. "If he or she was powerful—and nasty—while they were alive, then they could be plotting anything from simple revenge to world chaos and destruction as a spirit. From what I've seen up to now, this isn't simple revenge."

"That is also my opinion."

"Philomena, what are you doing?" Kwan snarled. He stood next to their table, glaring at Agent Choi.

"We're talking. I have to touch him so he'll understand my words and vice-versa."

"You are not allowed," Kwan growled, his skin taking on a glow of power.

"Kwan, I am not his cup of tea," Phil said carefully, attempting to calm him down.

"She is correct," Agent Choi said, although he sounded uneasy. "My partner who died was also my lover. I am relaying what I learned recently from his spirit."

Kwan didn't hold back a growl, but the light around him dimmed. He slapped the table hard before taking a seat next to Philomena.

"If I take back my hand, will you translate?" Phil bit her lip as she took in Kwan's angry gaze.

"I will translate," Kwan hissed. "We will discuss your disappearance without my knowledge later."

"Right. Okay. Did your partner say anything else?" she asked Agent Choi. "Was he able to describe his death? I know this is hard, but the information could be more than useful."

"He had a warding charm that I gave him; it failed shortly after he went through the door of that building. What he saw then is what makes me think a *dalgyal gwishin* is responsible."

"Others have also put forward that idea," Kwan told Agent Choi.

"That gives more credence to my theory, then," Agent Choi nodded.

"What I want to know is this," Phil said. "Why is it killing people and then tying their spirits to spelled objects? What's in it for him or her? I see no other reason to go to this much trouble. Also, why did it choose its accomplices as it did?"

She was careful not to mention dragons, because Kwan hadn't identified himself and she didn't want to give his race away without permission.

"This troubles me as well," Agent Choi frowned. "There must be a reason, but I have no idea what it could be. Also, I understand that dragons are involved; agents Park and Yoon explained it to me, and also gave me your phone number."

"Maybe we should increase our efforts to find its accomplices, then," Kwan said. "Although the thought of it makes me want to defy the laws and kill them."

"We need information, first," Phil sighed. "If we can find them."

"Enter your phone number," Kwan handed his cell phone to Agent Choi. "Call me first from now on if you wish to speak with Philomena."

"Ah." Agent Choi entered his cell phone number, then handed the phone back to Kwan. "I will do so unless there is an emergency. I will include you on the calls or texts to Philomena," he held up a hand to stop Kwan's objections.

"That will do," Kwan sniffed. "Although it is not my first preference."

"I will go first," Agent Choi stood and dipped his head to Kwan and Phil. Phil watched as he walked out the door before turning to Kwan.

"I want to ask what century you were born, but I know better," she grumbled.

"Philomena, do you know how my heart stutters if I find you gone?" Kwan said.

"Then call me. It's not a secret. Were you hoping to catch me kissing some hapless man I pulled off the street?"

"You will never kiss a hapless man from the street."

"Because I would never," Phil began.

"Because I will not allow it."

"Okay, maybe I ought to go stalk Park Hae-jin, then," she named one of her favorite Korean stars.

"Absolutely not."

"Lee Min-ho?"

"No."

"Ahn Hyo-seop?"

"Not while I live."

"Dang."

"Is there anything you want to do while we're out?"

"You don't have to go back to continue the meeting?"

"The meeting is over, Philomena. The Prince is considering our hunt for Dal and his accomplices, and whether he should increase the number of dragons doing the search."

"We really need to know what they know," Phil agreed. "What a mess."

"That was my argument, as well as Secretary Kim's," Kwan said. "The Council members Jiah invited are divided in their opinions, so the Prince is weighing all advice before making a decision."

"I'm glad it was you in the meeting and not me."

"If Jiah hadn't trusted the ones he invited, you would have been there," Kwan said.

"Just dress me like one of his guards, then," Phil cushioned her head on an arm while blinking at Kwan.

"Philomena, you are far more precious than any of his guards. If I hadn't trusted those he'd invited, *I* would insist that you attend. In normal times, this would not be an issue. These are not normal times, and I am grateful for your talents."

"So, that's why you came storming into a coffee shop because I was touching a gay man's hand?"

"That is not," Kwan bridled. "No. That is certainly not the reason."

"Okay, fine. I want another latte, and then we can leave. I need to write some more."

"I will buy lattes for us, plus the Prince and Tae Yong."

"Awesome."

"I'D LIKE TO GO BACK TO VASHON ISLAND TO GET MY PRINTER," PHIL told Kwan when he arrived in her bedroom later to escort her to dinner.

"I will have Tae Yong get one for you."

"I was going to bring my easy chair setup, too."

"Easy chair setup?"

"I have a rolling desk that fits over the entire bed. It's adjustable, so the smallest setting is good for an easy chair or recliner. It can hold a full-size monitor, my tablet and lets me use a full-size keyboard. My small printer can stay in the study here."

"Fits over the entire bed?"

"Up to a normal king-size bed, yes."

"I can use it for my gaming?"

"Yes."

"You will show me this after dinner."

"Are we bossy today?"

"We are bossy every day."

"I think I know that, now."

"Are you skating again tomorrow morning?"

"After breakfast."

"Then I will go to the Internet café again."

"Awesome. You do you," Phil patted his upper arm.

"Tomorrow is Wednesday. Plan to take Saturday off from skating. We'll have lunch in Busan."

"Okay. I didn't get to see much of it last time."

"I know this. That's why I wish to take you there for an outing, rather than work."

"Sounds great. How should I dress?"

"Office casual will be fine."

"You know what office casual is? Congratulations, you've joined the twentieth century."

"It is the twenty-first century."

"Well, aren't we making progress?"

"What are you saying, Philomena?"

"That Joseon Era fit you threw in the café earlier has definitely outlasted its usefulness."

"I am old-fashioned in many ways. I will see to updating our agreement."

"Can't do it by yourself, remember?"

"Shall we not argue? It will upset our stomachs and ruin dinner."

"Well, I can't argue with that. Let's go." Phil wrapped her fingers around the crook of Kwan's arm and followed him out of their suite.

"I AM STILL CONSIDERING MY OPTIONS REGARDING THE SEARCH FOR Dal and his cronies," Jiah said as they were served dinner. "Tae Yong is writing a list of suitable dragons to perform the search, should I make that decision."

"I have several names already," Secretary Kim acknowledged. "I've only contacted one, however, to prepare him ahead of time."

"Good," Jiah nodded. "Very good."

Phil was curious but didn't ask who that one might be. Kwan sniffed but didn't say anything—he apparently knew who it was, too. *I'll find out later*, Phil told herself, recalling that patience was supposed to be a virtue.

"Philomena, I hear that you met with the Shaman NIS Agent this afternoon," Jiah said, cutting into his rare fillet.

"I did." She wanted to sigh and slide under the table, but that would lead to Kwan pulling her upright again.

"Kwan tells me that Agent Choi agrees with the idea that Dal's associate is a *dalgyal gwishin*."

"That's the prevailing theory," Phil said.

"I ask that you don't leave the palace again without informing someone."

"I won't."

"You're not eating," Kwan pointed out.

"I am answering questions," Phil mumbled her reply.

"This is dinner, not an inquisition," Secretary Kim said firmly.

"You're right," Jiah sighed. "Philomena, you worried all of us when we could not find you this afternoon—we were afraid for your safety."

Phil drew in a breath and closed her eyes briefly. "Okay," she whispered.

"You wish to say something?" Kwan asked.

"Koi pond," Phil muttered. "Times two."

"What does that mean?" Jiah asked.

"It is nothing," Kwan waved a hand in dismissal. "She and I have an agreement."

"Your food is getting cold, Philomena," Secretary Kim said gently.

"Yeah." Phil stabbed her steak with a fork and began to saw off a piece with the knife she'd been given. Kwan frowned deeply but didn't say anything. Jiah went back to his food without comment.

"We're not speaking."

"But you were going to show me your bed table," Kwan complained as they entered their suite after dinner.

"Oh, sweet Jesus," Phil rubbed her forehead. Grabbing his wrist, she transported him to Vashon Island.

"This is quite good—I want one for myself," Kwan studied the rolling table set in front of Phil's easy chair in her sitting area. "Where did you find it?"

"Online."

"Does it require assembly?"

"Yes."

"Is it difficult?"

"No."

"Does the desk come in other colors? I'd prefer a different wood stain."

"Yes."

"Are you planning to answer only with single words?"

"Yes."

"I have upset you."

"Yes."

"I will think on this. Take us back, Philomena. Please."

Phil refused to look at him as she transported Kwan, herself, the easy chair and the rolling desk back to the palace.

"There are notes everywhere," Kwan growled at breakfast. Phil had left ample evidence behind that she was going to a coffeeshop for coffee and a croissant before going skating and wouldn't be at breakfast.

"I have a text from her," Tae Yong said, dipping into his rice. "I wonder if she notified the Blue House as well."

"The human President of this country does not need to know her whereabouts," Kwan sniffed.

"I was joking."

"I told her to notify us; she has fulfilled her obligation," Jiah said. "Have you placed her in a cage, cousin?"

"In his defense, he has never been in this situation," Tae Yong pointed out.

"True enough, but," Jiah pointed at Kwan with his chopsticks.

"But what?" Kwan whined.

"You cannot take away her freedom, Kwan. Yes, she is as obligated as you to let the other know where and when they are, but you cannot take all her choices away."

"Has she not proven that she is capable enough to protect herself?" Tae Yong asked.

"She is capable of defending others as well," Jiah pointed out. "As you well know, she has protected the Crown without being asked or coerced."

"What if a male approaches her?" Kwan blurted.

"Now we get to it," Tae Yong sighed.

"Well?" Kwan snapped at Tae Yong.

"She is a widow and has been for three years. Do you think that if she wanted a human male that she couldn't find one quickly enough?" Secretary Kim stated baldly. "She is only with you because she fell into the Royal Dragon Law trap—is that not so? After all, she could touch any other dragons with no repercussions, only you failed to explain it fully. She had no idea you are First Heir until she came here."

"It was better than the alternative," Kwan argued.

"Do you think you could carry out a death sentence against her?"

"I doubt we could hold onto her if she hadn't signed your agreement, Kwan," Jiah said.

Kwan lowered his head—Secretary Kim and Jiah were correct. He had no idea whether he could hold onto Philomena, and he hadn't fully explained everything to her at the beginning.

"Dragons take familiars because," Secretary Kim began.

"Do not," Kwan held up a hand. "Don't curse this relationship," he bowed his head. "I am—trying."

"Kwan," Jiah said gently. "In all this world, you may have stumbled upon the most unique human in it. Just remember—a creature with wings was never meant for a cage. You should know that better than anyone."

"Go lose yourself in gaming," Tae Yong urged. "She will be done with her skating soon enough."

PHIL WAS PLEASED WITH HER PROGRESS—SHE'D ACCOMPLISHED SOME spins and moves that she hadn't done for months while skating. Olympic Park was so big that she had plenty of room to do whatever she wanted, without having to skate in a confined space.

"So nice, even if it is cold today," she sighed, removing her skates and stuffing them into the bag she'd brought. While sitting on her favorite bench and watching people on bicycles and skateboards roll past, she uncapped her water bottle and drank.

Time to go back to the dragon's lair, she reminded herself. Rising, she slung the bag containing her skates over a shoulder and began walking toward a convenient place to disappear without notice.

Once inside the palace suite, she texted Kwan and Secretary Kim. *Back at the palace*, she tapped. *Need a quick shower*, she added.

Secretary Kim sent her a thumbs up emoji.

Come to the Internet Café, Kwan commanded.

"Because my life isn't weird enough," Phil tossed her phone onto the bed and began pulling off her top and leggings.

"I'M HERE," PHIL SAT ON THE SOFA IN KWAN'S PRIVATE GAMING SUITE. She'd stopped at the café downstairs for a latte before heading upstairs to find Kwan.

Kwan, in the middle of an on-screen battle, didn't reply. *I've done my duty*, Phil mused while sipping her coffee. Leaning back on the sofa, she crossed her legs with a sigh, preparing to wait until Kwan finished killing digital monsters.

"Yes," Kwan hissed minutes later; the creature he'd battled finally died.

Phil watched him raise his arms in an elegant stretch, then remove his headphones with a satisfied sigh.

"Annnnd his majesty returns from successfully routing his enemies," Phil remarked.

"Are we speaking again?" Kwan turned to look at her.

"Hmmph."

"Is that a latte?" He eyed her cup of coffee with interest.

"Maybe. Who wants to know?"

"May I have some?"

"Here." She held out the cup. "There's still half of it left. You can have it."

"Thank you." He rolled his chair back to accept the offered drink.

"Yes," he breathed after drinking most of what she'd given him.

"Spoils of war," Phil shrugged when he offered to return the cup.

"It's delicious." He drank the rest of the coffee, then tossed the cup into the trash bin by the door.

"Two points," Phil said dryly, commenting on his marksmanship.

"Shall we have lunch?"

"What do you want to eat?"

"I do not care."

"No, seriously—what sounds good?"

"Anything."

"Okay, this could go on for a while. Noodles and meat of some kind sounds good to me," Phil said.

"I like that idea."

"Awesome."

"My father is planning a visit to the palace," Kwan announced over lunch. Phil, in the middle of slurping noodles, looked up at Kwan in alarm.

Her eyes still wide with shock, she chewed and swallowed.

"But," she stuttered.

"Did you think I was an orphan?" Kwan was clearly offended.

"No," Phil waved her chopsticks in denial. "Uh, why are you second in line, if your father is alive?"

"The reigning monarch chooses from among his relatives," Kwan replied, his words and posture stiff and unrelenting. "We are distant cousins to the royal family. Jiah offered the position to my father first. He declined, as Jiah suspected he would. Therefore, the position fell to me."

"How in the world did he ever choose Dal as the backup, then?"

"He is related, too, albeit far more distantly than Father and I. Choosing Dal was political as well as expedient, I assure you."

"Ah." Phil stirred her noodles and broth for a moment, before speaking. "Does your father know about," she didn't finish.

"He was informed recently."

"And now he's on his way."

"Yes."

"Great. I really want to go home, now."

"You cannot. My father is Jiah's first choice to search for Dal and his cronies. You and I are expected to assist if needed."

"Your dad is the Sherlock Holmes of dragons?"

"Something like that, yes."

"Wow, I was kidding."

"I assure you, I am not."

"Now I'm really worried."

"Why?"

"Dr. Watson I am not."

"My father's specialty is metals," Kwan turned his eyes to the ceiling with a sigh. "And, as metals are generally used to make weapons or to infuse with spells," Kwan lowered his head and shrugged.

"Is your specialty metals?"

"No. My specialty is air. If aerial acrobatics could solve this mystery, then it would be over by now. Dal did his worst to me with his dagger; I couldn't fly with that abomination stuck where it was."

"This sounds like a much larger plot than I imagined," Phil chewed her lower lip. "I need to think about this again."

"I believe my father will ask that you remove both daggers from Jiah's walls and remove any spell residue. He may be able to tell something from them regarding Dal and where those weapons were kept."

"I can do that," Phil nodded. "What a colossal mess."

"That may be an understatement. Also, my father may come across as strict, abrupt and unfriendly. He adheres to old customs, which many consider outdated. I assure you, however, that he is this way with everyone. Please do not be offended."

"Do I really have to do this?" Phil's voice shook.

"Philomena, you will be required to meet my father eventually; he is a member of the Council, as well as my closest relative."

"Awesome."

CHAPTER 11

"**S**he went to the kitchen last night, looking for yogurt," Tae Yong told Kwan the following morning. "Apparently she was awake and working when she should have been asleep."

"That's why I had to pry her out of bed, then. She's in a temper, too; should we serve her breakfast inside the suite?"

"We didn't have yogurt; it's not something the kitchen normally stocks," Tae Yong continued, as if Kwan hadn't said anything. "She settled for sliced pears. I have someone out shopping this morning for the kind of yogurt she likes."

"What are you really saying, Tae Yong?" Kwan frowned in concern at Secretary Kim.

"Something upset Philomena yesterday. It's obvious to everyone except you, apparently."

"What? I did nothing," Kwan insisted.

"Was there anything—think carefully," Tae Yong said.

"I only told her that Father was coming," Kwan said. "That shouldn't," he stopped when Tae Yong's palm appeared before his face, silencing his words.

"Did she," Tae Yong lowered his hand, "express any misgivings?"

"She said she wanted to go home at first," Kwan said. "I told her what Father is like, and that she and I would be expected to help in his investigation."

"Ah. Kwan, I realize you intended to be helpful. However, I believe Philomena is now terrified."

"She never said anything like that," Kwan huffed.

"Perhaps we should investigate her past—she was married, if only for a moment or two. She had in-laws, which may be comparable to this," Prince Jiah arrived and joined the conversation. "Do we know anything about that relationship?"

"I confess I have never asked," Kwan sighed. "I merely read the online newspapers regarding the wedding massacre."

"I will take coffee to Philomena," Tae Yong decided. "She can stay in her suite for breakfast or join us—that choice at least should be offered."

"Shall I ask that your father join me in my study, so I can be present when Philomena is introduced to him?" Jiah asked as Secretary Kim rushed toward the kitchen. "In case he talks down to her?"

"I do not know whether that will help," Kwan jerked his head in denial. "You know how Father is—he will speak his mind, no matter who is listening."

"You are correct. I must consider this carefully."

Tae Yong carried the insulated pot of coffee and two mugs on a tray, while hurrying to Kwan and Philomena's suite. He'd shoved his list of duties aside for the moment; he worried that Philomena would be agonizing over Kwan's father's arrival.

He found the door to the suite open when he arrived. Assuming it was safe to step inside, he carried the tray through the door, only to trip and fling the tray and contents forward at the scene before him.

Philomena, crackling with energy, had squared off against Kwan's father, Hwang. Lifting an arm, stiff with anger, Phil stopped the falling tray, coffee pot and mugs in midair.

Tae Yong, who'd frozen mid-step, jerked into action and gathered everything, setting the tray down on a nearby table.

"Welcome, Hwang," Secretary Kim bowed to Kwan's father. "The Prince is awaiting you in the informal dining room."

"I'll see to you later, wench," Hwang growled at Philomena.

"Not if I have anything to say about it, you old toad," Phil snapped before disappearing.

Kwan and Jiah, responding to Tae Yong's desperate mental call for help, appeared in the doorway just as Phil teleported away.

"I see we should have been more forthcoming with the Crown's Chief Investigator," Jiah sighed.

"YOU ARE SURE OF THIS, *DOKKAEBI*?" HWANG GLARED AT SECRETARY Kim. Tae Yong glared back; on this, he wouldn't lower his eyes or back down.

"Yes. I saw three separate spirits about her; she is a Soul Witch and quite powerful. You saw yourself how she can go wherever she likes whenever she wants. My kind are seldom wrong about these things."

"You see the evidence for yourself," Kwan slapped his chest where the dagger once was.

"I dislike my son's impudence," Hwang snapped.

"Then listen to your Prince," Jiah countered, raising his voice. "Philomena has saved my life—and Kwan's. Why did you choose to confront her first without notifying us of your presence within the palace?"

"My apologies, Prince Jiah," Hwang dipped his head.

"I shall attempt to contact Philomena," Tae Yong sniffed and left the Prince's study without asking permission.

"That wench called me a name," Hwang bellowed once Tae Yong was out the door.

"What did you say to her first?" Jiah asked, attempting to calm his anger.

"Ah," Hwang lifted a hand and held up his index finger. "Ah," he hesitated. "I forget."

"Tch," Kwan turned his head away in disgust.

MORE THAN AN HOUR OF FURIOUS SKATING PASSED BEFORE PHIL COULD begin to rein in her anger. *He's lucky I didn't send him someplace unpleasant,* she thought for the hundredth time.

Philomena? It's Tae Yong, Secretary Kim's mental voice slipped into her mind.

Don't worry, I'm skating away my anger, she replied.

Olympic Park?

Yes, but it looks like it may rain soon.

Then meet me at the coffeeshop outside the common portal building in half an hour. I'll buy breakfast.

Okay.

Thank you.

Half an hour would give her enough time to transport herself to Vashon Island to clean up and dress before meeting Tae Yong. Phil skated toward the usual bench where she'd left her bag, collected it and then skated to her favorite spot to disappear.

"DID YOU RETURN TO THE PALACE TO CHANGE?" TAE YONG ASKED AS Phil sat across the table from him at the designated coffeeshop.

"No. I went back to Vashon Island to do it."

"Ah. We're ready," Tae Yong lifted his hand and spoke in Korean to their server.

"I'm just too—scattered to eat more," Phil said later when Tae Yong asked her if she wanted more than just toast and eggs. "I'll take more coffee, though."

"Bear in mind that I'm not defending Hwang for a moment," Tae

Yong released a pent-up breath. "But he is one of our more ancient dragons, which makes him rather—inflexible."

"I figured that out for myself when he blasted me for not being a virgin and ruining Kwan's life and reputation."

"What?" Tae Yong croaked.

"I had no idea that previous familiars had to abide by such stringent rules just to play the game of pretending to be honored by the high and mighty race of dragons. Frankly, if I'd known what Kwan was planning after I removed the dagger, I'd have hidden myself behind a barrier he could never compromise."

"Philomena, please say you don't mean that."

"What is in this for me?" Phil asked, slapping her chest while tears shone in her eyes. "What did I do to deserve this?"

"Ah, uh, normally, the situation provides financial security and protection," Tae Yong explained.

"Neither of which I need." Phil wiped moisture off her cheeks. "One good deed and I'm screwed for life."

Tae Yong's phone vibrated. Turning it over, he saw the name of the caller. Holding up the phone so Phil could see, he said, "It's *sasin* Moon."

"See what he needs," Phil hastily wiped away the tears on her cheeks and attempted to compose herself.

"*Ne*?" Tae Yong answered.

A spate of Korean ensued, while Tae Yong's expression grew more and more concerned.

He replied in Korean, although Phil could almost read the conversation in his face. "Who's in trouble?" she asked the moment Tae Yong ended the call.

"Agent Choi," Tae Yong gathered his phone and coat. "If I give you the address, can you get us there quickly?"

"Yes. Let's go."

You're where, dealing with what? Kwan replied to Tae Yong's telepathic message.

A rogue spirit has infiltrated a shaman and refuses to leave, Tae Yong replied. *The NIS asked Agent Choi to deal with this, at Agent Yoon's urging. Both are at the scene of what has become chaos, and several have already been injured. Agent Choi is overmatched in this, so Philomena is attempting to help.*

"What's going on?" Hwang demanded, while Jiah expressed concern and alarm; he'd been included in Tae Yong's telepathic messages.

"Let's go," Kwan grasped his father's arm and ran toward the common entrance door. Hwang protested the entire way.

Kwan gasped as he and his father arrived at the street market. It resembled a scene from a terroristic attack; every stall and cart had been destroyed, with food, housewares and clothing blood-speckled and scattered everywhere.

"Philomena has the shaman trapped within a shield so the spirit can't cause more damage," Tae Yong raced to Kwan's side.

"Everything is already destroyed," Hwang snapped.

"But the rest of the humans are still alive," Tae Yong growled. "Nineteen have been transported to the hospital, but only after Philomena forced the shaman into an invisible cage. Before that, nobody could get close to the injured."

Not far from Philomena, Kwan could see both Agents Choi and Yoon. They'd commandeered the local police, who were now holding a gathering crowd back.

"She should just kill the wretch and get this over with," Hwang complained.

"We are in public, or have you not noticed?" Kwan rounded on his father. "She is doing her best to save the human the spirit has invaded, or can you not see that, either?"

"Waste of time," Hwang muttered.

"There are cameras everywhere," Tae Yong hissed. "While they cannot see you or Kwan, they can certainly see what's happening to the shaman."

"I'll let you pass the barrier, if you leave the shaman intact," Philomena called out.

"*Ani-o*," the spirit's bellow emanated from the female shaman's mouth, making the crowd gasp and draw back. There was no mistaking that the deep voice belonged to a male.

"Then you don't get out," Phil shrugged, making the crowd whisper. Many didn't understand English, so others were translating for them. "I'll keep you imprisoned forever. Would you prefer that?"

More whispers raced through the crowd.

"The negotiations aren't going well at the moment," *sasin* Moon sidled up to Secretary Kim. "I'm here to take the shaman, should the spirit kill her."

"Philomena had the good sense to disguise herself, too," Agent Park joined the group. "We can see her as she is. The crowd is seeing and hearing something different. Their cameras will record those same sounds and images. Quite inventive on such short notice."

"Why can't she just pull the spirit out of the body, if she's so talented?" Hwang asked.

"Because the spirit will claw the human's insides to shreds as he leaves," *sasin* Moon answered. "This is a battle to save a life. While that has little meaning to you as you do not deal with humans more than once per century, it means something to my kind, as well as the *dokkaebi*."

"I doubt he's dealt with a human in the past three centuries," Tae Yong declared. "We *dokkaebi* do not answer to you, dragon," he said when Hwang growled. "I chose to serve the Prince and the Crown. I will not bow down to others when my friends are being attacked."

"Father, I believe you are outnumbered here," Kwan said. "Perhaps a judicious exit is best."

Hwang disappeared with an angry pop. Kwan's shoulders sagged. "What did he say to Philomena this morning?" he asked Tae Yong.

"As insults go, he couldn't have done much worse," Tae Yong

shook his head. "It is quite personal, too, so I shall tell you later in private."

"That doesn't sound good," Kwan sighed. "Is Philomena making progress?"

"It is a standoff, still," *sasin* Moon replied. "I am confused by the spirit's tactic, here."

"I worry that the tactic may be the idea of another, more malicious entity," Tae Yong said.

"Will her disguise hold in that case?" Kwan's worry increased.

"Let us hope so. For now, she appears to others as a dark-haired woman in her fifties—with glasses. That is what the recordings will reflect."

Kwan's cell phone rang, causing him to jump. He jerked it from a pocket, then stared at the caller's ID.

"Xinnie?" he answered quickly.

"I couldn't reach Phil," Xinnie said.

"Ah. Well. Philomena is quite busy at the moment—she is negotiating a contract of sorts."

"That sounds like her," Xinnie laughed. "I just wanted to let her know that Ray and I are back home, now."

"I am pleased to hear it," Kwan replied.

"When will she be back?"

Kwan realized this was what Xinnie really wanted to know. "Her stay has been extended—she is scouting locations for a future novel," he fabricated an answer.

"That also sounds like her. Just let us know when you two will be back; we'll make sure everything is ready."

"Tell Ray to drive the Jaguar once in a while—if he wants to, that is."

"Are you kidding? He'll take it to the grocery store. Are you sure you want that?"

"I do not mind in the least."

"I'll let him know. Tell Phil we miss her."

"I will. Thank you for calling, Xinnie. Philomena misses you and Ray as well."

"Bye, then."

"Bye." Kwan ended the call and stuffed the phone back in his pocket.

"Trouble?" Tae Yong asked.

"Nothing that can't be handled," Kwan replied. "Philomena's adopted family," he added.

"What?" the spirit bellowed in Korean. "You cannot prevent me from invading other shamans."

"I can and I will unless you get out now. I won't let you do this again if you harm any part of this woman," Philomena shouted her reply.

"You will not hinder me in the future?"

"Unless you pull this stunt again. Just expect the worst of me if that happens."

The crowd gasped as the shaman collapsed to the street; the spirit had chosen to flee. Phil let it go; she'd delivered her warning and tagged the spirit at the same time. She'd know if it entered another shaman. It was up to the spirit to mind his manners going forward.

"Shall we collect Philomena, then?" Tae Yong pulled Kwan forward.

"That saves me from some messy paperwork," *sasin* Moon crossed his arms in satisfaction.

"Us, too," Agent Park agreed.

"Call me if you want to drink soju," *sasin* Moon called out as Agent Park followed Kwan and Secretary Kim.

Agent Park waved a hand in agreement. *Sasin* Moon grinned.

"He said that—to her face?" Jiah was shocked by Hwang's rude outburst.

"I heard some of it before entering the suite—he left the door wide open for anyone to hear. Philomena confirmed the gist of it later."

"If I find out he entered without knocking," Kwan hissed.

"He's your father—what do you think?" Jiah said.

"I knew his opinions were outdated, but I had no idea," Kwan breathed.

"It is apparent that he asked some of his acquaintances for the latest news and gossip regarding Kwan's selection of a familiar," Tae Yong observed. "There's no telling what he heard before bursting in on her with those awful comments."

"Dragon gossip is worse than social media at times," Jiah said. "Very well, I have made a decision," he slapped a knee.

"What decision is that, my Prince?" Tae Yong asked.

"Philomena does not have to cooperate with Hwang and will not be forced to stand before the Council. I decree it, as a reward for special services rendered to the Crown."

"Very good, my Prince," Tae Yong smiled and bowed. "I shall prepare the decree for your royal seal immediately."

"This sucks big time," Phil muttered as she watched one of the numerous recordings of her interaction with the possessed shaman earlier.

"What is it, Philomena?" Kwan knelt beside her chair; she was viewing the social media sites from her easy chair setup.

"At least the cameras didn't get a hint of the real me in this mess," she shook her head. "Look—it's at half a million views and counting. At least the skeptics are poo-pooing the incident as a fake."

"At times, we should be grateful for skeptics and lies," Kwan philosophized.

"No kidding," Phil sighed. "Is the old toad still at the palace?"

"My father?"

"Yeah."

"He is, and I've called him worse," Kwan admitted.

"This day has been total crap from beginning to end."

"I forgot to tell you that Xinnie called while you were negotiating with the spirit," Kwan said. "I told her your stay was extended because you were scouting locations for a book."

"That's good enough," Phil said. "Thank you. I'll send her an email in a minute; she'll be asleep right now."

"Should we send her one of these recordings?" Kwan teased, tapping the enter key to play the next one.

"Please don't. My heart won't take it," Phil begged.

"I won't," Kwan patted her arm. "Are you hungry? Dinner will be ready soon."

"Will your father be there?"

"It's possible."

"Then I'm not hungry."

"I'll have something brought to the suite, then."

"I've blocked him from entering this suite without our permission," Phil said, leaning back in her easy chair with a weary sigh.

"That sounds reasonable. Also, our small refrigerator has been stocked with yogurt, in addition to the drinks we like. Lee Min says that spoons are now located in the top drawer of the chest next to the refrigerator. The small tray added to the top of the chest is for dirty spoons. Those will be collected by the cleaning staff and returned after they've been washed."

"I feel like such a slug; so many people are taking care of me now," Phil closed her eyes.

"You have been busy nearly every minute of this day, and some of those minutes have been mind-bendingly terrifying."

"That explains why I'm so tired."

"That explains it." Kwan pushed her rolling table away. "Scoot over—this chair is large enough for two."

"It really isn't," Phil complained as Kwan squeezed onto the chair beside her. "Here," she opened her eyes and frowned after pulling a leg over to make room for Kwan.

"No, now you are completely leaning on your side," Kwan lifted her with one arm.

"This isn't working," Phil's arm tangled with Kwan's.

"This way," Kwan pulled her off the chair altogether and settled her on his lap. "That's better," he declared as Phil gave him a grumpy frown. "Close your eyes and rest until food arrives." He settled her head on his chest. "Don't move; I'm comfortable," he breathed against her hair. "Everything is fine, now," Kwan's voice was suddenly mesmerizing. "All is well. Philomena is tired. She will rest."

"Leave it on the table," Kwan instructed the kitchen worker in a hushed voice. Their dinner had arrived, but he didn't want to wake Philomena; she slept peacefully in his arms.

The server bowed after setting the tray down quietly, then walked out the door moments later. Philomena hadn't twitched once and Kwan was glad.

"The daggers will wait until morning; Philomena is asleep," Jiah told Hwang. "You may study this in the meantime." He set the small, gold turtle taken from Dal's home in Busan on the corner of his desk.

"This held a spell?" Hwang lifted the object with careful fingers.

"Yes, and the spirits of murdered children were tied directly to it, making the spell even more difficult to remove," Jiah said. "Whatever you learn from it, I wish to know."

"I will study it diligently."

"If you need anything, contact me through Undersecretary Oh," Jiah dismissed the older dragon.

Hwang's long fingers stroked the gold turtle as he left Jiah's study; he was already searching for evidence within the precious metal.

Phil's eyes opened; she found herself in bed, staring at the ceiling inside the palace suite. Her stomach growled. Rolling onto her side, she reached for her cell phone on the bedside table. "At least it isn't noon," Phil flopped onto her back again after checking the time. She discovered she'd slept late.

"No, it is not noon," Kwan said, making her jerk and squeak; she hadn't realized that he stood on the other side of the bed.

"You should have gotten me up; I forgot to set my alarm," Phil pushed her hair back.

"I made sure you could sleep until you awoke on your own," Kwan's mouth quirked into a half smile.

"And now I'm starving." She slid off the bed and padded toward her bathroom.

"Get dressed; I'll take you out to eat," Kwan called out.

"Yeah, okay. Sounds good."

Half an hour later, they left the building which housed the common entrance and walked into a misty morning.

"I'll take you to the hotel coffeeshop; they cater to world travelers and their appetites," Kwan steered Phil in the proper direction.

"As long as they have coffee, I'm good with just about anything," Phil said.

"They serve good, western omelets," Kwan said.

"Oh, that sounds like heaven," Phil breathed.

Once inside the hotel's coffeeshop and café, they were led to a table and offered coffee and juice. Kwan asked for coffee, Phil ordered coffee and juice. Soon enough, she was served a mushroom, ham and cheese omelet with added tomatoes.

"So good," Phil stuffed another bite into her mouth while Kwan sipped his coffee.

"After you eat, will you remove the daggers from Jiah's walls and make sure there is no spell residue left behind? Jiah has commanded that you do not have to deal with my father again, but he needs the daggers to study them."

"I have to thank the Prince for that," Phil cut into her omelet again. She'd eaten nearly half of it already.

"It was an appropriate response to yesterday's—events."

"Do we know how the shaman is doing?"

"Tae Yong says that she's still in the hospital after suffering so much trauma."

"I'm not surprised. What I could sense of her emotions yesterday was pure terror."

"*Sasin* Moon was grateful he wasn't forced to escort her spirit; it wasn't her scheduled time," Kwan said.

"Can you sense when it isn't someone's time?"

"No. Any reaper would know, however."

"I do, too," Phil admitted. "I knew it when I saw the shaman yesterday. Occasionally, I'll hear of a death and I'll know immediately that it wasn't supposed to happen when and where it did."

"There are writings in the Prince's library that speak of such," Kwan nodded. "It is a phenomenon that has been remarked upon throughout the centuries."

"I wonder if *sasin* Moon will talk to me about it," Phil mused aloud.

"If he agrees, I will be with you."

"That's fine," Phil waved off Kwan's concern. "I just can't stop thinking that the entire episode yesterday was staged, somehow."

"Staged?"

"To get a feel for the opposition, maybe?" Phil's eyes met Kwan's. "I didn't pull out all the stops yesterday, for that reason alone. That's why it took as long as it did."

"You believe that spirit was acting on another's behalf?"

"I'm worried that it could be, although there's no absolute proof, yet. My concern is whether it will happen again—with a different spirit."

"Why wouldn't it be the same spirit?"

"I tagged this one; if he tries the same thing, he'll be blocked from entering a human body."

"That's possible?" Kwan leaned toward Phil and hissed.

"Shhhh," Philomena placed fingers over Kwan's mouth. Kwan's eyes widened at the unexpected touch.

"Sorry, didn't mean to get personal," Phil pulled her hand away. "I just don't want to call attention to us."

"Do you want something else to eat?" Kwan leaned back in his seat.

"No—I'm full," Phil assured him. "I just want to finish my coffee and we can leave."

"Shall we ask for lattes to go?"

"Yes," Phil smiled. "That sounds great."

"There we go," Phil set the second dagger on the table. "Nothing left to harm anybody; just normal metal and jewels."

"I'll inform Hwang," Undersecretary Oh told her. He and Tae Yong had come to witness the dagger removal, while Kwan observed the process.

"Thank you," Phil dipped her head to the Undersecretary.

"So, back to the suite, or would you like to come with me to the Internet café?" Kwan asked Phil.

"I think you need to exercise your fingers—I'll come with you."

"You will?" Kwan's face brightened.

"Sure. I can read or work while you're doing your thing."

"Thank you."

Fifteen minutes later, they made their way inside the Internet café. Phil followed Kwan to the desk to reserve the couple's suite.

While Phil stood beside Kwan, the whispers began. She didn't understand what was being said, but Kwan's head jerked up immediately. Both turned around; behind them stood several people, some covering their mouths while they spoke softly.

Phil had seen too much of that sort of thing in her past. Had someone released information on the wedding massacre? Fear gripped her, making her heart pound and her hands curl into fists.

Philomena, why are they calling you the Princess of Olympic Park? Kwan demanded mentally.

CHAPTER 12

"When did they?" Phil blinked while gaping at the cell phone recordings posted online. Kwan couldn't tear his gaze away from the images—of Phil performing an elegant spin on one foot. The move was strikingly similar to what a figure skater could do on ice.

He'd seen other moves, too—lazy, backward bending figure eights, with arms stretched wide like a ballerina's. A sit-spin, small jumps and choreographed movements; he could barely believe what he was seeing.

"I used to do demos at skating competitions," Phil sighed. "I had no idea people would pull their cell phones out for this; I was just having fun. Actually, it would be better if you heard the music with the moves."

"You had earbuds in?"

"Yeah. You said to keep my cell phone with me, so I listened to music while skating. It's my normal thing to do anyway."

"This person wishes to marry you," Kwan tapped one of the comments, which was liberally peppered with pink hearts.

"I don't want to marry him," Phil said.

"Good. What is this?" Kwan leaned forward to see the move better.

153

"Biellmann spin," Phil explained. "It's not easy to do on rollerblades."

"I had no idea you could do that," Kwan breathed. "Pulling your foot so high over your head while spinning on the other."

"Don't you watch figure skating in the Olympics?" Phil frowned at him. "That's a typical move for them."

"I don't watch television, as a general rule."

"Because you've been miserable for the past two centuries," Phil blew out a breath.

"It was a half-life, lived in partial twilight for me," Kwan admitted. "I barely recall the passage of time for the first century and a half."

"So gaming was something of a lifeline?"

"Yes. It took me elsewhere and allowed me to forget—many things."

"How do you feel now?" Phil rubbed his back.

"Like the sun has broken through dark clouds."

"Good." Phil dropped her hand.

"No—that feels good. Please continue."

"How about I give you a neck and shoulder massage, then?"

"That will be fine."

Kwan drew a shaky breath the moment Phil touched bare skin at the back of his neck. "Is something wrong?" Phil pulled her hands away.

"No. Quite the opposite. Your touch is magic, Philomena."

"All right. Let me know if it's too hard anywhere."

"I will."

Kwan's game was forgotten as Philomena worked her way down his neck and then moved to his shoulders. He was asleep before he knew it.

"What's this?" Phil lifted the heavy envelope off the table inside the palace suite.

"Oh. That's the invitation to Jiah's birthday celebration," Kwan replied. "My neck feels so much better, now."

"You slept for an hour, too. That could have something to do with it. When is this wing-ding happening?" She tapped the envelope with a finger.

"Next Wednesday. The envelope will list the dress requirements."

"Dress requirements?"

"There's always a theme. Last year, it was white and blue. What is it this time?"

"Um," Phil pulled the invitation from the envelope. "Let's see," she scanned the thick card. "Oh. Red and black."

"Then we must wear at least one of those colors," Kwan said.

"I don't have anything formal in either color," Phil informed him. "I brought a white dress."

"We will shop. I will buy," Kwan insisted.

"Can we do that in Busan tomorrow?"

"Of course. In fact, that is an excellent idea."

Both turned at the knock at their door. Kwan moved to answer. Tae Yong stood outside. "It seems that Min-ha, Min-Joon and Myeong are deeply embedded in Dal's doings, if your father's judgment is correct," he said the moment Kwan invited him inside.

"Does he have knowledge of their location?" Phil asked.

"He found traces of a lair, but when he and the guards arrived, they found it abandoned. Philomena, will you consent to go there—to search for spell residue?"

"I'll go," Phil nodded. "If Kwan comes with me."

"He and I will accompany you," Tae Yong replied. "I've left instructions that they should not touch anything until you deem it safe."

"Good. Thanks. We don't need a trap blowing up in our faces. What's the location?"

"I will explain on the way to the common entrance."

"They were here?" Kwan expressed his dismay as he, Philomena and Tae Yong walked through a home which once housed a CEO and his family. It was obvious to him that those the Prince hunted had left the place after rendering it unlivable.

"They even broke the stained-glass skylight," Phil complained as she stepped carefully over broken shards.

"Illustrating their contempt for us, no doubt," Hwang rumbled.

"Can you tell how long they've been gone?" Tae Yong asked Phil, drawing her attention away from Kwan's father.

"Maybe three days at most. I think they figured out we were hunting them. Did you sense the blood? They tried to clean it up, but there are still minute traces of it."

"Blood?" Hwang's anger increased. "Whose blood?"

"Probably human servants," Phil hunched her shoulders in distress. "You see there isn't a layer of normal dust on anything—they had someone cleaning and probably cooking for them. Now they're dead, I think."

"Have they committed *geumji haeng-wi*?" Kwan stared at his father in alarm.

"What?" Phil turned to Tae Yong.

"The forbidden act," Tae Yong answered. "Consuming humans as food."

"Ewww," Phil made a face and shivered. "That's just—ewww."

"If we cannot locate bodies, it is a possibility," Kwan said. "Shall we continue?" He held out a hand, indicating that Phil should go ahead.

Phil found nothing noteworthy on the lower level, other than the blood traces she'd initially discovered. The second floor contained the sleeping quarters of four dragons, one of whom Phil hadn't come across before.

"I haven't seen this one," she indicated the bedchamber. "I can't put a name to him yet."

"Another of Dal's allies, and an unknown," Kwan sighed. "This looks more and more like a plot to achieve a coup."

"I am very concerned that this may indeed be the case," Hwang agreed with his son. "I was there when the King was slain. It began like this," he nodded, his eyes clouding with memory. "Prince Jiah's elder brother also died, and Jiah was severely wounded. Had we not fought back successfully, the race of dragons would be very different today."

"If we survived what the opposition created." Tae Yong's words held anger. "Many of my kind died in that war."

"All of the powerful races were targeted," Hwang agreed. "None escaped unscathed."

"Okay, I'm really worried, now," Phil said. "Let's check out the other floors and then decide what to do with this place."

"This is a false wall," Phil later pointed toward a wall in the attic.

"What are your thoughts on finding another lair entrance behind it?" Tae Yong asked.

"I'd say it's ninety-nine per cent," Phil shrugged. "I can feel it from here."

"We've already closed the one downstairs," Hwang sniffed. "It will only take a moment to tear down this wall and close this one, too."

"Wait," Phil held up a hand before Hwang could change to dragon form.

"For what?" Hwang rounded on her.

"Let's think about this for a minute. You found the obvious one downstairs, right?"

"Yes."

"This one—you didn't find it. It wasn't on your radar, so to speak."

"Correct."

"How about this, then? Let me lay a trapping spell."

"Trapping spell?"

"A spell that will effectively toss a magical net over any dragon or dragons that come through that entrance," Phil tapped her chin thoughtfully. "I'll know if the trap's activated. That way, you can come and do whatever you want with the detainees."

"I am—listening," Hwang nodded.

"I can arrange for you and anyone else to know if the trap's sprung," Phil added. "So you won't have to communicate directly with me before acting."

"I will give you names of guards and individuals I trust," Hwang replied.

"Okay, then. Let's get this started."

I'VE NEVER SEEN ANYTHING LIKE THIS, KWAN TOLD TAE YONG telepathically as they watched Phil create the trapping spell.

The knots and lines are so intricate, yet I can feel the strength she's laying in each, Tae Yong replied. *At least they are visible to us until the entire spell is set.*

Is she part spider? Hwang entered the silent conversation. *I have only witnessed a few spells placed by witches, but I have never seen anything like this.*

All of them watched as Phil created each glowing line of power, connecting it to other glowing lines. All of them would form an impenetrable web, designed specifically for dragons.

She's tying off the last thread, Tae Yong spoke reverently.

There was a collective sigh when Phil released the final knot and the entire spell became invisible.

"All done," she said. "It won't harm anybody, but it will get pretty tight if they continue to struggle."

"If the trap is sprung, I hope to be here quickly," Hwang sniffed. "Thank you." He bowed his head briefly.

"No problem. I'm starved. Is dinner ready, yet?"

"THIS IS REALLY GOOD," PHIL CUT ANOTHER PIECE OF STEAK. "MY compliments to the chef."

I can't believe she's eating at the same table with your father, Jiah silently told Kwan.

He was civil earlier. I hope things remain this way. You see that he's not sitting near her, however.

After today, he ought to be afraid to sit near her, Tae Yong observed. *She could truss him up like a goose before he could react.*

"Philomena, are you attending my birthday celebration?" Jiah asked aloud.

"Of course," she told him. "What would you like as a gift?"

"A set of your books, perhaps? For my personal library?"

"Absolutely. Plus a pan of lasagna, whenever you want one."

"That sounds wonderful."

"Philomena and I are going to Busan tomorrow," Kwan announced. "If anyone would like to join us."

"I hear she leveled Dal's home there," Hwang lifted kimchi with his chopsticks and set it on his plate.

"It leveled itself," Phil replied. "It held a destruction spell."

"Which I triggered," Tae Yong confessed. "Philomena instructed me to stay back, but I entered the building anyway. She cast a protection spell about me; I was unscathed when pulled from the debris."

"Not your fault," Phil told him. "At that point, if a squirrel wandered in, the result would be the same. I set it in motion when I untied souls from the spelled tortoise."

"My Prince, this sounds more and more like an elaborate plot to either gain or destroy the Crown," Hwang observed.

"We believe this, too," Jiah replied "but who has allied with Dal and the others to accomplish this? The last we saw of Dal, he attempted to kill me and Kwan."

"Both of you were together, eh?"

"Yes. Without Philomena's intervention, we would likely be dead."

"Perhaps it would be wise to separate, unless a meeting is necessary," Hwang suggested. "This is how your father and your older brother died, do you recall?"

"I do. I came running in and was nearly killed myself."

"Father," Kwan objected.

"No, he's right," Jiah intervened. "As much as I enjoy having you here with me at the palace, it could serve to destroy everything."

"Have you named a Second Heir to replace Dal?" Hwang asked.

"Not yet. I was hoping you'd consent," Jiah began.

"Then publicly announce that you made the offer and I accepted," Hwang said. "And then choose another in secret."

"Who can I trust?" Jiah snapped. "At this moment, the only ones I have complete faith in are sitting at my table."

"Perhaps I can be of assistance, then—if the witch agrees to help," Hwang sat back in his seat with a sigh.

"Philomena?" Jiah turned to her.

"Yeah, I could probably help with that."

"Tell Xinnie and Ray that we'll be back next Thursday, and that we may bring a few guests with us," Kwan said as he opened the door to their suite and indicated that Phil should go in first.

"Guests?" Phil turned toward Kwan.

"Unless I am quite wrong, Jiah will send Tae Yong with us and allow Undersecretary Oh to take care of things here. Also, Tae Yong will choose one or two of the *dokkaebi* who serve to go with us. I imagine that Lee Min will beg to go. Then, at least two guards will be provided," Kwan lengthened the list.

"Where will we put all of them?" Phil asked.

"You don't use the wine cellar," Kwan sniffed.

"That's true." Phil flopped onto a chair with a sigh. "We may have enough room for the others that way."

"I can take your sitting room—it is quite large."

"Huh?"

"It won't be that different from sharing this suite," Kwan pointed out. "It has a door, does it not?"

"Xinnie will have a heart attack."

"I doubt very much that Xinnie will do anything of the sort. Le Min can help her in the kitchen. Lastly, I believe that if Jiah chooses another heir in secret, then he will also be with us."

"What about your lair entrance?"

"I can move it to the sitting room; as long as it is in the same location, it is no trouble and does not require permission from the Prince. I will buy a new bed for that space; I don't spend much time in a bedroom except to sleep."

"Fine. I don't use half my closet anyway, and the bathroom has double sinks."

"I appreciate your kind offer."

"Will the others be leasing cars? I only have garage space for six."

"I believe there will be enough space; vehicles can be shared."

"Except for my Mercedes."

"That is quite obvious, dear Philomena."

"Pack an overnight bag; we will spend the night in Busan," Kwan told Phil the next morning. "Jiah and a few others are coming with us. Father wishes to see the remains of Dal's home; Jiah is arranging to have the rubble removed and is meeting with an architect to build a new home on the site."

"Who will live there?" Phil asked.

"Ah, he has not yet settled the decree of ownership," Kwan said. "I feel sure it will happen soon enough. We can do our shopping while he and Father settle that business, then we can meet for lunch and decide which sights to see."

"All right. I'll go grab a bag. Do we have hotel reservations already?"

"We do."

"Cool."

"Yes, it will be cool there. Pack accordingly, and then we'll go to breakfast."

"I don't have to ask whether you're packed, do I?"

"Not even."

"*HAEUNDAE* DISTRICT," KWAN INSTRUCTED THEIR TAXI DRIVER, THEN named an upscale dress shop in Korean after settling Phil and himself in the back seat.

"I feel like I'm playing hooky," Phil giggled.

"Hooky?"

"Skipping school," Phil explained. "Like the day is ours to do whatever we want."

"The day *is* ours to do whatever we want," Kwan confirmed. "We have no responsibilities today."

"Feels nice," Phil leaned her head back and closed her eyes. "The sun through the window is nice, too."

"Red or black dress?" Kwan breathed against her cheek.

"Hmmm?" Phil opened her eyes and turned toward him.

"I will be wearing black with a red tie."

"Then I suppose I ought to get a red dress. What do you think?"

"I think you will look beautiful no matter which color you choose."

"Uh," Phil's mouth dropped open.

Kwan chose to take the advantage.

Phil's breaths were stolen by Kwan as he drew her lower lip into a mind-bending kiss. When her breathing resumed, it became shudders and small moans. Kwan's mesmerizing kisses didn't let up; Phil couldn't think—she could only feel as Kwan's hands cupped her head to continue the onslaught.

Oh, God. Oh, God. Oh. My. God, Phil's mental words echoed in Kwan's mind. Dragging his mouth away, he pulled her close to his chest while she gasped for air. Glancing up, he noticed the cab driver staring in the rearview mirror in fascination.

"Eyes on the road," Kwan snapped in Korean irritation.

Kwan hid a smile as he helped Phil out of the cab later; she could barely stand. "Hold onto me," he instructed as he led her down the sidewalk.

"That's," Phil couldn't gather her thoughts to finish a sentence.

"I've wanted to give you pleasure for days, now," Kwan breathed against her hair.

"That was two for two, then," Phil blushed and hung her head.

Kwan threw back his head and laughed.

ꙅ

"Not that one—it's too tight," Kwan told the shop assistant, who'd dressed Phil in a form-fitting, beaded red gown.

"Thank you," Phil told him. *I wasn't sure how to tell her I didn't like it*, she added mentally. *I can barely walk in this thing.*

Phil had already tried seven dresses, and neither she nor Kwan had liked any of them. Kwan gestured with a hand, indicating to the assistant that the dress Phil currently wore wasn't suitable. Both returned to the fitting room while he watched.

Taking a seat in a chair provided for him, he waited for the next dress. *Kwan?* Tae Yong's voice entered his mind.

Is something wrong? Kwan asked.

Agents Yoon and Park came to find me. I believe Philomena's assistance may be required.

When?

After lunch? They say it shouldn't take too much of her time. A man was arrested yesterday and is currently in a holding cell, but there is something strange about him. They hope Philomena can discover the reason before it becomes a larger problem.

Where is he?

Here in Busan. Tae Yong gave the address for the police station. *He's been arrested before for petty theft, but there are no records of this behavior in the past.*

Very well, Kwan agreed. *Do they understand that I will be with her?*

As will I. They know this already.

Good. Ah, Philomena is coming out in another dress. We will speak again at lunch.

"This one I like," Kwan nodded in satisfaction as Phil held up the skirts of the red ballgown she wore. The sleeveless dress fit her perfectly, down to the gold, beaded belt that circled her waist.

"This one lets me breath and I feel good in it," Phil said, smoothing the skirt and turning so Kwan could see the back.

"Yes—I like this very much," Kwan informed the assistant. "We will take it and matching shoes, please."

"THEY WERE CALLED IN EARLY THIS MORNING; THE NIS DOESN'T SPEAK of it openly, but they allow Park, Yoon and Choi to deal with anything that doesn't appear ordinary or human," Tae Yong told Phil over lunch.

"That's the usual human reaction," Phil said. "Turn away and let somebody else deal with it because it doesn't fit into their view of the world."

"True enough," Jiah sighed. "This sushi is quite good. I haven't had Japanese cuisine in a long while."

"I love avocado rolls," Phil said. "And this one," she tapped a plate before her, "where I come from, they call this a cowboy roll." She lifted a piece of the tempura shrimp, avocado and cream cheese-filled roll and set it on Kwan's plate.

"Have some gyoza," Kwan placed a dumpling atop her rice.

"These are good," Phil lifted it with her chopsticks and bit off half.

"Is this what you usually order?" Tae Yong asked.

"Most of the time, plus fried rice with extra egg. My favorite Japanese restaurant in Seattle knows I'm going to ask for extra egg every time. Usually I order takeout on weekends, since that's Xinnie and Ray's time for themselves."

"If you remember to eat," Kwan pointed out, setting another dumpling on her rice.

"Hey, now," she nudged him with an elbow.

"Xinnie told me to ride herd. I am riding herd."

Jiah snickered.

"This way." Agent Park ushered Phil, Kwan and Tae Yong into the area where the prisoner's holding cell lay. Agent Yoon followed.

"These are the violent crime detectives who arrested him," Agent Park introduced two men who stood outside the cell. Both blinked in surprise at Phil; they didn't often see Westerners like her inside the police station.

"Holy crap," Phil mumbled as she ignored the wide-eyed looks cast in her direction. Instead, she went straight to the bars of the cell. "This isn't good," she turned toward Agent Park after considering the hissing, growling man inside the cage.

"He's like a rabid dog," Agent Park began. "He wants to fight anyone who comes near him, and the sedative he was given didn't work."

"Rabid could be a good description," Phil sighed. "But that's not what's happening here. He's rotting from the inside, but the spell laid on him is keeping him active."

"What are you saying, Philomena?" Kwan demanded.

"Somebody is attempting to make a zombie, I think."

"Nobody can hear us," Agent Yoon told Phil after she and the others were brought to an interrogation room. "The cameras and microphones are turned off."

"If I remove the spell, he'll drop over dead," Phil began. "I really don't want to be accused of who knows what afterward. If you send him to the hospital, I'm not sure that anyone who touches him will be safe. You certainly can't let him go. Honestly, I don't know what to do or say in this situation."

"A delayed spell, perhaps?" Tae Yong asked.

"I still have to unravel the threads of the spell on him first," Phil began.

"What about placing your own spell to achieve the same results and set it up to run its course hours after we leave, then remove the original spell itself?" Kwan asked.

"A timed spell, huh?" Phil considered the idea. "It might work. I still need to be close enough to set the new spell and remove the old one. Without drawing attention, you understand."

"The cell next to him is empty," Agent Yoon pointed out.

"But," Phil began.

"I know you can disguise yourself," he countered. "We will leave, you will create a disguise and I will arrest you."

"Please say he's joking," Phil frowned at Kwan.

"This may be the only opportunity to deal with the problem, Philomena."

"That's not the answer I was looking for, Kwan."

"We will go first," Kwan gripped Phil's wrist and pulled her toward the door. Tae Yong, wearing a doubtful frown, followed.

"What is that smell?" Phil didn't want to touch anything in the alley where she ended up with Kwan and Tae Yong.

"You don't want to know," Tae Yong said. "Disguise yourself quickly; Agents Yoon and Park are almost here."

"What will I be charged with?"

"Assault," Kwan said.

"Right now, I'd like to make that a fact rather than fiction," Phil glared at him. "I have no desire to," she didn't finish—gunshots rang out and Phil screamed.

Then, the air stilled, every noise was silenced and everything else went in the strangest of directions.

CHAPTER 13

"*S*hootings are rare in South Korea," Tae Yong snapped at Kwan. "Why and how did this come about, and exactly where Philomena would be?"

"I don't know." Kwan shook his head. "Agent Yoon says the shooters are still so confused and disoriented they can't speak, and the firing mechanisms of all three weapons were melted and are now worthless. Philomena is still shaking inside her jail cell."

"We should have taken her to a physician, rather than continuing with the plan," Tae Yong rounded on Kwan.

"I understand that—now."

Kwan and Tae Yong were invisible to anyone else inside the police station. Their conversation was also muted while they kept an eye on Phil. She sat on the floor, her back to the bars farthest from the hissing, crazed man in the adjoining cell. She'd rested her head against her knees while wrapping arms around her legs; Kwan couldn't see her face.

He'd already attempted to contact her telepathically, but she wouldn't—or couldn't—reply. Disguised as a middle-aged Korean man, none of the humans at the station would think to render aid. She hadn't asked for anything either, so she was ignored while the agents and officers were busy attempting to get information from the shooters.

Pull yourself together, Philomena. Get this done and we can leave, Kwan told her. *If this isn't dealt with soon, you may be transferred to another facility and lose the opportunity to do anything at all.*

Raising her head, she stared at the man in the other cell. Kwan could see clearly that her eyes were red and cheeks tearstained. He drew in a shuddering breath; Tae Yong turned toward him, anger clouding his features.

"She's ah, she's building a spell," Kwan breathed, causing Tae Yong to turn away sharply to watch Phil.

"Is she all right?" Agent Choi arrived sounding out of breath. "Agent Yoon called after the arrest and asked me to come. I was forced to take the train from Seoul."

"She's building the spell now, but as you can see, her hands aren't quite steady," Tae Yong explained.

"I understand she has had trauma in her past?"

"She still has scars from the bullets," Kwan sighed and hung his head. "This could not have happened at a worse time."

"I scent—ah," Agent Choi closed his eyes. "Death," he whispered.

"Philomena says the man in the other cell is rotting from the inside, and that only the spell cast on him is keeping his body animated," Kwan explained.

"I can sense it, even from here," Agent Choi nodded. "This isn't something that any shaman could deal with."

"She's layering her spell over the first," Tae Yong reported.

"She has to remove the first one, now." Kwan crossed his arms while he watched, hoping Phil's strength didn't fade while performing the task.

"I HAVE THE TRANSFER REQUEST," AGENT CHOI HANDED PAPERS TO THE Inspector. "The previous charge of assault is incorrect; this one may have information relating to another incident in Seoul."

"The NIS can have him," the Inspector replied. "We have our hands full with the shooting incident earlier. Two witnesses are in the hospital, and we can't get anything from the ones who were arrested."

"Thank you," Agent Choi dipped his head to the Inspector.

Minutes later, he lifted Phil to her feet; she couldn't rise or stand on her own.

"Hold on a little longer," Agent Choi said softly while he held her upright. "I'll get you out of here—can you walk at all?"

"I'll try," Phil told him. "I can't—promise anything."

"Just enough to get to the door. The others are waiting outside to help."

"Tch," Phil mumbled.

"How long will it take for your spell to activate?" Agent Choi did his best to hold Phil upright while she staggered toward the door.

"Around four hours, if you're asking about the spell," she breathed.

"I'll let the others know."

"Thanks. I hope I'm asleep somewhere by that time."

"I'll take her." Kwan pulled Phil away from Agent Choi the moment they were out the station's door. He ran lightly down the steps with Phil in his arms, with Tae Yong and Agent Choi running after him.

If she was jostled during the trip, Phil didn't know—she lost consciousness quickly.

"Will you cancel the hotel reservation and go home?" Jiah asked Kwan after he settled Phil on the bed. She'd lost her disguise and her consciousness at the same time. The *dokkaebi* physician had arrived and was currently checking her over while Kwan and Jiah talked.

"I don't want to, but the physician will have the last say," Kwan admitted.

"My concern is the same as Tae Yong's—why were weapons fired near Philomena's location? Does the enemy know who she is? This sounds more than suspicious to me."

"It probably isn't difficult to sort it out," Tae Yong sat on the hotel room sofa next to Kwan. "I'm sure our enemies are very curious, and, as a few of your kind have seen her—you understand how quickly news and rumors travel throughout dragonkind."

"Father certainly received plenty of information, most of it false or misleading," Kwan grumbled. "What is the Prince's command in this?" he asked, turning to Jiah.

"I think we should take her to the palace; I doubt she'll have enough strength to do anything for the rest of today and most of tomorrow. Also, I worry that we are being followed. We cannot expose ourselves like this in the future."

"It concerns me, too," Kwan admitted. "Very well, we'll go back when the physician is finished with the examination. Busan will have to wait."

"Philomena?"

"Hmmmmm?" Phil responded to her name breathed softly against her cheek.

"Hungry?" was whispered as a kiss was laid beneath her ear.

"Tired," she mumbled, attempting to burrow under bedcovers.

"I know, but food is on the way. You need to eat something. I'll help you sit up."

"Noooo," Phil complained as she was pulled away from her pillow.

"Open your eyes, now." Fingers brushed hair away from her face.

"We have resistance?" Jiah's voice jerked Philomena out of her stupor; she was awake and bristling in half a second. Kwan sat on the bed beside her while Jiah, Tae Yong and Hwang stood at the end, watching and listening.

"Who knew that an audience was necessary?" Hwang noted dryly.

"What are you doing?" Phil snapped at Kwan as she jerked the sheet up to her chin. Someone—probably Kwan—had dressed her in a thin, sleeveless, V-neck nightie.

That she hadn't brought with her.

"You've slept sixteen hours, Philomena. You need to eat."

"Does food require spectators? Honestly, I should dump you in the Atlantic." Pulling the sheet around her, she teleported off the bed and into the bathroom, slamming the door in the process.

"As a tactic, it worked. As an experiment, I'd suggest we not try it again," Tae Yong sighed. "We could all end up in an ocean, and I dislike cold seawater."

"We must assume going forward that our enemies know who she is," Hwang observed. "Perhaps they are testing her strength and abilities under these circumstances."

"Do you suppose these traps have been laid so carefully? Who knew of your plans to visit Busan?" Tae Yong asked Kwan.

"Only those of us here and," he hesitated. "I gave a false name at the hotel, but my card number—they've traced my card information, haven't they?"

"I know of someone who'd give that information freely—especially after you fired her," Tae Yong mused. "I will begin the process of replacing all the cards and financial information Ms. Nielson had."

"Can you do the same for Philomena?" Kwan struggled to hold back his anger and think rationally.

"I can and will," Tae Yong agreed. "I'll have it done soon."

"Do you have enough currency to get by?" Hwang asked. "For here and the US?

"I do," Kwan replied. "I'll check on Philomena's resources."

"Be prepared to go to Seattle immediately after my birthday celebration," Jiah said. "I dislike all of us being in one place."

"Perhaps you should go now, and come back for the celebration," Hwang suggested.

"Xinnie and Ray aren't expecting us back until Thursday," Kwan said.

"What's wrong with an early arrival?" Jiah queried.

"Because we'd disappear again in two days," Kwan pointed out.

"Does Philomena have another place to go for two days?" Tae Yong asked. "After all, those of us planning to go to the US with her won't be ready until after the birthday celebration."

"Phil does have other resources," she announced after exiting the bathroom fully dressed. "We don't have to upset Xinnie and Ray just yet."

"Food first, then pack only what you need," Kwan ordered. "I can get us back to the house, but you'll have to handle everything past that since I'm not familiar with where we're going."

"I can get us both there," Phil said. "And don't think you're off the hook for what you did earlier, because you're not."

"*Aigoo*," Kwan sighed.

"WHERE ARE WE?" KWAN SET HIS AND PHILOMENA'S BAGS ON THE tiled kitchen floor of a large apartment.

"You're in the penthouse suite of the *Le Texte Enluminé* building," Phil explained. "Of course, it's only six floors so it's not that impressive, although you can see Elliott Bay through the windows."

"*Le Texte Enluminé*?" Kwan's eyes widened in surprise. "The Publishing house that only puts out thirty-six books a year, and all of them are best-sellers?"

"That's the one," Phil said. "Living room is that way," she pointed past the kitchen island. "Have a seat. Want something to drink?"

"Do you know the owner? Are we borrowing their suite? Do they know we're here? This could prove dangerous, Philomena."

"Let's see," Phil tapped her chin. "The answers are yes, yes, yes and not likely."

"Who is the owner, then? I've only seen a CEO from time to time, making an announcement on the current crop of books."

"Well, Gran started the company. It's mine, now. I make the final decisions on what gets published, just like she did. All my correspondence is handled by an assistant, who acts as a go-between with the CEO and me. They make a truckload of money for their services and I'd trust them with my life—and yours, too."

"This person's name? And where are they? Do they know we're here?"

"Muki doesn't know yet; they're asleep. They live in Vancouver, Canada, which isn't a long way by train. Muki handles most of my business from their home and only comes to the office once a week unless there's a meeting or something important."

"Not a US citizen?"

"Originally from Bolivia but now a naturalized Canadian. Loves to read. Gran hired them. I'll let Muki know I'm here in an email. They won't mind and will only ask if I need anything."

"You keep cash here?"

"In a safe inside the bedroom closet."

"I'll take that drink, now."

"Awesome."

PHIL, ARE YOU AWAKE?

Phil lifted her phone when it buzzed. In Seattle, it was early morning. She hadn't gone to bed since she'd slept for sixteen hours before coming to the US. Kwan slept peacefully in the bedroom; Phil was having coffee and a croissant she'd taken from the freezer and zapped in the microwave.

Hey, Muki, how are you? Phil texted back. *I'm here at the penthouse for a couple of days—just wanted to give you a heads up,* she replied.

Want anything delivered? I'm coming in today for a teleconference with an author and a cover artist.

Could you have some groceries delivered? Just some basics, please, and have them leave it at the door. If you want to come up when you're done with the conference, just let me know.

I haven't seen you for ages. I'll be there when I'm finished with the call.

Awesome. If you're hungry, we can order in or go out.
Ordering takeout sounds great. I want lobster rolls.
You can have all the lobster rolls on the west coast, Phil teased.
Three will do for now. Gotta go catch the train. See ya.
KTHXBAI.

S

"WE NOW HAVE FRESH GROUND COFFEE, CREAM, SUGAR, HONEY, bagels, cream cheese, eggs and bacon," Phil told Kwan when he shuffled into the kitchen. "Plus a few other things. I can fix an omelet or a sandwich for you if you aren't feeling the bacon and eggs thing."

"We got delivery?" Kwan frowned at Phil. "Doesn't that take a credit card?"

"Relax, Muki ordered it for us on their company credit card while they were on the train to Seattle. They offered, and they're very thorough. If you need anything else, though, I have a company card in the safe with the cash. I don't use it often, as you can imagine."

"Good. Very good. I see you're taking this seriously."

"Why would you think otherwise?"

"I'd like an omelet, please. I'll make my own coffee."

"Awesome. Get your coffee, then. What do you want in your omelet?"

Twenty minutes later, Phil set a ham, tomato, mushroom and cheese omelet in front of Kwan, who sat at the kitchen island drinking coffee.

"Good," Kwan mumbled after taking a bite of the omelet.

"Muki will be dropping by later; we'll order takeout. There's a seafood place nearby that makes their favorite lobster rolls. The menu is in the top drawer next to the fridge."

"I haven't had lobster rolls since I left New York," Kwan said, pointing his fork at Phil. "I'll try these, but I warn you, I'll judge which place makes the better ones."

"Well, I'm getting a big bowl of clam chowder, with crab and lobster topping," Phil sniffed. "Plus garlic and cheese toasted baguettes."

"I'll look at the menu. Sounds like there may be more to order besides lobster rolls."

"Have you checked in with Jiah and Tae Yong?"

"Yes, and Father as well. They all send regards."

"Your father, too? I'm not sure whether to believe that."

"He's coming around; give him time," Kwan said. "You impressed him when you constructed the spell net. He has a gleam in his eye every time he thinks about trapping the ones who used that place. We consider the consumption of human flesh to be amongst the worst of crimes."

"What will happen to the ones we trap if they show up?" Phil asked, pouring herself another cup of coffee.

"Judged by the Prince and the High Council."

"High Council?"

"Jiah chooses the High Council, which consists of six other members. Those are the ones he trusts the most. My father and I are on the High Council, but it hasn't convened in more than a century."

"Why doesn't the High Council hear treason cases, then?"

"That's the way I'd like it to be, but Jiah still wants the entire Council to hear them. Of course, that has its negative aspects."

"Which we've recently seen," Phil nodded.

"Nothing is perfect, Philomena, although Xinnie's lasagna comes close."

"Perfection may be a matter of opinion, Mister Kwan," Phil pointed a finger at him. "My grandmother's lasagna recipe *is* perfection, in *my* opinion."

"I'll accept that, but only because you said it. I have to brush my teeth, now."

Kwan scooted his chair back and slouched toward the bedroom and the bathroom within.

He looks good in faded jeans and a knit shirt, Phil mused while watching him walk away. He hadn't combed his hair back, either, which left him looking more relaxed and approachable. He scuffed along in his inevitable slippers; Phil wore her usual socks.

"Write or not write?" Phil asked herself after Kwan disappeared down the hallway.

Her cell phone rang, ending her deliberation. "Xinnie?" she answered right away.

"Your ex-father-in-law just called. He and his wife want to drop in for a visit, beginning next Friday."

"Please, no," Phil moaned. "For how long?"

"About a week."

"Can we send them to the adjoining property?"

"You know they don't want that; they want to stay in the fanciest house available for free and boss the cook around."

"Dammit," Phil breathed. "This—why do they always wait until the last minute to spring this on us—so we can plan on being conveniently out of town? Xinnie, I'm bringing a few people back with me, but this really puts us in a bind. Besides, I know neither of us wants to listen to Paulson Muir's bullshit for a week."

"You got that right."

"Look, I can get somebody else to come in and wait on them hand and foot. I don't want you to have to deal with them, okay? Why don't you and Ray take the adjoining property for that week?"

"But what about you? Paulson still blames you for living while his son died in that massacre. He does this just to bully you—you know that, don't you?"

"I know it, Xinnie, but what else can I do?"

"Xinnie?" Kwan pulled the phone away from Phil's hand and held it to his ear. "What is happening?"

"Kwan—it's so nice to hear your voice," Xinnie said. "Phil's former in-laws are coming for a visit on Friday. They're insufferable and Phil doesn't have much of a choice in the matter."

"I say go to the alternate location, as Philomena suggested. I and my friends will handle any misbehavior from former relatives."

"Kwan, they're prejudiced up to their eyeballs," Xinnie stated baldly. "They like to order me around because I'm married to Ray. They'll make your life miserable, too."

"We'll see about that," Kwan said. "Do as Philomena suggests; we'll see you on Thursday as promised."

"Do you need a ride home from the airport? Ray and I can come get you."

"Don't worry about us; we're getting in quite late. We will hire a taxi."

"All right, but we were looking forward to having you both back home."

"Don't worry, Xinnie. Tell Ray the same, all right?"

"I will."

"FORMER IN-LAWS, EH?"

"Yeah." Phil slumped onto the sofa with a heavy sigh. "Trey was the exact opposite of his father. He took on pro bono civil rights cases, which aggravated Paulson to no end. He was the only son, though, and Paulson wanted him to take over the law firm when he retired. Now, he's pushing Rayne to marry a lawyer so the son-in-law can do the same thing. Rayne is going nuts because her parents want to dictate her life."

"Rayne?"

"Trey's younger sister. She's twenty-three and still trapped in the same house with her parents. That's not a good thing for her, I assure you. I've offered to get her a place, but she doesn't want the fight to start with the family. I really didn't need this headache right now." Phil raked fingers through her hair, leaving her curls fluffed out like an angry lion's mane.

Kwan settled on the sofa beside Phil. "Take a few deep breaths, Philomena. You aren't alone any longer in this fight."

"Can my life get messed up any more than it is?" Phil moaned, leaning her head back and closing her eyes in resignation.

"You are not alone, Philomena," Kwan leaned in to breathe against her ear. "Tae Yong and I will deal with this."

"Evidently, you've never met Paulson and Patricia Muir."

"Not yet. I look forward to it." Kwan lightly kissed Phil's cheek. "Would you like a nap, or can we go for a short shopping trip?"

"Huh?" Phil opened her eyes and blinked at Kwan's face, which hovered over hers.

"Nap or shop? Which will it be?"

"I think I'd like some fresh air."

"Good answer. Shall we?" He rose and offered a hand to pull her up.

"You look—really nice," Phil told Kwan as they strolled a sidewalk not far from *Le Texte Enluminé*. They'd taken the private elevator down to the underground parking area and left the building that way.

"I do?"

"Yeah. Eye candy, for real."

"It is my duty to serve."

"Annnnd there's the matching ego," Phil teased. A corner of Kwan's mouth quirked upward, while the almost dimple in his chin made her smile. Pulling her close, he kissed her, leaving her breathless.

"You have no idea how happy I am that nobody can see us," Phil leaned her forehead against Kwan's chest when she was able to breathe again.

"Shall we continue kissing or walking?" Kwan asked.

"Um, I don't think having a climax in public is a good idea—even if people can't see us," Phil leaned away from Kwan. "I'd still be embarrassed."

"Let me know when you want more kissing, then." Kwan tucked her hand in the crook of his elbow and led her away.

"Where are we going again?" Phil asked five minutes later.

"The jewelry shop on the next block."

"I still haven't worn the earrings you got me last time."

"This you will wear, going forward. Remember, this won't be just for show or as a tactic. Tae Yong is already preparing the paperwork for the other half of this."

"Okay—now I'm worried."

"Don't be. Shall I kiss you again?" He leaned in, but Phil covered his mouth with her fingers.

"Your mouth is beautiful and dangerous at the same time," she told him. "Let me just look at it for now, okay?"

"That will be fine—for now. Shall we appear nearby? It is time for us to be seen," Kwan said.

"All right. Fine."

PHIL'S CHEEKS WERE WARM AND FLUSHED AS SHE WATCHED KWAN discuss rings with the clerk at the jewelry shop.

She wanted to argue with both, but Kwan wouldn't give an inch on his decision to buy a matching pair.

"I like these very much," Kwan pointed at the bands studded with groups of three small diamonds in an upward swirl all the way around. Made of gold and platinum, the rings were both eye-catching and expensive. "You have these in stock?"

"Yes. Do you want an engagement ring with this?" The clerk sounded hopeful.

"No," Phil waved off the idea while her cheeks flushed a brighter red. "something like that tends to get caught in my clothes or on other stuff."

"If she wants a diamond, I'll buy it for other occasions," Kwan placed a hand at the small of Phil's back. "That way, she can wear it only when she wants."

"Later, please," Phil wanted to hide her flaming face against Kwan's denim jacket sleeve.

"I'll box up your rings," the clerk smiled. "Will this be cash or charge?"

"Here," Kwan lifted a card from his jacket pocket. "Put it on this, please."

"I'll be right back, Mister Drake." The clerk took off.

Phil's shoulders sagged and her head fell forward.

Philomena, it is all right, Kwan mentally soothed. *The card is under a new alias. Besides, these rings serve many purposes. We will discuss things later, all right?*

Fine.

Good. Come here—you look flustered. Kwan placed an arm around her shoulders and pulled her close.

Kwan—I, Phil searched for words.

Shhhh, all is well, Kwan said. *Trust me. Please.*

"THERE." KWAN SLIPPED PHIL'S RING ONTO HER FINGER, AFTER putting on his own. "This should deter your former in-laws."

"Or piss 'em off," Phil's head dropped onto her arms at the kitchen island.

"Both are perfectly fine with me." Kwan reached out to lazily wind a honey-blonde curl around his fingers.

Phil's cell phone buzzed. Lifting her head, she scanned the text message.

"Muki's on the way. We'll order when they get here."

"Good. I'm starved."

"Yeah. Clam chowder sounds really good right now."

"Do we have something to drink besides soda, water or milk?"

"We have several bottles of various white wines in the fridge, plus some red in the pantry. We also have Scotch, vodka, rum and a few mixers."

"Wine will do."

"Awesome. I'll get some glasses."

Phil stepped around the island to retrieve wine glasses from an under-counter rack when the doorbell rang.

"I'll get it," Kwan's slippers scuffed along the wooden floor toward the front door.

Phil set the glasses on the island and rushed after Kwan, worried about their initial meeting.

Kwan opened the door, then was forced to drop his eyes. His entire body stilled for several seconds; Phil arrived at his back.

Muki looked up at Kwan in curiosity, before nodding. "Dragon," they acknowledged.

"Cavern elf," Kwan dipped his head respectfully.

CHAPTER 14

"**Y**ou're much taller than most cavern elves," Kwan poured white wine for Muki.

"True." Muki's smile was a thing of beauty, as were their eyes and the shape of their face. With pale blond hair tied in an elaborate knot atop their head, Kwan understood the gender fluidity of this particular cavern elf. "In the regular world, I'm considered a little person. In the Andes where I was born, I'm a giant at three-six."

"Does this make your life difficult?" Kwan asked.

"At times it does, but like you, I can become invisible to humans whenever I want. Now," they turned to Phil, "in my wildest imaginings, I never thought you'd involve yourself with another race, and dragons least of all."

"It—sort of just happened," Phil turned away to hide guilty embarrassment.

"The rule of touching a royal came into play, you understand," Kwan explained.

"Phil, are you saying you couldn't keep your hands off him?" Muki pretended to be shocked. "Really?"

"It's not what you're thinking," Phil began.

"Way too many K-dramas," Muki shook their head.

"That's not it," Phil stammered. "Not in the least little bit."

"I love ticking her off," Muki told Kwan. "When her temper rises, the energy around her crackles. It makes me feel alive."

"She dumped me in the koi pond a few times," Kwan admitted. "It made me feel wet and messy."

Muki laughed and slapped the island's surface.

"Drink your wine, Muki," Phil grumped.

"I hear the in-laws are coming for a visit," Muki said soberly. "For how long?"

"They told Xinnie about a week," Phil replied, her voice glum. "When they see this," she held up her left hand and wiggled her ring finger, "they'll probably have the biggest conniption ever."

"They can try," Kwan huffed.

The doorbell rang; their food had arrived. "I'll get it," Kwan waved off Phil's and Muki's offers to answer the door.

Shortly after, he piled takeout bags on the island to be sorted and served.

"I got an extra order of lobster rolls," Muki said. "For sharing. There are two servings of clam chowder, too, it's really good."

"My second favorite," Phil said, carefully pulling back the lid of her chowder bowl.

"It's your second favorite clam chowder?" Kwan lifted an eyebrow.

"Her favorite is from a place in Pismo Beach," Muki arranged lobster rolls to their liking and opened a container of clam chowder. "If she decides to pop down there, I'm always good to go with her."

"You will also take me, next time," Kwan stated.

"Why would I leave you home?" Phil poked his shoulder with a finger.

"There is no reason at all to do so."

"Okay, I'm too curious, now. Phil, why did you have the temerity to touch a royal dragon?" Muki asked.

"First of all, I had no idea he was a royal dragon," Phil frowned at Muki. "Second of all, the dagger stuck in his armpit pushed me toward that fateful decision."

"She distracted me with a vanilla latte," Kwan explained. "Before I could stop her, she'd disintegrated the dagger, touched my chest, healed most of the wound and hauled me to a safer location before I could refuse the contact."

"And I ended up reforming the dagger and removing the spell on it later," Phil sighed. "After I was forced to sign a contract with Kwan."

Muki's eyes widened as they stared at Kwan in surprise. "She's your familiar?"

"As recorded by the Prince himself."

"Mostly he likes to order me around—hence the koi pond," Phil dipped into her clam chowder.

"You got yourself into something you didn't expect," Muki snickered.

"Which one of us?" Phil asked.

"Both of you."

"You're not wrong," Kwan nodded at Muki. "I had no idea."

"Phil exists for a reason," Muki said. "It's my good luck to be so close to her."

"We're not officially back, yet," Phil said, changing the subject. "That will happen on Thursday, and a few others will be coming with us. One or two will help Xinnie, Kwan will have a guard or two, plus Secretary Kim. This way, the dragon royalty won't be in the same place at the same time."

"It's wise to split up unless a combined front becomes necessary," Muki sighed. "I can feel the coming troubles in the earth itself."

"Yeah," Phil crunched into a slice of toasted garlic cheese baguette. "We have to be on guard from now on. We may have troubles on top of troubles anyway, with the coming dry season on the west coast. At least one of our enemies is able to pull moisture from the ground itself, and with it already drying out faster than it should, we could see even more catastrophic fires."

"That would be a dragon enemy, then," Muki considered Phil's words. "How did this happen?" They locked eyes with Kwan.

"We believe it may have started more than two centuries ago, but has only become apparent recently," Kwan replied.

"What set it off at this point?" Muki asked.

"I think that's on me," Phil hung her head. "I just couldn't leave that dagger where it was."

Kwan stilled for a moment before slowly turning toward Phil. "That's—you believe that was the trap?"

"Yeah." Phil dropped the rest of her baguette on the plate with a sigh and dusted her hands. "I'm sorry, Kwan, but I think that was the catalyst."

"Someone was waiting for you, then," Muki nodded thoughtfully. "But that's really no surprise, is it?"

"What are you talking about?" Kwan demanded.

"Dragon, aren't there prophecies in your royal archives?" Muki asked. "You may find your answers there."

"I haven't researched those—they're in the Prince's private library."

"Yes—his father and elder brother died at the same time," Muki observed. "Perhaps there was information not passed to the youngest heir before their deaths."

"What?" Phil and Kwan echoed one another.

"I suggest you tell the Prince that research may be a very good thing—and soon," Muki replied. "My kind are born with the knowledge our race has collected. We know there is a prophecy; we only know of it as the *fulcrum war*."

"You mean tipping the balance one way or another?" Kwan's eyes widened.

"Yes."

"This doesn't sound good," Phil tilted her head back and moaned.

"Muki, I would very much like it if you could join us on Vashon Island and offer advice," Kwan tapped the kitchen island with a finger. "If you and Philomena consent, that is."

"That's fine with me—I could use a change of scenery for a while," Muki shrugged.

"No problem—they've been for visits before," Phil agreed. "Muki loves Xinnie and Ray, and vice-versa."

"They think I'm young," Muki laughed. "They adopted me—unofficially, of course. Xinnie will cook anything I want if I ask."

"I need some private time to have a telepathic conference with

Jiah," Kwan rose from his seat. "Thank you, Muki. You've given us much to consider."

"You are welcome. I will do everything I can to help Phil—and, by extension, the races intent on saving the Earth."

Yes—now and then I come across a reference to particular prophecies while doing my hobby research on witches, Jiah remarked. *I admit, I hadn't considered reading any of them, thinking them old and irrelevant in these times.*

The cavern elf knows of them, but not their contents. Muki referred to this prophecy as the fulcrum war. *Have you read anything regarding that?* Kwan asked.

Not using that particular term—no, Jiah said.

Could there be another term—in anything you've read? Something that may not have made sense at the time?

I will check my notes and think on this, Jiah said, *and I will keep you informed. I'm glad you met the cavern elf—the advice could prove invaluable.*

Agreed. Has Tae Yong completed the certificate?

Yes. It is now official. I realize this was a momentary weakness where you are concerned, but it has turned out to be the best of luck— for all of us.

I know. Even in the Pacific Northwest, the sun was shining on me that day.

"Muki will stay at the adjoining property with Xinnie and Ray until the Muirs leave," Phil informed Kwan when he came back to the kitchen. "They left to catch the train back to Vancouver."

"What, exactly, is the adjoining property?" Kwan thought to ask.

"When the house next to my property line went up for sale, I bought it," Phil said. "It's nice but not nearly as big—four thousand square feet and four bedrooms. There's a trail we built between both houses; takes about five minutes to walk if you're in a hurry, ten if you're not."

"Where will the Muirs sleep—which bedroom?" Kwan asked.

"The one two doors down from mine. They'd love to shove me out of my suite because it's the nicest, but that's one thing I refuse to allow."

"Shall we put Tae Yong in the bedroom next to ours?" Kwan asked.

"Uh—I forgot about that," Phil said. "Yeah, the one next to ours. He can use the library as his office if he wants. There's a desk and chair in there already, and I can find other stuff for him if needed."

"Good. We'll sort the rest out when we get there."

"Awesome. I'm tired." Phil yawned. "Make yourself at home; I'm going to bed."

"It will be a paid leave of absence," Agent Yoon explained to Agent Choi. "I've been informed that there is an adjoining property where we can stay once the houseguests are gone. Secretary Kim believes the more eyes to observe there are, the safer the heir will be. Your job at the NIS is secure; we will see to it."

"I've never been to the US," Agent Choi studied the location displayed on Agent Yoon's phone. "The area is quite scenic."

"Expenses will be covered while you're there," Agent Yoon said. "There is no need to worry about such things. We will coordinate day and night shifts with the other guards."

"Understood. Yes, I'd like to do this," Agent Choi said.

"Very good—I will inform Secretary Kim."

"Did you find something?" Tae Yong asked Jiah as the Prince strode into his office.

"I took photographs of the references with my cell phone, and sent them to you and to Kwan," Jiah answered Secretary Kim's question. "We must now search the prophecies to learn whether there is a reference to those designations."

"*Lebeo manyeo*?" Tae Yong pulled the information up on his desktop. "Lever witch? That makes no sense."

"I glossed over it as it didn't appear often, and some of the other information I read was just as vague regarding witches," Jiah said. "Plus, each time it was mentioned, there was no consistency regarding the type of witch described. I took it to mean either a level of power or authority—perhaps both."

"That would also be my assumption," Tae Yong agreed. "I'll read through what you've sent; please let me know if you find an associated prophecy."

"I will. What is Eun-Kyung's reply?"

"She has agreed, my Prince."

"Good. Inform Kwan that he and Philomena will host two more houseguests."

"I'll ask if she wishes to bring a servant or two with her—providing they have Philomena's approval."

"I trust you'll assess the housing situation and arrange for everyone's comfort?" Jiah asked.

"Of course. Kwan has already sent the house plans. I believe the guards can make use of the rather large wine cellar, if privacy screens are installed."

"Very good. Keep me informed, please."

"I REALIZE HOW LUCKY I WAS TO KNOW MY FATHER," DAE-WON TOLD his mother, Eun-Kyung. Both stood inside the columbarium, where Dae-won's father's ashes were kept. "So few of us know the other parent."

"I wanted this—for both of you," Eun-Kyung leaned against her son for comfort. "He was loved by both of us, as was deserved."

"Yes," Dae-won sighed and placed an arm around his mother's shoulders. "It's just so difficult to lose them this quickly."

"But the knowing and loving are better than not knowing or loving, don't you think?"

"I wouldn't trade those years for anything."

"Neither would I. The Prince wouldn't have contacted us had things been otherwise, I believe," Eun-Kyung continued. "We have wisdom, tolerance and talent."

"When will we join First Heir?"

"After the Prince's birthday celebration. He will announce you as Second Heir, and Hwang will step into Third Heir's role."

"Do you know First Heir?"

"Vaguely. You've read what Secretary Kim sent—the reason Kwan didn't socialize during the past two centuries."

"I did. I want to learn more about the witch."

"You can ask, my son, but please don't be disappointed if the answer is no. You'll be introduced at the celebration."

"Father taught me manners," Dae-won sighed. "I won't pester."

"Your father did very well. I miss him daily."

"Me, too."

PHIL AWOKE DISORIENTED, HER BRAIN FRANTICALLY SEARCHING FOR her current location, time and date. She found herself confined in some way. With a rapidly increasing heart rate and desperate, shallow breaths, she began fighting against what held her down.

"Philomena," Kwan's voice was rough from sudden waking. "It's me. I'm here. You are not in danger." Both his arms were wound around her, now, as he struggled to calm her fright.

"Oh, sweet Jesus," Phil's breaths were now ragged as she recognized her surroundings.

"It's all right," Kwan soothed. "I'm right here." Phil's head was tucked beneath Kwan's chin as he stroked her hair.

"I didn't know where I was," Phil said when her breaths and heart rate reached a more normal rhythm.

"It happens," Kwan said. "You're okay where you are," he added when Phil showed signs of moving away. "Stay here for a while," he kissed the top of her head.

"Kwan, I," Phil began.

"Shhh. I like this." Kwan carefully pulled Phil's curls away from her neck and planted a kiss. "I like this very much," he breathed against her skin before kissing her collarbone. "Oh, what's this here?" He pulled the neck of her pajama top aside to reveal the beginnings of a breast curve.

"My willpower is low right now," Phil's breaths became ragged.

"As I prefer it," Kwan's voice purred. "Will this be mine?" His hand moved downward and found the hem of her top. "Philomena?"

"Huh?" Phil turned her head. Kwan captured her mouth in an all-consuming kiss.

Philomena was his—and he wasn't letting go.

"I should have gotten a necklace to match the ruby earrings," Kwan studied Phil, who was now dressed in the red ballgown they'd bought in Busan. "Never mind; you are stunning, Philomena."

"And you're not? Look at you—all dressed up and spiffy," Phil wrinkled her nose at him.

"That goes without saying." Kwan straightened his shirt cuffs and the sleeves of his black tux. To complement Phil's dress, he wore a deep-red bowtie and ruby cufflinks.

"That's what I love about you," Phil patted his shoulder. "You're so humble."

"Tch. Come along or we'll be late."

"To our palace suite or somewhere else?" Phil thought to ask before teleporting.

"Our suite will be fine; Jiah wants us to walk into the ballroom with him."

"Sounds good. Let's go."

"First, you will walk in behind the Prince and First Heir," Secretary Kim studied Dae-won's appearance with satisfaction. Eun-Kyung, Dae-won's mother, stood nearby, her eyes shining with pride.

"Then," Secretary Kim continued, "After a short speech, Prince Jiah will announce you as Second Heir. Next to the Prince himself, you are the youngest heir to be named by dragonkind."

"I will work and study diligently in the days to come, so the Prince's trust in me will not be misplaced," Dae-won dipped his head to Secretary Kim.

"Is everything packed and ready to go?" Secretary Kim turned to Eun-Kyung. "You will be leaving with Kwan after the celebration tonight."

"Yes," Eun-Kyung replied. "Our belongings were placed inside Kwan's royal suite until the proper time to leave."

"If you wish to travel by lair entrance, that is your choice. I have the idea that Kwan will ask his familiar to transport the rest of us."

"She has that ability? Is that not impossible?" Dae-won asked in surprise.

"I will go with her—she is that powerful and trustworthy. Only a few of her kind in recorded history have been capable of relocation."

"Shall we go with them, Mother?" Dae-won turned toward Eun-Kyung with a hopeful expression.

"If Secretary Kim deems it safe enough," Eun-Kyung agreed.

"That's settled, then," Secretary Kim smiled. "Please, make yourselves comfortable; the Prince is awaiting Kwan's arrival. We will enter the ballroom shortly afterward."

Jiah, we have arrived, Kwan announced. Are these ah, Dae-won's belongings in our suite?

His, his mother's and three servants', Jiah admitted.

I hope the servants are prepared to share quarters.

They understand that space may be limited. They are eager to go anyway. Will you and Philomena join me in my suite? I've already asked Dae-won to come. Secretary Kim will arrange for an escort to the ballroom for Eun-Kyung.

We will be there shortly.

"What's up?" Phil blinked at Kwan.

"Let's go to Jiah's suite; he is waiting for us. You'll get to meet the new Second Heir, too; his name is Dae-won and he is only fifty-nine years of age."

"Only fifty-nine?"

"Any dragon under a century in age is still considered a juvenile. We mature slowly, you understand."

"Um—gotcha," Phil deadpanned.

"Take my arm, Philomena, and we will join the Prince."

"Mmm-kay."

"Wow," Phil breathed as she took in the magnificence of Jiah's royal robes. Black silk was richly embroidered with gold dragons against blue skies. "That's—gorgeous. Resplendent. Amazing."

"You like it?" Jiah's smile was wide.

"I love it. You really know how to shine, don't you?"

"Thank you for your compliments," Jiah said.

"Prince Jiah." Someone else entered Jiah's receiving room. The newcomer bowed for the required amount of time before straightening.

"Welcome, Dae-won," Jiah smiled at the newcomer. "I hope you are not feeling anxious about any of this—it is only a formality, you understand. Allow me to introduce Kwan, my First Heir," he indicated Kwan, who dipped his head to Dae-won. "And this is Kwan's familiar, Philomena Muir."

"Pleased to meet you," Dae-won spoke in accented English, before dipping his head to both.

He looks twelve, Phil told Kwan mentally.

He will be sixty next month, Kwan replied.

He's so cute, I feel like I should buy him school supplies, Phil countered.

Kwan was forced to dip his head and press his lips together to keep from smiling.

"I'm very pleased to meet you," Phil held out a hand to Dae-won. "I hope you'll enjoy your time at my home on Vashon Island."

"I have read information on the area," Dae-won shook Phil's hand. "I am looking forward to seeing it for myself."

"Is everyone ready?" Tae Yong arrived.

"We're ready," Jiah agreed.

"I've got feelers out," Phil said. "In case anybody has nefarious plans."

"Feelers?" Dae-won asked.

"I'll explain later. We have to do the *Pomp and Circumstance* thing first. Don't worry, I've placed a protective shield around you. Prince Jiah and Kwan already have theirs in place."

"I felt nothing," Dae-won sounded confused as he and Philomena walked behind Jiah and Kwan.

"You won't feel it," Kwan turned his head to explain. "Just be grateful it is there."

Jiah's speech was in Korean; Phil was relegated to a position off to the side and couldn't touch anyone to understand its meaning. When Dae-won was introduced as Second Heir, she understood the motions but little of the language.

She did understand, however, the angry murmurs among certain knots of guests. *Somebody's got their panties in a bunch*, Phil considered as she amplified the anger in individual emotions to sort out those who could be Jiah's enemies.

She didn't miss the frequent, angry glances in her direction, either.

Pairing those with the ones who were angry about the choice of Second Heir, Phil began collecting images to give Jiah later.

"Have you discerned anything from the guests?" Hwang sidled up to Phil.

"Plenty. I can't give names, but I can show you faces."

"I have spelled the gold within the flooring, to listen for names and pertinent information. Perhaps we can put our findings to good use afterward."

"I'm okay with that."

"I was hoping your trap would be sprung, but alas," Hwang released a heavy sigh.

"Just give 'em time. I don't think they'll abandon it completely," Phil replied. "They wouldn't have covered it like that if they didn't have a use for it."

"True enough."

"Jiah is considering adding you to the High Council, since Dae-won will be added. It's to keep it at an odd number, you understand."

"But," Phil argued.

"It can be done—if the Prince decrees it. There is a *dokkaebi* on it already."

"Tae Yong?"

"Yes. I have no objections to your addition."

"Oh. Thank you."

"Has anyone in particular stood out as a specific point of interest?" Hwang went back to the previous subject.

"Yeah. Let me send his image to you." Phil mentally relayed the dragon's facial appearance to Hwang.

"Sung-hoon," Hwang muttered. "I have my eye on him, too."

"I think he's up to no good," Phil said. "I get a bad vibe from him, and I have the feeling that it has spread to some who are hanging around him."

"Shall I introduce you?" Hwang pulled Phil's hand into the crook of his arm and took off before she could object.

Dragons in human form parted to allow Hwang through; apparently, most of them were frightened of Kwan's father.

Good enough, Phil thought. *Let them be afraid. I'll back Hwang up if I have to.*

As if he were expecting them, Sung-hoon, a glass of champagne in his hand, stood his ground, waiting for Hwang and Phil's arrival. The few knotted about him took a step or two away but didn't leave, as if waiting for a coming conflict.

All of them were already on Phil's radar, but she strengthened their images in her mind anyway.

"Sung-hoon," Hwang dipped his head. "Good to see you again," he spoke in English so Phil could understand.

"Always a pleasure," Sung-hoon replied, although his smile was more of a sneer and Phil noticed a calculating glint in his eyes. "Is this the little witch your son has chosen?" His expression changed to one of disdainful speculation.

"Philomena," Hwang turned to her. "This is Sung-hoon, a member of the Council."

"Pleased to meet you," Phil dipped her head while grinding her teeth at the *little witch* comment. She felt it, then—a buildup of power within Sung-hoon.

He's building power, Phil warned Hwang. *And he's pulling it from those around him!*

Several things happened at once; Hwang's dragon roared as the lights went out in the ballroom; Phil shouted as she felt her trap spring at the hidden lair entrance.

I'll trap all of them, Phil informed Hwang before she sent Sung-hoon and his cronies to the hidden lair to join their colleagues.

Protect the Prince, Hwang ordered mentally, *Guards, with me!*

Mother's hurt! Dae-won's anguished voice filled Phil's mind.

Be right there, Phil attempted to reassure him while frantically racing through what had become a darkened cavern.

Lights, Phil, she chastised herself as she ran along. Gathering Sun Magic and flinging out an illumination spell, she bathed the ballroom with light, only then finding the damage Sung-hoon had managed to do while she'd been otherwise occupied.

CHAPTER 15

"We lost two of ours." Jiah let his ceremonial robe fall into a puddle on the floor of his suite. "Without Philomena's help, it would have been much worse."

"The enemy sacrificed six of his own to do this damage," Tae Yong's fury was barely held in check. "Do you imagine for a moment that they understood their lives would be forfeited?"

"I doubt it," Jiah growled. "They were spaced carefully at pivotal points around the ballroom. Kwan and Hwang will be bringing the miscreants caught in Philomena's trap to us shortly. The High Council will pass judgment upon them. How are Dae-won and his mother doing?"

"Philomena and Lee Min are with them now. Eun-Kyung is resting comfortably; her wounds have been cauterized and bandaged."

"Will she withdraw Dae-won from his position as heir?"

"I don't know. I believe that Philomena has now placed a shield about her, just as she did for Dae-won." Tae Yong lifted Jiah's royal robe and carried it toward the closet.

"My concern is that one of the enemy's living weapons was close enough to kill us, without our knowledge," Jiah dropped onto a comfortable chair with a sigh. "That is how Eun-Kyung was wounded."

"At least Philomena's shields protected you," Tae Yong was back.

"Yet two died. We must find the source of this uprising and soon, before other dragons are caught up in this vile treachery."

The prisoners are now being held in the cavern beneath the palace, Kwan informed Jiah.

How many? Jiah asked.

Twelve, Kwan replied.

Is Dal among them?

Yes.

Good. I have questions.

As do Father and I. Is Philomena available?

I'll send Tae Yong to find out. She's currently tending to Eun-Kyung.

Ask her to come if she's able. Father and I want to know how those spelled barbs were encased within bodies, with none the wiser.

I'll bring her myself if she isn't exhausted.

Thank you.

BRISTLING WITH ANGER, PHIL STOOD BESIDE KWAN OUTSIDE Sung-hoon's spelled jail cell. "I see the little witch isn't as powerful as she thought," Sung-hoon gloated in English.

"And yet here you are, caught like a rat in a trap," Phil sniped back. "If you think you're getting out of there anytime soon, think again."

"You thought to kill many more," Jiah's voice was calm and deadly. "We lost two. You lost six. Did they understand they were sacrifices, Sung-hoon? Did they give their lives freely to your cause, or were they unwitting pawns?"

"I have nothing more to say," Sung-hoon waved a hand in dismissal.

"They didn't know—I can read it in his face. In fact, he didn't know they'd die, either. Did you?" Phil accused.

"I have nothing more," Sung-hoon began when Dal hissed, "Shut up," from another cell nearby.

"Wait your turn, Dal," Hwang rounded on him in fury. "We'll get to you soon enough."

Philomena, do you have enough strength to lay a shield and trap around the entire cavern? Jiah asked.

I think I can do that.

Good. I am weary. We will allow these to wallow in their self-created misery for the rest of the night, then begin our questioning again tomorrow.

Sounds awesome. You can leave if you want to.

I'll stay and watch.

Okay. Will you and Kwan render us invisible? I don't want any of our guests to see what I'm doing.

We can. Kwan, we will render Philomena and ourselves invisible, Jiah commanded.

As you will it, my Prince.

"I promise I'll transport you another day," Phil told Dae-won later. "Tonight, I have to let Kwan take us through his lair—I'm too tired."

"Please, don't worry about me," Dae-won assured her. "My mother and I wish to thank you for helping us."

"I will assist with the belongings," Hwang volunteered. "Son, take them through; I will be right behind."

"Lee Min and I will help Hwang; go first," Tae Yong nodded at Kwan.

"How weary are you?" Kwan asked Phil softly. "Should I carry?"

"I'm okay, as long as I can hold onto you," Phil replied.

"Good enough. Jiah, I will speak with you later," Kwan met the Prince's eyes over Phil's head.

"As will I," Tae Yong promised. "Keep us informed, and if you have need," he didn't finish.

"Undersecretary Oh and I will keep you advised, as will Hwang. Be safe in your travels; your Prince commands it."

Before Phil could stop him or complain, Kwan lifted her into his arms and allowed lair magic to pull him and the others through.

"It's ten minutes after three in the morning in Korea," Tae Yong sighed. "Here, it's ten after ten the morning before—and daylight." He squinted through the tall, curved windows of the Vashon Island house.

"Go to bed, I'll show you to your room," Kwan ordered. "We all need rest. For now, we'll send Eun-Kyung and Dae-won to the adjoining property—with their guards and servants. We may have to put Xinnie and Ray up in a hotel beginning on Friday."

"They can go to the apartment in Seattle; they know where it is," Phil flopped onto a barstool. "It'll give them a nice break. Muki can stay with them if they want."

"Give me the visual information on the adjoining property," Hwang told Phil. "I'll get Dae-won and Eun-Kyung settled there."

"It's clean and ready," Phil said. "Thank you."

"Philomena, you have a lovely home," Tae Yong said. "I'm sorry I'm too weary to see more of it right now."

"Go to bed; we'll see you when you wake," Phil said. "Sleep as long as you want."

"Come with us," Kwan pulled Phil off her barstool. "It's bed for you, too."

"Phil?" Xinnie sat on the edge of the in-ground spa outside the house on Thursday morning.

"Xinnie?" Phil pulled down her sunglasses to see better.

"When did you get in?"

"After three. We're exhausted."

"Is everyone else asleep?"

"I hope so. Man, I hate jet lag. I'm tired and I ache all over."

"Need more coffee and something to eat?"

"You don't have to wait on me. I can do it myself as soon as I haul my ass out of this thing."

"Are you kidding? Stay here; I'll be back in a minute with coffee and yogurt."

"Okay—that I'll accept. Thanks, Xinnie. It's good to see you. I'd hug you, but you'd get wet."

"We'll hug later, and discuss the in-laws coming tomorrow."

"Right. Are they here just to hang out, or is there another reason?"

"Paulson has a legal seminar on two of the days, but it's not until next week."

"Figures. Xinnie, we'll have a house full, and there are folks at the other property, too. Would you and Ray like some time at the Seattle apartment? Muki may come for a visit while you're there."

"Phil, I think Ray and I want to stay. Maybe it's time Paulson learns he's not top dog here."

"Yeah, well," Phil pulled her left hand out of the water and held it under Xinnie's nose. "Kwan may stand with you on that issue."

"What?" Xinnie's eyes grew round as she stared at the ring on Phil's finger. "Did you—Philomena Muir, I have no words."

"Yeah, same here. All I can say is that Kwan is very persistent, and generally gets his way."

"That's not what I meant," Xinnie slapped Phil's hand. "We didn't get an invite, and I'm hurt."

"Xinnie, if you're that intent on having a wedding, then plan it here and we'll have one. You have to convince Kwan first, though."

"This means you're married in Korea?" Xinnie held Phil's hand to see the ring better.

"Yeah. We're married in Korea. The South part. We got papers and all that stuff."

"Xinnie, how are you?" Kwan sauntered out of the house carrying a large mug of coffee and wearing sunglasses, a T-shirt, jeans and sneakers.

"I hear you're part of the family, now," Xinnie said.

"You heard correctly." Kwan held up his left hand to show her his ring.

"You're a lucky man, Kwan. I didn't think Phil would even consider getting married again."

"Because the first time turned out so well," Phil muttered.

"Philomena, you resemble a lobster. Come out now and have breakfast with me," Kwan said.

"Somebody's hungry," Phil stood and stepped out of the hot spa.

"Here," Kwan lifted her terry robe and helped Phil into it.

"What would you like for breakfast?" Xinnie asked Kwan as he herded Phil toward the house.

"Don't humor him," Phil told Xinnie. "He's overbearing enough as it is."

"Just sit at the island; we'll have breakfast ready in a few," Phil told Tae Yong as he walked into the kitchen. "Want coffee or a latte? Cappuccino, maybe?"

"Can you make a cappuccino?" Tae Yong asked.

"She has a nice espresso machine in the butler's pantry," Xinnie set a plate of food in front of Tae Yong. "She likes to play with it."

"Are you knocking my previous life's experience?" Phil made a face at Xinnie.

"Previous life?" Tae Yong frowned.

"I earned my keep in college by being a barista at a coffeeshop," Phil said. "I know how to make a cappuccino. Want it plain or flavored?"

"He'll have a caramel cappuccino," Kwan intervened.

"Coming right up."

"Here's some juice while Phil makes your drink," Xinnie set a glass of fresh-squeezed orange juice in front of Tae Yong.

"Here ya go," Phil set a thick ceramic cup and saucer in front of Tae Yong minutes later. An impressive topping of velvety foam covered his coffee drink.

"Very nice," Tae Yong nodded after taking a sip.

"Looks like we need more bacon and eggs," Phil said as two guards, plus Lee Min and one other, approached the island.

"We can help," Lee Min offered.

"Sit down—we'll have your food ready in a minute," Xinnie ordered. "You can help with dinner if you want."

"I can't wait to see what Paulson and Patricia have in store for us," Xinnie told Phil later, after everyone was fed. The others were now gathered in the library, which had already become Tae Yong's new office. The topic of discussion was everyone's safety. Dae-won had arrived with a guard to join the conversation.

"I'm not in a good mood anyway, so things could go downhill fast if they don't like the circumstances. I can find a hotel room and put 'em in it really fast." Phil finished cleaning her espresso machine and set her drink mixing utensils on top.

"They could get their own hotel room—and should have," Xinnie agreed. "Ray is out with the landscaping crew, but we ought to go to the grocery store in a little while.

"We'll have to take Ray's van," Phil sighed. "We're feeding an army. Lee Min and Si-woo can help. They can read English, so that won't be a problem."

"Good. I'll start a list."

"We'll let them know that weekends are their days off, too. We can order takeout if nobody else wants to cook."

"I can take care of the rest of this," Xinnie said. "Go write."

"Yes, ma'am."

Phil tapped a pen on a pile of printed pages, pondering manuscript changes when someone knocked on her office door.

"Come in," she called out.

"Kwan said to be prepared," Dae-won stepped inside her office, curiosity evident in the way he studied everything inside it.

"I'm a stacker," Phil explained, expecting judgment any moment.

"I feel it's very much like someone's brain," Dae-won touched the triton's trumpet shell displayed on one of Phil's bookshelves. "I see no dust anywhere, so it's not dirty."

"It's a spell," Phil said. "So any dust, dirt or grime disappears. I do the same thing for the gallery ceiling and outside windows. Nobody has to climb up and risk their lives for that."

"Kwan and Secretary Kim will be here soon; they want to know about the spelled projectiles."

"Yeah. I think I have an explanation for those, and why they didn't trigger anybody's radar."

"How was it accomplished?"

"Do you know what ghost guns are?" Phil asked as Dae-won continued his perusal of her bookshelves.

"The selling of gun components, in order to build a complete weapon?"

"Yes. I think the projectiles were inserted as tiny pieces, which were designed to join with other pieces at a particular moment. The spell was the same way—weak and ineffective until it combined with the other parts. How's your mother doing?"

"She's fine, although a bit shaken, still."

"More than understandable. If she needs anything, just ask."

"Can you do a spell like that—in pieces?"

"Yes, but it could come at a very steep price. The enemy didn't care who got hit—and destroyed his own allies to do it, you understand."

"More than enough reason to hold back on such an atrocity."

"Yes," Phil agreed. "It's exactly that—an atrocity. In legal terms, it could be called reckless endangerment."

"Are you well-acquainted with the law?"

"No. My deceased husband was an attorney, though. I picked up a few things from him."

"His parents are the ones arriving tomorrow?"

"Yes. They aren't particularly nice people—isolationists may be the politest term to use in describing them."

"Ah."

"Yeah. Bluff, bluster and bigotry, anyone?"

"That's what I like about your books," Dae-won turned a smile toward Phil.

"You've read them?"

"Your grandmother's, too. I enjoy reading. Reading in other languages builds my vocabulary. Studying is my primary objective during my first two centuries."

"What do you do for fun?" Phil asked.

"This and that. My favorite is skateboarding."

"I do inline skating," Phil said. "There are skateparks all over the area."

"I've never tried inline skating. Might I join you?"

"Sure," Phil shrugged. "We can go two or three times a week if you want. You'll need a pair of skates, though. One of the indoor rinks has a shop. We can go there."

"You will have guards when you go," Kwan insisted as he and Tae Yong walked through Phil's office door.

"Philomena says the projectiles were a product of ghost spells," Dae-won told Kwan. "Harmless enough in smaller pieces, but deadly when joined together."

"That—makes sense," Tae Yong sighed.

"I'll make the detection spells more sensitive," Phil leaned back in her chair and moved her head from side to side to relieve muscle aches.

"You have more guests," Xinnie arrived at the door. Behind her were Agents Park, Yoon and Choi. Behind them stood *sasin* Moon.

"We're not picky about our quarters," Agent Yoon said. "Agent Choi has been learning English recently."

"Philomena, what, exactly, is going on?" Xinnie frowned.

"When Ray gets back, I'll uh, tell you," Phil said. "In the meantime, see if you can find room for our new guests."

⚶

"I KNEW YOUR GRANDMOTHER WASN'T TELLING US EVERYTHING, BUT this is—out there," Ray shook his head in disbelief.

"Philomena is particularly talented," Kwan explained. "She didn't want to frighten you; you are her family."

"Are you sure you're a," Xinnie couldn't comfortably say the word *dragon* to Kwan's face.

"Yes. As is Dae-won, his mother and three of the guards," Kwan answered. "We also have *dokkaebi* with us."

"Goblins," Phil sighed. "They're on the good side," she added quickly. "Muki is a cavern elf. Also on the good side."

"Ignorance is bliss," Ray sighed and slapped his knee.

"We are still the same; only a few labels have changed," Kwan soothed. "Philomena has protected this area. You are safe here. From now on, we will make sure you are protected if you leave the island."

"All this—and just in time to deal with Paulson and Patricia," Xinnie moaned.

"Xinnie, you can go to the Seattle apartment. Talk things over with Muki if you want. They have plenty of good information to share if you'd like to hear it."

"But that means we need a guard to go," Ray said.

"I can get you there as soon as you pack a bag," Phil reassured him. "Let Muki arrange for food and necessities."

"Philomena, do they have protective shields?" Kwan asked.

"Yeah. I can make them more sensitive, just in case."

"We have what?" Xinnie blinked at Phil.

"It's a spell that's harmless to both of you," Phil replied. "If anybody tries to hurt either of you, well, they won't be successful, okay? Gran had one around you, too. I just improved on it when I got here."

"It doesn't work on verbal abuse, does it?" Ray snorted.

"Unfortunately not—that would be too noticeable," Phil said. "If you want to quit, I'll understand, but you're my family, just as Kwan said."

"Phil, we're not going to quit," Xinnie said decisively. "We just need time to digest this. Okay?"

"Okay. Go pack a few things. I'll call Muki."

"THERE ARE TWO BEDROOMS INSIDE RAY AND XINNIE'S SUITE; IF YOU don't mind sharing, you can use that space for the next week," Phil told Yoon, Park and Choi. Agent Choi spoke in Korean; *sasin* Moon nodded his agreement.

"Choi and Moon will share a room," Yoon translated.

"We'll get more beds brought in; there are at least two in storage inside the garage," Phil said. "We'll try to make this as comfortable as we can. After the week's up, we can probably use the media room as your new quarters. There's a full bath nearby, you'll just have to share or go to another one farther away."

"We will work this out," *sasin* Moon said.

"Awesome. Can any of you cook?"

"HUH?" PHIL BLINKED AS TAE YONG, A MUG OF COFFEE IN HIS HAND, supervised a massive cleaning explosion.

"Xinnie told me the regular cleaning was canceled, due to so many arriving simultaneously," he said. "Kwan allowed me use of his lair entrance. I asked for help from the palace servants."

"They're—really efficient," Phil gawked at the supernatural pace being maintained.

"When they learned it was for you, we had many volunteers. Jiah has given permission for them to come twice per week; this many people in the house will likely require more frequent cleanings."

"Yeah. Well, Dae-won wants to learn inline skating. We can go out on those days if we want."

"He has a youthful curiosity that I very much appreciate."

"Me, too."

"Will you show me how to use your espresso machine?"

"Sure."

"KWAN?" XINNIE CALLED OUT AFTER TAPPING ON THE SITTING ROOM door. Kwan, poring over loose parchment nestled inside a leather cover, looked up from his reading.

"Come in," Kwan said immediately.

"I just wanted to tell you something before Ray and I leave for the Seattle apartment," she said.

"Sit," Kwan indicated the chair opposite his.

Xinnie took the offered chair; she wore a look of deep concern.

"Tell me," Kwan said softly.

"Paulson and Patricia—don't ever call her Patty," Xinnie began. "Have you ever seen one of Phil's shaky days?"

"I have," Kwan acknowledged. "They drain her energy reserves, I think."

"That's exactly what happens," Xinnie agreed. "Paulson and Patricia drain her dry, along with getting on her last nerve. Phil has one of her daddy's denim shirts in her closet. It's more than three sizes too big and on the worst days, she wraps herself up in it and wears it everywhere. She always says it's like a hug from him, and it's a bit of comfort for her. Both her parents died at the wedding, while Paulson and Patricia are still alive and wearing down anybody who crosses their path."

"She should refuse the visit," Kwan growled.

"Easier said than done," Xinnie replied. "It's like trying to stop a speeding train when you're tied to the tracks."

"I'll let the others know," Kwan said.

"Make sure they're prepared for insults and rudeness, too. Paulson doesn't hold anything back."

"Let me think on this, then," Kwan said. "Thank you for telling me."

"Call me if there are problems," Xinnie told Kwan. "We can arrange for repairs or deliveries if needed."

"I'll keep that in mind."

"Thank you, Kwan. You have a calming influence on Phil, and

that's worth a lot more than you think. Ray says the same—that he hasn't seen her this steady since before the wedding, and she's actually eating regular meals."

"How do you think the visitors will take the news of our marriage?" Kwan thought to ask.

"Not well," Xinnie admitted. "Please don't let them drive you away."

"As if," Kwan snorted. "Perhaps I should ask my father to visit."

"As the new in-law? How tough is your father?"

"He is of the *heads will roll* variety," Kwan said.

"Maybe he ought to come, then. Well, I need to finish packing," Xinnie rose from her seat.

"Thank you for the information, Xinnie. We will deal with this crisis as best we can."

⚡

"PHILOMENA?" KWAN SETTLED ON THE EDGE OF THE BED. IT WAS after midnight, yet Phil was still awake and staring at the ceiling.

"Huh?" Phil turned toward him. "You just now coming to bed?"

"I had things to discuss with Tae Yong and the others. What time will your guests arrive tomorrow?"

"Their plane gets in around eleven in the morning. Give them another hour or so to get their bags and get here. At least I don't have to pick them up at the airport."

"Thank the skies," Kwan murmured. "Should we prepare lunch?"

"Probably. Be prepared to hear them complain about whatever it is —while they eat it."

"Will you lend them a vehicle?"

"They can use the compact SUV—the keys to the Mercedes are currently hidden in my safe."

"Good to know," Kwan said. "Time for sleep, Philomena. You need your strength for tomorrow."

"Fine. Just so you know, I put together a bleeping spell."

"Bleeping spell?"

"Yeah. If anything racist or derogatory comes out of Paulson's or Patricia's mouths, you'll hear the word noodle instead."

"Are you kidding?" Kwan's face was now inches from Phil's.

"No. It's a kind of trapping spell, but for certain words instead of people or things."

"What gave you that idea? Not that it isn't brilliant, but out of curiosity, you understand."

"Ray, plus the find and replace option on the computer."

"I love you, Philomena."

"Huh?" Phil's next words were drowned by Kwan's kiss. He put most of his mesmerizing skills to work with it. Phil was asleep before he drew his lips away from hers.

"I TOLD YOU TO PACK MY LEATHER JACKET, GAWD-DAMMIT," PAULSON yelled at Patricia the moment they exited the airport. The weather was cold and foggy, as it often was in the Seattle area.

"You did no such thing," Patricia sniped. "I packed every single thing you asked me to, and you never said leather jacket to me once. Philomena still has Trey's jacket—you can borrow it while you're here."

"That bitch should give it to me," Paulson muttered as they rolled their bags toward the taxi line.

"She should. I don't care if she did get it for his Christmas gift before the wedding; we got everything else back except that."

"She ought to be the dead one," Paulson muttered while the taxi driver placed his bag in the trunk.

"Well, it's too late for that. We should have smothered her while she was in the hospital." Patricia didn't attempt to lower her voice.

"Ma'am?" the taxi driver asked.

"Nothing. It's nothing," Patricia waved off the driver's concern. "Here's the address on Vashon Island." She handed a slip of paper to the driver before sliding onto the back seat beside Paulson.

"This will involve a ferry ride," the driver informed the Muirs. "It'll take about an hour to get there unless there's a long wait."

"Don't bother us with details," Paulson snapped. "We've been here before."

"Yes, sir."

"Damn right," Paulson cursed softly. The driver put the taxi in gear and pulled away from the curb.

"Their taxi just drove onto the island," Phil sighed. She and Kwan watched as Lee Min and two others put lunch together for everyone.

"Remember to be polite," Tae Yong walked into the kitchen and reminded the staff. "These two may offend intentionally; don't take the bait."

"Yeah, you got that right," Phil nodded in Tae Yong's direction. "They're not nice people unless you have more money and status than they do, and even then they're only nice to your face."

"Should I show them my bank account?" Kwan asked dryly.

"Please don't. *I* have more money than they do, and they still treat me like crap," Phil patted his arm. "Anybody connected to me will get the same treatment, guaranteed."

"Perhaps we can ensure that this will be their last visit?" Hwang walked into the kitchen, wearing an expensive suit and Italian leather shoes.

"If you can accomplish that, I'll owe you big time," Phil said.

"I believe the debt is mine to pay," Hwang sniffed. "I understand now why the Prince and my son have such faith in you. By the way, the trial of those we captured will be held by the High Council on Monday. Philomena, you have been added, along with Dae-won."

"We will be there, most certainly," Tae Yong dipped his head to Hwang.

"Get ready, they're here," Phil announced, while pulling the denim shirt she wore tighter about her.

"I'll get the door," Tae Yong strode out of the kitchen looking quite grim.

"Shall we?" Kwan offered Phil his arm.

"Will you hold me up if my knees buckle?" Phil asked.

"Most certainly."

"Awesome."

Hwang followed Kwan and Phil as they headed for the front door.

"WELCOME, MR. AND MRS. MUIR," TAE YONG HELD THE DOOR OPEN and dipped his head to Paulson and Patricia.

"Who the noodle are you?" were the first words out of Paulson's mouth. "Philomena," he glared at Phil, "what the noodling noodle are all these noodling noodle noodles doing in your house?"

Kwan bit his lip and ducked his head to suppress a snicker.

"I believe you are out of line, sir," Hwang stepped forward. "My daughter-in-law deserves better from former family."

"*Your* noodling daughter-in-law? What in the noodling noodle are you noodling talking about?"

"Married," Kwan held up his left hand, then lifted Phil's, to display their matching rings.

"Well, that stupid little noodle," Patricia shouted. "You can't get married again! You're disrespecting our son, you noodling noodle."

"I married a widow if you recall," Kwan's anger began to rise. "Now, we can either show you to your quarters, or show you the door. Which will it be?"

"It'll be a cold day in noodle before you ever put your gawd-noodled hands on either of us," Paulson shouted, making Phil cringe.

"That is enough," Hwang's voice rose to a near-roar.

"Philomena is kind enough to offer a place to stay," Tae Yong intervened. "But we will remove you, make no mistake, if you continue to insult her. We have orders to protect her and her new family. Unfortunately, you are not included in those orders."

"Then we want to stay in Philomena's suite," Patricia demanded.

"That will never happen," Kwan hissed. "You will stay in your assigned bedroom, or not at all."

"Lunch is ready," Lee Min rushed in to announce.

"Our food is being prepared by more noodling noodles?" Paulson roared.

"You're not obligated to eat here," Tae Yong said. "We will be happy to find a nice hotel for you elsewhere."

"Take our bags upstairs," Paulson shoved both his and Patricia's rolling suitcases toward Tae Yong. "We'll eat now, and it better be something good." Grabbing Patricia's hand, he hauled her toward the kitchen.

"Oh, sweet Jesus," Phil breathed as her knees buckled. Kwan kept her from falling.

CHAPTER 16

"I'd rather have a tuna sandwich, gawd-noodle-it," Paulson shoved his plate of chicken with mushrooms in wine sauce away.

"We will have one ready shortly," Lee Min gestured for one of the helpers to comply.

"You get one menu change," Hwang said. "After that, you get no food at all and the kitchen will be closed."

"Who the noodle left you in charge?" Paulson demanded.

"I am currently your host as Philomena is not feeling well and my son is tending to her. As you and your spouse are the reason for her illness, I suggest you no longer provoke us."

"If you try to throw us out, we're calling the cops," Patricia glared at Hwang.

"There's no need for that," Hwang smiled, allowing a bit of his dragon persona loose. "We will escort you off the property, and you will never be allowed entrance again."

"You can't do that, you noodling idiot," Paulson sneered. "Patricia, dial 9-1-1."

"I am so grateful for metal phone cases," Hwang's smile became toothier. Patricia's phone glowed in her hand—she shrieked in pain and dropped it on the table.

"I believe you have been dismissed, sir. Follow me," one of the dragon guards appeared beside Paulson's chair, while a second guard materialized beside Patricia's.

"You dropped this?" The guard next to Patricia's chair handed the now-cooled phone back to her. "Shall we?" He gestured for her to rise from her seat.

"We're not leaving, you noodling noodles," Paulson insisted.

"Take them out," Hwang shrugged to the guards. To the Muirs, he said, "You have no transportation, so you'll be forced to walk back to town. Good luck."

Paulson attempted to shove the guard next to him. The guard remained rock-still and stared into Paulson's eyes. "You will walk with me to the property line. You will not be allowed to return," the guard mesmerized Paulson Muir.

"You will do the same," Patricia's guard said, imprinting his will over hers.

Hwang watched as Paulson and Patricia marched toward the door, followed by both guards.

"I'll send their bags with them," Tae Yong smiled grimly. "It's a mile or two for them to walk. I hope they survive it."

"You should eat something, Philomena. Xinnie and Ray are on their way back and Tae Yong is supervising the repurposing of the media room for our agents and *sasin* Moon," Kwan soothed.

Phil had woken from a nightmare after Kwan put her to bed earlier. "I must say, your spell worked so well," he smiled down at her. "Also, we had Paulson and Patricia followed when they left the property; they got a taxi and are now headed for a downtown Seattle hotel. We will not be paying their expenses."

"They left?"

"They left. It only took a small bit of convincing. If Paulson isn't arrested or reprimanded for disturbing the peace or destruction of hotel property while he's here, I will be much surprised."

"He's on the list of several hotel chains that refuse to allow him to stay," Phil sighed. "They're really gone? That's almost a miracle. I really do owe your father."

"My father enjoyed himself and was happy to do this for us. As for your former in-law, Paulson Muir has bullied you for the last time—if I have anything to say about it," Kwan snorted. "I will also ensure that he is never welcome in South Korea."

"He'd probably fit right in with the leadership on the North side," Phil grumped.

"We won't talk about that. They're gone and we should eat something."

"All right. Can we take the elevator down?"

"If that's what you want."

"I do."

"THIS IS A GOOD IDEA," PHIL SAID WHEN KWAN TOOK HER THROUGH the media room later. "Cubicle dividers give them some sense of privacy."

"Xinnie and Ray arranged to have more beds delivered; we were short by two," Kwan said. "Tae Yong found the cubicle dividers at an office furniture warehouse. There are more in some of the shared bedrooms. They'll be easy enough to remove once they're no longer needed. Also, Xinnie said that she and Muki made peanut butter cookies for everyone; they and the cookies should arrive shortly."

"I love peanut butter cookies."

"I think that's why they made them. You look tired, Philomena. Shall we find a sofa and sit for a while?"

"Yeah."

Saturday morning arrived drenched in fog and mist. Phil stood at the front windows, a mug of coffee in her hands as she studied what little of the front yard she could see.

"Philomena?" Tae Yong came to stand beside her after making a cappuccino for himself.

"Good morning." Phil sipped her coffee.

"Is it often like this?" Tae Yong asked, peering through the windows at the fog outside.

"Yeah. I like it, but not everybody does. In South Texas right now, it'll be bright light and the sun heating up—that's how it is in April on the gulf coast."

"That is where you were born, as I recall."

"Corpus Christi," Phil nodded. "Gran, too, but she moved here when I was little. She and I were a lot alike."

"Did your mother have abilities?"

"Some. She never used them much. Gran always told me that not everybody is cut out to be a witch, even if they have the talent."

"Your grandmother must have been very wise."

"She was. I miss her—and my parents."

"Something is troubling you; I can feel it," Tae Yong sighed.

"I got an email from Paulson this morning. He sent a copy of the hospital bill for Patricia's burn treatment, says he's going to sue me, and demanded that I give him Trey's leather bomber jacket. I will bury that jacket with Trey before I'll ever give it to Paulson Muir."

"You may do whatever you want with the jacket; I will ask the attorney I have on retainer in New York to deal with Paulson Muir's threats," Kwan joined Phil and Tae Yong, carrying a cup of steaming coffee in his hands.

"Thank you," Phil hunched her shoulders. "I'm really not in the mood to deal with his tantrums today."

"You should never have to deal with that again," Kwan said, using his free hand to pull Phil against him. "Put it out of your mind. My father asked for a meeting this afternoon with the three of us plus Dae-won; it's to discuss the High Council hearing for Dal and his cronies on Monday."

"Okay. I was hoping to get some information on the procedures to follow," Phil admitted.

"We will answer all your questions," Tae Yong reassured her.

"I also want to see the prisoners again before we hold the hearing," Phil said. "In case any of them have low-level power emanations that I didn't think to look for earlier."

"That's—a frightening thought," Tae Yong blinked at Phil. "I will alert the Prince."

"Tell everybody to keep their distance, just in case," Phil agreed. "We don't need more assassination attempts."

"And if they have been made into living bombs?" Kwan thought to ask.

"It will make questioning them a big problem," Phil said. "Unless I can figure out how to deactivate what they have."

"Kwan, I will be using your lair entrance," Tae Yong said before striding away.

"Jiah must be informed," Kwan sighed, hugging Phil tighter.

"Yeah," Phil mumbled against his chest.

"HE'S A GUIDE," PHIL SAID WHEN XINNIE ASKED ABOUT *SASIN* MOON.

"He always wears that hat and black clothes when he goes outside?" Xinnie whispered, although *sasin* Moon had already left the house and couldn't hear her.

"He's a Korean guide; that's how they dress," Phil shrugged. "He likes drinking soju with the *dokkaebi* agents."

"Is that why there are so many bottles in the recycle?"

"Probably."

"I had a few drinks with them last night," Muki said, climbing onto a barstool at the island. "It was fun."

"Are you going to order in or go out tonight?" Xinnie asked Phil, changing the subject.

"Xinnie, this is the weekend; you shouldn't be worrying about the rest of us," Phil pretended to scold her.

"But what if Ray and I want to join you?"

"Well, that's different. Is there something calling your name?"

"Ray wants either Mexican or Chinese."

"Either of those would be good—or we could get both as takeout," Phil mused.

"How about we set it up on that gigantic dinner table you never use?" Xinnie grinned.

"Now there's a thought," Phil nodded. "In fact, we could throw in anything we like and serve it as a buffet."

"I'll order a whole cheesecake and some other stuff for dessert."

"You want to take point on that? I'll see about getting drinks and stuff," Phil offered.

"Yeah. Let's do this."

ꙅ

"Do you suppose they and the one behind them suspected I would assign this hearing to the High Council?" Jiah set his teacup down and blinked at Tae Yong.

"I'd say it's entirely possible—especially after the shooting incident in Busan. That, in my opinion, was a carefully planned trap for Philomena."

"Perhaps they were gauging whether she would be up to the task of dealing with their zombie after such a traumatic event, and how long it might take for her to accomplish it," Jiah nodded thoughtfully. "This does not bode well for us."

"I will discuss it with Kwan—I hope we can arrive at a solution for the future, so Philomena will not be debilitated for hours afterward."

"Yes. That is certainly a good idea. If a war is brewing, we will need her abilities."

"Time grows short, my Prince, before the hearing. We must plan carefully from now on."

"Agreed. Please keep me informed. How is Dae-won doing?"

"Better than expected. He has adapted well; he is becoming good friends with the cavern elf and Philomena."

"Good. Dae-won's mind is curious and quick; he will learn much from this experience. Also, if the cavern elf agrees, bring them with you on Monday."

"I will extend your invitation to Muki."

⚞

"WE'LL BE GETTING A MASSIVE DELIVERY AT THE GATE, THAT'S WHY," Phil explained to Kwan as she dropped another marble-sized Sun-sphere into the basket Kwan held. "Ray will be there, but if you want another guard, that's your decision to make. I don't want to overstep my authority."

"Philomena, they would be honored if you asked them," Kwan sighed. "How many spheres do you plan to make?"

"I did all the other spheres earlier—Earth, Air, Water and Tree, but the Sun spheres have to be made while the sun is shining."

"I see. There is a purpose for all these, I assume?"

"Yeah. There'll be enough for everybody to have a bracelet or a watchband made of them. It's just extra protection," Phil explained.

"Very well. I will ask the guards to accompany Ray to the gate for the food deliveries."

"I don't usually close the gate to the property, but things are different, now. I should have known Paulson would buy a gun here if he hadn't brought one with him."

"His mistake is in threatening you in another email. As for closing the gate and requiring a passcode and a guard, I would have advised it, had you not made that decision. Stop worrying; we will take every precaution from now on."

"That man has lost his mind, threatening somebody with violence in an email," Phil complained.

"My attorney has already turned the information over to the Seattle area authorities. No doubt, Paulson will be visited by the police at his hotel."

"If the hotel doesn't throw him out, first," Phil said. "Honestly, he should fly home now to avoid questioning."

"Paulson's screw-up is bad timing for everybody," Muki sauntered onto the boat dock where Kwan and Phil stood. They watched as Phil pulled more sunlight into her hands as if it were a corporeal substance, before shaping it into a ball. She then shrunk the ball of golden light into a small marble.

"I've only seen her do this once before," Muki whispered to Kwan.

"What did she do with the spheres?" Kwan expressed his curiosity.

"They're buried all along the property line—and around the adjoining property, too."

"Muki, do you want a bracelet or a watch band made from your spheres?" Phil dropped another sun sphere into Kwan's basket.

"Bracelet, please. I don't always wear a watch."

"Awesome."

"How much trouble is it to make a watchband?" Kwan asked.

"Not too much—I just need to flatten your spheres and join them together. They'll expand to fit over your hand and then contract to fit your wrist comfortably. For yours, your father's and Prince Jiah's, I'll make them look like multicolored dragon scales."

"Now I want a watchband," Muki sighed.

"How about I make your bracelet like that—flattening out the spheres and making it wide?"

"I'd love that."

"You got it. Here—that's the last one," Phil dropped another Sun sphere into the basket with a satisfying plink. "Now, to get all these put together before dinner."

"Want something to drink? I'll make a virgin piña colada for you," Muki offered.

"That actually sounds good," Phil agreed. "Let's go."

"I like this very much," Tae Yong admired the watchband Phil made for him. "The colors are lovely without being ostentatious. It's almost as if they reflect whatever I'm wearing."

"They come from nature, and that's how things should be—a balance between all things," Phil smiled at the *dokkaebi's* compliment.

"The gold that holds the other colors together—you say that's Sun magic?"

"Yes. It's like sunlight itself, flowing in, around, and often through other things. As for the other colors, blue is Water magic, green is Tree magic, "brown is Earth magic, and the white opal is Air magic."

"The Prince will be very pleased with his gift, I think."

"He's curious about which types of magic I control. Now, he'll know for sure," Phil said. "This isn't something I'd tell anyone, if it weren't necessary."

"That information will not go astray," Tae Yong promised.

"Thank you. I have a few things to do in my office before dinner; tell Xinnie to let me know if she needs help when the food arrives."

"I think we can handle those things easily. Do what you must; I'm sure Kwan will pull you away if you don't come for dinner promptly."

"Yeah. He's predictable like that," Phil agreed.

PHIL LOOKED UP FROM HER COMPUTER WHEN MUKI WALKED INTO HER study. "Phil, what are you planning, exactly?" Muki frowned at her.

"Shut the door; we need to talk," Phil sighed.

"I was afraid of that," Muki echoed Phil's sigh.

"HOW DOES ONE DRESS FOR PASSING JUDGMENT?" PHIL STUDIED THE contents of her closet after dinner; Kwan placed his arms around her from behind.

"You smell nice," Kwan kissed the curve where her neck and shoulder met. It was one of the things he loved to watch—the gentle slope from ear to shoulder as she moved about.

"I just got out of the shower," Phil mumbled. "You're not being helpful in picking out something to wear for the hearing."

"No jeans with rips or holes. No T-shirts with profanity or political slogans. No spaghetti-straps or midriffs showing. Sensible shoes with no open toes. It will be cool to cold inside the hearing chamber; depending on the outside weather, layering would be most prudent."

"Business casual?"

"That will do."

"Awesome."

"If you could leave that word behind, I would be grateful."

"I'll try."

"Thank you." Kwan kissed her neck again.

"When should we leave, local time?" Phil's breath hitched when Kwan kissed the sensitive spot beneath her ear.

"Tomorrow morning, due to the time difference. Plan to leave shortly after breakfast since you wish to see the prisoners before the hearing starts. Also, Jiah wants to see everyone in his study beforehand."

"Uh, okay." Kwan's fingers had wandered to the bottom of her T-shirt, making Phil's breaths erratic.

"I should have found you sooner," Kwan whispered in her ear. "If only I had known," he added, before turning her in his arms for a proper kiss.

Kwan, Philomena, Tae Yong's mental voice interrupted. *There is a situation between your ex in-laws and the police in Seattle.*

"HE HAS TWO HOSTAGES?" PHIL'S VOICE EXPRESSED INCREDULITY. SHE and Kwan sat before a detective's desk in downtown Seattle.

"We've just got off the phone with the Texas authorities," the detective sounded weary. "They informed Mr. Muir earlier today that they have two suspects in custody regarding the wedding massacre. Apparently, the suspects had a disagreement with Mr. Muir and were intent on murdering everyone at the wedding out of revenge. Unfortunately, they missed their main target and ended up killing many others instead."

"Oh, sweet Jesus," Phil closed her eyes and dipped her head backward. "Did they say how the suspects were arrested?"

"It was a second attempt at Mr. Muir; they broke into the Muir residence fully armed. Their daughter is at college out of state, so the house was empty. The alarm notified the police and they were captured running away from the property. The guns and rifles they had with them will be tested to see if they match the ones used in the massacre three years ago."

"So they didn't know Paulson was out of town," Kwan mused.

"It looks that way," the detective frowned and shook his head. "Now we've got a lunatic with two hostages at a hotel, waving a gun and screaming that none of this was his fault."

"As he's prone to do," Phil pulled her head upright with a sigh.

"He's also claiming that you threw him out of your house earlier," the detective leveled his gaze on Phil.

"We did; he was rude and threatening to all of us," Kwan said. "He was politely escorted to the gate afterward."

"Can you provide a statement?" the detective turned toward Kwan.

"Yes, as can my father; Paulson Muir upset Philomena so badly she became ill; my father stepped in to act as host and serve them lunch. We couldn't calm Mr. Muir down—he only wanted to insult and belittle the staff and everyone else in the house. The amount of profanity he employs exceeds the limits of most people, including sailors, I believe."

"That's—what we've discovered as well," the detective nodded. "What I need to ask next, Ms. Muir," he turned back to Phil, "is this; do you have any idea how to convince him to release the hostages and surrender?"

"Philomena does not do well when guns are present," Kwan's voice turned to steel. "If you think to place her at the scene to beg that man to surrender, I suggest you choose another way. She bears both physical and mental scars from gun violence."

"I supposed that makes sense," the detective nodded. "Is there any other way, then?" he asked Phil. "Can we offer something in exchange for the hostages, at least?"

Phil slumped in her chair, which alarmed Kwan.

"Trey's bomber jacket," Phil mumbled. "Kwan, ask Xinnie to get it out of my closet; she knows where it is. If Ray and Tae Yong can bring it—it might convince Paulson to let the hostages go."

"I will make the call," Kwan said, his voice stiff. "Excuse me." He rose from his chair and stalked away, pulling the cell phone from his pocket as he went.

"This jacket you're talking about—do you really believe," the detective began.

"Paulson wants it more than anything. It's the only thing I have left of my late husband," Phil's eyes were bright with unshed tears as she blinked at the detective. "He and his father wore the same size; Paulson's wanted that jacket ever since Trey died."

"This is hard for you, I can see that," the detective attempted to placate Phil. "But," he leaned back when Phil quickly held up a hand.

"Don't patronize me," Phil said. "I've heard every kind of sympathetic statement to my face and all the gossip behind my back for three years. I'm no longer willing to listen. If this upsets you, then I apologize. Let's just get this over with and send those hostages home to their families."

"Understood." The detective tapped his desk with a finger. "You're right—that's the main objective."

"Xinnie, Ray and Tae Yong are on the way," Kwan returned and sat beside Phil. "Xinnie is in tears but refuses to stay home."

"I knew she wouldn't," Phil leaned forward and covered her face with both hands.

"I'll send an escort to the ferry landing," the detective rose from his desk. "If you need coffee or anything else, just let one of the officers know."

"Leave it to Paulson to screw everything up at the worst possible moment," Phil said, sitting up and looking at Kwan. "If we get any sleep tonight, it'll be a miracle."

"I was thinking the same," Kwan admitted.

"Do they have the suspects' names?" she thought to ask.

"Let me check," Kwan pulled out his phone. "Ah—it appears that the names have been withheld from the public for now."

"Too bad," Phil muttered. "I can't place a curse if I don't have a name."

"You have Paulson's name."

"Huh?" Phil jerked at Kwan's words. "I was kidding. I don't do that kind of thing."

"That makes sense—you could have dealt with Mr. Muir long ago," Kwan leaned back in his seat with a weary sigh.

"That's what I'm saying. Even if I could place a curse, I wouldn't. That's dark magic and its path leads to chaos. Definitely something to stay away from."

"Philomena?" Kwan turned his gaze toward the ceiling. "Are we fighting against dark magic now?"

"Kwan, don't say those words out loud."

Kwan was out of his chair and on his feet quickly. "I will return in a moment." He stalked toward the door.

"Sweet Jesus," Phil sighed.

How do you think it's possible? Jiah asked.

No idea, and I don't fully understand it anyway. Since you've studied the subject, I was hoping you'd know more, Kwan replied.

There is very little I've come across in the library concerning dark magic, Jiah admitted. *I don't know the source of it, either. Philomena pulls energy from natural sources to construct her spells. Would dark magic also come from those sources?*

I didn't get that idea, Kwan admitted. *When she spoke of dark magic, I scented her unease with the subject.*

Perhaps there is something that we're missing? Jiah speculated.

I am certain of it.

How do we find it, then?

No idea.

Aish. How did we come to this? Jiah moaned.

Do you suppose Dal can answer our questions?
We can hope.

"THE OFFICERS TOOK THE JACKET AFTER WE GOT OFF THE FERRY," Xinnie admitted, her arms wrapped around Phil at the police station. "They should be at the scene already, I think."

"Trey's jacket—it's gone from us, now," Phil sniffled against Xinnie's shoulder.

"I know. Trey was a good man. We won't ever forget that."

"He should still be here. There's no justice in this for him."

"I know," Xinnie patted Phil's back. "Don't let them keep hurting you, Phil. If they can still hurt you, they're winning. Don't let them win."

"You're right." Phil pulled away and wiped moisture from her cheeks. "Is Kwan back, yet?"

"Not yet," Ray spoke from behind. "He's with Tae Yong outside."

"Do we know how the negotiations are going?" Phil turned in her seat to ask Ray.

"They're not telling us anything at this point," Ray admitted.

"They should let us take Phil home, then," Xinnie grumped.

"You can take her home," the detective strode into his cubicle. "Paulson Muir was captured shortly after he put on the jacket. He'll be booked into the jail soon enough. If we have further questions, I'll contact you."

"Thank goodness," Xinnie muttered. "Phil, grab your purse and jacket; we'll leave right now."

"Do you want the jacket back?" the detective asked as Phil gathered her things.

"Not after Paulson Muir's had his hands on it," Phil shook her head. "It lost its magic the moment he touched it."

"WILL YOU BE ABLE TO SLEEP, PHILOMENA?" KWAN ASKED AS SHE SAT on the edge of her bed.

"I hope so; I don't need to be awake much longer if I want to stay alert for the hearing."

"Shall I help you sleep?"

"If you would."

"Then lie down beside me and get comfortable."

"Okay." Phil flopped her head onto the pillow and wriggled her body to find a comfortable spot.

"Hold on," Kwan's hand appeared before her face.

"Huh?"

"This," he leaned in to kiss her.

She was asleep when he pulled away.

CHAPTER 17

"Coffee," Phil mumbled as she shuffled into the kitchen around nine Sunday morning.

"Coffee and an omelet," Lee Min corrected, setting a freshly brewed mug on the island. "Please, sit. Food will be ready soon."

Two of Lee Min's associates bustled about the kitchen, preparing food.

"Am I the last to get up?" Phil frowned.

"No," Tae Yong arrived and took the seat next to hers. "I am last. I waited until Paulson Muir was safely ensconced in a cell last night. Also, Patricia was arrested for assaulting a police officer."

"Sounds about right," Phil nodded. "Did you get any rest at all?"

"I did—enough to get through the day," Tae Yong accepted his mug of coffee from Lee Min and drank.

"I hope I make it through the day, and I got more sleep than you did."

"Your outfit is appropriate for the hearing," Tae Yong smiled. "Although I've never seen you wear bracelets before."

Phil wore matching bracelets on both wrists, which bore red, orange, yellow, white and blue stones. The jewelry stood out against the black pants and black cashmere turtleneck she wore.

"I don't normally," Phil shrugged. Lee Min set plates of food on the bar and dipped his head to both. "I just wanted to lighten up the outfit a little," she continued after thanking Lee Min and the others. "The earrings match the bracelets, too."

"Good job," Tae Yong cut into his omelet.

"Yeah."

"I just need to brush my teeth before we go," Phil told Kwan, who was doing his best to rush her without being obvious about it.

"The Prince is waiting, Philomena."

"I know, but I don't want to see him if I have egg in my teeth and bad breath."

"Fine. Brush thoroughly, then."

"Thank you."

Five minutes later, Phil was pulled toward Kwan's lair entrance in her sitting room; the others had already gone through with Hwang, who'd arrived to assist. She'd offered to transport everyone, but Kwan and his father insisted on using the lair entrance.

"Wrap your arms around my neck and hold onto me tightly, Philomena," Kwan instructed. "I will shield you from the shock as much as I can."

Phil drew a shuddering breath after wrapping her arms around Kwan's neck, as he'd asked.

"Don't worry; I'm right here," Kwan breathed against her ear before pulling them both into the lair entrance.

"I just need a quick walk past their cells," Phil explained to Jiah. "And someone who's willing to go with me."

"Tae Yong and I will go," Kwan spoke quickly.

"Very well. Philomena, I ask that you keep yourself and your escorts safe; both have their own defenses, I know, but you can provide extra if necessary," Jiah commanded.

"We will be safe enough on this short journey," Phil dipped her head to the Prince. "I merely need to sharpen my spell detection skills."

"Very well. Go and return quickly," Jiah said.

DAL, HIS LONG FINGERS WRAPPED AROUND THE BARS OF HIS CELL, glared as Phil, Tae Yong and Kwan walked past. He remained silent, although his eyes and expression displayed hate and anger. Sung-hoon in the cell opposite Dal's, wasn't as circumspect.

"You'll pay for this," he hissed, shoving his body against the metal bars of his cage. "All of you will pay for this."

"My father sends his regards and wants you to know he's always found your pettiness a complete bore," Kwan replied.

"Bastard!" Sung-hoon shouted as he threw himself against the bars a second time.

"My lineage is proven," Kwan sniffed and walked away.

The remaining prisoners refused to speak as Phil walked past their cells. Some pretended to be asleep; others sat against the wall or in a corner, glaring at the spectators as they passed.

Have you noticed anything different? Kwan sent a mental question to Phil.

Difficult to tell, Phil replied. *Let's see what they have to say at the hearing.*

Very well. Take us to Jiah's study.

THE THREE DRAGON MEMBERS OF THE HIGH COUNCIL THAT PHIL hadn't met were waiting in Jiah's study when she, Kwan and Tae Yong returned from the dungeon. She studied each carefully, searching for hidden spells or anything else that could prove them untrustworthy.

Finding nothing out of the ordinary, she bowed as each was introduced. Dae-won sidled up to her after the introductions.

Did you find anything? he asked.

Nothing to speak of at the moment, she responded.

Good. Tae Yong says this could take hours. I hope we can get through this; Mother will worry the entire time.

All mothers do that I think, no matter what.

I wish my father were still alive; I'd appreciate his patient advice at this time.

Same here, Phil admitted.

What was your father's occupation?

He was a judge, Phil said. *And a good one.*

My father retired as a prosecutor.

Fist bump? Phil held up a hand. Dae-won bumped his knuckles against hers while giving her a grin.

"Fighting," Dae-won said, pulling his fist up.

"Fighting," Phil echoed his action and encouragement.

"Shall we go to the hearing chamber?" Tae Yong asked after coming to a stop beside Phil and Dae-won.

"May as well," Phil sighed. "Lead the way, friend."

THE HEARING CHAMBER WAS UNDERGROUND, MASSIVE, AND NOT FAR from the holding cells. Phil found herself seated between Kwan and Hwang, and not far from Jiah's seat at the center of the massive, U-shaped table.

Dae-won and Tae Yong sat on either side of Jiah; the remaining High Council members sat together opposite Phil and Kwan, talking quietly among themselves.

Beyond the table lay a large, well-lit circle of light; Phil knew it was designed to hold prisoners of any kind. Some sort of ancient magic formed the spell, which fascinated Phil as she examined it carefully.

"What's directly above this space?" Phil asked.

"Kitchens and servants' quarters," Hwang replied. "Why do you ask?"

"Just curious," Phil shrugged. "I still don't have my bearings because the palace is so big."

"They're bringing in the first three," Kwan whispered, pulling Phil's attention to the massive double doors leading into the hearing chamber.

Dal was with two others, his head down and anger vibrating in every cell as he was propelled to the circle of light by four guards.

The same scenario occurred three more times, until all twelve prisoners were bathed in spelled light.

Phil, we're okay to go, Muki sent telepathically.

Go now, she replied, as the cavern and the palace above it exploded in a reality-shattering, light-bending cloud of fire and debris.

"YOU'RE INSIDE AN ABANDONED MISSILE SILO IN TEXAS," MUKI attempted to calm Kwan, Hwang and Jiah. All three were in dragon form; Hwang's red dragon clung easily to the curved ceiling of the man-made cavern into which they'd been forcibly transported.

Jiah's gold dragon had been shoved behind Kwan's red-scaled persona as he hissed and spit at Muki.

Behind them, Dae-won, many dragon guards and *dokkaebi* servants stood, waiting for orders from the Dragon Prince.

"Exxplain quicklee, cavern elf," Hwang's claws ticked against concrete as he made his way to the floor.

"The one controlling all the prisoners planned this," Muki began. "Phil expected an attack; right now, the enemy thinks you're all dead."

"We will disabuse him of that notion," Kwan snapped, regaining his human appearance. "Where can we find him?"

"That's what Phil is doing right now. We can't get a location any other way—or an identity any other way. This silo has been modified to hold everybody, and there are enough supplies here to feed all of us for at least a week. This is the entrance; it was left this way to fool the curious. If you'll follow me, I can get us past the door and into the living quarters."

"I will have a discussion with Philomena," Kwan growled.

"Don't distract her right now; she may be following a difficult trail. If you want results, then leave her be," Muki warned. "Come with me; the living area is much more comfortable than this."

"Lead the way, then, cavern elf," Jiah straightened his robes after turning human. "I want a full explanation and quickly."

Muki led a whispering crowd toward the concrete wall at the back of the tunnel. Once there, they placed their hand on the wall, which morphed into massive, steel-and-titanium doors.

Tapping a keypad which was also revealed, Muki stood back while the heavy doors opened outward.

"Go inside quickly; it's climate controlled and we're well-hidden," Muki instructed. "We can have a conversation and tea at the same time."

"ALL THE LAIR ENTRANCES ARE NOW BLOCKED," MUKI TOLD JIAH, who'd asked the obvious question first. "Your palace, understandably, no longer exists."

"What happened to the prisoners?" Hwang demanded.

"Dead, just as their master intended them to be."

"I thought Sung-hoon had plotted against us," Jiah set his cup of tea on the table.

"He's just a cog in the wheel, I believe," Muki responded. "Perhaps an important cog, but an expendable one, as you've seen for yourself."

"Who could possibly be forming such an elaborate plot?" Jiah turned to Hwang.

"That's what Phil wants to know. She thinks the main perpetrator won't be able to stop himself from visiting the palace ruins to gloat. If that happens, she intends to follow him afterward."

"What?" Kwan exploded off the chair he occupied.

"Dragon, please sit," Muki begged. "Phil is more than careful. She only wants to gather information and put puzzle pieces together. My only concern is how long this will take."

"What if the perpetrator fails to take the bait?" Hwang asked.

"Then at least we're alive, eh?" Muki answered. "We were all targets, and without Phil's intervention, we could all be dead. Call this being proactive, if you will."

Tae Yong, who hadn't said anything during the exchange, nodded thoughtfully. "It could have been another trap, my Prince," he told Jiah. "One to test our ability to deflect and respond to the enemy's attacks. Tell me," he turned to Muki, "did Philomena arrange to leave evidence behind of our deaths?"

"She ah, did," Muki sighed. "The enemy would have to be more powerful at deception than she is to believe otherwise."

"How did we end up here—all of us together?" Dae-won asked.

"The bracelets and watchbands that she made for all of us got those of us at ground zero out of the cavern beneath the palace. Carefully-laid spells sent us here once the spheres were activated. Those were formed by natural sources, so no evidence of our exit was left behind."

"Cunning," Dae-won nodded thoughtfully.

"She should have told us," Kwan complained.

"That was a risk," Muki replied. "If I were you, I'd check on the others brought here to see if anyone is missing. Only those who support the Prince would be carried away."

"I'll do that now," Tae Yong rose from his seat and walked out of the makeshift meeting room.

Minutes later, he reported telepathically to the others. *Two of the other three High Council members are missing, along with three lower-level guards. All dokkaebi are accounted for. All of them ask when Philomena will return.*

"How did she accomplish this?" Dae-won mused.

"Her magic may be able to differentiate, where we could not," Hwang leaned back in his seat with a deep sigh. "I wish to speak with her about this and soon."

"As do I," Jiah agreed, examining the watchband on his wrist with renewed interest. "Is the magic in this still active?" He asked Muki.

"Until she deactivates it," Muki replied.

"My concern is with the apparent spies in our midst," Kwan muttered. "And how much information was transmitted to the enemy."

"Clearly, their intention was to report on our strengths and weaknesses, before attacking us while we were together," Jiah said. "I wonder whether the debacle at my birthday celebration was meant as a test or was a real attempt at killing us then."

"There's something else about this recent attack, as opposed to the previous one," Muki said.

"What is that?" Hwang asked.

"You were shielded from the sounds of gunshots before you were pulled away," Muki explained.

"We were fired upon?"

"Yes, although I could not determine the source or direction. One of Phil's last spells before the prisoners were led in was to change the sound of gunshots to that of handbells ringing. She did it to keep her mind clear in the face of danger."

"Her defense against Paulson Muir also helped with her gunfire phobia," Kwan pinched the bridge of his nose. "I hope this spell remains active in the future."

"We have to trust her, now. We're safe, and that is likely a great relief to her," Muki responded.

"Besides sitting and waiting, is there anything we can do?" Hwang asked.

"I have already contacted Ray and Xinnie. Dae-won, your mother is fine and knows you're safe."

"Thanks," Dae-won began, before he was rendered speechless by the electronic tablet that clattered onto the table out of nowhere.

"We have our first message," Muki said, reaching for the device.

"How is Guk still alive?" Hwang slapped a hand on the table, making the wood shiver beneath his strength. He and the others watched the recorded video for the tenth time, unable to believe what they were seeing.

"This is the one who killed your father, uncle and brother?" Muki asked Jiah, whose rage was evident as he watched the video with the others.

"The same," Hwang growled. "How can he not be dead? The guards killed him and dumped the body."

"Apparently, he had help," Kwan huffed. "My guess is that the one who helped him then is also the one helping him now."

"You know he was angry at your father for disallowing the ritual," Tae Yong kept his voice even and his words reasonable.

"The ritual?" Dae-won breathed. "The one where," his eyes widened in sudden realization.

"Yes. He asked for dragon immortality for his familiar. After much questioning, Father denied the request," Jiah said. "The familiar in question had—issues."

"She was also a witch, although her talents weren't as formidable as Guk would have everyone believe," Hwang said. "I was at your father's side when he made the determination," he directed his words at Jiah.

"That was centuries ago," Tae Yong observed. "She would be long dead," he stopped short. "Do you suppose?" he blinked at Hwang.

"There are several possibilities, none of which I like," Hwang said. "A *dalgyal gwishin* is the simplest explanation—but fails to cover much of what we've seen so far."

"How can a dead spirit, no matter how powerful, control that many other spirits?" Tae Yong asked.

"Perhaps we should consult *sasin* Moon," Kwan suggested. "He may know something."

"I'd like to hear his opinion," Dae-won nodded. "But what are some of the other possibilities?"

"Dragon blood," Hwang shrugged. "It will give certain humans an extended lifespan."

"There is also another option, more frightening than that, even," Jiah shook his head. "It is difficult to contemplate, and even more difficult to achieve."

"Guk would never allow anyone to stand in the way of something he wanted," Hwang noted dryly.

"He had no knowledge of the ritual," Jiah began.

"He had access to your father's library, through those who proved disloyal," Kwan frowned at Jiah. "We merely assumed that your father's, uncle's and brother's deaths were the only things Guk wanted. We could be very wrong."

"Still, unless royal blood is employed," Hwang argued.

"What if it was—but not from a living royal?" Tae Yong had gone still as he contemplated the possibilities.

"This could be very bad," Jiah rose to his feet, his face turning pale as he considered Tae Yong's suggestion.

"What, exactly, would that mean?" Dae-won whispered.

"Pretty much the worst thing you can imagine," Phil appeared, dropping another tablet onto the table. "This is really, really bad."

CHAPTER 18

"I had to put a spell on the tablet to get the recording; the witch has everything else blocked," Phil sipped the glass of juice she'd been given.

"Her other spells were tied to spirits of the dead," Tae Yong said. "How has she tied herself to living specimens?"

Hwang, Jiah and Kwan were studying the images recorded on the tablet while Phil answered Tae Yong and Dae-won's questions.

"I can't say for certain, but I think the only people she will allow to live are those with a witch's talent of some kind," Phil said. "My theory is this; that she gained a half-life with the help of the black dragon who is with her, and now wishes to become a dark magic soul witch by gathering as many to her as she can find who have the slightest touch of power. You can see how many people she's tied to herself. They've been taken over, body and soul, to provide the witch with power. This is the blackest of black magic."

"If my library were still intact, I could find her name in the archives," Jiah lamented. "Alas, it is now gone forever."

"Huh?" Phil frowned at him.

"You sent us photographs of the smoking ruin of it," Hwang sniffed. "Of course it is gone."

"You guys, you guys, you guys," Phil rubbed her forehead. "Remember Dal's daggers?"

"What about them?" Jiah demanded.

"Remember when I told you that anything I dematerialize I can rematerialize?"

"You saved my library?" Jiah's voice held hushed reverence.

"I saved your palace and everything in it," Phil shrugged. "I can put your library inside this bunker if you want. I don't think rematerializing the entire palace here is a good idea, though. Texas charges a lot in property taxes."

"Then the destruction of the palace was faked?" Tae Yong's eyes shone with admiration.

"Yeah. I guess you could say that. I'll put your library in here, but I need to rest and eat, first," Phil told Jiah.

"Take as long as you need," Jiah waved a hand. "You must be exhausted."

"She used Earth, Air, Water, Tree and Sun magic," Jiah tapped his watchband. "There are only two other magics. There is no record of a Soul Witch commanding this many talents."

"You haven't been paying attention," Muki set their drink on the table and climbed onto a sofa inside the silo's common room.

"What do you mean?" Jiah asked.

"The other two magics are Fire and Moon magic," Muki said. "We wore all the others; Phil herself wore Fire and Moon. Fire magic made the destruction of your palace appear authentic."

"I—am at a loss for words."

"It's the first time I've seen her use Fire magic," Muki shrugged. "I know she's used it in the past, but I've never seen it firsthand until now. In the wrong hands, it's too unpredictable to use. I think she tied it to Moon magic to keep it under control."

"How?"

"It's just a theory, but Moon magic has phases, from full brightness to darkness. That, applied to Fire, can allow full effect to no effect, I think."

"Interesting. I'd like to ask her about it sometime."

"Save it for later—she's kept all this hidden for a reason," Muki said. "For now, my questions concern the self-made Soul Witch—which is an oxymoron in this case. None of the souls she employs were willing."

"That certainly clarifies the situation."

"I'm sure Phil has already calculated the number of deaths attributed to this pair. She'll agonize over every one of those lives, including the ones tied to the black magic witch now. There may not be a way to save any of them."

"Philomena will be forced to deal with that one; Guk's life is owed to me and my kin."

"He may have dark spells wound about him; are you prepared to deal with those?"

"I hope Philomena can provide protection against whatever he has."

"That's my hope, too."

"For six centuries, Guk has survived without our knowing. More than two centuries ago, that bastard arranged to disable my dearest friend who is also First Heir. We must move swiftly to counteract what he has had centuries to plan," Jiah cursed.

"If Phil hadn't intercepted Kwan and removed the dagger," Muki shook their head.

"We'd be dead," Jiah stated flatly.

"I WANT TO HOLD YOU AND SCOLD YOU AT THE SAME TIME." KWAN, lying face-to-face with Phil on their bed, gently pulled a stray lock of hair away from her face. She slept deeply, thanks to his mesmerizing skills. "The scolding will wait," he decided. "I'll be here beside you, my love."

Kwan? Jiah's voice sounded inside his mind. *Where are you?*

With Philomena at the Vashon Island house. She sleeps better on her own bed.

When she wakes, let us know. I'd like a dinner meeting.

I believe that can be arranged.

⚘

"They're on the North side of Korea," Phil told Jiah, when he asked where Guk and his dark witch were.

"Why take the time and trouble to import slaves to the South, then?" Hwang asked.

"I believe they were waiting for their opposition to appear," Phil replied. "Plus, the people they imported had likely been drained of their essence long ago by our dark witch. Consider them walking dead, transported to the South to die. Their souls were tied to the objects we found—which were then left as traps to cause problems for us and assess my skills at the same time."

"Now that they believe we're dead, what are their plans?" Jiah asked.

"I'm waiting to see exactly that," Phil replied. "I hope they start out small, to give us an idea of what they intend. After all, they should be cautious as there are still dragons out there who could rise against them."

"True enough," Kwan sighed. "They must realize that not all of dragonkind will align with their nefarious goals."

"What can we do in the interim?" Tae Yong asked.

"I think we should find Guk's lair," Phil said simply.

"Yes," Hwang hissed, turning toward Jiah. "His seat of power will be there."

"How do we find it?" Kwan interjected. "He's hidden it for six centuries, and his witch has probably placed so many shields about it, we can't find it through ordinary means."

"I think I may be able to help," Muki cleared their throat. "I must make a trip to the Andes, however, to convince others of my kind to join the hunt."

Philomena, I love you, Kwan sent. *For making friends with a cavern elf, along with many other reasons.*

Gran recruited Muki, Phil reminded him.

Yes, but Muki loves you.

I love them, too.

"Are you strong enough to rematerialize my library?" Jiah asked.

"Yes. Everybody needs to clear out of this room, first; I don't want any stray books or objects falling on you."

"We'll go now," Jiah declared and strode toward the doorway. The others fell in line behind the Prince and followed him out.

Lifting her arms, Phil employed Tree, Sun and Moon magic to rematerialize Jiah's massive library. Even the smallest motes of dust appeared, just as they'd existed before. Phil dropped onto one of Jiah's reading chairs with a sigh as she surveyed her work.

If this war is lost, this will survive, she thought. *If I die, the spells on this library will hide it until Jiah or one of his heirs comes to claim it.*

It's done, she mentally informed Jiah and Kwan.

"It feels so different—without the walls," Jiah breathed as he took in the shelves, tables and furniture from his library.

"The palace itself is a separate spell," Phil told him. "It would be more difficult separating one part of it from the rest."

"Don't concern yourself; I find this miraculous," Jiah said.

"I'll be on my way," Muki announced. "I have a meeting with the elders."

"Do you need anything before you go?" Phil asked.

"Just a hug. I have my own way of getting there. I'll be back with an answer soon."

"I want a hug, too," Phil held her arms open. Muki went to Phil; their hug lasted for nearly a minute before they parted.

"Take care," Phil cautioned.

"Always," Muki grinned and disappeared.

"I see I must do research on cavern elves," Jiah sighed.

"I wish to work with you, with your permission," Dae-won nodded.

"Of course."

"Ask Muki. They have as much information as you might want," Phil said. "They're a walking library."

"I find this fascinating," Hwang observed. "Does anyone have thoughts on how we bring down Guk and his witch, once we find his lair?"

"I'm thinking about it," Phil said. "But I have some questions first, about lairs and what, exactly, they might contain."

"Most lairs contain treasure and priceless collections of art, as a beginning," Hwang replied.

"But we have no idea what Guk's lair contains, do we?" Phil turned from Hwang to Jiah and then to Kwan and Tae Yong. "It could be filled to the brim with spelled objects and traps. He and his black witch have had six centuries to do exactly that."

"Ah, this is untenable," Hwang's forehead creased in a deep frown.

"I'm hoping Muki and their people can give us better information," Phil said. "I can give protection spells to the searchers if their elders agree to help us. If you need a bargaining chip, open your library to them."

"But," Hwang began.

"Do you think they'll choose to use the information against you?" Phil asked. "I suggest otherwise. Information is more valuable than gold to them, and any secrets they find will be hidden and treasured better than gems and precious metals."

"Are you saying that even if the Prince's library is destroyed, the cavern elves will hold that information within themselves?" Dae-won asked, wonder in his voice.

"Yes," Phil smiled at him. "That's exactly what I'm saying. Muki has held my information close to their heart for three years."

"I will think on this if they ask," Jiah sighed.

"If I were you, and should you choose to share, then make it an exchange," Phil offered. "Use them as a card index. They'll know where any bit of information is stored, so you can put your hands on it easily."

"I hadn't thought about that," Jiah's eyes lit up. "That would certainly be of great help to me."

"And to your heirs," Hwang observed. "Perhaps one or two cavern elves could be assigned as librarians?"

"That goes without saying," Jiah chuckled.

TWO DAYS LATER, MUKI RETURNED WITH AN OFFER FROM THEIR elders; in exchange for the knowledge contained in the Prince's library, they and others would search for Guk's lair.

"I accept," Jiah said immediately.

"Phil guessed right, didn't she?" Muki grinned.

"Yes," Jiah laughed. "I've had two days to consider, and that's my answer."

"I'll relay your answer. I must warn you; there may be a swarm of elders arriving quickly while the library is this close."

"I hadn't thought about the distance," Hwang observed. "That makes sense."

"Perhaps we should leave it here until they're finished with it," Tae Yong suggested.

"How long do you suppose that will take?" Jiah asked. "If my palace is returned to its original location, I will feel the emptiness where the library should be."

"It is similar to his lair," Hwang offered. "Every piece a dragon collects becomes a part of him in some way."

"Let me work on that while we're waiting for the cavern elves to find Guk's lair," Phil said. "In the meantime, would you like to visit Vashon Island, Prince Jiah? Xinnie is making lasagna."

"I LIKE THIS VERY MUCH," JIAH STOOD OUTSIDE PHIL'S HOUSE AND took in the view. The day was clear enough that he could see Mount Ranier in the distance. "Still an active volcano—I can feel its presence."

"As can I," Kwan asserted. "I haven't been this close to a volcano since I last flew over Paektu."

"Paektu?" Phil blinked at Kwan.

"The volcanic mountain on the border between North Korea and China," Kwan explained. "It's sacred to Northern leadership—it's where they believe their country originated."

"Is that the one involving a ride on a white horse?" Phil frowned at Kwan.

"That would be the same one," Jiah acknowledged. "Only it means far more to dragonkind, and for far longer."

"Back in the times before dragons chose to shape themselves into humans," Hwang sighed.

"Huh?" Phil gave Hwang a puzzled look.

"Long ago, dragons were dragons and humans were humans only." Jiah clasped his hands behind his back while taking in the evening sunset reflected on the water surrounding Vashon Island. "That was the way things were—until human populations began to overtake suitable breeding grounds. Dragons were in danger of extinction, as a result."

"The solution to the problem is a great secret, known only to the Dragon King's heirs," Hwang interrupted. "Suffice it to say, that era of our existence ended, and dragonkind was reborn when Mount Paektu erupted more than a thousand years ago."

"So it was sacred to the dragons first?" Phil asked.

"You could say that, yes," Jiah agreed.

"I learned something new, today," Phil stretched in the fading sunlight. "Is anyone else thirsty? I need a glass of water."

"You're learning this faster than I did," Phil smiled at Dae-won when they stopped skating the following morning. "I fell a lot when I first started."

"We have a very good sense of balance," Dae-won replied. "I like this very much. Will you teach me the spins and other moves?"

"Yep. Whenever you're ready, we can work on those things."

"How long do you think it will take for Muki and the others to find what they're looking for?" Dae-won took a seat to remove his skates.

"It depends on how far they have to go, and what kind of precautions need to be taken. They can feel irregularities in the earth itself—anything that isn't natural will draw their attention, but it's necessary to be within a certain distance to make an accurate determination of what it is they're sensing."

"Will they be vulnerable to traps set by Guk and his witch?"

"They've dealt with all kinds of spells—objects and other things, too, in the past. I gave Muki a few spelled spheres to help detect low-energy spells. That's what fooled us at the Prince's birthday celebration."

"Good thinking." Dae-won shoved his skates into the backpack he'd brought with him. "Are you hungry?"

"Maybe a little. How do you feel about Chinese?"

"I would love that," Dae-won grinned.

"Let's go."

We've found three former lairs so far that have Guk's lingering vibrations, Muki informed Phil.

I didn't consider that—that he'd move around, but it makes sense in retrospect. He'd be forced to hide himself and his messed-up lover. After a while, even a low-level person or creature with power will detect the wrongness.

Exactly—all three locations drew our attention. We wonder how many times he may have moved in the past six centuries.

I get that, Phil agreed. *Have you gotten any idea yet how long he may have stayed at the ones you've found?*

That is under discussion. We will let you know if a consensus is reached.

Okay. Thanks for the info. Let me know if you need anything.

We will. Muki withdrew from Phil's consciousness.

"Muki?" Kwan's arms dropped around Phil's shoulders from behind.

"Yeah. They've found three of Guk's former lairs. They're trying to determine how long he may have stayed at each location, but they haven't finished discussing it yet."

"Philomena, I can feel the tension in your body," Kwan breathed against her neck before kissing a sensitive spot.

"I'm trying to keep it from leaking out and upsetting everybody," Phil sighed. "You have no idea how much I'd like to get this over with."

"Jiah says the same; often, waiting is the worst part of any experience."

"Yeah." Phil leaned back against Kwan, surprising him in her willingness to allow him to bear part of her weight.

His arms tightened around her. "That's right," he breathed against her ear. "Let me help."

"Thank you," Phil breathed. "I feel so stressed."

"I know. Let it go for now, my love." Kwan allowed a thread of his mesmerizing skill to infiltrate his words. "Just relax. I will never allow you to fall."

Phil became boneless in his arms. Just as he promised, Kwan lifted her in his arms and carried her toward their suite.

MUKI'S FACE WAS PALER THAN USUAL AS HE AND THE FIVE WHO'D COME with them shared information on what they'd discovered.

Not just a lair; level upon level of lairs, built into a series of volcanic vents in Mount Paektu. All the lairs were filled to the brim with spelled objects, coins, gold, silver, gemstones and priceless items stolen throughout Guk's history, which spanned millennia.

This dragon and his perverted witch have planned this carefully, the eldest among the cavern elves observed silently.

The stench of her permeates all of it, Muki complained.

As the scent of death permeates any dwelling if left too long. This is an evil against nature itself, the elder confirmed. *Will your friend be able to deal with all of it?*

We must tell her what we've found and let her decide, Muki replied.

We see your worry and misgivings, the elder responded.

If this can be destroyed, will anyone near it survive? Muki closed their eyes and shuddered.

Doubtful, the elder sighed. *We have heard from those studying the Dragon Prince's library. The prophecy gives little hope. We are debating whether to release that information to the Prince and his heirs, in addition to your witch friend. It can be construed as interference, you understand.*

We dislike holding fate in our hands, Muki snapped.

Yet in this case, we must. Not only the balance but survival of the planet itself rests upon our impartiality.

Then we request the right to recover remains, should we survive.

Muki, that right will be granted only if it is safe enough to do so. Often, something such as this should remain buried—if it can be destroyed at all.

We will abide by the decision of the elders, Muki hung their head.

We will rest now, the elder said. *Then, we must take our findings to those who are destined to fight this battle.*

As you say, Muki stifled a sob. *But we do not like it.*

CHAPTER 19

The drawing Muki brought was detailed and accurate, with as many descriptions as could fit onto the parchment provided by the cavern elves.

Phil was devastated by what she saw and read.

Kwan, Jiah, Hwang and Dae-won wore identical, worried frowns as they studied the map with Phil. "How have we not known of this?" Jiah sighed.

"He and his witch managed to hide it," Phil spoke grimly. "The other lairs were probably set as traps, just like their recent tests of my ability. I don't have sufficient words to describe this evil bastard and his zombie witch," Phil cursed.

"Do you think that every trap on every level is set to activate at the same moment?" Hwang asked her.

"No doubt. There's no way to get in at the vent openings without setting everything off and effectively shouting a warning for them to get out before we can even get to them."

"I believe you have the right of it," Hwang nodded. "This is indeed the cleverest of traps, meant to kill us or thin our numbers while they escape to attack us again."

"Then we must outthink them," Dae-won sniffed.

"You're right," Phil told him. "But this could take time."

"I doubt they're going anywhere soon," Kwan pointed out dryly. "This is the final trap. They're waiting on us."

"I fear you are right," Jiah sighed. "They want us to come to them—and die."

"My Prince, you must stay behind for that very reason," Hwang insisted. "We cannot risk the Prince and all his royal heirs."

"I dislike that notion," Jiah argued. "We will discuss this again. I want ideas from each of you in two days. Show me the advantages of including and excluding me in your plans."

"What if we don't reach a viable solution in that time?" Hwang asked.

"Then we'll take another two days and try again."

"As you say, my Prince," Hwang dipped his head. The others copied Hwang's gesture, Phil included.

"THIS IS A NIGHTMARE," PHIL SIGHED, TOSSING A PAPER COPY OF Muki's map onto a table in her office. "Without being there, I have no reference as to how strong any of the spells are on all of this junk."

"It isn't junk," Kwan pinched the bridge of his nose. "Guk wants to lure us with what he has. You see this?" He pointed to one of the images that he'd enlarged on Phil's copier.

"Yeah. What is it?"

"The amber room—taken from Russia during World War II. In my estimation, much of Hitler's stolen treasures are also within Guk's labyrinth—the items unaccounted for, anyway."

"Great. We're dealing with the biggest asshole ever. Did he give Hitler lessons, do you suppose? What about the jerk in charge of North Korea at the moment? Him, too?"

"I cannot say for certain, but that idea cannot be wholly discounted."

"So, a bunch of human puppets could have Guk's scaly claws up their—well," Phil grimaced.

"Don't forget his witch's involvement in all of this," Kwan reasoned.

"Yeah. Were they both like this before Guk extended her lifespan, or did one poison the other?"

"No way to tell. We only know that they are together in this assault against every living thing on the planet."

"We need answers, and there's no way to find them," Phil muttered. "Are you hungry? I'm hungry."

"Let's find something to eat, then."

"THIS IS WORTH THE TRIP," JIAH SIGHED AFTER FINISHING A BOWL OF clam chowder topped with crab and shrimp. Phil had transported everyone at the Vashon Island house to Pismo Beach, the home of her favorite clam chowder restaurant.

"I ordered more to take home," Phil rested her head on Kwan's shoulder. "I'll want seconds later."

"Xinnie and I love the food here," Ray grinned and draped an arm over Xinnie's shoulders. "If Phil asks if we want clam chowder, we know she'll bring some back for us. We just never realized how far away the restaurant was until today."

"You'd freak if I did," Phil teased.

"Before we knew better, we would have," Xinnie confirmed. "Now, we want to come with you."

"Of course," Phil said. "Who else would I bring?"

"THE CAVERN ELF LIBRARIANS HAVE PAID MORE ATTENTION TO ONE specific area of the Prince's library," Tae Yong reported to Hwang. "Your suspicions proved correct."

"Let me know when they leave for the evening," Hwang nodded. "I will search that section myself."

"If you need assistance," Tae Yong offered.

"If you are willing," Hwang replied. "Tonight, then?"

"Yes."

"*Sasin* Moon, we have questions," Tae Yong spoke softly to the reaper after breakfast the following morning.

"If I can, I will answer," *sasin* Moon agreed.

"Very well. Meet me at the boathouse in half an hour. Hwang and I have a dilemma to solve."

"Of course."

"You may want a drink afterward."

"That serious?"

"It would so appear."

"THIS IS A COPY OF THE CAVERN ELVES' MAP," AGENT CHOI spread the rolled paper out on a folding table Xinnie found for him.

"Are these vents natural, or were they created by the rogue dragon and his witch?" Agent Park asked.

"I've never seen a volcano with this many natural vents. I believe these were manufactured," Agent Yoon replied. "You see how the interior dome curves outward within the depleted mantle, like a fat vase? A natural vent wouldn't have a dike built at the inside opening to keep its contents from spilling out. Our rogues have built these to contain what they've stored within."

"So many spelled objects, which could maim or kill whoever comes close," Agent Choi leaned back in his seat with a weary sigh.

"Look at the way these vents are positioned," Agent Yoon pointed out. "You see that the back end of the one above the next vent roughly matches the beginning of the one beneath?"

"What's your point?" Agent Park asked.

"If the space at the back of each vent were greatly weakened, then the contents of the vent above it could break through and spill into the one below."

"Are you saying to weaken the end of each vent, to create a cascading event?" Agent Choi sat straight in his chair and studied the map with renewed interest.

"If it can be done without the rogues' knowledge, yes."

"How?" Agent Choi frowned while tracing the line of the depleted mantle with a finger.

"Who got in there to provide us with a map in the first place?" Agent Yoon smiled.

"But that would require a partnership, or an exchange," Agent Park countered.

"What do we have that we can give?" Agent Choi considered the problem.

"*Dokkaebi* are not without resources," Agent Yoon smiled. "I shall speak with Tae Yong."

"How do we accomplish something so delicate without," Tae Yong argued with Hwang after their meeting with *sasin* Moon.

"Leave that to me," Hwang rumbled. "I have what is needed—do not concern yourself."

"What about Kwan?" Tae Yong lowered his voice.

"This is what the Americans would refer to as a *need to know* situation, eh? My son doesn't need to know until later."

"You're his father," Tae Yong admitted. "You have the right to withhold the information."

"As written in Dragon Law," Hwang nodded sagely. "I will find the proper time. Do not fear; there will be no harm done."

"I have your full assurance on that?"

"You do."

"Very well. Will you keep me informed?"

"Of course."

"Are you coming to bed?" Kwan frowned at Phil.

"Soon. I need to spend about an hour in my office—the new crop of titles that have passed the first hurdle for publication by *Le Texte Enluminé* have been handed to me for the final selections," Phil sighed.

"It only takes an hour?" Kwan blinked at Phil.

"I get a feeling from each manuscript. I don't have to read the whole thing to know whether it'll be successful or not."

"Then I will wait for you in the sitting room. I have emails waiting for responses," Kwan said.

"Okay. You do you," Phil grinned at him before heading toward the door of their shared bedroom.

Forty minutes later, Phil considered the final three entries; only one of them would make the publication list for the following year. A knock sounded on the door.

"Come in," Phil called out.

"I have a question," Hwang announced as he opened the door.

"What's that?"

"Are there any caves or hollow trees on your property?"

"Um, no caves," she shook her head. "Does the hollow tree need to be a big one?"

"No, but it does need to be hollow at the base."

"Yeah, there's one not far from the front gate," Phil said, grabbing a piece of copy paper to draw a map.

"Here you go," she handed the sheet to Hwang minutes later. "I hope the drawing is good enough to get you there."

"I'm sure it will be fine," Hwang smiled. "Thank you."

"Oh, my gosh, look at the time," Phil said when her phone alarm beeped. "Let me know if you need more help," she called out as Hwang walked out the door. A text interrupted; Kwan was asking where she was, what she thought she was doing, and why she refused to answer his telepathic queries.

"What telepathy? He can't even wait two seconds before getting all impatient and huffy," Phil complained. *Coming, your majesty*, she tapped in reply and rose from her desk.

⚔

"IDEAS? LET ME HEAR THEM," JIAH SAID AFTER THE LAST STRAGGLER joined the meeting the following day.

"We have something, but it will only be secondary to the actual attack," Agent Yoon stood and bowed to the Prince.

"Secondary is still good," Jiah nodded. "Proceed."

"We made a copy of the map, to show how all the vents are lined up, plus the distances between them. We doubt more than one or two of the sixteen are natural. The rest must have been created by the rogues involved."

"We know this to be true," Muki agreed. They hadn't been at the Vashon Island house until that morning and hadn't spoken much until now.

"Confirmation by the cavern elves is noted," Jiah acknowledged Muki's statement.

"We noticed the way all of them are lined up inside the depleted mantle," Agent Yoon continued. "Observe how the end of a previous vent lines up with the beginning of the next one."

"How does that help us?" Kwan asked.

"If we can weaken the area between the ends and beginnings," he drew a pattern with his finger between vents, "perhaps with a spell or such, then, at the right time, we can create a cascading event, where each cache of spelled items drops into the vent below it, until, as you can see, it reaches the undepleted mantle."

"How do we accomplish this feat without the enemy being aware?" Hwang steepled his fingertips.

"It can be accomplished," Muki offered. "But it will take both Phil and me to do it."

"What kind of spell?"

"Earth magic," Phil shrugged. "I think we can employ something similar to what Guk and his witch have been doing—making the components of the spell so small that they're undetectable—until the spell is activated. This will require an invasion of Muki's personal privacy," she turned toward Muki with a frown.

"We do not mind that," Muki's eyes were downcast as they spoke. "But Phil is the only one we will allow."

"What will happen to the spelled objects when they reach the heated interior of the chamber—or the magma near the core?" Jiah asked.

"Armageddon," Phil grimaced. "That means we have to go on the attack at roughly the same time the first vent collapses into the second. Once that happens, then we may have two or three minutes at most before the whole thing blows up in our faces."

"Then we must find a way to locate both rogues before we begin the cascade," Tae Yong shook his head. "And we must keep them from escaping while we deal with them."

"Two minutes to take down a witch who's tied herself to so many souls," Phil's shoulders sagged. "What about Guk? How long will that take?"

"It depends on who faces off against him," Hwang admitted. "I will be one of those, as I didn't finish the job the first time."

"I will be there to fight beside you," Kwan told his father. "You will have power over weapons if he has them; I can attack from above. Either way, one of us will distract while the other takes advantage."

"I can form fog to obscure his vision," Jiah said. "I will fight beside you."

"My Prince, you know that is not the best idea," Tae Yong began.

"If we have Water, Air and Metal fighting against a single Fire dragon," Dae-won interrupted, "are there any Fire dragons available to join us?"

"Unfortunately, there are not," Hwang murmured.

"Then, as an Earth dragon, I would also like to fight beside you. Four of the five types should have an advantage, even against one Fire dragon protected by many spells."

"Have you taken lessons in attack and defense?" Kwan frowned at Dae-won.

"I have the basics, yes," Dae-won replied.

"He's being modest; I have his records from the instructors," Jiah said. "If Dae-won wishes to join the fight, I will allow it."

"I dislike the thought of the Prince's involvement," Hwang reiterated, glaring at Jiah.

"Your opinion is noted," Jiah sniffed. "The final decision in this is mine, as you know. My father and older brother are dead because of Guk and his witch. They owe me their deathblood."

"They also owe the *dokkaebi* their deathblood," Tae Yong agreed. "I and many of our best will be there to help. We will provide powerful distractions, as well as direct hits whenever we can make them."

"All this hinges on where, exactly, Guk and his witch are located within the volcano," Phil pointed out. "Higher is better for us; lower is better for them."

"Then they'll go low; you can count on it," Kwan stated baldly.

"We ought to figure out how long it will take to get everybody out if we have to get anywhere near the magma chamber," Phil sighed. "Two minutes to gather any of the injured, even if we win the fight, isn't very long."

"What you're not saying is that if we lose the fight, it won't matter anyway," Muki declared. "I have been given permission to do what I physically can to support Philomena."

Phil's head jerked around; something in Muki's voice drew her attention. They were hiding a deep concern—one that decidedly worried Phil.

"Are you sure you want to do this?" Phil asked Muki.

"I do," they replied. "I will not have it otherwise."

"How long will it take to prepare the attack?" Jiah asked.

"Five days at least, if I want to have enough energy to handle Guk's witch," Phil answered.

"Very well. Report to me on all progress during this time. Kwan, Dae-won, Hwang and I will practice our maneuvers until then."

"The *dokkaebi* will join you," Tae Yong announced.

"Good. Everyone, we have our plan. Get to work," Jiah announced.

"How close can we get to those vents?" Phil asked Muki.

"If the witch has set traps, I cannot speculate," Muki replied. "We must do this from a distance. I will provide the information, but our minds must be linked. I suggest we do this from a mile away, at least."

"Okay. If there were any other way," Phil sighed. "I honestly hate the thought of being in North Korea. The bad vibes may be overwhelming."

"I know this," Muki mused. "But you're forgetting that half the volcano's crater is on China's side of the boundary. Why don't we set up there? Perhaps the bad vibes will be muted somewhat. Phil, you're the only one I trust enough to complete the link, and the only one with enough power and talent to get the job done."

"Then we'll go tomorrow," Phil decided. "I need to get a good night's sleep before we do this."

"As do I."

"Philomena, do I need to remind you to be careful?" Kwan expressed his skepticism during breakfast the following morning.

"Honey, I don't need a lecture," Phil sighed while lifting her coffee cup. "Muki and I have already had a discussion about all the bad stuff."

"Where will you set up to achieve your goals?" Jiah interrupted before Kwan could say anything more.

"On the China side," Phil answered while casting a wary glance at Kwan. "I think I'll feel more comfortable from that side of things."

"Don't forget that Heaven Lake is still covered in ice—and normally will be until June," Tae Yong pointed out, naming the body of water that filled the volcano's crater. "Vibrations or the production of heat to change that fact could reveal your actions or your intent, you understand."

"We'll be careful," Phil promised, ignoring the glare Kwan sent her way.

"When has Phil let you down, dragon?" Muki frowned at Kwan. "I'm ready whenever you are," they turned to Phil with a nod.

Before Kwan could express his misgivings, Phil and Muki disappeared. "I'm not sure my heart can take much more of this," Xinnie dropped onto a barstool with a heavy sigh.

"Kind lady, do not fear," Hwang said gently. "Today will go well enough, I think."

"We will wait patiently for their return." Jiah pointed his words in Kwan's direction. "We should practice our battle drills during that time." Obediently, Hwang, Kwan and Dae-won followed their prince toward the door.

MUKI KNEW THEY'D BOTH FREEZE WITHOUT PHIL'S WARMING SPELL. She'd cast a shield around them first, then filled the small sphere with warmth. Together, they huddled inside a small crater that Muki had excavated upon their arrival.

"I've never seen you work—I had no idea you could make a hole like this in only a few seconds," Phil complimented Muki.

"We're cavern elves; this is what we do," Muki replied with a modest shrug. "This is how we hollow out our homes underground. We fill them back in when we move. Staying in one place for too long invites human discovery."

"So it's for self-preservation, huh?"

"Every creature on the planet has gone through some sort of evolution as time passes. When humans began to dig deep, our abilities were turned toward the specific goal of surviving."

"Even dragons?" Phil asked.

"Hmmph," Muki snorted. "You would be most surprised at how they evolved—and it was also for self-preservation. They will refuse to reveal that secret, but the cavern elves know it anyway."

"Of course they do," Phil gave Muki a nervous smile. "Should we talk more, or will we only get more uncomfortable as time passes?"

"We should do this," Muki sighed. "The others are waiting anxiously for our safe return."

"Yeah."

"Take my hands, then," Muki instructed. "We will do this together."

MUKI'S MIND WAS A MAZE; ONE THAT PHIL COULDN'T NAVIGATE without the cavern elf's assistance. So many neural passages were closed or blocked off; she understood those were unique and personal to Muki.

Could she have broken past those barriers with her power?

Probably.

Phil refused to consider that breach of basic courtesy. Muki's privacy was just that—private. *Here,* Muki interrupted Phil's thoughts. Following Muki's guidance down a difficult passageway, Phil saw the inner structure of Mount Paektu, beneath the caldera. In clear, three-dimensional images, Muki led her mentally to the first vent, where she would begin to lay the delayed cascading spell.

The difficult part would be setting the threads of the spell separately, to be joined later. Otherwise, Guk and his witch might detect Phil's presence. If that happened, all the work done up to that point would be useless, in addition to placing both Muki and herself in grave danger.

Take your time, Muki soothed as Phil's physical body drew a shaky breath before beginning.

Yeah, Phil replied and cleared her mind of the fears that threatened her concentration. *I'll take my time,* she added, as a reminder to herself. *No need to get in a hurry. Do it right, Phil.*

CHAPTER 20

"It's done?" Kwan questioned Phil the moment she and Muki appeared in the kitchen, six hours after they'd left.

"It's done. We're exhausted. Food. Sleep," Muki mumbled as they climbed onto a barstool at the island.

"What Muki said," Phil breathed, slouching onto another barstool.

"We have pot roast and vegetables warming in the oven," Xinnie moved Kwan aside to reach the appliance in question. "Give me a minute and you'll have food."

"Thank goodness," Phil pillowed her head in her arms on the island. "That was nerve-wracking, and to top it off, a few Chinese hikers came along."

"If Phil hadn't disguised our temporary cave and put a heavy shield over it, we'd have been stepped on," Muki explained.

"Eat," Xinnie commanded, setting plates of food in front of Phil and Muki. "Then go straight to bed. Both of you look like you've been through a battle."

"Says somebody who's actually been there," Phil reminded Xinnie. "We were scared and anxious. That's about it."

"The battle is yet to come," Hwang pointed out. "Let's not get ahead of ourselves."

"It's decided, then," Jiah declared. "We will go in two days, rather than tomorrow. Our witch and our cavern elf need the rest."

PHIL TURNED AND STRETCHED ON THE BED WHEN SHE WOKE, REALIZING then that Kwan wasn't in bed with her.

"Where is he?" she muttered, forcing her eyes open. "What time is it?" Sitting up in bed and shoving hair away from her face, she attempted to gauge the time by the amount of light shining through filtered shades.

"I'm here and it's after ten," Kwan announced from the doorway. He then cleared his throat in a disapproving fashion.

"Crap." Phil rubbed her forehead. "I was tired, but I had no idea I'd sleep this long."

"You can thank my father for your late waking—he wanted you to sleep as long as you could."

"Thank you, Papa Hwang," Phil sighed and sank back onto her pillow.

"You should thank me as well," Kwan sniffed. "I considered waking you for breakfast many times."

"Is there any food left?" Phil's empty stomach growled at the mention of breakfast.

"Go see for yourself. I am not your servant."

"Dang, you're grumpy. What is wrong with you?"

"He's attention deprived," Muki stepped around Kwan and walked into the bedroom. "Mistreated. Ignored. Neglected."

"Ahhhh," Phil nodded. "Now I get it."

"Will you put my hair in a bun?" Muki stepped to the side of the bed and held out a hair tie.

"Do you even have to ask?" Phil sat up straight and took the hair tie with one hand, while a hairbrush appeared in the other.

"Tch," Kwan sniffed and stalked away.

"Xinnie says he's been in a snit all morning," Muki sighed while

Phil brushed their hair. "I feel so relaxed when you do my hair," they added.

"Any time," Phil said and continued brushing. "You think he's mad because we left him at home yesterday?"

"I believe so," Muki agreed.

"I'M SORRY WE DIDN'T TAKE YOU WITH US," PHIL SLUMPED ONTO THE sofa next to Kwan. He'd ensconced himself in the sitting room connected to the bedroom, a book of poetry in his hand.

"Tch."

"I'm really sorry we didn't take you with us," Phil said. "Really, really sorry. I should have known better. Really."

"Did you eat?" Kwan asked without glancing away from the book.

"I did. Xinnie made bacon, egg and cheese biscuits for me."

"Good." Kwan turned the page, still without looking at Phil.

"You're gonna milk this for all it's worth, aren't you?"

"Dragons may be petty at times. It's best to humor them."

"And how might one humor a dragon?"

"A trip to the local coffeeshop, perhaps?"

"Sure. I'll even let you drive the Mercedes."

"What are we waiting for, then?" Kwan dropped the book onto the coffee table and pulled Phil to her feet.

Twenty minutes later, they stood in line at the Bean Brewery, waiting to order vanilla lattes. "That's her," a woman's voice whispered loudly from a nearby table. "The widowed," the voice stopped abruptly as Kwan leveled a murderous glare at the woman.

"She is remarried. I am her husband. This talk will end immediately," Kwan snapped, holding up Phil's left hand with his to display both rings.

"Well, I," the woman stuttered.

"It's rude, and you've already told me three times," her female companion said, before turning toward Kwan and Phil. "Don't mind her—she's just a busybody."

"Well," the woman snapped before rising and storming out of the coffeeshop. Several patrons clapped at her exit.

"And the world rights itself," Phil sighed as her shoulders slumped.

"Lean against me, my love," Kwan pulled her against his chest. "Our turn to order will come soon."

"What would you like? I'll order and pay for you," the guest at the counter turned around to say.

"They want two large vanilla lattes," the cashier supplied the information. "Go sit down—they'll be ready in a minute."

"Sit here," the busybody's companion stood and gathered her purse. "I should go find Nelda before she buys everything she sees while spreading gossip. Congratulations on your marriage," she smiled at Phil and Kwan. "I hope we meet again sometime."

"Thank you," Phil smiled back. "I'm sure we'll find one another from time to time."

"It's a small island. My name's Marie Butler—I run the real estate office across the street."

"We will invite you for coffee whenever we come here," Kwan dipped his head. "Thank you for the table."

"Your lattes," two cups were set on the table as Phil and Kwan settled on their chairs. "Enjoy," the cashier smiled before going back to the counter.

"Cheers," Phil tapped her cup against Kwan's before drinking.

"THAT WAS A WORTHWHILE TRIP," PHIL SIGHED AS KWAN CAREFULLY parked the Mercedes in its spot in the garage.

"Yes, it was, although you probably should have given that gossip-monger a case of acne long ago."

"I don't do that," Phil argued. "Otherwise, many politicians and world leaders would acquire unexplained medical conditions. If I did do something like that, I want them to know *exactly* why they have that condition."

"Ah. Otherwise, it would remain an unexplained phenomenon."

"Without affecting their behavior one bit," Phil sighed. "It's better to remain neutral in these cases. It's why I stopped watching the news. Before then, I fantasized about some of them regurgitating caterpillars every time they lied."

"I think that would be more than effective," Kwan appeared thoughtful. "Certainly, it would become a deterrent. What stops you from doing this?"

"Well, I don't want to start witch hunts, okay? Most witches don't have the ability to do anything of the sort, but they can fall prey to those who might blame them for the malady."

"Ah. I see your point."

"Just as dragons hide themselves for a reason, well, anybody who has this level of ability should also hide themselves."

"A rule the *dokkaebi* have long followed," Tae Yong walked into the garage to meet them. "Prince Jiah wishes to dine out this evening. We ask for your input before choosing a location."

"How many, and what's the general consensus? It may be easier to do tonight, since it's a weeknight," Phil replied.

"Steaks and seafood are the most requested items," Tae Yong smiled.

"Let me see what I can do," Phil grinned.

"Is the owner one of your fans?" Kwan lifted an eyebrow in obvious curiosity. Phil didn't reply; her gaze was locked on Xinnie and Ray, who displayed delight at finding themselves at a popular steak and seafood restaurant in Las Vegas.

"I'm getting them a hotel room. They can go home whenever they want," Phil tapped her phone while ignoring Kwan. "They like to stay at this casino hotel anyway, and this is their favorite restaurant."

"The Emperor's Palace is one of the highest rated in Las Vegas," Muki joined the conversation. "I like the lobster and filet here at the Date Palm Oasis."

"Your table is ready; follow me, please." Their host had returned with a waitperson whose arms were loaded with menus.

A long, narrow table awaited; seats were taken, water glasses filled and the daily chef's specials were suggested.

"Order a Caesar salad, they serve it with anchovies," Phil bumped Kwan's elbow with her own. "I don't normally like anchovies, but these are amazing."

"All right. What else do you suggest?"

"Any of the side dishes is enough for three or four people, but they're all good," Phil studied her menu. "Xinnie and I like the creamed spinach, but not everybody likes spinach."

"I'll share one with you," Xinnie beamed at Phil from across the table.

"That was already in the works," Phil laughed. "You can take any leftovers with you. There's a fridge and microwave in the suite I reserved for you. Use the business card to get yourselves home in the next week or two."

"Did you hear that, sweetheart? We have a suite and transportation back home," Ray bumped his forehead against Xinnie's.

"I heard it. Just make sure you don't come home with bumps and bruises," Xinnie pointed an accusing finger at Phil.

"Noted," Kwan slipped an arm around Phil's shoulders.

PHIL SHIFTED RESTLESSLY IN HER SLEEP, CAUGHT IN A DREAM SO ALIEN, she couldn't have reconciled it with any part of her reality in waking moments. Beside her, Kwan's regular breathing rumbled in his chest—he slept so deeply he failed to register Phil's unconscious restlessness.

This is a dream, a part of Phil's mind informed her, while the images filling her mind were as bright as the sunlight in which she floated over a snow-and-ice covered lake.

Volcano crater, a gentle voice informed her.

A *female* voice.

Speaking in Korean.

Phil's restless movements increased; Kwan continued to sleep as if drugged.

Why? Phil demanded of the voice, as she found herself making a lazy turn high over the lake-filled crater.

The others still don't understand the why of this. You must understand, Philomena. He wants to undo everything that I sacrificed to create.

Within Phil's dreaming vision, as her slow, lazy turn was made above the frozen lake, Phil caught sight of something that stopped her breath.

A tail curving behind her.

Covered in gold scales and finned in gold and white, the tail fanned out much like the most beautiful betta fish anyone could imagine.

Breathe, Philomena, the voice urged. *Do not lose your focus now. I have much to tell you, and time grows short.*

"DUE TO THE TIME DIFFERENCE, WE WILL BE STRIKING AN HOUR BEFORE dawn comes to Paektu," Jiah spoke with quiet authority over breakfast the following morning.

Philomena, is something wrong? Tae Yong's voice made Phil jerk in her seat.

I think I had a nightmare last night, but I can't remember any of it, Phil confessed.

And now you feel uneasy, yes?

Yes.

Don't let it trouble you. If you need to recall it, then surely it will resurface.

I hope you're right. I just feel unsettled, I think.

As do the rest of us. While we have made the best preparations we can, none may predict Guk's true mind in this—or that of his false prophet.

Wait—that's, well, I think that's the best description I've heard of that bitch-witch so far, Phil admitted. *Thank you for that insight.*

Hwang and I share a similar view in this, Tae Yong admitted. *Hwang is most familiar with Guk before he met that woman. In Hwang's opinion, Guk has been swayed mightily in order to do these deeds.*

Not good news, if she's so cunning she can con a dragon, Phil sighed mentally.

It is as you say, Tae Yong dipped his head to Phil.

"We have two hours before we leave," Jiah spoke again. "Meditate, rest or do whatever you must to prepare yourselves physically and mentally for this battle. Survival of the Earth itself may depend upon the outcome."

"What do you want to do, Philomena?" Kwan's lips brushed her cheek. He'd sat beside her, unaware of her silent conversation with Tae Yong.

"Whatever you want to do, I think. I want to be with you, no matter what it is," Phil replied.

"There is a coffeeshop in New York," Kwan leaned away and smiled wickedly at Phil.

"There are coffeeshops all over Seattle," she countered.

"Yes, but this particular one is frequented by a certain woman, who once assumed you were overweight and unsuitable to be my wife," Kwan's smile became a malicious grin.

"So you're saying we ought to make her feel small and petty?" Phil blinked at Kwan.

"Ah, if you don't think," Kwan began.

"No—I rather like it. Besides, you're so handsome, I can't say no to this face," Phil patted his cheek.

"This face?" Kwan tapped his chin.

"Especially this mouth. This mouth makes me feel weak and positively sinful." She pressed a finger against his lips.

"Ah. Well, then. Shall we?" Kwan stepped back and offered Phil his arm.

"We shall. I'll get us there, but you'll have to make introductions."

"With pleasure. But first," Kwan pulled out his cell phone to make a call. Phil listened in.

"Kwan?" the female voice was breathless with anticipation. "I haven't heard from you in so long." Phil imagined the feigned pout coming through in the woman's tone.

"I'm heading for your favorite coffeeshop now. Want to meet? I have something to tell you," Kwan almost purred.

"I'll be there in ten." The call ended abruptly.

"If she's afoot, she'll be running there in heels," Kwan sniffed. "Take us there, Philomena. We should arrive first, don't you think?"

"I don't want Philomena to know that Paektu is where my mother sacrificed herself for dragonkind's continued existence," Jiah frowned at Hwang. "Yes, we have always considered it sacred as her final resting place, but Guk's presence there has defiled it and we cannot attempt to save any part of it, now."

"Guk did this purposely, knowing this would be a crushing blow against you and your heirs," Hwang growled. "As well as making us furious, he is likely hoping it will make us reckless when we arrive to do battle."

"He is expecting us; of that I feel certain," Jiah agreed. "Had it been anywhere but there, my heart would feel more at ease."

"Guk wants us to feel uneasy. He wants a rushed attack," Hwang counseled. "This is why I think you should be far away while the rest of us battle him and his witch."

"Deathblood," Jiah muttered angrily. "He owes me that and far more than that. He knows things—has deprived me of the life I would prefer to live, as Second Heir only."

"I know this, and my heart weeps for you," Hwang replied. "My case—it is similar, as you know. Only your father could convince me to have a son; he was wise in his decision, as you well know."

"Kwan is much loved—not only by you and me, but by Philomena as well. Without her help in the past few weeks, we would be far worse off than we are."

"I regret that I considered her unworthy in the beginning. Now, I know that there could be no other who is better suited for my only child."

"You are not alone; I was jealous—and angry at first," Jiah admitted. "Who could be worthy of him, in my eyes? And, when I learned she was a Western witch, I thought my blood would boil. I was more than ready to activate the royal death decree against such an arrogant, presumptuous human, had Kwan not designated her as his familiar."

"We both know what a mistake that would have been," Hwang snorted.

"In every aspect. Now, I find myself caring and worrying about her —just as much as I do about Kwan."

"We both acknowledge our mistakes in this, yes?" Hwang asked gently.

"Yes. I feel that I owe the entire royal treasure inside my lair to Philomena, and it still would not cover my debts to her."

"She would not accept it."

"And that, dear Uncle, is why I've come to love her almost as much as I do your son."

"THIS IS MY WIFE, PHILOMENA," KWAN DRAPED AN ARM AROUND PHIL as Paige Nielson, his former property manager, approached their coffeeshop table.

His words stopped Paige in her tracks. *Stand with me and toss back your lovely hair, Philomena,* Kwan instructed.

"Philomena, this is my former property manager, Paige Nielson," Kwan continued smoothly. "She assumed you were overweight and insulted you. That's why I fired her."

"Wh-what?" Paige blurted.

"Also, she pestered Secretary Kim almost to death, asking for personal information on me, to which she was not entitled," Kwan went on. "Now that you know, I suggest you never overstep your boundaries again, Miss Neilson," Kwan smiled. "Philomena and I have something important to do later, so we'll take our leave."

"Well, I never," Paige stamped a foot as Kwan led Phil toward the door.

"And you will never," Phil turned in Kwan's arms and smiled at Paige. "Never, ever, ever. Trust me."

Kwan laughed as he and Phil emerged onto the sunny, New York sidewalk, while Paige Neilson shrieked in anger behind them.

"Remember, we only have information provided by the cavern elves, and they have sensitivities regarding the interior of Paektu that we do not, whereas we dragons have a certain affinity for the volcano itself," Jiah instructed, once everyone had gathered around him for the impending journey.

"This means that we should remain in contact if anything unusual is detected," Hwang took up where Jiah left off. "Muki cannot be there with us; they are forbidden from interfering in any way."

"We *dokkaebi* have no power against dragons; we can only provide distractions, and those have to do with the interior of the volcano itself and perhaps the spelled objects collected there," Tae Yong said. "If more time is needed, we hope to help in that way."

"That may prove invaluable," Jiah blinked slowly at his *dokkaebi* secretary, acknowledging Tae Yong's assistance. "We dragons must deal with Guk. Philomena must deal with the witch."

"Yeah," Phil sighed. "Her and all the slaves she's gathered, who had no choice but to die in her service."

"I know this troubles you," Jiah said. "But, by your own admission, they can never survive on their own, now, even if we set them free."

"I know. I'm ready to do what needs to be done," Phil drew in a deep breath and closed her eyes for a moment.

"Very well. Shall we go, then?" Jiah asked, making the question a command, as only the Prince of Dragons could.

"I'm ready to have Guk's blood on my claws," Hwang rumbled.

"Philomena, take us to the battleground. We have business with Guk and his witch."

"THEY COME," THE WITCH SMILED AT GUK, HER TEETH BLACKENED BY age and the dark spells she'd spent her life casting.

"How little they know of what awaits them," Guk smiled back, his teeth stained with blood from consuming more than fifty of his witch's spelled servants. "Your power is mine, and mine is yours. Their witch will never survive—and without her, neither will they."

SO DARK, A TINY VOICE NAGGED AT PHIL AS SHE AND THE OTHERS settled onto a ledge inside a widened area between the volcano's conduit and the magma chamber. From there, most of the side vents were accessible; Phil could feel the witch's spells in each of the false vents created by that malevolence.

No light, Jiah snapped mentally when one of the *dokkaebi* began to glow. *We have memorized this interior. We wait for the collapse of the false vents. Guk will be alerted to our presence then. Everyone, remember your duty and execute it flawlessly.*

The dim light snapped off immediately; Phil couldn't decide whether she felt grateful or even more worried than before.

Something isn't right, she breathed into the minds around her before she could stop herself.

Philomena? Kwan barely had time to express his question within her name before Guk struck. His first victim died immediately.

Hwang perished before he could become dragon and fight back.

Phil shrieked in pain; the power in her shields was snatched away like a hat in a hurricane. She cried out a second time as invisible claws raked her mind, searching for the source of her power.

She barely had time to gather energy to fight off that attempt, when, their plan of attack all but forgotten, dragons exploded into being around Phil. Their roars filled thickening, sulfurous air inside the chamber, before they scattered like a flock of startled pigeons.

Dokkaebi relocated away from the point of attack as Guk, who'd disappeared after killing Hwang, reappeared, breathing a powerful shaft of fire. Phil, standing alone on a narrow ledge which began to crumble beneath her feet, could only shield herself and Hwang's bloody remains against Guk's attack.

"She's mine!" The witch slowly rose from the depths, floating above the slaves still tied to her by cords of darkly glowing power. Guk, black scales bloody from his earlier feast and Hwang's death, laughed, the sound low and guttural in his dragon's throat.

"I will not deprive you of your victory, dear one," Guk chuckled.

Dragons, to me! Jiah's mental shout shook Phil to the core; she swayed as she considered that the shields covering all of her companions had been cut away, like a sharp knife slicing through tofu.

In horror, Phil watched as Jiah, Kwan, Dae-won and the royal guards formed a phalanx to attack Guk, only to be rebuffed as if they were feathers in a whirlwind. Jiah's scream of pain and anger echoed throughout the volcano, shaking volcanic dust and fist-sized clumps of solidified lava down about her.

"Now you see what you deal with," the witch screamed at Phil. "You have no power against me; I've had centuries to build this magic, while you barely know what to do with what you have."

Phil blinked at the witch for a moment as the dark-spelled creature completed her journey from the depths of Paektu, floating in midair a dozen yards away from Phil.

"I want to suck the power away from her with my own hands," the witch turned to Guk, whose dragon eyes creased in amusement.

"Do you think you can have it?" Phil demanded, struggling to calm her trembling voice and shivering body. "Your souls are stolen. Mine have all willingly given what they had to me. They can leave me whenever they choose. Try to take them. I will not allow it."

Philomena, Jiah is injured, as is Dae-won, Kwan's mental sending was soaked in terror. *We are trapped within a vent; we cannot allow the vents to collapse, now, or we will die here.*

Philomena, transport yourself away from here, Tae Yong begged. *You cannot allow this creature to take what you have. Go now.*

Do you think they won't follow, no matter where I go from here? Phil replied. *They've been testing me all this time and forming a defense against my shields and my power. Save yourself and the others. Get the Prince and Dae-won to safety and call for the physician. If I don't get out of here, you and they have to find a way to destroy these two.*

I will stand beside you to the end. Lee Min and the others will take the Prince and the heirs away from here. Tae Yong appeared next to Phil. Her eyes widened; Tae Yong was dressed in ancient Korean battle gear and held a spear and shield in his hands. The shield was painted red with a gold dragon coiled upon it.

His battle gear from when he was human long ago, a faint voice informed Phil. *This is why he chooses to serve the Prince.*

Do you think I will leave you here to die alone? Kwan's dragon appeared on Phil's other side, his claws clutching precariously on the narrowing ledge. *Lee Min and the other dokkaebi freed us and took the Prince and Dae-won away*, he added. *My father is already gone. We will die beside him or win the day. It is now up to us.*

"*Dokkaebi*, I have no argument with you or your kind," Guk rumbled. "Our war was in the past."

"And yet we continue to have an argument with you—and your witch," Tae Yong snapped, pointing his spear at Guk. "Prepare for battle. I do not fear death; I have died before, as you know."

"That one is still mine," Guk's witch pointed at Phil. "Take the other two and kill them quickly. I have souls to consume."

"Look, if we're all going to die anyway, I'd like some light in here while it happens," Phil hissed, pulling sun magic to her and flooding the area with sunlight.

"What?" Guk's witch shrieked as the interior walls of the area were suddenly illuminated with crystals in all the colors of magic; green, gold, blue, white, brown and red.

Phil's body absorbed the colors—as if they were pouring out of the volcanic rock and soaking into her like water into dry earth.

Remember, the faint voice became stronger. *Hwang died to give you this. Do not turn his sacrifice into ultimate defeat. Our lives depend upon it. I am here. Pull me into existence, Philomena. The four of us will have to be enough.*

Four? Enough? Phil squeaked.

Enough, the voice replied. *Do this now, or time will run out—for the Earth and everything upon it.*

The last of the magical colors leeched from the walls and soaked into Phil, after which her sun magic died like a candle flame snuffed in a high wind. Instinctively, Phil pulled the magic together as requested, only then realizing that she'd absorbed something other than magic from the main vent's surface.

Someone, not something, the voice was even stronger, now. *I sacrificed then, hoping someone with the power would come to release me. Release me now, Philomena, while there is still time.*

Push, another voice coaxed. *She is within you. Push her out, now.*

Others whispered into Phil's mind—showing her what and how.

Phil pushed, although it weakened her greatly.

Once more, and I will be free.

Dropping to her knees, Phil pushed again, the pain of it much like the pain of giving birth, had Phil known of it. Phil's eyes closed—*have to stay conscious*, she struggled to convince herself.

I am here, Philomena, the voice was now strong. *Transform now. Hwang gave this gift to you. Remember what I taught you; there is no time to adapt—you must be perfect from the start.*

"Huh?" Phil said aloud without meaning to.

"Guk, you filth, you owe me your life!" the scream was from the throat of a dragon.

A female dragon.

A Queen.

Now, Philomena. Transform now.

Light so bright it blinded Guk's witch momentarily flashed inside the cavern, lighting the interior so brilliantly that few could withstand it.

The Queen Dragon hovered above Guk, who cowered away.

Kwan's dragon had already taken flight; there was no space left for him to cling to.

No—that space was now occupied.

By a second female dragon.

The Queen's golden scales lit the cavern by themselves.

The second female was gold as well, but dispersed among the golden scales were those of blue, green, brown, opal and red. Her beautiful fins and tail trailed and floated about her as she stared at Guk's witch like one who'd been starved and now viewed a feast.

One of the vents collapsed at that moment; Tae Yong leapt toward Guk, his spear aimed at a massive eye, Kwan bellowed a roar that shook the walls, the Queen sunk her teeth into Guk's throat and breathed fire—and Tae Yong's spear found its mark.

Philomena, now! Kwan's voice shook Phil from a temporary stupor. Before she could react to Kwan's mental images of attack, Phil was thrown against the conduit's wall by a blast of malicious, death-fed power. Kwan roared and aimed his tail at the witch, who was momentarily distracted with buffeting the attempted attack.

The counterattack against Kwan hurled him against the opposite side of the conduit, next to a false vent. The impact was severe and set off whatever had been stored inside the vent; the resulting explosion shook the volcano to its core and the hardened cap over the magma chamber collapsed.

One by one, the false vents exploded outward as Kwan screamed in pain. Philomena woke from her stupor at Kwan's cry of agony, her fury rising to the fore.

He's hurt was the only thought that echoed through her mind as she gathered the energy from all the magic and power she'd absorbed earlier.

Do it, the Queen commanded while power built around Phil. Guk's witch hurled a series of powerful blasts against Phil while Guk, one eye ruined by Tae Yong and the Queen's teeth and fiery breath still in his throat, roiled in anguish, weakly attempting to dislodge the angry Queen.

Philomena, we can't hold back time any longer, Tae Yong

interrupted. *The remaining vents and the volcano itself are ready to detonate.*

Philomena, Kwan's pleading was weak as she garnered power to send him to safety.

"Whore," Guk's witch increased her attacks against Phil. The witch wavered in midair—she'd pulled everything she could from her remaining, mindless slaves.

Guk's dead, the Queen snapped. *I have Tae Yong. Get on with it.*

"Bye-bye, bitch," Phil's dragon laughed and released everything she had.

CHAPTER 21

"No!" Xinnie shouted as she and the others left behind watched in horror; satellite images showed the moment Paektu erupted in North Korea before a dense cloud of ash blocked the site from view.

Beside Xinnie, Ray stood while tears tracked his cheeks. He pulled Xinnie against him when she sobbed.

Agent Choi, too stunned to speak, sat heavily on a barstool at the kitchen island, his eyes glued to the television screen at the end of the counter.

"The Prince and my son are safe; I received word from Lee Min," Dae-won's mother sighed. "I'm sorry; that's all I know right now."

"Kwan and Tae Yong are safe but both are injured," Lee Min appeared inside the kitchen. "Guk is most certainly dead; I also have verification of that fact. I'm sorry to report, however, that the volcano erupted with the witch and Philomena still inside."

"MOTHER, I DON'T UNDERSTAND HOW," JIAH MUMBLED, HIS HEAD bowed before Queen Seondeok.

283

"I know. The tale of my survival is one to be told later. For now, we must search for Philomena. I hold hope that she has survived somehow. I wish for her to take her place at your side as your wife."

"What?" Jiah's head jerked up and his eyes locked with his mother's. He'd believed her dead for too many centuries to count, yet here she was, alive and breathing again.

"It is required for you to become King," Seondeok replied.

"But she and Kwan," Jiah argued.

"If she lives, I will set those attachments aside myself. This is the one worthy of my son. I will hear no arguments on this subject—not from you or from anyone else."

"She and I have nothing between us except close friendship," Jiah ventured before dropping his eyes. He knew he didn't have the power to argue; the Queen herself had returned and the dragon race as a whole was still rejoicing—not only for her return but also because she'd taken down Guk on her own to avenge her husband and her eldest son.

"Marriages have been based on far less, as you well know. I wish to see a King on the throne again, and I will only accept Philomena as my daughter. That is the end of this argument."

"We don't know that she survived," Jiah spoke softly.

"I wish Hwang were here; he would discover the truth quickly. I dare not ask his son, for obvious reasons."

"You think Hwang would support me over his son in this?"

"Jiah, I said the subject was closed. If I must search for Philomena's fate myself, then I will do so."

"As you will it, Mother. I had no idea that our eventual reunion would result in such disharmony." Jiah, flipping his gold-embroidered robe, stalked out of the throne room.

"You can't; the volcano is still spewing lava," Tae Yong glared at Kwan.

"How long do you think it can erupt?" Kwan lifted pain-filled eyes to Jiah's *dokkaebi* secretary.

"This is no ordinary eruption, my dear Prince. You know it was filled to the brim with the witch's magic and with spelled artifacts, along with the witch herself. That power has to be burned clean by the volcano itself."

"I worried it would be so. If she is truly gone, what will we do?" Kwan brushed moisture from his eyes.

"I don't know. Without her, I doubt any of us would have survived Guk and his witch. That includes humans as well as the hidden races. We must pay homage to your father, Kwan," Tae Yong continued. "Without his action in this, we would certainly have died."

"Who knew he held scales from Jiah's father, brother and uncle, along with one from the Queen herself?"

"I ah," Tae Yong cleared his throat. "Philomena held all those scales, that is so. She also held one from your father."

"He sacrificed himself on purpose? Is that what you're saying?" Kwan rose slowly from his chair, never taking his eyes off Tae Yong.

"I believe that to be true," Tae Yong dropped his gazed first. "He bet everything he had, including his life, on Philomena."

"Did you see her—when she changed?" Kwan wept. "So beautiful."

"I did. I have already changed the dragon's image upon my shield to reflect the colored scales of all the magics Philomena commanded."

"So she would be the one you serve, should she live?"

"Yes. I and my kind are agreed on this." Tae Yong now wore a fiercely determined expression.

"You know something I don't," Kwan took a step toward the *dokkaebi*.

"I do, sadly enough. Minds can be changed, however. At least, that is my final hope should we find Philomena alive. Everything hinges upon it."

"You won't tell me until we find out, will you?"

"You can't force me to say it, and I refuse to do so. Pain is not something I like to experience or to inflict upon those I love."

"Then I'll wait. I have enough pain as it is. I should visit Xinnie and Ray, but I'll break down in front of them," Kwan admitted.

"Then I will take you, and we will break down together," Tae Yong took Kwan's arm and led him toward his lair entrance.

⚡

"I'M SORRY. I DIDN'T MEAN TO CRY ALL OVER YOU," XINNIE apologized to Kwan.

"I don't mind; I've cried all over myself since the eruption," Kwan's smile held deep sadness.

"What will we do if she doesn't come back?" Ray choked on his words.

"The *dokkaebi* will see to it that this home stands forever as tribute, and that your place here will be assured," Tae Yong replied. "Place your hope in Philomena and do not worry about anything else."

"Dae-won's mother and her guards left last night," Ray sighed. "We miss them already."

"Lee Min will arrive tomorrow with two others," Tae Yong said. "You will not be alone unless you desire it."

"We haven't heard from Muki, either," Xinnie brushed fresh tears off her cheeks.

"Ah. Perhaps the cavern elf is doing what we cannot at this time," Tae Yong appeared thoughtful.

"What's that?" Kwan jerked around to face Tae Yong.

"Attempting to fight their way through a volcanic eruption to search for Philomena."

"They can do that?" Ray sounded hopeful.

"We don't know the full extent of a cavern elf's abilities," Tae Yong admitted. "Shall we hope for Muki's success? Surely they will contact us, one way or another."

"My heart can't take much more of this," Xinnie pulled out a barstool to sit. "We found out yesterday that the trial date for the two who killed Phil's family and her husband has been set. Texas wants it started in ninety days. The trial will begin exactly then. I figure

Paulson Muir's name will come up a lot during the trial. There's already a petition in the works to get him disbarred."

"He ought to be disbarred, getting his own son killed like that," Ray growled. "Phil still hasn't gotten over that mess."

Should we tell them about Philomena's transformation? Kwan silently asked Tae Yong.

Not unless she lives, the *dokkaebi* replied. *Philomena should tell them herself. For now, it isn't relevant.*

You are correct. We shouldn't muddy the waters—isn't that the proper term?

It is appropriate.

"Do you want to spend the night?" Ray asked.

"May we take you to dinner tonight?" Tae Yong asked. "If so, then my answer is yes."

THREE MONTHS LATER

"Thank you for bringing us; this may be the only justice Phil gets," Xinnie patted Lee Min's hand. With Ray on Xinnie's other side, the three of them sat in a San Antonio District courtroom, waiting for the judge to arrive. "If she were alive, she'd be here for this."

"We know. I've sent a message to Tae Yong already," Lee Min sighed. "Nevertheless, we will wait for justice in Philomena's place," he added.

"I'm worried about Muki," Ray whispered. "They should be here for this, too, and we haven't heard a thing from them, either."

"Ah, just in time," Tae Yong arrived and scooted onto the bench next to Xinnie.

"All rise," the bailiff intoned when the Judge walked into the chambers and took his seat.

The audience and the jury were seated, then, and the case before the court was announced—*The People versus Curtis and Quentin Gorsham.*

Xinnie cast an unfriendly gaze toward one person sitting on the opposite side of the courtroom; Paulson Muir, arms tightly crossed over his chest, wore an angry expression as he studied the brothers accused of killing his son and many others.

"Like he didn't start the whole damn thing," Xinnie muttered beneath her breath.

Tae Yong patted Xinnie's hand—he understood her words very well.

Ray pulled a pen and small pad of paper from his shirt pocket to write a message. *Will Paulson get disbarred after the evidence is presented?* He wrote and held the note out for Xinnie and Tae Yong to read.

If he doesn't, then something is very wrong, Tae Yong wrote back. Xinnie nodded her agreement as the first witness took the stand.

"I DON'T KNOW WHY THEY DON'T JUST PLEAD GUILTY AND GET THIS over with," a reporter complained to a colleague during recess in the women's restroom. Xinnie, who was washing her hands at a nearby sink, shrugged her shoulders.

"You disagree?" the reporter turned to Xinnie.

"I want those two bastards to have their say on the stand and implicate Paulson Muir in his own son's death," Xinnie snipped. "He ought to be charged with accessory to the crime, in my opinion."

"That would be difficult to prove," the colleague said. "I hear rumors that a jail sentence might be deserved, though, in this case. Oh, well, justice doesn't always get served—I've seen too many get away with murder. Literally."

"Yeah. You're right," Xinnie agreed. "I guess we'll wait to see what happens."

"I wonder where the widowed bride is," the reporter pulled paper towels from the dispenser to dry her hands. "There's been no word from her, even though the DA sent at least a dozen subpoenas."

"Maybe this is still too painful," the colleague surmised. "That's enough grief and trauma to last a lifetime, don't you think?"

"It is. I wish she were here, too," Xinnie tossed her paper towels in the trash and strode toward the door. "Just to make Paulson Muir sweat."

"Did you have friends who died in that massacre?" the reporter called out, causing Xinnie to turn back.

"I worked for Beatrice Lang, who died at that wedding," Xinnie replied. "She treated me like family. My husband and I loved her. Now do you understand why I want to see Paulson Muir in jail?"

"That would do it," the colleague nodded. "I miss her books."

"I do, too. Do you have a card? I'll be sure to read your articles," Xinnie said.

"Here." A business card was placed in Xinnie's hand. "It was good to meet you, Mrs. ah," the reporter realized she didn't have Xinnie's name.

"Xinnia Owens," Xinnie replied. "But people call me Xinnie—with an X."

"If you'd like to do an interview about Ms. Lang, call that number. I'd be happy to sit down and chat," the reporter offered.

"I'll think about it."

"Thank you."

"THE VOLCANO STOPPED ERUPTING, JUST IN TIME FOR A HEAVY snowstorm to hit. It's been snowing on Paektu for three days, now," Lee Min informed Tae Yong. "What are your thoughts on the trial today?"

"So far, only minor witnesses have been called," Tae Yong replied. "I think the District Attorney wants to build this story from the beginning, and slowly work his way toward the day Paulson Muir made his initial offer to the Gorshams, their commission of arson and then Paulson Muir's refusal to reimburse them for their ah, work."

"Xinnie would call that a train wreck, wouldn't she?"

"She already has. She and Ray went straight to their suite when we brought them back. They're exhausted after hearing what they have so far, and this hasn't touched anything truly important as yet. I worry that the brothers will make a deal and plead guilty to take the death penalty off the table."

"I read the same thing in an online article," Lee Min said. "But if that happens, Paulson Muir may not be as heavily implicated as he should be."

"We can't interfere," Tae Yong shook his head. "I hope we'll be able to get through this, for Xinnie and Ray's sake."

"I worry that Philomena is lost to us," Lee Min hung his head.

"As do I. Had she survived, she wouldn't miss this, I think."

"What is the latest from the palace?"

"The Queen stands firm, but I believe she is also having doubts. Jiah has resigned himself to the worst, I think. Kwan hasn't come away from his lair for a week. That concerns me greatly."

"Do you feel that this—disagreement—will sully Philomena's memory? I don't want to see that happen, as she is the reason the dragons survive."

"Jiah knows. While I appreciate the Queen's return, I dislike the conditions she placed upon a Dragon Princess who didn't survive her final ordeal."

"A part of me wants to mourn. Another part wants to refuse it. Ah, my heart hurts," Lee Min mumbled.

"Hmmph," Muki walked into the kitchen and pulled themselves onto an empty barstool. "Is there anything to eat? I'm starving."

"MUKI REFUSES TO SAY ANYTHING," TAE YONG TOLD KWAN. HE'D coaxed Kwan out of his lair by sending messages regarding Muki's reappearance. "All they said was that when the palace backed down, they'd relay their discovery."

"When the palace backs down?" Kwan felt confused.

"Meaning the Queen, I'm sure," Tae Yong replied dryly.

"What does that mean?"

"Kwan, what will make Jiah a King?" Tae Yong's hand dropped heavily onto Kwan's shoulder.

"A Queen at his side," Kwan's answer was simple. It was something he'd learned at an early age from his father.

"The Queen wants to ah, elevate Jiah to King. Then, she will accept the role as Queen-Mother to the King and retire."

"But there aren't any female dragons of royal blood," Kwan began.

"Unless Philomena has survived somehow," Tae Yong nodded once at Kwan. "She holds scales from the Queen herself, the former King, the King's brother and the King's eldest son, all of whom were killed by Guk. She also holds one of your father's scales, making her more than royal in any dragon's eyes."

Kwan's breath caught and his chest hurt. "Would they force that on Philomena? *My* Philomena?"

"The Queen wants to set aside your marriage—and the writ declaring her your familiar has already been vacated."

"That—this is unacceptable," Kwan fumed. "We don't know if she's alive, and the Queen makes this her first official act? I am infuriated."

"Jiah isn't happy about it, either. In his eyes, you are closer than a brother. He doesn't want to hurt either of you."

"Yet, if I were out of the picture, he'd surely take Philomena as Queen without a second thought," Kwan fumed.

"That is not how things are, and that is why he has consistently argued with his mother about it, when they should be working on other things."

"Like putting a working Council together," Kwan's words were bitter. "Father would be furious."

"I think we all know that."

"Has the trial started in Texas?"

"It has. It was my hope that it would serve as a catalyst to bring Philomena back to us, had she survived. My hopes are taking heavy blows because of it."

"Is there some other way to convince Muki to tell us what they know?"

"None, to my knowledge."

"Untenable."

"Yes."

⌇

"Are you ready to leave?" Tae Yong walked into the kitchen to find Xinnie and Ray drinking coffee and looking dejected.

"No need," Ray lifted his cup. "After the first day of trial, those two murderers are making a deal with the DA's office."

"And that means we may not get justice against Paulson for his part in the massacre. We're hoping there's enough evidence to charge him in the prior arson and murder incident, but there's no guarantee that anybody other than the Gorshams will go to jail on those crimes," Xinnie said. "Paulson Muir has to be the luckiest asshole I've ever met in my life."

"And he still has his license to practice law in the state of Texas," Ray shook his head before emptying his coffee cup. "Want coffee or tea, Tae Yong?"

"I'd take coffee, if you don't mind."

"Not a bit." Ray slid off his barstool and headed toward the coffeemaker.

"Ah, you're here," Lee Min strode into the kitchen, Muki close behind. "Want breakfast? I hear our dear Muki is hungry."

"You're chipper today," Xinnie gave Lee Min an odd look.

"Today is a better day than yesterday," Lee Min smiled at her. "Shall I make omelets or eggs and sausage for you?"

"I want an omelet," Tae Yong decided.

"I'd take one," Xinnie nodded.

"Me, too," Ray returned with two cups of coffee, setting one down for Tae Yong. "Muki, want coffee or tea?"

"I'll take coffee," Muki gave Ray a lovely smile before clambering onto a barstool. "We should be fully awake to see what the day brings."

"What will the day bring, then?" Xinnie asked. "Just so I'll know how much coffee to drink," she added.

"I'd say two cups at least," Muki replied.

"That's what I normally have, and then another one or two around ten," Xinnie sighed.

"Then treat this as an ordinary, extraordinary day," Muki grinned. "Somebody turn on the TV. We should see this for ourselves, I think."

Tae Yong gestured with a hand, causing the television on the counter to come to life and display the news from a twenty-four-hour news station.

"While it should come as no surprise that the Gorsham brothers have pled guilty in exchange for life sentences without parole, we may hear other news before the morning is over," a Texas newscaster told a well-known national reporter.

"Can you give us any insight as to what that might be?" the reporter asked.

"I can't at this time. Stay tuned, however. The news when it comes could be big. Oh, wait," the local newscaster turned around. Behind him, people began approaching an outside podium.

"Isn't that the DA in the Gorsham case?" Ray leaned in to get a better look.

"That's the one I saw yesterday," Tae Yong agreed.

"Look—oh my goodness, is that?" Xinnie sounded breathless.

"It's Paulson Muir. Is he—are those handcuffs he's wearing?" Ray was now standing, his eyes widening in surprise.

Just as the DA reached the podium to speak, Paulson Muir, who was also escorted by two police officers, dropped to his knees. "I offered to pay the Gorshams to burn down that office," he shouted.

CHAPTER 22

"He's jumping every time he admits to a new crime, like somebody is poking him in the back with a gun," Xinnie cut into her omelet as she and the others settled in to listen to Paulson Muir's confession.

His list of crimes was longer than many of the criminals he'd defended during his career.

Tae Yong, with Lee Min sitting beside him, snorted or chuckled every time Paulson Muir jerked and admitted a new crime.

"Too bad Phil's grandmother couldn't be here to see this," Muki shoved the last bite of omelet into their mouth with a smile. "Bea would have enjoyed this. She loved Trey but never cared for his father."

"And the reason we left the wedding early," Paulson Muir jerked again, "Was because I saw the Gorshams park their truck down the beach and I didn't want to run into them."

"So you just ran, leaving everybody else in the dark when you should have warned them?" the local reporter sounded incredulous.

"Why should I tell them anything?" Paulson whined on the screen. "They were after me."

"Piece. Of. Shit," Ray cursed.

"Definitely," Muki nodded.

"You left your own daughter behind," someone else accused.

"She didn't get hurt," Paulson shouted. Someone threw an egg, hitting Paulson square in the face.

"That's all for today," The DA said before cutting the mic and urging the police to move Paulson Muir inside the building.

"Look," Tae Yong tapped Lee Min's arm.

"I see," Lee Min chuckled.

"What do you see?" Xinnie turned toward the *dokkaebi*.

"What only we or another dragon might see," Tae Yong smiled.

"What's that?" Ray asked.

"Justice," Lee Min coughed. "Beautiful justice."

"I can't believe it," someone inside the Seoul restaurant exclaimed. A television was on in a corner, and a well-known South Korean newscaster delivered the latest from North Korea—that the snowstorm hadn't abated over Paektu but somehow, that country's leader was now offering to engage in talks to reunite families that had been separated since the Korean War.

"That will take a miracle," someone else said.

Agents Choi, Yoon and Park, who sat at a table having lunch with *sasin* Moon, laughed and slapped one another on the back.

"What?" Queen Seondeok exclaimed. Jiah dipped his head respectfully to his mother. "You can't force her. It's written in our own Dragon Law," Jiah held out the leather-bound sheaf of papers with both hands, offering it politely to his mother.

"How did you find that?" Seondeok demanded.

"Ah, with a bit of scholarly research," Jiah bowed again when his mother accepted the book.

"I knew you made a mistake, letting those cavern elves have access to our library," she snapped.

"Mother, you knew. You also knew years ago that it would take Philomena's help to pull you into existence again, once you'd separated your magic. You did that so humans could bear dragon children, remember? You expended everything—made that sacrifice—to ensure the continuation of the race."

"And that was also my goal in having her marry you," the Queen turned away from her son.

"That doesn't mean you can't have an heir—that I can't have a child," Jiah said. "Mother, you know my heart; I'm sure you discovered things quickly when you returned, if you didn't already know. Before you left us long ago, I felt the beginnings of it. I think this is why Guk left me alive. In all my life, I have never felt an attraction to females. However, modern science can ensure an heir—if Kwan and Philomena are willing to carry my child and birth it someday."

"Eh?" The Queen turned swiftly back to her son. "Is this true?"

"I have this, too, Mother," Jiah produced another, more modern book, which he held out for the Queen to take. "It explains how this is possible. The child will be mine and Philomena's, if she is agreeable."

"I will study this." The book was snatched away quickly. "We still have no idea as to her survival, however."

"Perhaps the next few days will bring new information to light."

"Hmmph. Go amuse yourself. I have reading to do."

"WHOA—THIS ONE, TOO?" XINNIE AND RAY READ THE NEWSPAPER articles online—in the past three days, so many politicians had confessed to crimes committed, and handed evidence over to the appropriate authorities, that those agencies were swamped with work and calling for additional funds to hire more employees to handle the load.

"Being able to mesmerize is a beautiful gift. I told a few of those assholes to stop lying, too," Phil knelt beside the sofa where Xinnie and Ray sat.

"Phil?" Xinnie's eyes were wide. Tears ran down her cheeks as she sat, stunned, for several seconds.

All at once, Xinnie and Ray exploded off the sofa to embrace Phil—hard enough to crack bones.

Phil laughed—it would take far more than human strength to ever crack her bones again.

⌇

"WHAT DO I DO? THE QUEEN HAS SET ASIDE THE MARRIAGE AND THE familiar contract," Kwan paced before Tae Yong.

Tae Yong, listening patiently, waited for Kwan to calm himself.

"Ah, perhaps you should ask her—properly this time," Tae Yong suggested after Kwan had fallen silent for several seconds.

"What if she says no? What if she doesn't want any of us? Why didn't I know that Jiah loved me—and not just as a brother? I feel stupid," Kwan confessed. "How did he not feel jealousy after I found Philomena?"

"He did, I assure you. But, because he knew you cared for her—almost from the moment you saw her," Tae Yong said, "he forced himself to accept it. While he reluctantly welcomed Philomena at first, he also knew you could never love him in ah, that way. He wanted you to be happy. Once he learned the dagger had been removed, and by an extremely talented witch, may I add, he gave his blessing to whatever union the both of you might have."

"He loves me that much?"

"He does."

"This—is far beyond my imaginings. Where is Philomena now? Should I send a note? Flowers, perhaps? What should I do?" Kwan moaned.

"Send a note and a gift to Jiah. Send flowers and a note to Philomena. See if either accepts your gratitude, and whatever love you can give to them. Jiah is at the palace. Philomena is with Xinnie and Ray at the Vashon Island home."

"Then I must make my plans carefully. I don't wish to lose either of them, I think."

"HERE IS THE PRECEDENT, MY QUEEN," MUKI HANDED AN ANCIENT scroll to Seondeok. "It is a case very similar, involving Jiah's great-great-grandfather."

"And this worked?" Seondeok unrolled the scroll.

"You ought to know it yourself, if you recall the royal history."

"Yes. I suppose I must have glossed over much of this. I knew that the King had a Queen and two consorts, both male and female, but disregarded that in favor of learning the history of the time instead."

"If you recall, human Kings of Korea had *naemyeongbu*, but that applied to female consorts. Only the dragons could be so bold as to have a male consort."

"Ask Secretary Kim to attend me in an hour; I wish to ask for a meeting with Jiah, Kwan and Philomena. The Queen commands they attend."

"I will pass the message," Muki bowed.

"You know Philomena will make you Royal Archivist, should she choose the position offered," Seondeok said softly as Muki turned to leave.

"Phil is my best friend, first and foremost," Muki replied. "Everything after that matters little to me."

"Do you think that one day she and I might be friends? I may have started all this off badly," the Queen admitted.

"It—could take some work," Muki shrugged. Seondeok watched as the cavern elf left her study and softly closed the door.

"PHIL?" XINNIE'S ARMS WERE FILLED WITH A BOUQUET OF PINK ROSES so large she could barely hold onto it.

"Wow." Phil's shoulders sagged. "I guess he's serious, huh?"

"These are from Jiah. There's another van completely full of red roses from Kwan."

"What?" Phil, using dragon talent, omitted the rising and stepping portion of her actions, disappearing in a liquid motion from the easy chair and coalescing before Xinnie.

"Phil, stop that or you'll give me a heart attack," Xinnie complained. "It was hard enough coming to terms with you being a witch. Now you're a dragon witch, and I'm still having to work my way through that bit of information."

"Just put the flowers wherever there's a flat surface," Ray instructed as two floral delivery employees carried several large bouquets through the front door.

"This will take a while," Xinnie smirked at Phil, who pulled Jiah's card from the pink roses to read.

Please share the throne with Kwan and me, the message read.

"Huh?" Phil turned the card over and over in her hand.

"Card," Ray handed a larger envelope to Phil as deliverymen continued to carry bouquets in the house.

Phil pulled the card from the envelope to read. *It has a historic precedence with dragonkind,* Kwan's note read. *I love you, Philomena. I love Jiah, too. I will work to make you both happy. Please share the throne with Jiah and me.*

"What in the name of the holy hand grenade is this?" Phil demanded, holding both cards out to Xinnie.

"Well, you're a dragon, now. While you didn't get a choice in all that, I figure things are gonna be different for you from now on."

"You're not helping, you know," Phil glared at Xinnie.

"The Queen requires your presence in a meeting with Princes Jiah and Kwan," Tae Yong appeared, holding out a third envelope.

"I think the day just got better, huh?" Phil's sarcasm had risen to its highest level as she lifted the envelope from Tae Yong's outstretched hands.

"Oh, and look—the meeting is in less than an hour. Joy," Phil mangled the word, making it sound like jooooey.

"Please use proper English when you meet with the Queen," Tae Yong breathed while bowing to Phil. "Please."

"All right, but only because it's you," Phil slapped the card into Xinnie's hands before disappearing.

"Where?" Tae Yong began.

"She's dressed in a track suit. She can't go looking like that," Ray hid a smile.

"Ah. Yeh," Tae Yong agreed.

"SHE LOOKS LIKE SHE'S DRESSED FOR A BUSINESS MEETING—ONE where she intends to fire all her employees," Kwan whispered to Jiah.

The Queen sat at the head of the long conference table inside the library; Jiah and Kwan sat next to one another farther down.

Phil walked in wearing a black silk suit and turtleneck, her feet in black heels that clicked authoritatively as she walked across the marble floor. She took the chair opposite Kwan's and Jiah's, her eyes never meeting theirs.

"I see we have a mountain to climb to reach the Princess," the Queen noted. "Tae Yong," she nodded at Secretary Kim, "Have the kitchen provide tea and snacks."

Philomena, please bear with us, Jiah begged mentally. *Please. We can work this out, I think, and appease Mother at the same time.*

Don't cause trouble, Kwan's message came on the heels of Jiah's. *We are in the presence of the Queen.*

Oh. You mean the Queen who couldn't make it back on her own, so she had to drag herself out of a volcano using my power? That Queen? The one who made my shields fail from the start so she could make a comeback?

Did that actually happen?

Yeah. It took a while to figure out, but yes. That's exactly what happened. If I didn't have fire magic, I wouldn't have survived. I had to become one with the volcano's eruption to keep myself from dying. It wasn't a pleasant experience. Jiah doesn't know, and don't you dare tell him. He has enough on his plate as it is.

Ah. At least you care about him.

I care about him. I don't want to bring more trouble to his door than is already there.

Then please cooperate now. Jiah is ah, gay, Kwan admitted. *All this time, he has been in love with me. What am I supposed to do, Philomena? Please tell me. I have no desire to hurt him, either.*

But if you serve as King's consort, Phil began.

There is a way—it is called flying happiness *among dragons.*

Flying what?

A dragon couple can engage in this, without actually coupling, if you understand my meaning.

You're saying having sex without actually ah, Phil floundered.

It is more of a mental pleasure, but the physical climax is the same —without actual touching. I'm not saying this properly, Kwan hung his head.

And you're an expert at flying. I get it, now.

Philomena, please. I don't wish to see you exiled.

Tell me—before the dagger, did you and Jiah ah, Phil didn't finish.

We were young and experimenting. I had no idea it meant so much to him. For me, it was only sex at the time—it is permissible in dragon culture.

Right. I don't know what to say—or do in this situation.

Please, trust me—and Jiah in this. We will not mistreat you.

Uh-huh. Sure.

Phil? Muki's sending intervened.

Muki?

You love Kwan. You know you do. I see no harm in this to you, and he loves you more than anyone or anything else. Within my culture, I am special. This means that I am all and everything, should I choose to take a mate or mates. Tell me; what troubles you the most in this?

That they'll gang up on me. I've had a hard enough time dealing with Kwan alone in the past. I can't fight two at once.

"She's afraid," Muki walked into the library. "That her voice will be lost if she has to deal with both of you, rather than only one. Admit it, Kwan. You have done your best to make her cower before you in the past."

"Wha?" Jiah turned to blink at Kwan. The Queen cleared her throat uncomfortably.

"And I usually ended up in the Koi pond," Kwan argued.

"Except you wrote it into the contract that she couldn't do that, remember?"

"Look, I am still exhausted after the volcano," Phil stood. "I don't know who I can trust as far as dragons go. So far, the only person in this room that I have full faith in at the moment is Muki, and they're trying to convince me that a threesome is a great idea."

"You are weary, Princess," Tae Yong appeared and set a cup of tea on the table. "Please, sit. An agreement can surely be reached, and a new contract can be written. I will write it myself, and ensure you have full rights to make your voice and your opinions heard and heeded. Without you, dragonkind would no longer exist."

"This much is true," Jiah lowered his eyes. Scooting his chair back, he rose and bowed to Phil. "*Gamsahabnida*, Philomena," he said, thanking her in Korean.

"*Gamsahabnida*, Philomena," Kwan rose and copied Jiah's words.

"*Gamsahabnida*, Princess," the Queen rose and dipped her head. "I exist because you exist."

"Please, Philomena," Jiah continued. "Give us a chance. I promise we will faithfully listen to you, now and forever. You have saved my life more than once, and I owe you far more than I can ever say."

"I beg you to sit the throne beside my son," Seondeok said.

Phil's shoulders sagged and her head drooped—she really was too tired to be dealing with such stress, yet here she was, in the strangest situation of all.

"I didn't plan on becoming a dragon," Phil lifted her head and stared at Kwan and Jiah. "Hwang made that happen and then made me forget until the day I found myself fighting off that filth inside a volcano. That choice was taken away from me. The choice to become a familiar and then a wife to a dragon also was made without my consent. Wasn't it?" She focused on Kwan, who turned his head away. "The Queen has vacated our marriage. I'm single, now.

"Tell me, Kwan," she went on, "how you'd have gotten along if you'd still had that dagger stuck in your armpit inside the volcano?"

"Guk would have killed me," Kwan admitted. "Easier than he killed my father."

"I would have died without your help when Dal stabbed me with a spelled dagger," Jiah stated baldly. "The physician couldn't have saved me. He freely admits this. I know it as a fact."

"Our lives have been spared too many times, by Philomena's willingness to protect us," Kwan admitted. "We are grateful."

"Then I have a few conditions to all this," Phil said. "But first, I need to sit down. I am really, really tired right now."

"SHE'S SLEEPING," MUKI WALKED OUT OF PHIL'S SUITE, ONLY TO FIND Jiah and Kwan waiting outside in the hallway. "She went to work almost from the moment her dragon broke out of the lava that encased her inside the volcano. No wonder she can barely stand."

"Mother has agreed to Philomena's conditions," Jiah sighed. "I never thought I'd see this happen."

"Once you become King, your mother will become the Queen-Mother and take the newly-built house in Busan as hers," Kwan patted Jiah's shoulder. "Although I dislike some of the other ah, conditions."

"Hmmph. Just because I have first rights to the throne," Jiah huffed.

"That isn't, ah," Kwan pinched the bridge of his nose. "This is most unacceptable to me."

"I knew what you meant. I merely wanted to divert your attention away from this. Philomena's refusal to be married to either of us— Kwan, if anyone can convince her to marry in the future, surely you can. We will rule as equals on the throne, I guarantee it, although mother insisted that I have first rights, Philomena second and you have third rights."

"I never would have imagined this," Muki blew out a breath. "I need a drink. Do you wish to join me?"

"Most certainly," Jiah agreed. "Let's go to my study. I feel the need to be quite drunk, actually. If that doesn't happen, I may force Kwan to engage in *flying happiness* before the crowning ceremony."

"Depending on the level of our hangover, I will take you tomorrow or the day after," Kwan promised. "At least she is with us, rather than refusing the throne outright, which is what I feared."

"Shall we discuss Philomena's lair, then?" Jiah placed an arm over Kwan's shoulders.

"She should have my father's, don't you think?"

"What if there are things inside that shouldn't see the light of day? Your father was very old," Jiah reminded Kwan.

"Can you think of a better dragon to guard it, then?"

"Absolutely not," Jiah nodded after thinking it over.

"Very well. It's settled if Philomena agrees."

"I wondered if anybody would bother to ask her," Muki grumbled.

"From now on, that's exactly how it has to be," Jiah said.

Six Weeks Later

"By signing this agreement, the three of you will abide by all the terms inscribed therein, and rule dragonkind with an attitude of benevolence, justice and honesty," Queen Seondeok announced.

Next to the throne was a table, and upon that table were three identical pacts. Behind each written pact stood Jiah, Kwan and Phil. "Sign now," the Queen commanded. Each lifted a pen and signed their names at the bottom of the papers.

Each pen was capped carefully and set beside the contracts.

"It is with great pleasure that I renounce my throne in favor of King Jiah, Queen Philomena and King Kwan," Seondeok shouted.

Roars arose from the throats of dragons in and around the palace, as a new era for dragonkind began.

Epilogue

"Sun magic. It makes me deliriously happy," Jiah turned his face toward the sunlight overhead.

"Here," Phil handed him the golden watchband she'd just created. "You can carry this day with you forever. It holds a spell to recreate any of its memories that you like."

"Thank you." Jiah accepted the piece of jewelry with a smile.

"There you are," Kwan arrived, brushing fallen cherry blossoms off his robes. "Time to celebrate your birthday with your subjects, my King."

"I'd prefer to spend my day with only the two of you, but then we can't always have what we want, can we?"

"Or often enough," Kwan agreed. "Come, your mother will arrive soon. We can't have her in a bad mood because her son wasn't waiting to greet her."

"True. Philomena, this is such a wonderful gift," Jiah leaned in to kiss her cheek. "Will you help me put my watch on this band?"

"With my eyes shut," Phil smiled at him. "Come on King One, let's get this day over with. I know you want to go flying with Kwan."

"I do, but I don't want you left out of it, either."

"Three can fly at once, or so I'm told," Kwan sounded shy, suddenly.

"What? I don't want to interrupt," Phil snorted.

"You will be welcome with us, Philomena," Jiah told her gently. "Always."

"Then I'll think about it," Phil replied.

The End

Author's Note:

If all goes well, Phil, Kwan, Jiah and the others will appear in the sequel to this book, currently titled *The Dragon Queen of Seoul.*

Thanks for reading!